# RED ISLAND

A. A. DARK

Mad Girl
PUBLISHING
PITCH BLACK™

# AUTHOR'S NOTE

The timeline for Red Island takes place approximately 6 months from the fall of Whitlock from the 24690 series but BEFORE the opening of the Garden of the Gods series. The A. A. Dark world follows the Mistresses and Masters who occupy it. Mistress and Master is a title showing nothing more than ownership. The scale of darkness in the stories will range from Pitch Black, Static White, to the extreme, Oblivion. Red Island is classified as STATIC WHITE, walking the edge of OBLIVION (for some). Please be aware of this before you dive in. If you're not familiar with the triggers that are in STATIC WHITE or OBLIVION, please visit the Home Page of my website where it explains all three tiers. If you are not comfortable with dark reads, and this one is DARK, please DO NOT read this book.

Red Island
International Bestselling Author
A. A. Dark
Copyright © 2023 by A. A. Dark

All Rights Reserved

# PROLOGUE

## THE DRAGON

*I*t was a glimpse at a fairytale—a moment stolen from when I thought I had everything. Love wasn't supposed to be mine. I was never meant to feel happiness…but I did. I gave my entire heart, only for fate to completely shred it in its greedy hands. Or maybe I was the greedy one. After all, wasn't this my fault? Hadn't I been the culprit that triggered the events of what I was now suffering through?

She was all I had ever wanted. Layla was a slave—raped by countless men before she got to me. The main one, Ram, I'd had the pleasure to burn alive. She'd almost died on her way to my island because of him. The pregnancy wasn't expected or wanted on her behalf, but I claimed those babies. The twins *were* quite possibly mine given the timeline, and I made her see nothing but the possibility. We were going to be happy. I was going to be a father of twins. *I was*…a father. Or had been.

Evil won. That should have meant victory was mine. Once, I was the devil, himself. Once, I was feared across all oceans and countries. They thought my coveted love would be the end of me like with Bram Whitlock. They dreamed it would. Like all things stolen, the universe found a way to set the taken free. It stole Layla. It almost took them all.

*"No! Layla, wake up. Layla!"*

Aamir's screams could no doubt be heard clear across the island. He wouldn't let his twin go, and me, I wouldn't let her murderer free. Blood-soaked hair was tangled in my fingers as the woman's severed head swayed in my grasp. I was walking in circles. Gasping with broken-up breaths of disbelief and panic. I couldn't believe...I didn't want to face that on some level I'd done this.

Not an hour ago we'd all been so happy. I'd been smoothing back black hair, whispering words of encouragement. Feeding her all my strength through each push. Then, Jamison was born, blue, and not breathing. The moment went from miracle to tragedy faster than I could process. Eimine left to work on the baby, and Layla didn't have long before she was pushing again.

*"Eimine!"*

*"Gavin. Gavin!"* Layla clawed at me, trying to push and see after our son at the same time. *"Something's wrong. Go to him. Gavin, please!"*

*"Aamir."* Layla's twin didn't need me to tell him what to do. Aamir was already rushing over to my son. I was torn, confused on where I should go. I wanted to see my child, to try to help, but there was no way I was leaving the woman I loved. Not after the complications she'd experienced the entire pregnancy. *"Look at me, Lovie. He's going to be okay. Aamir is there. Focus on you right now. Do you need to push?"*

Layla's scream filled the room, nearly cutting me off. The baby's head was already crowning. My attention snapped to Eimine. I called to her, but when she paid me no attention, I didn't hesitate to grab gloves and slide them on.

*"You're doing so well. I need you to keep pushing. Jasmeen's almost here. She's—"*

*"I can't. I—"* Layla's screams echoed from the stone walls as

4

she jerked to the side, penetrating the deepest crevices in my being. Still, she kept looking to where our son was.

*"Was he just crying? Gavin, is he okay?"*

*"Focus, baby. You can do this. You're strong. Jasmeen needs you right now."*

*"Something's...wrong. Something...What is the doctor doing? His eyes had been open, Gavin. I saw...His eyes... when...she laid him down. Why isn't he crying, anymore?"* She took a deep breath, yelling out again as she pushed hard. When she went right into another, Jasmeen's head was free. I reached down, providing support for the baby. Maybe had I not been so awestruck, I would have done something different. I would have realized what Layla did. Perhaps, I could have gotten Mandy to help sooner as I checked out Jamison.

*"You can do this. She's almost here. One more push. One more."*

Layla screamed, bearing down. One second I was encouraging her, and the next Jasmeen was in my arms. She was flailing and letting out the loudest cry I'd ever heard. Her dark hair was thicker than I'd expected, and I felt my chest nearly explode as tears blinded me. My stare shot to Layla's and we both smiled. Aamir raced to my side, pale as he brought me a blanket and helped dry off my daughter. I didn't have to ask what was happening and neither did Layla. She was already back to moving to her side, trying to see around me. Despite that she was reaching for Jasmeen, her eyes never looked our way again. The tears she cried as she reached her other hand towards our son gutted me. What Layla felt, I lived. She was part of me in ways I couldn't begin to understand. I would have died for her. I would have *lived*, and almost got to...

*"Have her bring him to me. I don't want her...I want my. I want..."* The color was draining from her face by the second. Rationality left me in that moment.

*"Eimine, now."* The midwife glanced up from Jamison's

small body. She gave Layla a brief glimpse, then me, slowly heading in our direction. For the time it took her to reach us, my world stopped, and Layla's concerns hit like a punch to the gut, putting me on guard. This white-haired, older grandmother type wasn't a panicked doctor concerned for her patient. She wasn't showing any emotion at all. There was a coldness I suddenly couldn't ignore. I knew the look she held—that disassociated stare as she stayed focused on what was mine.

I handed Jasmeen to Aamir, eyeing the woman suspiciously as she cut the cord and began pushing against Layla's stomach. She grabbed a syringe from her bag, shooting something in the IV before I could open my mouth. My glare could have engulfed the world in flames for what I feared.

*"What was that?"*

*"For the pain."*

*"Gavin? Where's...Jamison? Jasmeen?"*

Layla's words were slurred. Breathy.

*"They're right here. Aamir has our daughter. She's perfect and safe, Lovie. Beautiful, like you. Don't worry about them right now. Let's focus on you, okay?"*

*"Jamison. Where's? You have to."*

The raw pain at Aamir shaking his head had bile pushing to the back of my throat. My heart tore, raw and bleeding as I tried to keep the shakiness from my voice. *"Layla, baby, listen to me. Hear what I say. I love you more than anything. More than these beats,"* I said, bringing her left hand to my racing heart so I could bring attention to her wedding band. *"More than air. More than—"*

*"Money and...this island."*

I smiled as she finished for me. The words were something I'd repeated now for months.

*"We're going to leave here. We're going to move to some small town to raise our family. You'll have Aamir and your parents. I promised you we'd come up with the perfect story so*

*that you could have your life back. I'm going to keep that promise."*

Layla tried to smile, but her eyes looked distant. It was as if she couldn't even see me. She blinked hard, sucking in a deep breath as she became alarmingly paler.

*"What the fuck is going on?"* I growled to the side. Just as my stare landed on the midwife, her hand was already surging forward, towards Layla's stomach.

*"You have to get back, Main Master, and let me work. She's bleeding out."*

The scalpel sliced through layers of Layla's stomach, but I was the one who felt the pain serrating my insides. *Main Master.* The condescending tone she'd used for my title sent my blood to ice.

*"Gavin...Gavin you have to take the baby."* Aamir swayed, barely catching himself as he took in his twin sister.

I pointed, but all I saw was the mask this woman wore. *"Put her in the bassinet. Get my guards. Find Mandy, and fast."*

Each word was clipped. Did I already have my knife in my hand? I did, and the sight of it brought back the corner of the woman's mouth. It was all I saw as I lurched forward, wrapping my hand around her throat.

*"If she dies—"*

*"She will die. I've made it so, just like with your son. The powers that be have decided. You are the Main Master of Red Island. You will stay that way."*

*"Powers that be? What the fuck are you talking about?"* I already knew as I let go. The fact that I tried to leave here the right way was my mistake. There was no escaping this life. There were no families or wives associated with leaders of sin. I ran an island of sea and sex slaves. Did I really think they'd let me walk away from this alive? Walk away like former Main Master, Bram Whitlock? God, I had thought myself that lucky, completely ignoring what I had gone through to be placed here.

Love blinded me. It fed my ego. It made me think the impossible when reality was nothing more than imprisonment. This island was open and free, but there was never any leaving it. Didn't the burns covering my body speak for themselves? They were the cost of my life—*this* life.

Guards burst through the room as I pushed towels into Layla's stomach with one hand and pointed the knife with the other. Mandy was already running to take over for me with Layla's twin right behind.

*"Aamir told me what happened. I sent for The Babke—"*

*"Blood,"* I rushed out. *"Layla's bleeding out and that bitch was trying to speed up the process. I made sure to have bags brought in for an emergency. Blood, now!"* Two of the guards raced out as I turned back to Mandy. *"You sent for her? The Babke..."* I stopped myself, feeling too many emotions drown me all at once. Layla didn't like the tribal woman who inhabited the island. She didn't trust her ways of healing, and thought she was evil. From the rumors, she was. They all were. The tribe were unruly. The best killers I'd ever come across.

"It's her only chance. Layla needs her. I can't…"

Mandy trailed off as I nodded and looked down. We couldn't do this by ourselves. We needed help, and more than some shaman witch doctor who had a dark reputation on my island. "My hands are covered in blood. Aamir, get the phone from my pocket. Call Bram and put it on speaker."

But he was slowing. His eyes were on his sister, and they weren't leaving.

*"Aamir, now!"*

"I can't lose her. I…I can't." Aamir grabbed my phone, dialing and putting it on speaker. Jasmeen's cries mingled with the rings, but all I heard was the long beep from Layla's heart monitor slowing. Stopping.

"Fuck. Fuck! Aamir, put the phone on the bed and start compressions."

I gave Layla one breath, two. Bram's voice broke through the room nearly taking my own oxygen.

*"Well, well, if it isn't The Dragon. What do I..."* he got quiet. *"Gavin, is that a baby I hear? Did Layla—"*

*"Bram, I'm in trouble. I...I saved your life. You and Everleigh owe me a favor. You and my brother... you and Luke have to come to the island. Layla."* I stopped, giving her more breaths as Aamir sobbed and paused from pushing on her chest. Mandy was still working on her stomach, and I had no idea what was all happening there. All I knew was whatever we were doing, it wasn't working. There was so much blood. Too much.

*"You have to come get Aamir and the baby. Layla."* Still, I couldn't say it. *"You have to get them!"*

*"Baby? Just one?"* He stopped, his tone deepening. *"Gavin, I need you to slow down and be blunt. Tell me exactly what's happening."*

*"It was a lie. They were never going to let us leave. They sent her to kill my family. I don't even think she's a doctor,"* I exploded. *"We lost Jamison. Layla, she's not...breathing. She's... her stomach is...cut open. I don't know how bad. I'm going to kill that bitch; I'm going to fucking shred her apart."* I tried to stop the deep, animalistic pants that were coming with the truth, but I was homicidal, and it was taking everything for me not to act on it. *"You have to come take Aamir and Jasmeen before they come."* The room was spinning, but it was my mind that was fading from reality. All I suddenly saw was the blood on my hands as I went to grasp Layla's face to give her more air.

*"Gavin, listen to me; you're not safe. I don't think they'll come, but they may have more insiders. Get as many trusted men as you can to be on guard. We're already in the air and only a few hours away. We'll be there soon. Have Aamir and the baby ready. We won't be long."*

*"Thank you."*

Wetness trailed down my face causing my hand to lift. I

wasn't crying, and yet the tears dropping from my jaw were undeniable. I cupped Layla's lifeless face, kissing her as Aamir's cries echoed my own. This wasn't supposed to be how the day turned out. It wasn't supposed to have happened at all. Not until we were old and had lived our lives together. I promised her freedom. A real family. Decades of happiness. *She promised me she'd be here for it.*

"*Lovie...I love you. Do you hear me? I love you. I...love you. Don't you fucking dare leave me. Come back to me. You promised. You—*"

I did sob then. My breath caught and my heart pounded in some offbeat cadence. My gaze left Layla's, locking on Eimine who was surrounded by guards. One minute I was on the bed with my wife, the next my knife was thrusting into the lower stomach of the woman I'd flown in for the ultimate protection. Woman. Not a team like I tried to push for. Woman. One who said she had this under control.

Had I truly been so stupid and blind?

Blood flooded over my hand while I jerked the blade up towards her bellybutton. I was beyond speaking, beyond all rational thought as Layla's monitor went off and on with irregular beats. *Stop. Start. Stop.* I twisted, not satisfied with the direction. Her screams drowned out Jasmeen's and Aamir's. I sliced over towards one hip, and then the other. I cut at every angle I could as I made my way up. Intestines spilled free, waterfalling out as I added more force to the pattern I was making up to her chest. I hit bone. I cut through muscle and organs. Resistance pinged against my blade from her ribs causing me to withdraw and stab into her chest mercilessly before redirecting my wrath. By the time I got to her neck, I was straddled over her dead body, on the floor. My aggression knew no bounds. Not even when I was out of breath, chopping and sawing through her throat, or when I was pulling her head free to hang in my grasp. I was gone from this room. Enraged and broken beyond sanity. I didn't want to live if I didn't have Layla, but no one was coming to kill me. Deep inside, I knew that.

*Life. Death.* Red Island was my curse. This land was nourished with the blood I'd fed it from kidnapped men, women, and children from around the world. There was no escaping my haunted destiny. It lived here, surrounded by a paradise rivaling heaven. It was my hell, and I would forever be its ruler.

# CHAPTER 1

## LAYLA

"*We stitched her up and stopped the bleeding. The transfusion accompanying your ritual should be helping, but she doesn't stir.*" Mandy's voice cracked, echoing and sounding so far away. "*I don't understand what's happening. How long is it supposed to take for her to wake up?*"

"*I gave her something special. She'll wake when it is time.*"

"*Time?*"

"*You love her very much.*"

"*Babke...I*" Mandy paused through what sounded like a small cry. "*I care for her, yes, but it doesn't matter. I'm only Layla's personal servant. My love is unworthy of anyone. I am nothing.*"

"*I disagree. What an awakening you're about to embark on, child. If we're lucky...you both.*"

Language I didn't understand followed me into a rollercoaster of unconsciousness. It came. It went. Chants. A blur of colors and images flickered turning to a dark fog.

Silence.

It stretched out and was heavy in my ears as I fought to wake up. My babies. They needed me. Had they been able to save

Jamison? Why couldn't I hear Jasmeen? She had been crying before, hadn't she? The doctor. I didn't like that woman. I'd seen my son open his eyes. He had been awake as she carried him away. I saw it. I swore I had heard him crying.

Fatigue nearly stole me from remembering. I was so cold and numb as the darkness nearly suffocated me. The hum of voices was back, but they were so far away. I couldn't make out but maybe every other sentence, and even then, my brain wouldn't process what it meant.

*"Death was summoned here, child. That's all that woman wanted for the Main Master's wife. Death. It's here. Can you feel it? It calls to her, but it obeys me. Death will not get her today. I'm not sure how long I can hold it off, but for now, she will live."*

*"No."* Gavin's rumbling response made me jump inside my skin. The power in his tone was undeniable. So was the pain and anger. *"It's too much of a risk to speak it out loud. Layla is dead to everyone outside of this room. To Bram when he gets here. To Everleigh."* He took a shuddering breath. *"To Aamir, and even to the guards. No one must know she's alive. She's in too much danger. She's dead until I can figure out who's behind this. Dead, do you hear me? Layla is no more."*

*"What of Jamison?"*

A sniffle. Was Gavin crying? I could feel my wedding band spinning on my finger. Spinning. Spinning.

*"Find a slave close to Layla's appearance. We need a body, and...I will not bury my son alone. He needs protection. A caregiver. I...Just find one, dammit. We put them to rest tomorrow at sunset. The sooner, the better. The island must believe it's her."*

Spinning. Spinning. Pressure as my ring left my finger...Gone.

*"Yes, Sir."*

*"Mandy..."* Hesitation. *"I'm sorry for yelling at you. Thank you for bringing Layla back to me."*

14

*"It wasn't me, Main Master. Not really. I kept losing her. Babke's the one who did it. Layla was...dead. She...But...She stopped the bleeding, and then the ceremony...Sir. I'm scared,"* she whispered. *"The blood from that vial. The words the Babke spoke,"* Mandy's voice shook. *"I don't know much of my native language, but I know enough. She called them."*

*"Called whom?"*

*"Them. The tribal...demons. They watch over Layla guarding her from Death."*

*"Guarding her? Why is that bad? Angels, demons, I don't give of fuck who it is, so long as she's safe and alive."*

*"Main Master, this isn't your culture. You don't understand. Nothing is free. Layla will not be herself when she wakes. She may never be the same again. They will never part from her. Not even when Death does get its way. Her soul is their responsibility now. For always. Eternity. It's the price for life."*

*"Have you thought that nonsense through? The only one Layla's soul belongs to is me."*

More silence. Dead silence. Had I been cold before? Even though I didn't exactly know what was happening, the ice in my veins only seemed to grow colder. The scent of dirt grew closer, and I recognized the smell. The voice. Or maybe it was the presence that made me aware. Thick accent. Husky tone. Earth. It was her. The devil witch. The evil one.

*"Babke—"*

*"You worry about what I've done, but you don't care. You love the wife you have taken; for this I am certain. You want to thank me. Don't. Your payment will come the moment I need it. Red as wine. White as salt. The darkest night calls out to those it sees."* She paused. *"It calls to you. Fire whispers over your shoulder and awaits your sacrifice. It is part of you and talks to me, just as all elements."*

Gavin cleared his throat, continuing in a scratchy tone. *"What do they say? Is Layla going to be okay? Will she live?"*

*"I can't tell you anything other than 'it's time'. The air and death want the pieces left from your kill. We will offer it as our gift. In return, Death will temporarily be sated, and the air will cleanse the dark stain left upon this room."* She stopped and creaking followed. *"Let us open the windows. Rejoice in the scent of flesh. Set the fire in your pit on the balcony, Dragon. We must satisfy the forces, or the hours will grow long and uncertain for all of us. We wouldn't want that."*

*"**I** know you're mad at me for coming to your room, Gavin, but your brother and I are not leaving here until we talk. You're grieving. I'm so sorry about Layla, but you're not thinking rationally. Please, let me in. Tell me exactly what happened. Maybe I can help you."*

*"You are helping me, Bram. You're taking Aamir and Jasmeen. They're safer with you than me. I wouldn't trust anyone else with my...daughter."*

The words were choked out as Gavin's heartbreak pulled me from the depths of sleep. I was so close to becoming aware, yet I was further away than ever.

*"I'll protect them with my life. I owe that to you. Please, let me in."*

*"I can't. I'm sorry. I...I'm going to find out who ordered my family's death. I did everything by the book."*

The silence seemed to last forever as I floated in awareness.

*"The primordial book, as you call it, isn't real, Gavin. Yes, there's a protocol, but not one we're at liberty to have. There's no escape from this life. What happened with me was—"*

*"Luck. Yes. I know. I was just. I thought."* Gavin took a deep

breath. *"I thought reaching out and being honest would hold weight. I should have known you getting out was too good to be true. God...What the fuck was I thinking?"*

*"I wish you would have told me your plan."*

*"The damage is done. It's too late for wishes. My wife—"*

*"You married Layla?"*

Another voice. Luke? Yes, Gavin's brother. Of course he'd be with Bram and Everleigh. He was Everleigh's main guard. Their most trusted protector.

*"I did marry her. It was nothing big; a small ceremony at the beach. I...I didn't want her to have the babies and not be married. She deserved all of me."* A sniffle. *"This isn't fucking happening. I can't think. I want my son. My wife. My family. This isn't real."*

*"Gavin, please, let me in. I'm your brother. I need to be here for you. Let me do that."*

*"You want to stay?"*

*"Are you fucking kidding me? I don't just want to stay; I am staying. If you're going to be looking for who did this, I'm going to help you. Let us in."*

Another sniffle. A breeze blew against my skin, cooler than if it were midday, and I could hear the shells that hung from the trees bordering tribal land. It was night. Maybe even in the early hours of morning.

*"If I let you in, you can't go by the bed. I have the curtains drawn, but Layla, she's still not decent. I don't want you to see her like that."*

*"Of course."*

Luke's voice was soft as footsteps grew closer. My finger twitched, but with the small effort, I felt myself grow heavier. The witch. She'd given me something. I could still taste it. I was so tired, yet I couldn't seem to control my awareness. It was here. Fleeting at times, but here.

*"Start at the beginning,"* Bram said, growing closer. *"Tell us about the woman they sent. How did you find her?"*

*"I."* He groaned. *"I made orders at the beginning of Layla's pregnancy for a ton of medical equipment. As a safety precaution, I wanted everything she needed here. My ships took care of most of it, but there were a few things that I couldn't get instant access to. It was during a delay in one of the orders that I got a call from Austin Birch."*

*"Austin Birch out of Hong Kong?"* Bram sounded taken-aback. *"The same one who owns Imperial Shipping and works for the Main Master out of China?"*

*"That's right. He mentioned overhearing about my purchases at one of the docks and wanted to see if he could offer assistance. He was coming close to the island and for a favor, he would deliver. He asked for three days in one of the huts and slaves of his choice. As many as he wanted. Layla wasn't doing well, so I agreed."*

*"Did he ever see Layla?"* Bram's voice dropped. *"Tell me you didn't introduce them."*

*"And intentionally put her at risk? I'm no fool. It's the main reason I had everything coming in on my ships. I didn't want this to get out, but it did. I may be the Main Master, but this island talks. Maybe it was one of the slaves or guards. I don't know. All I know is he found out I was married, and she was expecting. He knew a woman who could help if I ever needed it. He spoke highly of her. She made calls for China, London, and Chile. Hell, everywhere. She was a specialist. He called her a jack of all trades. You can bet your ass with Layla so delicate, I didn't take his word for it. I called Ramiro from Chile. We've met on a few occasions so I figured if I could trust anyone, it's him. He vouched for her."*

*"He did?"* Bram made a sound that was skeptical. *"Chile doesn't do pregnancies. They run things very close to how we did*

*at Whitlock. Hysterectomies. Abortions. Whatever it takes. No children."*

*"I know that; that's why I called. It didn't sound right, but he said there had been occasions he had to use her, and I could get more information if I wanted to reach out to Redmond. I did, and George confirmed."*

*"Redmond?"* Again, Bram sounded aghast and skeptical. *"The Main Master of London. You're sure it was him?"*

*"Yes. He told me he used her quite often. London allows children to be born under its roof. Hell, they adopt them out when they're not serving them on the buffet. I didn't get any red flags. They made it sound normal, as if they were surprised I wasn't already using her for any situations here on the island."*

*"Gavin, London has its own medical center just like Whitlock did. They have surgeons, doctors. I'm sure they have their own pediatricians. I don't see why they would bring her in. What skills would she have that they wouldn't permanently acquire themselves?"*

*"I...don't know. I've had so much on my mind. I didn't think of that. Layla needed someone good. Someone trusted. I just wanted her safe and taken care of. I flew that woman in weekly for the last few months. Sometimes twice a week. Hell, I tried to bribe her to stay here but she refused, saying she had other patients."*

Nothing. The words faded in and out as I fought to listen. My mind wouldn't let me. It was finished trying to decipher what it all meant. I'd start to grasp their conversation when it would slip away to oblivion. Pieces here and there filtered through, and I knew enough.

We had been played. Maybe by one. Probably by all. The corrupt web woven around us was a mystery, and it all led back to a main source, but who? How were decisions made in a world like this? Who called the shots when everybody was at the top? Or were the Main Masters not the leaders of their own domains?

I had no idea how any of this worked.

Perhaps they were just as big of puppets as us slaves but with longer strings. I didn't know much about the trafficking world, but there was a burning in the pit of my stomach that wanted to find out. Something stirred around inside me that I couldn't explain. It was anger, yes, but bigger. Hotter. It was but a spark in a near combustible space, and it wasn't going to take much to ignite an explosion.

# CHAPTER 2

## THE DRAGON

There was something about the smell of burning hair and flesh that stayed in your lungs for hours. It didn't matter whether you were in the vicinity, you couldn't drown it out. As I stood looking over the ash and embers in my fire pit, I could still smell the doctor as if I had just lit her severed limbs on fire. It was satisfying and yet not. She should have paid a lot worse for what she'd done. If I would have been able to think at all, I would have come up with a genius plan to make her suffer instead of hacking her apart. It was too late for that now. Not that it mattered. I still had other people to question. What I wanted to know was, who told Austin Birch about Layla? He obviously had his suspicions when he came here, so who exactly set this plan into motion?

"Main Master."

Mandy's whisper had me turning as she waved her hand frantically. Just the thought that something was wrong with Layla had me heading across the fortress's main balcony in her direction.

"What is it? Is she okay?"

"She tried opening her eyes. I think she's trying to ask for you."

I barely heard the rest of Mandy's sentence as I raced toward my room. There was a guard posted on the corner. I slowed enough to bark an order at him as I passed. "No one but Mandy is allowed in this hall. Tell our guests I'll be with them soon."

"Yes, Main Master."

Running the few feet to the door, I threw it open, heading to the large bed. When I pulled back the curtain, Layla still appeared to be sleeping. I lowered to sit on the edge, leaning down to brush back the strands of hair from her face. I grabbed her hand, holding it to my cheek as I leaned in. I hated that her ring was going on a corpse, but it couldn't be helped. I'd buy her a new one. I'd do better than the simple band she asked for. I wouldn't give her a choice this time. She deserved more. She deserved the best.

"Lovie, it's me. Can you hear me? Are you awake?"

"G-G...avin."

I had never cried in my life like I had in the last few hours. Even tortured for months, the tears didn't leave me. Screams, yes, but not tears. Hearing her voice, I saw just how much of a broken man I was. She was my weakness. My entire existence.

"I want you to rest. You're gonna be okay. *We're* gonna be okay. I love you so much. God, I do."

"Ba-bies. I...want."

Had the phantom flames that haunted me moved up to my eyes? They were on fire worse than my scarred neck and chest had ever been. The tears burned as they filled up the space and fell to the small fingers kept at my cheek. I kissed against them, sniffling, and trying to hold myself together.

"Everything is fine. Rest, baby. Get stronger. I'll be waiting for you when you wake up again."

I wasn't sure what else to say. Never in my life had I lacked words when it came to Layla. I would have talked to her about the most boring thing in the world just to hear her speak. Right now, I couldn't bear the thought of her losing any more strength. Or facing anymore pain. And she would. This was going to destroy her. Destroy wasn't powerful enough. I feared for my wife's reaction when she found out both of our children were gone. Would she be angry? Would she understand why I was sending Jasmeen away?

Knocking on the door had my head whipping around. She already appeared deeply asleep again, but I couldn't be sure. I pulled back the curtain, hiding her in the bed as I went to answer it. Mandy clutched tightly to her hands as I pulled her in.

"I don't want her alone. If she wakes again, do not answer any of her questions. Call me immediately."

"Yes, Sir."

"Mandy...not a single question. Not one."

Fear clouded her eyes as she nodded her head. I left the room in angry steps. It didn't take me long to make it to my dining area. Bram was eating while Everleigh rocked Jasmeen. Aamir sat further down the table, resting his head along the surface, sleeping. I slowed as I approached my daughter, trying to hold the tears back that would not stop. I had no control over them. What did that say about me, or about what I had become?

"I think she's the most beautiful baby I've ever seen." Everleigh stood, meeting my stare. "She needs you. Hold your daughter, Gavin."

Had I been running from facing my own child? To see her without Jamison was almost too much to bear. I clenched my teeth, taking the tiny infant from Everleigh. She was swaddled in a pink and white blanket with a tiny matching outfit and hat. Her head immediately turned towards my chest as I brought her close. When she opened her eyes, I almost couldn't catch my breath. Her eyes. They were Layla's eyes. It was like looking at a mini spitting image of her mother. I knew it was way too early to tell, but I could so clearly see what I loved. It was the face in front of me.

I pulled the hat free, taking in the black hair. My bottom lip quivered at the sight. I bit against it to make it stop. There was no way I was going to break down in front of these people. They had seen enough already. I just couldn't get over how absolutely beautiful my little girl was, and I could have lost her had that bitch doctor had her way.

"I fell in love with her mother just like this: love at first sight. How does that happen? How could it, for a man like me?"

Fingers grabbed and squeezed into the bottom of my suit jacket as Aamir lifted his head with a sob. It was too much. My lids squeezed shut as I lowered my face to Jasmeen's. Breathing in her smell was a heartbreak of its own. It was all I had ever wanted since learning I was going to be a father. I dreamed this, and now my dream was ending—stolen from me.

"I w-want to see my sister. She can't be—I can't."

Aamir could barely speak he was sobbing so hard. This was a nightmare for me, but for Aamir...Layla was part of him. They'd been inseparable since his return from Whitlock. Now for him to think he lost her this way?

"I don't think that would be a good idea."

He pulled at my jacket to bring me closer, moving his head against his fisted hand to lean into me. He didn't have to say a word for me to understand it was his way of begging. I hadn't always liked Aamir. In truth, we damn near hated each other for a while, but that all ended on his return. His presence helped Layla. It made her strong. Happy. I was grateful for that.

"I can't leave here remembering her...seeing her like..." He stopped, catching his breath. "This doesn't seem real. I can't believe what I don't feel."

"Aamir."

"I have to see her again. She's not. She can't—I want to say my goodbyes the real way. I have to see again for myself."

How could I tell him no when his soul knew the truth? I was a bastard, but not heartless. Not to those who meant something to me. And hadn't Layla asked for her babies? I could never deny her. I wouldn't now. Not with what I was about to do.

"Jasmeen should say her goodbyes too. I will go with both of you." I turned to Bram and Everleigh. "Will you please excuse us?"

They nodded and Aamir stood. He was still holding onto my suit as we began to leave the dining area. Whether he was even aware of it, I wasn't sure. He was beyond devastated, drowning in his grief, and he was about to hate me when he realized it was for nothing.

"Before we see Layla, I need to talk to you."

For the first time, his gaze rose from the floor. Bloodshot eyes blinked, studying mine as we came to a stop halfway down the main hall that led to my room. He didn't speak. He didn't ask questions. Maybe Aamir was so lost he couldn't think of any.

"If you could turn back time and save your sister's life, would you?"

"What kind of fucking question is that?" Anger came out in a mass wave of rage. A rage I knew Aamir bottled inside from his time in Whitlock. He wasn't the boy who originally came to my island with his sister as a slave. This is the Aamir who killed to get here. Who murdered and fought to survive red light massacres and corrupt guards.

I glanced down at Jasmeen, dropping my voice as I leaned closer. "You're not my brother, but you're like a brother to me. You know I love your sister. You know I'd do anything for her."

Aamir didn't speak, but he nodded.

"I will ask you again. If you could turn back time and save your sister's life, would you?"

"Yes."

"Here's your chance to prove it. When you leave my room, Layla *is* dead to you. Do you understand me? *Layla is dead.*"

Seconds dragged as multiple emotions swept over his face. Aamir kept his eyes on mine, and I saw the moment realization finally clawed through the sorrow. He spun, but I grabbed his arm before he could race forward like he wanted.

"Slow. Calm. You're going to say goodbye to your dead sister. Nothing has changed to warrant a fast response."

"I can't believe you," Aamir growled under his breath. "If you weren't holding my niece—Why didn't you tell me earlier?"

"Be lucky I told you at all. I wasn't going to. No one can know. No one, Aamir. They tried to kill her once. If they know…"

It was all I had to say to have his anger receding. We got closer to the guard, both of us growing quiet. When I opened the door, Mandy stood from the side of the bed, pulling the curtain closed.

"It's okay, he knows. He's come to say goodbye."

Aamir took the room in fast strides, once again breaking down as he neared the bed. Sitting, he leaned forward, kissing her forehead.

"I thought I lost you. God, Layla. *My h-heart.*"

"Brother."

The word was but a whoosh of air, barely recognizable.

"Shh. I'm here. Don't speak."

"Babies."

I came closer. As if Layla sensed us, her eyes cracked open. Her attempted smile at our daughter was immediate. Her lids closed again, and I handed Jasmeen to Aamir as he brought her closer to his sister. For the first time since Layla had given birth, I walked to the bassinet that held Jamison. Mandy had wrapped him in a blanket and put a hat on his tiny head. I could barely see him through the tears as I picked him up and held him close. If I thought I'd broken down before, that was nothing. Seeing his face. Feeling him in my arms and knowing tomorrow night I'd never see him again…my knees nearly gave out through the truth.

"I'm sorry, son." I whispered against his cool cheek. "This is all my fault. I'm so sorry."

Maybe I should have listened to Layla. Would he have died if I would have walked over there when she told me to? Something told me I was already too late. Layla's brother had been there. Whatever she did was before Aamir had arrived next to them, only seconds after.

"Gavin."

At Aamir calling me, I turned and headed back towards them. I managed to hold in the sobs threatening to leave, but barely.

"Is she okay?"

Layla's lids were heavy but open as I rounded the corner and made my way past the halfway-drawn curtain. They widened at what I was holding, but with one look at me, she knew. Her lids closed and tears raced down the sides of her face through the near silent cry.

"Where…is she?"

"Baby, you're weak. Try to rest. You need to heal."

"Where?"

I knew she was referring to the doctor. There was anger in her barely existing tone.

"Dead."

"You?"

I hugged Jamison tighter to my chest as I nodded.

"Good. Good."

The last I could barely hear. Layla was leaving me again. The Babke told me to expect this. In truth, I didn't believe Layla would wake up for days from what the shaman woman said. That my wife was conscious, spoke volumes. The mother in Layla would not rest without answers, but now that she had them, there'd be no peace.

"Aamir, did you tell her goodbye?"

"I did."

"You told her that you and Jasmeen are leaving?"

He leaned down again, kissing her on the forehead one last time and whispering something I couldn't hear. When he stood, he nodded.

"I told her twice. She refused to acknowledge me. I told her I'd keep Jasmeen safe, but Gavin...*I don't want to leave.* I can stay with you and Luke and help. I need to make whoever did this pay."

"And you will, but Jasmeen needs to be guarded, and we need players on every side. That includes the Whitlock side." I moved in closer to him, keeping my voice down as our eyes locked. "If anyone can find out inside information, it's Bram Whitlock. You will shadow him. Learn everything you can from him, but you will say nothing. You and I will stay in contact. I'll give you a phone. What we're dealing with goes beyond one man. I'm going to need you, Aamir. When we find out who's responsible for this, you'll come back, and we're going to make them pay. *Together.* They're going to suffer far worse than we are. I promise you."

# CHAPTER 3

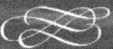

## LAYLA

The swirling, dark fog was endless. Each step, it swallowed me whole, taking me deeper into a comforting nothingness. Maybe I should have been afraid. The whispers in the far shadows implied I should. Even though I couldn't understand the voices, instinct told me I should be wary of what watched me.

Dew dampened my feet, and even though I couldn't see the ground I walked on, I could feel the grass. Had I been here before?

Yearning pulled me forward, and the wisps of tinted smoke wrapped around me like the softest blanket. A part of me wanted to lay down and let it put me to sleep. I was tired, wasn't I? There was something more that kept pulling me forward. There was something I needed. Something so a part of me, I couldn't have stopped if I wanted to.

"—don't look. She—can't."

My head whipped around at the barely audible whispers that grew closer. I scanned the area, despite seeing nothing more than thick fog surrounding me. The sky projected darkness, but even the brightest light wouldn't penetrate what enveloped me. I was trapped, or maybe I was being guarded. Thoughts were almost impossible as I felt my steps descend, only to rise. The whispers bit back and forth at each other; their jabs so sharp the words cut my skin. I was bleeding, but I wasn't afraid. Disorientation had me turning in a circle and I tried to grasp the cord that tied me to what I longed for. Who or what it was, I didn't know. All that was clear was that I had to keep going.

"*She—fall. Down. Down. Down.*" There was snickering between the deep-toned voices. Defensiveness had me standing taller as my eyes narrowed. I walked faster, almost looking for whoever it was that looked down upon me. Did they want me to fall? Is that what they meant?

"*Gavin?*"

My voice echoed around, going nowhere. Everywhere.

I swiped at the swirling mix of black, white, and gray.

"*Gavin?*"

"*Dragons burn things. Dragons—burn you. Burn me. He'll —the world.*"

"*Who are you? Where are you?*" More giggling and sneering. Three? Four? How many were there? "*Show yourself to me. Where's my husband? Gavin! If you've hurt him, I'll find you. Do you hear me? Gavin!*"

I'd never been one to make threats. Why I even was now, I didn't know. There was a sharp edge of madness boiling in my depths. I could feel it. Why, I couldn't remember. There was something. I had to keep going.

I pushed from the balls of my feet, starting off at a slow jog.

"*Gavin?*"

The bouncing had pain stabbing into my stomach. My palm pressed into the center, and the flatness had my eyes blinking hard. This wasn't right. The pain grew as I ran faster. This wasn't right at all. That turned my anger into fear so great, I could barely breathe. Something. There was...something. "*Gavin!*" I was sprinting, holding tightly to a stomach I was sure was going to split open at any moment. The whispers were getting closer. Pushing me faster. As I brought my hand up, the blood covering it nearly made my feet trip on themselves. I was going so fast; I could have been the wind. I could have been air, itself. Blood. Blood.

*"Dragon's burn. Burn the world."* Mischievous laughter. *"Burn, Layla. Be...fire."*

Orange bled into the sky, igniting a vibrant crimson as the fog separated, giving me a path. The faster I ran, the more my life left me. Time was running out, but salvation was ahead. If I could go faster. If I could reach the red. Gavin was there. He had to be.

*"Child, running will not save you."*

The musky smell of earth had a sound pushing past my lips. I knew that voice. It wasn't like the others. It was her. The Babke.

*"Gavin!"*

*"He will not save you either."*

I was suddenly glimpsing the cliffs ahead. Although there were different ones around the island, I recognized these as the same ones not far from the fortress we lived in. Even as I glimpsed over my shoulder, I could see my tower. I'd lived there before I gave myself to my husband. I'd cried right at that window, wanting nothing more than to throw myself from it and end my life.

*"Jump. Jump."* The wild laughter grew louder. *"Fly."*

Looking ahead, the cliffs grew closer. I was still running, feeling the invisible presence that plagued me grow so close, claws dug into my back. I cried out, Babke's voice joining me in my new nightmare as I continued to call for Gavin.

*"You can stop any time, child. Only strength will win here."*

I ignored her words, instead scanning the dim mountainside ahead. *"Gavin!"* He'd make this stop. He'd protect me. He always did. But he wasn't here now. I was the only one I could see, and no one was coming to save me from whatever it was that was chasing me.

Water for as far as the eye could see surrounded me as I neared the sharp edge of the cliff ahead. It couldn't have been more than three to four stories, but here, in this space, I was higher than any skyscraper I'd been in. Fear swallowed me whole, and even though my feet were trying to bear down so I could stop, I was still racing towards my death. Toward the precipice of some pivotal moment of live or die.

*"Gavin!"*

*"He's leaving you, child. Even now, he plans. It's time to be strong and find yourself."*

*"It's true. Gone. Jump. Jump."*

*"Fly."*

*"He's leaving."*

*"He leaves you because you're weak."*

A weaving of different sneers and hushed accusations floated around, almost encircling me.

*"Weak. Weak."*

*"Too young."*

*"A baby, herself."*

*"Fly. Die."*

*"Weak. Weak."*

Tears poured down my face, and I was internally screaming. What was I looking for? Gavin, yes, but something more? Yes, it needed me. I had to find it. I had to stop!

But I didn't. The sky grew a brighter red, coming alive in a sea of waving fire. Reds, oranges, yellows. Heat flared, and I tried screaming for my husband even louder. Just as I went over the cliff, my eyes flew open. My entire body jolted, and I was shaking through the ice cold that had me. My jaw was chattering, but I was covered in sweat.

"And you started the antibiotics? How long ago?" The twinge of fear in Gavin's tone had my head turning towards him, but he didn't see me. His wide golden-brown eyes were focused on Mandy. On my friend and servant as she wrung her hands on the loose, white slave dress she always wore. Gavin was in a clean black suit with a black shirt and tie, despite his hair was disheveled. The tie rested around his neck loosely, and the top of his tanned chest was exposed from the opened buttons. Thick scars from being tortured and burned peeked through with every shift of his frame. He was afraid. Upset, as he waited for her response.

"The antibiotics, Mandy. When?"

"An hour before the ceremony, Main Master."

"That was," he looked at his watch. "Four hours ago. Did you give her the fever reducer?"

Mandy's mouth opened, her gaze shooting to the other side of my bed. She was shaking, just as terrified as my husband.

"I told the girl no."

*The devil witch.*

"Why the hell not? Don't you see—"

Gavin's gaze shot down to me as he gestured, and his mouth parted wider as he dove to my side.

"Layla. God, Lovie." Tears nearly overspilled as he grabbed my hand and kneeled on the side of the bed, coming level with my face. There were dark circles under his eyes, and the fact that they were bloodshot and slightly swollen said more than I could even begin to process. Gavin never cried. Never. This was bad. I...was bad.

"Babies?"

The word came out as a hoarse whisper. Despair had his eyes lifting to the ceiling, so the tears didn't fall, but they did. Silence had me clearing my throat.

"Aamir. That's right." My lids closed as I shook my head through the recollection. Yes, he was taking Jasmeen to safety. Taking her away from here. And my son. My poor baby boy. The doctor killed him. Killed my newborn son.

Tears just wouldn't stop from either of us. Again, I was shaking my head, trying to erase the acid residue consuming my mind.

"No. I'm here, shhh. Try not to do this yet. Right now you have to be strong. You have to fight. I can't. I—" Gavin breathed out raggedly against my cheek, his tears only making mine flow worse as we both broke even more. His hand cupped to my bicep further away, and his face buried in my neck as I stared up at the ceiling. Movement had my gaze cutting over in nothing less than a glare.

I was seething. Raging inside, the moment I saw her. Something was changing deep in my depths. A rotting stain on the person I'd been before. Fear, I'd felt for the Babke and her tribe, but never hate. Maybe it wasn't even towards her. *It just was.*

"You." The words and warnings came back in a rush. My voice got choked on the sob, and Gavin's head came up as I stared her down. "Stay out...of my...dreams."

"You don't want me out, child, trust me. You want me there."

The voices kept repeating, making me even colder. "Stay. *Out.*"

I was so tired, and I was beginning to spin even though I lay still. Pressure built within, suffocating and hot as it grew. Gavin was holding my hand in both of his, looking between me and the Babke nervously. I was never mean. Never rude or threatening. He was taken aback by my tone, but I couldn't think on that now. I was fire and ice. Grief and rage.

"Babke says you're l-leaving. They confirmed it in my dream. They talk to me. They're not...good."

Gavin went rigid as he glanced at Mandy. He didn't speak. He didn't have to for me to know it was the truth. He *would* leave. He'd go after his revenge even if that meant death. Even if that meant leaving me forever. He'd never let this go. As much as that angered me, I couldn't blame him. I wanted to go after whoever had caused this too, but what could I do?

*"She's weak."*

*"Too young."*

*"A baby, herself."*

*"Fly. Die."*

*"Weak. Weak."*

Young, yes…I *was* young. Nineteen, but I didn't feel it. With what I had gone through with the birth, the rapes and difficult pregnancy, I could have been at least five to ten years my senior. I was more than tired; I was done on so many levels.

"Layla?" Gavin paused, waiting for me to open my eyes and bring my attention back to him. When I did, he brought my hand to his mouth, moving in closer. "I love you. You have to know that, but you're right. I may be gone when you wake up again. I'm sorry. I don't know how long I'll be away, but you have to stay hidden. You can't let anyone know you're alive. I have a plan, but it'll only work if you follow it. Do you understand?"

My eyes cut away from his to show I wasn't happy.

"They want you dead. If they know they didn't succeed, they're going to return. They may already be here, waiting. I'm leaving my instructions with Mandy. Do as she says. Please. *That is an order.*"

The deep tone brought my gaze jerking back to his.

"You order me now?"

"I'll do whatever it takes to keep you alive." He pressed his lips into mine, possessively. Claiming. There was such intensity as he pulled back to keep eye contact, but something was different. Gnawing at me as I watched his expressions shift. "The same goes for outside sources. *Whatever it takes.*"

My insides shook like an earthquake as a part of me broke. To save me, he could very well end up killing himself. Hadn't I lost enough already? My babies, they were gone from me. Now, him? I couldn't do this alone. I couldn't be without him. To do so was to live with who I truly was instead of who I'd forced myself to be. And not just with Gavin. I'd been a part of someone my entire life. First, my twin, Aamir, and then my husband. My identity revolved around theirs. Around Gavin's, I was safe and in love. I was a princess who had been rescued by a dragon. He was more than a knight to me, he was the ruler of my world, my God. Gavin was both savior and sword, and to deny the truth wasn't going to save me. Loving him had come at a price. One that nearly killed me. One that *was going* to kill me once I faced what happened.

"Can't we just leave? We could go get Jasmeen and Aamir and hide somewhere. Mistress Everleigh and Bram—"

"I will not put them in more risk than they're already in. We'd all be dead in days. Did you learn nothing from the Whitlocks? I was trying to prevent that for us, but I see now there is no other way. There's no leaving Red Island, Layla. Ever. There's only justice, which they will not fault me for when I get my revenge. I'm sorry I'm having to break my promise about us leaving. I said we'd have a new life and now we do. Just not one either of us want. I can't do this. I can't." He squeezed my hand, wiping his tears as he stood to leave. His steps were fast. Determined. Fleeing…

I was spinning again. Nothing was making sense. *He didn't want a life with me anymore? He didn't want this? Didn't want me?*

"Stop."

The order came out with more strength than I had. Gavin's shoulders caved in as he grew still, but he didn't immediately turn to face me. A broken breath filled the space, and he spun, hesitant as he returned. More, he wiped the tears. The expression on his face was hard. Distant. He wasn't the same man I married, or even the same one I'd seen only hours ago. His love was different now, changing, and I wasn't clear headed enough to be able to see through the walls he had up. Who was he becoming? It was as if my Gavin had died with our dream. Died with Jamison. The one being reborn…I didn't know. Already, he was so different, but *so was I.*

"You can pull back from me all you want, but you're not leaving without telling me you're going to be safe."

"My safety depends on you. I can't stress that enough. Follow my rules, and if you do, hopefully I'll be back before the month is out. Worst case, a month and a half. If you don't listen, and you rebel, like you sometimes do." He stopped, his eyes lowering. "I don't think I have to say it. You know the risk. We paid for it with our son. Do exactly as I say, Layla. Stay low. Give yourself time to grieve. Heal. I'll do the same…*my way.*"

# CHAPTER 4

## THE DRAGON

There were moments I was sure I couldn't exist for another second. Had Layla not lived, maybe I would have died on the spot. I'd been guarded from the world for so long that when I fell in love with her, I never thought not to love her with everything I had. It wasn't like she could leave me. I had plans to keep her as mine forever, whether she had wanted it or not. By pure miracle, she fell in love with me too. My mistake was thinking our love could live outside of Red Island. I was dead to the outside world—killed during my military career so that I could take my place here.

I'd never been a good man despite that I had stayed on the straight and narrow and excelled in my career. But the bad always found me. My personality couldn't be overlooked. I was perfect for this role. Killing didn't bother me. Morals…or what I had of them, disappeared during my recruitment and training process. They killed me. Literally. They made me into what they needed, and I was a fool to forget what I'd undergone to get here. My body was covered in a variety of different kinds of scars to prove it.

I rose from kneeling before the freshly covered grave of my

son and supposed wife. The sight of some veiled stranger holding my child nearly had me taking him from her arms in those agonizing moments only hours ago. He was meant for mine. For his mother's. Nothing about existence made sense. Life was fragile. Unfair. I'd been on the wrong side for so long, I was quickly seeing the power I had amid my fortress on the hill. Where I could berate myself forever, I had more pressing issues. Ones that called for blood and bone. I was going where fire and fate would collide, and the flames were coming to those who thought to cripple me through my family. First, I needed a direction, and I was about to get it.

"They're ready, Brother."

Emotion retreated to the depths of the oblivion inside, hiding from the new monster I was becoming. I turned, barely seeing my brother, Luke. What I focused on filled the grounds between the camps and the fortress. The captains I had in port, along with sea and sex slaves, were lined up next to each other in rows for as far as I could see. In front of them in two large groups off to the side were my guards, and the soldiers who lived in the underground bunkers within the island. They were the dishonorably discharged. The soldiers who couldn't leave war behind. They were killers to the core, and they were loyal to the Master who'd taken exceptional care of them. *They were mine.*

"Do we have any names yet?"

Luke ran his fingers through his short brown hair, standing taller as he inhaled through my question.

"Only two slaves survived that night. Neither are talking much. They say they weren't asked any questions concerning you or Layla. I'm not sure they know anything."

"Somebody knows something, and if I have to kill every single one of them to find out who, I will."

Luke kept a fast pace with me as we headed in their direction. It wasn't far, and from what I could see, they knew this was going to be bad. Fear was unmistakable on most of their faces as

I approached and stepped up to the elevated stage I rarely used. It had to have been almost a year since I had to address any situations. Since before Layla...

Grabbing the small mic from Lopez, I gave him a nod, not speaking as I ate up the width of the stage. I stared down everyone, from the slaves to the guards, letting my anger simmer so every single one knew I meant business.

"Some of you are going to die today. Maybe a lot of you. Because of information that was leaked from this very island, my family is gone from me. Dead. *Murdered.*"

I continued to pace, not taking my eyes off the large crowd.

"Since the word has already gotten around on what I want, I don't have to go into complete detail. A man stayed here months back. If you work the sea, you either know him or you've heard of him. He goes by the name Austin Birch. While he was here, he had access to all of you. Not just the female slaves, but guards too." I stopped, pointing towards the crowd. "Maybe you talked to him. Maybe he was asking questions. If you came across him while he was here and he spoke to you, you come to the front of the line right now. I want to know everything he said, and everything you know."

There was hesitation, but a handful of slaves began to weave between the rows, towards the small wooden stage. While they came forward, I continued.

"This man works for someone out of China. I do not know if that is who sent him here. *Someone* did, or communicated with him after he left, and I want to know who. Those of you who know Austin Birch through shipping, or have any information on him or his dealings, you stand in a second group off to the side." I paused. "And I better hear something of significance. If you were the one who gave him information, you tell me. You be honest, and I may be lenient. If I get nothing notable by the end of this, I will start with the first in line and work my way down killing all of you until I do. Let that be warning enough. Do not lie to me. Do not hold any information back. If you've heard *anything* about him or he said something to you, even hello, I want to hear it. Omission will only result in one thing. You all will suffer. There is no escaping it if you don't speak up."

Two large bonfires sparked to life, raging behind me. The ranks shifted as stares shot to the blaze. There wasn't a person before me that wasn't terrified. I didn't bluff, and they knew it.

"Let's go!" My voice boomed over the speaker. "I want two groups. Those who've had contact in this one, and the ones who may have information in the other."

More movement stirred as slaves began to hesitantly come forward. I headed for Luke, not able to stop the twitching of my hand as I handed Lopez the microphone. For a soldier, he could have passed for an average, everyday guy. He could blend in anywhere with his dark hair, brown eyes, and common features. That's what made him lethal. One minute you'd think you were making a new best friend, and the next he was slicing open your throat. I didn't trust many men to get near me, but I'd known Lopez now for over ten years, and I trusted him with my life. We served together. Killed for each other. We were brothers, just as much as me and Luke.

"I just got word." Luke stepped closer to me, lowering his voice. "The ships are being prepared. We'll head out on Sea Breeze tomorrow evening with the crew."

"Does Lui, the captain, know?"

Luke's head gave a swift jerk. "Nope, and he's not going to know until we're far away from this island. I have one of your men watching the vessel. He'll be our distraction while we take our place in the captain's quarters."

"Perfect." One more day. God, I felt sick at the thought of leaving Layla while she was so unstable. With the fever, what if she got worse? What if something happened while I was gone?

My head shook at the thought, trying to make it disappear. I gripped my brother's shoulder, giving a squeeze as I tried to catch my breath from the sea of emotions threatening to drown me. I had to act now. If I delayed, more information would be lost. They'd get away with it. I'd never find out who was responsible. Besides, if Layla had died, they'd expect me to come. If anything, it made her safer, even if it put me more at risk.

"Maybe you should go inside for a while, Luke. Things are going to get a bit—"

"Bloody? Gruesome? You're joking, right? Everleigh Whitlock removes faces for fun. I've helped her so many times, I've lost count. I'm here for you, Brother. Tell me what to do."

How had I overlooked that? His employers were no different than me, other than they'd already lived this nightmare and survived. *Barely.* There was no guarantee my fate would be the same.

"Okay. You take the second group and see what they've heard of Austin Birch. I'll talk to the slaves and guards and see what they recall from his time here." Luke nodded, and I couldn't stop from reaching to his shoulder as he began to walk their way. "Thank you for staying. For…helping me."

"You're my brother. I love you. I think for a long time, you forgot that."

I couldn't speak, and he didn't wait around for me to find words. I turned, making my way to the first group nervously eying me as I approached. There were four guards and three female sex slaves. Only two had lived after being used by Austin, but this third intrigued me.

"One at a time."

I pointed to the closest female, walking a few feet away, separating us from the others. The slave had skin the color of honey with eyes as green as the palm leaves. Her hair was to her lower back and wild with black curls. Her fingers slid to interlace, coming to a stop at her waist. She wore the typical white slave dress that ended just below the knees, loose and thin.

"What can you tell me about Austin Birch? You're in the contact group. Did you see him while he was here?"

"I did, Main Master. He didn't use me long. I believe I was his first on the trip."

"First. And you lived? Interesting."

"Lived, Sir, but not without undergoing suffering."

"So, he hurt you."

The slave nodded. "A lot. I was bruised over my face, neck. My chest too."

Her hand came to hover over her eye, cheek, neck and sternum, making its way down as she spoke.

"Sir, the man was…odd to me."

"Odd, how?"

"He was very much into our act, but I noticed he kept turning towards the door. I assumed he was waiting for someone, but no one showed up while I was there."

I was going to have to watch the video. I hadn't even gotten to that yet.

"Did he say anything to you concerning me or my wife?"

She paused, her lids narrowing before she finally shook her head. "I don't think so. At one point I must have passed out from the hits. I don't think he asked anything then, but I can't be sure. If he did, I don't think there was any way I could have answered him. Not since I was unconscious."

"What about the island? The boats? Shipping? Did he ask anything about this place? Anything at all aside from sexual acts he wanted you to perform?"

The slave got quiet again.

"He did say something I thought was a bit strange when he finished with me. I was on the floor, barely conscious, but I vividly remember him saying, *'I guess it is true. The pussy is sweeter on Red Island. Maybe I'll find me a wife here too.'* I was barely awake, and he was blurry. I tried rubbing my eyes, but that only made him angrier once he realized I was awake. I think he mumbled *'double or nothing'*. Once he said that, he immediately brought his leg back and kicked my face. I passed out again after that. When I woke up, I was outside of his hut, on the pier."

"He said wife?"

"Yes, Main Master."

My fists clenched as I glanced towards the pier, housing all the luxury bungalows. I should have gutted the bastard while he lay in the extravagance I provided, eating my food. *Killing my slaves.* What the hell was *'double or nothing'* supposed to mean? "Think back to when you first arrived and faced him. Did he say anything to you? Introduce himself?"

The slave's lips slightly parted.

"I was outside with the laundry. We were hanging up sheets. He walked up and said, *'you, come with me'*. Word had already gotten around the island that we were to go with him if we were called." She paused. "I put down the basket, and I followed him."

"He didn't say anything to you on the way back to his hut?

"No, Main Master. Not until we got inside. He said, *'take off your clothes'*. I did. Then he—"

"That's it? He didn't say anything else?"

Anxiety flashed, and her eyes made jerky movements as she thought back.

"I walked in, and he said, *'take off your clothes'*." Her brow creased. "I was nervous. The man didn't feel good to me. I wasn't fast enough. He...had his phone, looking at the screen. He told me to hurry up as he was putting it on the small table by the sofa. I was nervous at his tone. There was anger. A lot of it. I obeyed and followed him into the bedroom."

A long exhale left me. Who had he been on the phone with? Or who was he waiting on? She'd mentioned he kept looking towards the door. He was expecting someone.

"So, you had sex with him. You did as you were told. During, did he say anything?"

Her lip made the smallest shake before she shrugged. "He called me names. Slut. Whore. You're all whores. He said that a lot. The longer that went by, the more violent he became. The last hit…I flew off the bed. That's how I ended up on the floor. It's all a blur at that point. I only remember what I told you before."

I nodded. "Tell the blonde to come to me. You get back to the group and don't move. I'm not done with you yet."

Curls swayed as she backstepped, refusing to turn her back to me. It wasn't until she was a few feet away before she finally spun and ran back to the group. As I took in my brother and my soldiers, I couldn't help but wonder what we were missing. There was something…something. My eyes locked on Lopez, who never had his attention off me for long. At my wave, he came over.

"Lopez, do me a favor. I'm doing this backwards. Fuck, I can't think. Get into the feed of when Austin Birch arrived. I want you to watch and see if there's anything on there that could tell us something. I want to know everyone he talked to. Everyone he may have locked eyes with."

"Your brother and I already have. There's nothing out of the ordinary, Main Master. Aside from the female slaves, he never spoke to anyone else here. The girls who lived are in that group you're questioning. Aside from them, the only ones he talked to were his crew, and mainly before they were leaving."

"His crew. Of course. He was prepared for this. Austin's not stupid. He would have waited until he was back on his own boat to confirm any rumors or learn of them." My teeth ground. "I'm going to continue to interrogate the groups. Get back to the footage. Maybe you all missed something. My biggest mistake was not putting cameras in those huts. I plan to change that immediately. Someone revealed information about my wife and kids, and I want to know exactly who it was."

# CHAPTER 5

## LAYLA

"*I* know it's scary, but you have to try. Put the pillow to your stomach. Maybe it'll help with the fear."

"What if my stomach opens and everything spills out onto the floor?" I glanced at Mandy. She held on to me as we stood, but I was terrified to take a step. It'd been hard enough to stand with how weak I felt. "Are you sure this is safe?"

Mandy's lips parted and her scared eyes shot to Babke across the room. The older woman's long white hair was wild today, haloing around her darkly tanned face. Glacier blue eyes, almost white, watched us, but they didn't appear threatening. Just observative as they seemed to glow in the distance.

"I see. She told you to get me to do this."

"Babke says it is time. You have to walk, Leelee[1]."

The older woman's head tilted at the pet name Mandy used for me. She'd said it the last few months. I figured it was a cute nickname but given that look the devil woman wore, I wasn't so sure.

Bringing the pillow to my stomach, I winced as I took a step. Then two. Mandy's big smile lit up her face, easing the worry as her hands stayed locked on my hips.

"You're doing it. See, you're going to be okay."

That was debatable. I was so fatigued, and I was still cold, hours later. My fever lingered but had eased due to the drink Babke concocted for me. My higher self said I shouldn't have drunk it, but she had saved my life. I didn't think she'd try to kill me now.

Four steps along the bed and I turned to sit back down. Sweat was beading on my face and there was a pull to my stomach I didn't like. The damn doctor woman had cut me open good, but not nearly as bad as she could have.

"You did good, child. Tonight, you will eat vemki[2]. It will make you stronger."

Mandy cringed, and my gaze shot to the shaman.

"What's that?"

"Special soup."

"Horrible soup," Mandy whispered. "Sour."

"Not horrible, girl, healing." Babke pointed, shaking her long, thin finger. "You will eat some sour soup too. Maybe it'll chase some of that fear away from you."

Mandy's lip pouted, but she stayed silent. How could I think about eating when all I felt were how swollen and painful my breasts were. My babies weren't eating. Not from me. To feed them from myself was a miracle, a gift. All I was now was cursed. Probably in more ways than one.

"I'm not hungry."

"Not my concern. You *will* eat."

I opened my mouth to argue but couldn't speak as screams filled the fields below. I surged to my feet, doubling over from the shooting pain. Mandy rushed to my side, placing her hand at my lower back.

"You must go easy."

"What was that?"

Silence. More screams, and I couldn't tell if it was a man or a woman.

"What is happening down there?" As I eased to straighten, the Babke headed over, drawing the curtains over the wooden coverings that already blocked us from view. I eased back to the mattress, watching as she headed to light a mix of black and white candles. We had white, but I'd never seen black candles here before. "Babke?"

There was a pleading in my soft tone. A bending I wasn't sure I was good with as I waited for some sort of answer. Truth was, there was a heaviness within my wounded core. It made my heart race and my spine straighten. The stirring was undeniable; I just wasn't sure what exactly it was. I hated even more how uncertain I felt around the devil witch. I was so conflicted on everything.

"You fear. You should." A flame burst to life, igniting the end of a thin wooden length of timber. "Gavin Draper works with fire and Death tonight, but I think you know that. You feel Death close. He feels you too. Your husband appeases the force. He buys you time."

"You're saying Gavin is down there burning people alive right now?"

The candle's wick caught, jumping into a long flame. I kept going over his full name, wondering why the witch used it. The Babke didn't answer my question as she moved to the next. Her finger trailed the length of black wax, and she eased the firestarter forward, sending that flame higher than the last.

"Your Dragon seeks answers. He will find them, but not for hours more. He's only put aside three bodies to burn so far, so we have some time. Seventeen will meet their fate before it is over with. Not one more or less. It has begun." She inhaled deeply. "If you close your eyes, child, you can detect the hint of flesh starting to be carried through the air. Can you smell it? Gavin Draper. Draper. Gavin. Dragon." She whispered his name, closing her lids.

My nose crinkled as my hand came to flatten over my

stomach. The screams were turning crazed. Frantic. I was slightly faint just at the thought of how the skin had to have been bubbling and burning. After all, I'd seen Gavin burn people alive before. He didn't know I secretly watched, but I had. As his wife, I felt I didn't have a choice. He couldn't carry the burden alone, not that he saw it as a burden. More...a treat.

"You smell it. You recognize the scent." Her eyes were opened now, and she nodded as confirmation, turning to Mandy. "But not you. Not yet. You're pure. *Big heart.* You haven't suffered like your Leelee. You've been rather lucky with your time here. Or is it more than luck? The gift, perhaps? What made you call her your queen? I see no headdress or crown."

The servant shifted her stance as she looked between us.

"She's with the Main Master of the island. Is she not a queen? In the tribe, the chosen is the queen. Shouldn't it be for the island as well?"

The Babke shook her head. "A woman is a queen when she earns it. Marriage won't justify that title. It is gained. Deserved. Your mother should have let us raise you. Not," she flicked her wrist. "*Him.* Your father's coveting ways did more harm than good. He stole your mother and paid the price for it. The sea retaliated and took down his ship, but it was too late for her. What happened to your mother: a slave. What happened to you? Slave. Servant, but slave. The tribe would have welcomed you both home. Meshtu was always stubborn. Your father even more. Not you. You are broken by *their* ways. Not to worry. Your Leelee will change that soon enough. She's not going to have much choice."

I went to ask what she meant by that but winced through the new round of pains. I turned, letting Mandy help me back to my spot on the bed. I didn't even reach the pillows before more screams erupted in the distance. The Babke glanced over, lighting another candle, and closing her eyes.

"The night will be long. I will start preparing the vemki. We turn in early tonight. Much awaits us."

But I didn't want to know what she meant by that. Every time I slept, the voices were there with me. They taunted the woman inside. They angered the mother within. I was twirling and twisting in some never-ending nightmare I couldn't escape. They loved insulting me with their mean jibes. I could take that had the truth not hurt so much. I believed their demeaning words, and that only made me angrier at myself. At them, and the entire world. I was drowning in rage, and my new reality of being alone had barely even begun.

*The sway of grass*
*A breeze so soft*
*A moment trapped upon the loft*

*Brown eyes are sad*
*Tanned skin so true*
*He calls aloud to answer you*

*Dear girl, don't fret*
*Just turn around*
*She cries amid the haunting sound*

*She jumps, she leaps*
*The edge grows close*

*One more step to claim your ghost*

*H**e loves, she loves*
*A tale no more*
*The monsters here are worse than lore*

"*L*ayla. Layla, wake up."

A familiar voice pulled me from the red sky that called me closer. I gasped, still hearing the voices beg me to hurl myself over the cliff. Sweat drenched my lace camisole, and I was shaking through the chills that seemed to have me again. Gavin was talking and cursing angrily, but I could barely focus as I floated from the effects of whatever she'd put in the vemki.

"Enough of this. You get her fever reducer now and double the fucking antibiotics if you have to. She should not still be sick like this."

"It takes time, Dragon. Already, she's walking. Not far, but a few steps. She will grow stronger than you realize."

The Babke's words wavered, sounding slightly muffled with how far away she was.

"Gavin?"

I reached towards the blurred face that lowered to hover above mine.

"Lovie, it's a few hours before morning. My day is going to be...busy." He stopped. "I have to start preparing to leave now. I couldn't go without telling you goodbye." He stopped, making a deep sound in his throat. "I promise they're not going to get away with this. I'm going to kill whoever was involved, if it's the last thing I do." Lips pressed into my forehead as his long fingers pushed through my hair to hold. "I'm leaving my heart behind with you. I want you to take good care of it while I'm gone. I'm going to need it back when I return. Stay on guard. Protect yourself. *You're everything to me.*"

"But…you said." I cleared my throat, trying to push up to sit. Gavin didn't let me as he leaned down, nuzzling the side of my face. "You said you couldn't do this with me anymore. You don't want me now that I—*lost our babies*. You don't want me."

"Don't you dare say things like that. Of course I do. None of this was your fault. God, it's mine. It was all me. What I can't do is breathe. I can't…take the guilt. I brought her here. I let her near you."

"You didn't know."

"*I should have.* Do you know how close I came to losing you? *We lost our son.* Jamison is gone. Our daughter and family…gone. I can't." Tighter, his fingers gripped to my hair making me wince in pain. "When I get done, no one will ever think about coming after us again. I'm going to keep you and Jasmeen safe. I'll burn them all to make sure of it."

Lips pressed into mine and somehow I managed to grip Gavin's shirt, pulling him even closer.

"I'm not sure I can do this without you. I don't want you to leave me. What if something happens?"

"Baby—"

"*No.*" I met his eyes, trying to make them come in clear. All I saw were golden flames burning within. "What if something happens? I can't be without you. What am I supposed to do?"

Seconds went by as Gavin held my stare. Whatever passed between us was nothing short of terrifying.

"Luke doesn't know it yet, and he's going to be pissed when he wakes up, but I'm leaving him behind. I've already gone over it with the staff and soldiers, and they know he's in charge. I need someone to run Red Island, and he's the next best thing. He may even be able to convince others outside of here that he *is me* if he stays out of view. I can't risk that with you though. Layla, I need you to listen to me. You can't stay here while I'm gone. It's not safe. They'll be on the lookout for anything suspicious. Luke doesn't know the staff or slaves. It's too risky. The Babke has already agreed, and we've decided the tribe is the safest place for you until I return. They'll take care of you there. They'll protect you. Worst case... If you're discovered while you're with them, or you're in jeopardy, I have a source that will contact Luke, who will then contact Bram and Everleigh. They'll figure out a way to come get you."

I blinked through the words, trying to get him to come in clear. Was I still dreaming? He couldn't be serious. The tribe were murderers. They were dangerous. They were always in the distance watching us. *Hunting us.* I saw them. I'd watched them peeking around trees to point up towards our balcony. And not just one, but almost all. We were outsiders. We were their enemies. That's the way it felt, anyway. They weren't nice. They sure as hell weren't accepting.

"I...can't."

"You will. And if it comes down to it, you'll leave here with Bram and Everleigh. It's not safe for you to, and it puts them in worse danger, but it is the last resort."

"No. I don't care what happens, I'm not leaving the island. I'm waiting for you. I don't care if it takes forever."

"You'll leave if it keeps you safe. Just like you'll stay with the tribe until I return."

"...The tribe?" My head shook. "Gavin, are you listening to yourself? I can't do that. You've seen them bordering the field. Hiding behind the trees and watching everything. They hang shells from the branches to keep us out. You've seen the trees. Shells are everywhere as a warning. They won't want me there. They scare me. Soldiers have disappeared. *They eat them.* I... can't."

"We don't know that for sure. It's probably just scary stories people tell. And the shells are our border. They're nothing more than a fence on their part. They're cautious, but that's all. Just like when they watch. The tribe is curious. I've never had issues with them, so long as we leave them alone. The Babke is in charge and she says you can stay, and you will. This is the only way. Mandy will go with you. She'll take care of you."

"I don't need a babysitter," I spat. "I need my husband. *Don't do this.* We can plan our revenge later. Gavin, please, I can't. I just." To think of staying in the devil witch's territory, that was an entirely different thing. What Gavin spoke wasn't even accurate. He was watering down the truth to try to convince me, but he couldn't erase the facts. The tribe spoke a language I didn't understand. Most men didn't wear clothes. They had traditions and a way of life I didn't understand, like...blood sacrifice and cannibalism. Branding and death.

"Please don't make me do this."

"There's no other way, Lovie. I'm leaving this place and so are you. When you're well enough to walk, you're to head through the tunnels that lead to the far side of the island. That will get you past what's left of the guards and slaves. You're to stay with the tribe until I return. You're not to come back to the fortress for any reason. None. Neither is Mandy. Do you understand?"

Tears escaped as I tried to turn away. With his grip on my hair, I didn't move far.

"Lovie, do you understand?"

"The wife you see will no longer exist when you return." I met his confused gaze, letting the anger and abandonment roll through as I tried to bring him in clear. I understood everything he said, but the fear wouldn't let me accept it.

"What do you mean?" There it was. Anger. Enough to match my own. "If you're thinking of—*You're not talking about killing yourself.*"

"I have a daughter to live for. What I speak of is essence. Of being." I paused as my teeth chattered through the increasing shakes. "We will be strangers when you return, and I can't promise you'll love the person you come home to. I already don't know who I'm becoming. The voices."

"Layla." He let out a breath. "The voices are your grief. That's all. I may be becoming something completely different as well, but my love for you isn't going anywhere. Look at my face." His lids narrowed. "My love grows by the second. I would die for you. Kill everyone in the *world* for you. There's nothing out of my reach when it concerns proving my devotion." He dipped down, brushing his lips into mine. "I didn't make it where I am because I was weak. I'm unstoppable. Untouchable. Now inject that force with a love unrivaled with any before. Do you know what happens when that force is fucked with, Layla?"

"Death?"

A smile tugged at his lips as he kissed me and lifted higher to look down.

"That's too simple. Dragons guard their most sacred treasures, and they'll do anything to protect it. They're about to find that out. The statement I'll make will be what nightmares are made from. It'll be the warning given to Main Masters when they take their place. There won't be a person in the world my wrath won't touch. Just wait...*you'll see*. Hurting my family was their biggest mistake, and when they come to realize that it'll already be too late."

# CHAPTER 6

## THE DRAGON

*I*f I didn't think things could get any harder than burying my son and losing my daughter, I was wrong. Leaving my wife, the epitome of my existence, about killed me. She was sick. She needed me. Given what I saw when I went to her room, she may even be getting worse. I had no idea. What I did know was if I didn't find out who did this, I'd lose them all for good.

Last night's information hunt gifted me some promising leads, but I still had no smoking gun. That lay with Austin Birch, and I'd make it to him eventually. Until then, I needed more. Austin was a patsy. A pawn to a bigger fish. Whether that was the Main Master out of China, or someone else he was working for, I didn't have a clue. What I did know from my conversation with Bram was that everyone I talked to concerning the doctor more than likely lied to me. Men I considered allies. Men I thought I could at least trust. There was no trust in a circle of cold killers. But even they had an overseer. So did I. Rich Tilson was my contact and stayed so far behind the lines, he didn't exist. That had been his greatest strength. It could have been my biggest mistake.

*Ring.*

*Ring.*

My eyes cut to the boat I was meant to board at any minute. I was in the last fishing hut on the pier, hunkered down by supplies with Lopez, Fallon, White, and Pattinson; some of my deadliest men. Slaves were busy loading the boat, and I waited as the captain paced the deck.

"Yes."

The deep voice didn't come out as a question. It almost sounded like a response as I shifted to look back out of the window.

"You wouldn't have wanted me to leave. Did it come from you?"

Silence. Clinking sounded, and an exhale echoed over the phone.

"It's the middle of the night, Gavin."

"Was it you?"

"She was a pretty girl, but attachments like that never last in places like this. We taught you to be smart. To weigh the risks. You neglected to do that."

"Did the order come from you?"

"I flat out denied your request. Laughed at you. You know that, yet you decided you wanted it to go over my head. I gave you your wish. Besides, if you thought it came from me you wouldn't have called. You wouldn't be planning to leave. You'd already be here, or someone would be on their way to take me out. But you're not doing that. You're jumping a plane or ship. That's what you're doing, correct? Leaving on some grand adventure so you can get your revenge?"

"I know you know. I want a name, Rich. I deserve a name. I did everything I was supposed to."

"You were noble...*and stupid*. Did you think your marriage would never get out? That you could hide that girl and her condition from The Seers? Did I teach you nothing? The Collective High Council knows everything."

"Wait...*who?*"

"Gavin, let this go, and keep your head down for a while. Let the water settle and in time we can discuss what happened. You have potential. You made a mistake. Love does that to the best of us. In time it will be forgotten."

"Forgotten? They killed my children. *My wife.*"

"And you're lucky they didn't kill you too. They will if you don't let this go. For both of our sakes, look the other way until you're in the position not to. I've taught you better than spontaneous revenge. That will get you nothing but trouble."

"Perhaps. Or maybe it'll fill the hole these bastards blew through my chest when they took away the only thing I love. My family was everything to me. Someone's going to pay, and not in the future. *Right now.* I want a name."

"What you want is the list of this council I mentioned. That, I will not give you. Not because I don't want to but because I truthfully don't know who's on it. Even I'm not so privileged."

"But it was them? They're the ones who made the call?"

"No idea. I don't know the logistics, and that's the point. You answer to me. I answer to someone, and so do they."

"Who are The Seers?"

"Spies. They infiltrate. They're no ones. Mostly always overlooked as slaves or businessmen. Truth is, they're deadly, and they have more power than you could imagine. They're directly connected to the Collective High Council. Not through the supposed six men who lead it, but through a chain of people like us. Their voice has sway. Power. More than mine or yours."

"Why have I never been told about any of this?"

"Most don't know until they're either dead or chosen to move up in the ranks. I've heard them called 'the machine that rules the world'. I have no reason to question that. They are a machine. They're unstoppable."

"But was it them who decided my family had to die?"

A pause. "Gavin…truthfully, I don't know. It could have been anyone. The fact that I haven't heard whispers is a sign all its own. Whoever gave the order has power. That should be enough to deter you. What I can tell you is, if you do this, you will die. Whoever took out your family did so as a warning. Take that seriously, because if you don't, I doubt you'll make it anywhere near your first destination. Word travels faster than the wind, and your intentions are just as transparent."

"But are they? Don't underestimate me, Rich. I *will* kill those who were involved, and when I do, I better never hear my name in the mouth of another Main Master. They want me at Red Island, fine. *They have me.* But they're about to find out how my home got its name. It didn't come from you." I watched as one of my soldiers gave the signal, climbing on board to distract the captain. "I have to go. Don't worry about business. It will continue. Take care of the temporary Main Master because if you don't, I *will* come after you, and I will succeed in killing you. *You owe me this.*"

I hung up, shoving the phone in my pocket. I motioned with my hand, heading for the door. Inching it open, I watched as the soldier led the captain around to the other side of the ship.

Soon the clouds would be painted with vibrant pinks and oranges. The pier I was on was new. Layla and I would go on random walks when she was feeling up to it, and she refused to go down the old pier since that's where she'd shown up in chains with Ram. To make her happy, I tore the entire fucking thing down, old port pier, luxury huts not far from there, and everything in-between. What I had rebuilt in record time was a resort's wildest dream. It was top of the line bungalows, each with their own pools, floating islands, all in between a maze of multiple twisting and merging piers. At night, all lit up, it was its own community, and she adored it, even if it was just her looking down at it from our bedroom balcony. We were all about sunsets and sunrises. Those were our special times, back when every-thing was perfect, and we still had our babies alive and well in her belly. I'd never been happier in my life. *My arm around her. Her head resting on my neck. My other hand on her rounded stomach.*

My heart squeezed as I gazed into the darkness in the distance. The moon was full giving view to a slight glow from the horizon. I couldn't stop myself from glancing towards the fortress, wishing I was there with my wife. God, what was I doing? Was I really leaving Layla…like this? With her sick and recovering from being butchered? And to go to the tribe? The fucking tribe I wouldn't let her around on any normal day? Layla wasn't even allowed to leave the fortress without me. Not with the way they constantly watched and kept tabs on what I was doing. Was I really allowing this to happen?

For the smallest moment, hesitation had me. It was the scuffling of slave boys heading below deck that drove me faster. They were all so focused on their jobs. Busy. All of them but one. He'd happened to look up from carrying something below. He was a small-framed teen with a frail build and dark hair. He was frozen as we jogged forward. The moment my gaze connected with his, his head lowered. He knew better to move or run as I slipped onto the boat.

"Not a word boy. Not to anyone. You hear me?"

"Y-Yes, Main Master."

"Alright. Get to your duties and keep your mouth shut."

I swung the captain's door open, watching the sea slave scurry away as we slipped inside. The probability of Lui catching us here was slim. He'd stay up top in the bunk inside the wheelhouse, I was almost sure of it.

*Almost.*

I wouldn't think of that now. I secured the door, pushing my fingers through my black hair as I tried to stop the heaviness pulling me down. It was my body. My soul. *My entire fucking being*. The weight was a killer, confusing me on the right thing to do. Layla wanted me to stay. She needed me. And after everything she'd been through, wasn't that the least I could do? She said we could get our revenge later, but I knew that wasn't the case. We'd never discover the truth if I put this off. I didn't want to leave, but my son deserved better. He deserved justice.

A small glow filled the space from Fallon. It allowed us to see the surroundings without it being too bright.

"Start setting up the equipment. Every boat under my control has a tracker. I want to see where they are, and where they're going. If Luke's calculations are right, we can jump to the Sea Surf and pull into Lisbon on its scheduled port call. Nothing will seem out of character. That's if the captain is on his true route. I wouldn't say Keenan is the most reliable."

Footsteps had my finger flying to my mouth as the soldiers froze. I reached over, sliding the lock free and withdrawing my knife before someone could check the door. I didn't need a scene on the outside, and that's what would happen if they discovered the door was locked. In here, I had control.

Inching over, I put myself on the far side of the door, waiting to reach over and sweep someone inside if they were to open the barrier. The thuds from walking paused, and I listened as talking broke the silence.

"I'm sure it's nothing. The net obviously looks fine. It must have been a trick of the moonlight. I'll let you go. The Main Master wouldn't be happy if I knocked you off schedule."

"No, he wouldn't." The knob turned and my teeth clenched as I waited. "Hey, you wouldn't happen to be looking for another hand, would you? I don't have much fishing experience, but I can keep people in line. I'm a quick learner."

There was hesitation from the captain.

"Boat's full this time, but I may be looking in the future if this new guy I have doesn't work out. I'll be back in a few weeks. Find me, then."

Footsteps continued, merging in with the pitter-patter of a few more. The sea slaves were in full swing and it wouldn't be long before we were out to sea. Seconds passed. Minutes. The soldiers continued with their equipment, but I didn't move from my position. I couldn't risk a single mistake. Not when mine and Layla's lives were on the line. I may have feared for her more, but I sure as hell didn't want to die and lose her for good. I needed this to go through flawlessly. I needed us back together again so we could heal and try to make sense of any sort of future we'd have here. *If we had a future at all.* What if she didn't forgive me for causing this? For leaving? What if she grew to hate me for bringing her so much pain? Fuck, I had way too many questions and not nearly enough alcohol in my system. I wasn't much of a drinker, but liquor was about the only thing holding me together in my darkest moments.

"We're online, Main Master."

Pattinson stared down at the laptop, pushing buttons as Fallon, White, and Lopez messed with their devices.

"Excellent. Pull up all the boats. I want to see where they are. Fallon, can you get ears on the wheelhouse? I want to listen to Lui. I need to know who he's talking to, and what about."

"You got it, Double M. Give me a moment. I'll be right in."

My head nodded as I glanced to Lopez. He was eyeing me cautiously. It'd been a while since the two of us had really got to sit down and talk. Hell, before Layla, he practically lived at the fortress. Where had all those months gone? They flew by, and now they might be gone forever. I could die, or worse, Layla might realize exactly what I'd done. She might never forgive me.

Lopez stood, bringing his laptop with him. I pushed from the wall next to the door, glancing at the small round table he motioned to, not feet away.

"I'll take watch. You sit."

He placed the laptop down, making me go rigid as I watched Mandy help Layla walk along the bed. My heart was thudding at him remembering how to get into my system, but I didn't have to tell Lopez not to say a word. He knew my secret, and I had no doubts he'd die before he spoke it aloud. There was a reason he had my information to begin with. He was the only one aside from Luke I trusted.

"Sit, Boss. I got this."

My hand clamped to his shoulder in a silent gesture of gratitude. I took a seat, angling the laptop so no one else could look over and see the screen. A smile wanted to tug at my mouth, but I kept my face cold and unfeeling as I watched her place the pillow from her stomach back on the bed.

Layla was still awake, which had me frowning, but she looked better than she did when I left her sometime after midnight. She had the slightest amount more color, and there was a determination on her face that put me at even more ease. My girl was a fighter. She always had been. When we met, she was ready to die if it meant she could have her revenge. I'd never seen a woman so strong in my life. After what she'd been through, she would have let me kill her if it meant her rapist didn't get away with his sins. I didn't take her life the way she wanted, but I did burn that motherfucker alive. It was the best thing I'd ever done.

Banging outside had me glancing over, but I barely cared as Layla tried to stand straighter. Her eyes closed and she took a breath, easing Mandy back as she took another step. The Babke looked to be leaving the room. She liked Layla, despite my wife's fear of her. That didn't mean I was okay with the shaman woman. The witch saved my wife's life, but at what cost? Layla kept mentioning voices. That worried me after Mandy's warning. Surely, it was the guilt. We all had demons. Layla's were just winning because of what she experienced.

"Hey! Hurry up! I want to be out of here before the sun comes up."

The booming voice was loud outside the door. I knew immediately that it was the main deckhand, Kenneth, yelling at the slave boys.

"Let's go! You have three fucking minutes, or your ass is mine."

My eyes rose, taking in the three men on the other side of the small room. White was sitting on the cot, his eyes cut up over his laptop as he glared to the door. He was protective over kids, and this island was crawling with them. Fallon was focused on trying to get me into the wheelhouse, and Pattinson was just as focused on his own task.

As I glanced back down, I noticed Layla was talking. I could so easily turn up the volume but I couldn't with others in the room. I'd get Lopez's earbuds for next time. I had a few days to watch her before she left the fortress, and I planned on taking every minute of that I could.

# CHAPTER 7

LUKE

*I*t was gagging that drew me from a deep unconsciousness. The heaves came, causing me to stumble as I tried to race from the bed and into the adjoining bathroom. I crashed into the stone wall, feeling the skin on my bare shoulder break as I stumbled forward, barely making it in time. My balance was off, and I felt like I was riding waves as I collapsed to my knees, becoming ill. Colors blurred, merging with textures. As I got sick, I realized my entire body was covered in sweat. It was pouring from me, racing down my biceps and chest in little rivers. Literally. What the fuck was I seeing?

Tightening in my gut was crippling as I tried to catch my breath. My heart was racing, making my skin raise up with every thump-thump that echoed in my ears. I was fucking hallucinating. Somehow, I knew that. What I was seeing and feeling wasn't real, but it sure as fuck seemed like it as I managed to reach up and flush the toilet.

"Luke?"

The name formed in text before my eyes, bouncing around the room like a computer wallpaper. I followed its course over the elaborate walk-in shower, squinting as it pinged around the glass, spinning from *L* to *E,* eventually going right through the barrier to splat on the stone wall inches from me. Dammit. I was in trouble. I had to think.

"Luke?"

Louder I called, suddenly realizing...I was calling out my own fucking name, not Gavin's like I'd meant to. Was I so far gone I couldn't even remember who my own brother was? How did this happen?

Pushing to my hands and knees, I managed to crawl to the bathroom door. The room was still moving, rolling like the sea as I paused in the threshold.

"Much hate in you. Sadness. Fair amount of good. You'll do."

My head lifted, bobbing as I tried to hold it up to stare at the damn tribal woman who was sitting in the dark corner.

"You did this?"

"Eh. I made the vemki. You ate three bowls. You did this to you."

"The soup," I groaned. That's right. I'd come across it in the kitchen's refrigerator. It had been damn good. A bit sour but exotic tasting. Gavin...he'd told me to eat it. He—

"Where's my brother?"

Laughter dropped in pitch, turning so deep I expected my skin to start peeling back at the grating force.

"Gone. Soon...far, far away. You are the new Main Master. He needs you. You will run this place. He wrote you a note."

"Son of a bitch. I should have known. What time is it?" I groaned, trying to push up to my knees. I wasn't fairing well on all-fours and the nausea was returning.

"Late but not early."

"What the hell does that mean? Do you have an hour?"

"I have many."

I groaned, not able to argue or fight for an answer. "What was in that soup?"

"Truth. What do you see?"

I blinked, trying to make the colors stop slithering. They were slipping and sliding, rolling under my palms. Fear sparked, but I kept trying my best to convince myself none of this was real. My pulse didn't believe me. As I managed to lift the top of my body, I held to the door frame just to keep myself steady.

"The colors are moving."

"Look closer. What do you see?"

"I..." The darkness came alive, growing thicker and closer by the second. It rolled in whisps like fog or clouds, taking shape into tall, terrifying looking figures. I should have been afraid, but I couldn't get over the shock or awe of what was happening. "People. I see...cloaked figures?"

The witch nodded. "A fractal of your fate. What else?"

My eyes strained through the distance of the room. The black colors transitioned, rolling. I was back to the sea, feeling it move around me. I brought my fingers to my lips, trying to hold back the nausea.

"The ocean. It rolls. It's rough."

"It will be. What else?"

I winced through the pain and heaviness suddenly in my chest.

"You love him," she said, softly. "He's with you. You feel him. That's better for you as the new Main Master. What else?"

My stare was transfixed to the darkness ahead. It was constantly shifting and moving into different things.

"I see fire. Waves, fire, and...these figures."

The sound of footsteps had my concentration breaking. I turned, seeing the older woman as she stopped at the dresser in my guest room, picking up a paper. When she brought it to me, I couldn't stop my lips from parting at the power I felt from her.

There was no emotion attached to it. Just the side effects. I wanted to curl into myself. Maybe even yell with everything I had. Her power stabbed like needles along my arm, and the dots of blood had me swiping over my skin. This woman could destroy me. Maybe not by sheer strength, but I didn't doubt her abilities one bit. I feared her in that moment, if not respected her just the same.

"Read it out loud, Luke. Try not to get distracted at the letters moving around the page. Let your mind lead, not your eyes. Things are rarely what they appear."

The paper trembled in my grasp as I took it from her. Just as she said, a million tiny snakes appeared, all of them heading right for my thumb along the edge of the page. I rapidly blinked my eyes, forcing myself to focus on my brother's message.

"Luke,

I know you're pissed at me right now. I wish things didn't have to be this way. I'd give anything to have you here with me. I've come to realize that Red Island isn't safe without me there. That's impossible right now, but where I can't, you can. You're strong. You're brave. You're everything I've ever wanted to be. I may be the oldest, but never doubt how much I've looked up to you. Where I failed, you succeeded. If anyone could take my place, it's you. Not that I would wish this curse upon you. It is mine alone, and I see that now, but I can't let what happened to my wife and children go unpunished.

If something happens to me."

I stopped reading, shaking my head hard.

"Continue, Luke."

Again, I shook, not sure I could go on another word. I lost my brother once when he died to the outside world while he was in the military. I buried him. I truly thought he was dead. I couldn't do that again.

"Read, Luke. You must continue."

I managed to hold in the tears as I looked back down.

*"If something happens to me, I need you to take care of what's left of my family. This is the most important thing to do. They are everything. To think of someone killing them or turning them into slaves would decimate every part of me. Even dead, I would be destroyed, and even in death, I would avenge them."*

My brow creased. "Them?" I blinked repeatedly. "Jasmeen and Aamir?"

"Just keep reading."

*Luke, I know you're not going to want to be me and run this island. It's a shitshow job, and it's not for the faint of heart. You will have to hand out punishments. You will have to make decisions you don't want to enforce. You may even have to kill if it calls for it. You'll know if that time comes. I trust you to make the right decisions.*

*Hold everything in private and try to stay out of view if you can help it. The staff in the fortress know you're in charge and know not to* leave. All calls and records of who goes in and out is recorded. Watch carefully and if anyone disobeys, kill them. They know the consequences. If you need anything, call Tillin, I put his number next to your bed. He will be keeping in contact with you daily. All situations or issues outside of the fortress will be through him. I reminded Tillin, but make sure to keep the workers and slaves away from the far end of the island. That is tribal land and is forbidden for all of us. They are not safe to be around. Also, Rich, my boss, might call you. You can trust him to an extent, but always stay on guard.

Lastly...I love you too. Take care of yourself. Watch your back, and trust no one. I will try my best to get back as soon as possible. My estimated return is a few weeks. That's what I'm aiming for. I'll try to call when I can. Stay in contact with Bram. I'll be eager for any news he may have.

Goodbye, Brother. I'll see you soon.

P.s. Burn this damn letter. All of it. Don't leave the fire until nothing remains.

A fire erupted in the corner of the room making me jump. The witch was there, staring into the flames. Just seeing the vibrant mix of colors, my gaze got trapped there too. I inched along, crawling, stopping. Crawling. Stopping. Always staring at the beautiful blaze. How long it took me to get there, I didn't know. I didn't care. There was something about the fire. It was him. It was Gavin. I could see that, but it was more. It was me now too. Maybe not always, but in this moment as I took his place, I felt the connection click. I was the new Main Master of Red Island. I was The Dragon the underground world of trafficking feared.

# CHAPTER 8

## LAYLA

*I* didn't know the woman in the reflection who stared back at me. Dark unkept hair was pulled back in a ponytail. Swollen brown eyes. Puffy face. Pouty, full lips. I had finally stopped the tears that came from me eating the vemki, but it wasn't easy. For hours, I couldn't stop crying. I tried to go back to sleep at one point, but the nightmares were too much. They pulled me under a dark cloud. Even now, the emotional ties had me. My servant was gone, and the Babke had disappeared hours ago, leaving me to the pain as it washed over me in waves of unbearable agony. Mandy wasn't feeling the effects in the ways I did, so she had decided to make secret preparations as I mourned. I assumed the Babke was planning as well, but there was no telling where she was. They kept busy all morning. Me, I suffered as my demons tortured me with everything that had happened.

The truth in its entirety was something I could barely face. The memories started from my trip here on the slave ship and played out until the present. Every good moment. Every horrifying memory. I went from an innocent virgin on a vacation with my twin brother to being a slave bound for Whitlock. Ram's rape killed a part of me. Then, every rape after that chipped away at the hole. The entire crew of the boat had probably been inside of me at one point. The one that I couldn't bear to think about the most was my own brother. Ram threatened to kill me if Aamir didn't join in.

Even though I was unconscious during most of it, I could still remember hearing moans. My brother's cries. The sway from thrusts. When I arrived on Red Island, I wanted nothing more than to die. Life was unbearable. The *truth* was unbearable. But I didn't die. Aamir and I were ripped apart. He went to Whitlock to be sold as a slave there, and Gavin kept me here as payment. I went from suicidal thoughts to reckless in my need to end my life. I couldn't remember how many times I'd begged Gavin to kill me. Even seducing me, praising me, whispering sweet nothings in my ear, I pleaded to him for death. He didn't give up on me.

When I found out I was pregnant, I expected to get worse, but I couldn't when all I kept hearing was how these babies were Gavin's. He wouldn't listen to me when I told him about the rapes. He didn't care. I was his now. These babies were his. But had they been? Three days. That's how long it took him to make his way into my bed. I'd fought at first, but it didn't last nearly as long as it should have. I gave in, not able to deny the attraction to a man I should have hated. But how could I with his words? His actions? He catered to me. Protected me. Reassured me. Gavin was every bit the villain, yet he turned out to be my prince. But he wasn't the good guy. If he wasn't the hero of the story, *what did that make me?*

I slid my finger over the spot where my wedding ring used to sit. It was on a dead woman now. One who held my son. One who took my place when it should have truly been me. How did I let this happen? Who was I that I didn't fight harder when I knew something was wrong?

There were so many questions, and I couldn't answer those

right now when the past was determined to make me face it. There were too many memories I'd pushed away. I couldn't anymore, but it was understandable how I had for so long. It was easy to ignore the truth when every day was filled with coddling and cuddles. Gavin and I had been inseparable, and now that he was gone, my past was quick to creep in. It was quick to remind me who I was before my husband blinded me from the truth.

A small knock sounded, and I glanced in the mirror of the vanity, watching as Mandy slipped in. I hadn't moved or feared anyone seeing me. I was too mad and upset for that. I wasn't ready to leave my home. To leave the only piece of Gavin I had left. A few more days, and it would be time. I was already walking a little, and the pain had miraculously lessened with the cream and medicine the devil-witch continued to make me drink.

"Layla."

My name was but a whisper as Mandy took quick steps towards me. She was ringing her hands, barely looking at my reflection. I turned, searching my emotions as I watched her nervously shift under my stare. The rage and sadness were still eating me alive. Other than those, there was a slight curiosity in her fear, but not concern or empathy for her current state. It was so unlike me, yet I could barely summon the energy to search it out or pretend to worry. *The past...the present...*

"You're upset. What is it?"

"I've been gathering clothes, blankets, and food. Anything I thought we might need. I've been careful, but I've also been watchful. Word travels around the fortress faster than you can believe. When I was in the back pantries, I could overhear the kitchen slaves whispering about the new Main Master, Luke. They say he was sick last night, but on a rampage this morning. I was curious, but I didn't want to eavesdrop either."

My brow drew in as I glanced towards my door. "You did, though, right? It could be important."

"I thought so too, that's why after they left, I headed to the floor he's staying on. He was yelling from inside his room."

Worried for Gavin, I sat on the edge of my chair. "And? What was he saying?"

"I'm not sure. Something about the locations of ships. I couldn't stay around long. Havaan showed up and asked what I was doing on the fourth floor. You know she's always on my case. Luckily, I still had the linens I had hoped to pack and told her I was delivering them to the new Main Master. I sat them down right there at his door."

"She found you at his door? With linens?"

"I'm sorry. I never heard her approach. It was the only excuse I could come up with on such short notice."

Slowly, I stood, my lips parting as voices began screaming in my head. Terror should have been what I felt, but the only thing making my blood race were the calculations that were flipping through my mind. They were going so fast, I could barely make sense of them. I kept seeing the doctor. My babies. Gavin's heartbreak as he stared down at me. And he was gone from me now. We weren't together to keep each other safe. Everyone was a threat. Everyone was out to get us.

I scrambled into my vanity drawer grabbing a stainless steel nail file. The end was pointed, but I didn't think it would do the job. *I had to hurry.*

"Leelee, what are you doing?"

"You're not a maid or servant anymore, Mandy. I'm dead. There was no reason for you to be anywhere near Gavin's brother. She's going to figure it out if she hasn't already."

"No." Brown wavy hair swayed over her chest as she shook her head. "I don't think so. I was careful. I put the linens down and left immediately."

"Linens are not your job. That is beneath you. Everyone has their place here, and no one goes outside of it. You know that. You know how Gavin runs things. Your presence is mine, and that puts both of us too close to the man taking my husband's place. Havaan won't be able to ignore that. It'll hit her, and when it does, she'll tell people her suspicions. Think about it, Mandy. If I were truly dead, you'd be sent back down to the slave camps. Not a few days later. Almost immediately. Or at least put in a new position. You haven't been. You've been...doing your own thing. Free, not at all like the slave you are. It was a mistake to have you running around. It draws attention and that invites questions. Did anyone else see you?" I bit hard into my bottom lip, opening the next drawer. There had to be something sharper. *Something.* I stopped, wincing as I spun for mine and Gavin's bed.

"No. I don't think so. Layla, you're scaring me. What are you doing?"

I didn't answer as I jerked the bedside table open on Gavin's side. The folded pocketknife wasn't but a few inches long, and it sent my heart exploding in rhythm.

"Leelee?"

Seconds went by as I stared at the black metal. Gavin always had a weapon near. He was never not prepared, and he'd done everything he could to make sure I was protected while I was here. *Everything.* Didn't he deserve that from me? Did I have a choice if I wanted to keep us safe?

Swallowing hard, I grabbed the closed knife, fisting it as I shut the drawer and turned to face Mandy.

"You will go back to the fourth floor and find Havaan. You will tell her that you're packing my things and you need her help."

Mandy's mouth opened, but she didn't speak as I gave my head a hard shake and continued.

"You will tell her, and you will not give her a choice. She's to come up here with you and help. Once she's inside, lead her to my tower. When you're both inside, you will close us all in."

For seconds she searched my eyes and hers filled even more with tears.

"What do I tell the guard at the front of the hall? No one is supposed to be back here but me."

I glanced at the clock on the far side of the room. "It's almost time for a shift change. Tell him it's okay, that she's helping you pack. If he continues to give you trouble, tell him you're going to send for the Main Master. Do so if you need to. Luke will understand and let her through if you tell him it was Gavin's orders you're following."

"What if he comes to the room?"

"He won't see me."

"Are you sure? I think—"

"*Mandy.*" Fire ignited in every inch of me at the mere thought there was a chance Havaan might discover the truth. Gavin said no one could know, and I wasn't going to take the chance of it putting his life at risk. "We're running out of time. We only have forty minutes until shift change. We need to get her through before the new guard takes his place. Now, go get Havaan and bring her to my tower."

"Master Gavin would never let me pack your things if you were dead, Leelee. He never would have buried you either. All of this...*it's all wrong.* Even if it killed him, the Main Master would have lived with your corpse for the rest of his days. How he leaves you now is beyond me. We're all spinning, and everything is not turning out as it was supposed to be. Your excuse to get Havaan here isn't any better than the one I told, nor better than the one Master Gavin tells. I fear by adding another lie, we're making a mistake. It's one more death. One more body added to this terrible tale."

My eyes closed, and for the first time, aching and need nearly sent me crashing to the floor in a sobbing, broken heap. I wouldn't think about him being gone. I wouldn't think about anything but keeping him safe. These men responsible were going to pay, and that's where my focus would stay. With revenge. With doing whatever it took to keep with the plan.

"I will not risk my husband's life because of Havaan. *Go.*"

Footsteps grew further away through my deep breaths. It wasn't until the door shut that I opened my eyes. What met me was a room that used to terrify me. It was Gavin's space. His dark domain of giant, heavy furniture. Throughout, there were grotesque statues of mangled soldiers, and on the walls, paintings of the massacres of war. I'd been so afraid when I was first put in the tower. I saw the projections of death. What I hadn't seen was the pain from his past.

It was all here. *All of him.* Looking around, I wasn't sure how I hadn't picked up the change sooner…I was here too. Pale green blankets instead of black. Bassinets over where blood had been spilt on these stone floors. That did nothing to hide the truth. Weren't all the beds empty now? Wasn't love eradicated by other devils of this realm?

I was in the crossroads of the worst of humanity and the best moments of existence. They were folded in a fabric so tightly woven in grief and passion, I wasn't sure if what I saw was good or bad. How could a room be both night and day? Life and death? A nightmare and a dream? How could an innocent, traumatized girl fall in love with a real-life monster? How could they all be one, and what did that even mean?

I didn't know as I headed for the adjoining tower. My life was not easy. It was not hard. I was starting to see that it was only just beginning. This was the evolution of my survival. I wasn't dead, but soon they were going to wish I was. I was married to a monster. I loved a monster. The only way I'd be able to keep him or my daughter, was to match him and become an even bigger monster myself.

# CHAPTER 9

## THE DRAGON

We'd been in the captain's quarters for nearly twelve hours, and the soldiers were feeling every minute of it as the boat pitched forward and rocked with every wave. White wasn't faring well as he lay on the captain's bed, and Pattinson, Fallon, and Lopez were holding on by a thread as they stared down at screens. Me, I wasn't seasick, but I was getting restless in the small, suffocating cabin. It wasn't helping Lui was a fucking chatterbox to everyone but the ones who mattered. I was losing it and seeing Layla cry throughout the night and morning wasn't helping me hang on. Her pain riled a beast I wasn't sure I'd ever be able to put away. They did this to her, *to us*, and every tear she shed was going to be the blood I was going to drain from their dead, lifeless bodies.

"Double M?" Fallon got quiet as his eyes squinted through a confused gaze. He leaned in closer to the monitor, only to twist his mouth.

"What is it?"

"I think we're close to another boat, but I'm not detecting it on radar. They may have their signal off."

Pattinson was scrolling, only to pause to glance up. "All boats are accounted for that I can see. It can't be one of ours."

"Can you tap into their wheelhouse through their radio as well?"

"Already on it."

I glanced down again, taking in Layla as she spoke with Mandy. With the earbuds out, I couldn't hear what they were saying, but my wife didn't look happy. If anything…she was… angry, but more than that. She was suddenly so hard for me to read when that had never been the case before.

"Almost got it. I think if I—"

A voice echoed through the space—a language I wasn't familiar with. White immediately sat up, diving for the small bowl he'd found tucked away in the bedside storage. As he got sick, his finger was raised, but he didn't speak until he was trying to catch his breath afterward.

"Tribal. Nigerian. Money. They're getting together an amount for—" He heaved again, nothing coming up as he let out an exasperated sound. "The boys. Sea slaves."

"I beg your fucking pardon? They're not taking my slaves."

Pushing the laptop closed, I stood, holding to the window's ledge for balance. The voice was still going as White listened to their fast words.

"I don't think they're taking the slaves. They're not buying them for…work." His fingers pressed into his mouth. His eyes closed, and his head went back and forth as he listened. Disbelief quickly melted to an expression I knew all too well. Anger. "Sex, Sir. That's what they're here for."

"Sex?" I saw red as clarity dawned. "Of course. Fucking bastard. Lui's piggybacking off me, prostituting out what is not his to sell."

Had it really come down to this? Had I lost my touch by losing their fear? The captains should have known better. It would appear it was time for me to remind them.

"Do we know how far out the boat is? I need a name and to know whether we're dealing with Nigeria, or that's just the crew's nationality. Pattinson, work your magic. Find me that info."

"On it, Boss."

"White. Suck it up and get your recorder out. Translate as we go. I want everything they're saying, word for word. I want it documented, so we don't miss anything."

He rolled over, putting down the bowl as he unzipped the top of his backpack.

"Fallon—"

"Way ahead of you, Double M." He bit against his lip, looking between his monitor and Pattinson's screen. "The radio signal is close. A mile out, give or take. AIS isn't being picked up. They have their system off. Not to worry. Give me a few seconds, and I'll tell you exactly who we're dealing with." He leaned over to Pattinson, pointing as they began to talk to each other. Lopez had been quiet up to this point, but I knew he was deep into a plan as Fallon began translating the foreign words that filled the space.

"They're laughing, making fun of the captain. They say Lui is...dirty...I think they said pushover. A dirty pushover. But he always has...the goods."

"Got it, Main Master." Fallon cut in. He pointed at Pattinson's screen but moved back to look at his own as he continued. "The King Fish. Eighty-five-foot fishing vessel out of Nigeria. Owned by David Nalls, who's also owner of Second Wind Seas, a fishing fleet specializing mainly in tuna."

"Do we have the name of the captain for The King Fish?"

Pattinson glanced up. "Says Wesley Niles, but I got a hit for some aliases with that name."

"Aliases?"

"Korbin Hahns, Justin Hathaway. Willard Fischer—"

"Wait." My hand shot up. Did you fucking say Willard Fischer?"

"Yes, Sir. *Oh*." His eyes widened as he glanced between me and the screen. "Isn't that the captain of the Black Double we searched for a few months back?"

"The same one. That boat fucking went down." My eyes narrowed. "The bastard's supposed to be dead." Heat ignited inside as I thought back to the last time I'd seen him. It wasn't weeks after I had gotten Layla. She'd come to the island on his ship, and he was lucky I hadn't killed him for the condition she arrived in. But I'd been distracted with trying to get her mind back somewhat stable. She'd been so broken in those days, and all my attention was on her. There had been a really bad storm. I assumed the entire crew had gone down with the Black Double. There had been debris from what I'd been told. A lot of it. The story had sounded legit, but it was anything but. If Willard was alive, he could have easily told others about the island or Layla. He could have been the root of suspicion. It only took one word. One slip up. I didn't think he'd be stupid enough to talk. He'd know he was a dead man, but he might have gotten too comfortable at running his mouth about the small things, and that's all it would take.

"Gun up if you need to. White, keep translating into the recorder. I need to take care of something real quick."

As I sat back down, the other men didn't move. We were all the same. We were always ready.

I opened the laptop, taking in the window where I'd been watching Layla. The room appeared empty, giving me pause, but I quickly opened a messenger box attached to the secure phone I'd sent with my brother-in-law. Aamir deserved to know what was about to go down. He'd lived his own personal hell under Willard's crew, and I'd give him any closure I could for what he'd gone through.

Me: Having a run-in with the former captain of
the Black Double. Sending you a present
soon.

Within seconds text appeared.

Aamir: I hope you're fucking killing him.
Bastard. Before you disappear, I have to know.
How is she?

Warmth and aching collided.

Me: I plan on it. And she's better. Starting to
walk around now. How's my girl?"

Aamir: She sleeps a lot. Everleigh hardly puts
her down. She's so good.

My breath hitched as a picture of my daughter came through. All I saw was the woman I loved in miniature form. She was perfect in every way, and she only instilled my reasons for being here. I had to protect her future, no matter the cost.

I took in the pink onesie and beanie on her head, smiling.

Me: She's so beautiful. Take good care of her.
I'll send your gift soon. Got to go. Text me
information Bram may come across when you
have it. I'll check this when I can.

Aamir: Be safe.

Me: Always.

I closed the box, going back to Layla's window. I still didn't see her, but the door to the tower was opened. Was she inside? I couldn't remember the last time Layla had gone in there. Not since the beginning. Since I brought her into my bed and my life.

A soft sound of aggravation left me as I exited out the

window there too, closing the laptop. The weight of my knife rested in my belt. I usually only wore a suit, per the position of my job, but blacked-out tactical gear was my comfort clothes. It was all I knew from my years of training to prove my worth as a Main Master. I wasn't born into this position like Bram Whitlock. I had to earn my title with the price of blood, and I was damn good at draining people of it.

"Lopez, what do you got?"

Dark eyes came up from his screen.

"These men are prepared for anything. They may be fishermen, but they're in the illegal trade. Some may be carrying. We need to get control before this ship arrives. I have the blueprints of the boat here. If Pattinson and Fallon go around—"

"Around? I can get control of it right now."

"Gavin, you're not in this."

My head jerked back the smallest amount. "Like hell I'm not. This piece of shit works for me."

"We talked about this before we ever left land. No risks. You agreed. We're here for you. Let us do our job."

His voice was stern. My eyes lowered to the laptop, only to come up.

"Sneaking up on Lui would be the risk. Not me getting control. You want to do something, prepare for the oncoming ship. Fallon, jam the radio long enough to buy us a little time."

"You got it, Boss."

Within seconds he gave a nod. Lopez made something short of a growl, pulling his gun free as he scrambled my way. The other men were jumping to their feet as well, catching up as I turned and opened the door. White's face dropped a shade of color from the fast movement, but he stayed close as I stepped through the threshold, heading for the captain.

Boys of all ages slowed at my presence, some of their smiles fading as fear overtook them. Even the wind seemed to die down as I glanced up to the elevated pilothouse. Yelling immediately erupted from the deck above.

"What the fuck do you think you're doing? Get back to work! Hey!"

I didn't slow as footsteps pounded against metal. Narrowed, angry eyes projected down. The deckhand, a man in his early twenties, was ready to scream again, but he froze, his eyes widening as he jerked to a stop.

I took the stairs two at a time, my own anger exploding with my every movement as I got closer.

"M-Main Master. I…" Words escaped him as he took in me and my men. I glanced in the distance, a boat so far away, I could barely see it.

"Round up the crew. It would seem we need to talk about a few things." I turned to White who already looked to have more color. "Assist."

"Gladly."

I gave him a nod, going right for the door. When I jerked it open, Lui was already standing, staring at me in nothing short of shock. He had the radio in his hand, and I had no doubt he'd tried to steer away the boat in the distance. Luckily, he wouldn't have been able to.

"Main Master. I…What are you doing here?"

My eyes scanned the small room, stopping on a young boy who was cowering in the corner by the bunk where the captain would have slept. A cloud of hate grew and spread through my chest as I headed over, kneeling. I took in the boy's dark hair, light brown eyes, and tanned skin. He could have easily been Jamison in a few years. For the first time since I'd been brought to the island, I looked into the eyes of a child and saw innocence. Saw…what a monster I was, and what I'd allowed. The truth tore into me like the dullest blade. It sawed into my heart, taking its time in excruciating stabs of regret and shame. What the fuck had I become?

I took his hand, lifting him to stand as I stayed kneeling, so we'd be face to face. The boy couldn't have been much older than five. "What is your name?"

Fear. Uncertainty. Trembling.

"Lucas."

"Lucus? That's a good name." I forced a smile, but all that would come was a half-assed fucking grin. "Go outside with the others, okay? Can you do that?"

Despite whatever the boy had been through, teeth appeared with a big smile. His relief that I wasn't going to hurt him punched a hole right through what was left in my chest. The boy took Pattinson's hand, and I turned more than a death glare to Lui. I could have burned him to ashes with the emotion overflowing through me.

"A little young to pass off as crew, don't you think? Last I checked with my guidelines, ten was the minimum age for this fucking job. *Job*," I roared with everything I had. "Work. Lines. *Fish*."

I had my hand and knife at his throat, and his large body slamming into the wall before I could stop myself.

"I…It's better to teach them young."

"Is that right?" My grip tightened, cutting off his air. "What exactly are you teaching him? What about the others?"

"M-Main M-M—" His words were impossible as I cut off his air completely.

"You wouldn't happen to be piggybacking from me, now would you, Lui?"

Red turned to purple as his eyes bulged and he tried jerking out of my hold. He was beginning to slide down the wall as I kept him pinned from pushing me back. It wasn't until his eyes started to roll that I let go, allowing him oxygen. Coughing immediately filled the space.

"Now would be a good time to answer my question. What's your plan with my slaves?"

"Nothing." He gasped repeatedly, holding to his neck. "Work. That's it."

"Hmm." I turned, pointing at the ship in the distance through the large glass windows. "And them? What's their intentions for my slaves?"

Lui hesitated as he looked between me and the boat.

"Before you lie, I want you to think long and hard if that would be wise."

"I'm not the only one. *It was all Willard's idea.* Nothing big. A few stops between some boats for some extra cash. Fifty-fifty to each captain. I mean, the boys don't get hurt. Just some quick play here and there."

My hand shot up to hover over his face.

"You're going to write these names down. Every single one."

"Yes, Main Ma—"

"Now! Right fucking now."

Lui dove for the counter, grabbing a pen and paper. I glanced over at Lopez, shaking my head through the gall of these men. Children? And under my rule...? This wouldn't do.

Fallon and Pattinson were standing by the door, and I could see they didn't like this anymore than me. Outside, the crew was sitting, waiting as White held to his gun and walked the width of the ship, keeping an eye on them. Some were young, but there were a good number of late teens that were responsible for the heavier end of work. It was a mixed lot, and I was seeing first-hand how my operation was being run.

"Hurry your ass up." I leaned in, lowering my voice to Lopez. "We need to have the younger boys taken below until we can have a handle on The King Fish. Have the older boys work the top or at least appear to. I don't want to spook Willard. He won't suspect, but he may notice if anything is different."

"We'll take care of it. Fallon, stay with the Main Master. Pattinson, come with me."

The boat was growing closer, but not at an increasing

alarming rate. With our slow pace, we still had maybe half an hour, depending on if The King Fish increased their speed.

"Where's my fucking list?"

"I'm trying, Sir. I don't want to forget anyone."

"You better not because when I confirm your story, and I get names, I'm burning a body part for every one you leave off. Would you like to guess which one I'm starting with?"

Lui's eyes flew open, and the shaking of his hand increased as he continued writing on the wrinkled paper. I took out my lighter, taking a seat in the captain's chair while I watched him sweat and squirm at the flicks of my finger. The flame jumped to life, but not my heart. It was mourning for these kids. It was... scheming for them. If this man thought he'd live through this, he was sadly mistaken. The Babke mentioned Death and his hold over Layla. I knew she was out of the woods this time, but I was about to start a spree that would offer him enough souls to grant us immortality, together...*forever.*

# CHAPTER 10

## LUKE

"*D*on't you fucking tell me it can't be done. I want to know the exact location of that boat, and I want it now. There are satellites all over the fucking place. You get me eyes asap. And don't you dare call me back until you have it figured out. The clock is ticking, Mr. Frazer. I better get a call from you soon. *Real fucking soon.*"

I hung up the phone, cursing as the witch woman watched me from a recliner across the room. I had no idea why she was still here, but she didn't get the hint when I told her I had shit to do. She didn't leave either after I asked for privacy. The damn woman was glued to my side, and I was running off of rage and regret. Why the fuck had I had three damn bowls of that soup? I had the worst migraine, and her presence was only adding to it.

"If you're going to be in here, can you at least work your magic and make me feel better? Maybe get me a satellite signal on my brother so I can make sure he's okay?"

"You want food? I can get you good food."

"No food from you. You almost killed me last night. I'm not eating for days." I put down the phone, heading to check the email on my laptop.

"I'll make you potcha[1]."

"No food. I know you understand me. No. Food."

"Yes, potcha."

"No." I stopped at the desk, throwing her a look as I collapsed into the leather office chair. "Why don't you get me something for this migraine instead. For fuck's sake. I think my head is going to explode." I squeezed my eyes shut, pressing my thumb and index finger to the bridge of my nose. A hand settled on my shoulder, and I jumped at the contact. My eyes shot open and herbs were blown into my face, nearly taking my breath away.

"Jesus." I sneezed and coughed at the same time. Blurriness took over the room, and I blinked through the powder sticking to my face and eyelashes. "Is that cinnamon? Dammit, it burns. Do you know people can die from that shit? Allergic reaction. Asphyxiation. It closes your lungs." Again, I sneezed, cursing once more as I tried to get the room to come into focus.

"You're such a baby. Give it a few minutes. Drink water."

She didn't have to tell me twice. My damn lips felt like they were going numb.

"What did you blow at me?"

"Luck. Drink."

"Does this luck come with a solution to my headache?"

I grabbed a bottle of water, drinking until it was empty. Plastic popped as I crushed it in my palm, growling at the burning that was increasing in my eyes.

"If my lids swell shut—"

"Go get your phone. Luck."

My lips parted and ringing filled the room. I jumped up, racing forward.

"Hello?"

A pause. "Don't you sound eager. Are you all off the island?"

"Bram." I sighed. "Off? I was drugged and left to run this place. I could kill Gavin. I'm no Main Master."

"Ooh." The word drew out, and he laughed. "It would appear now you are. Welcome to the life. You're going to fucking hate it."

My lips tightened as I glanced over to the older woman who was watching me from the window facing the fields that held the shell-covered trees. Even now I could hear the soft clinking in the distance.

"I already do, and I haven't even done anything yet. What's going on? Any news? How's everything on your end? How's…?"

"If you mean your niece, she's doing great. She's…she's beautiful, Luke. Everleigh is in love. She'll take good care of Jasmeen and Aamir for your brother."

"I know she will. What about anything else?"

He let out a long sigh. "I don't even know where to begin. Your brother would have gone through his contact when he chose to leave. If my own connections are correct, that would be Rich Tilson."

"Yes, Gavin mentioned him in the letter he left me. Do you know him?"

"I do. Believe it or not, he's a good man. I've actually met him a handful of times when I was based out of Chicago. He was close with my father until their falling out. I could be wrong, but I just don't think he would have done this."

"If not him, who?"

"It's hard to say. If he routed up the request…I don't know. This world we live in is run in layers. Levels, if you will. Being a Main Master is high, but we're talking entry level into the machine."

"Machine?"

"That's what they're called. Or what my father and my own connections always called it. The makeup just 'is'. We don't question; we leave it alone. It's the way it goes. The way we're taught. We worry about our own domain, and we forget everything outside of it. We only go to them if we have a problem we can't solve on our own. Even then, we're not encouraged to reach out. They watch us and step in if needed...or they should, but sometimes they don't. They have their own role to play. I'll keep asking around though and see if I can get more information. I don't plan on being successful, but it's worth a try."

I got quiet as my mind raced.

"You said they watch. Are they watching me now?"

"Gavin wouldn't have left without informing Rich. I'm almost positive he knows. Whether he's watching or not, I can't be sure. Gavin's system is impossible to get into. We've been trying for hours with no success."

"I've been doing the same so I can get in and monitor the ships. My guy can't do it either. He's trying like hell."

"We'll figure something out. Call on the daily if you can. I don't like not having tabs on you there."

"I'll aim for this time tomorrow. I should go. Bram..."

"You're concerned for your brother. I'll find out what I can. Don't worry, Luke, he'll be okay. All I'm waiting for is a location for where he pulls into port. I can have people there in a matter of hours. Less, if he sticks to Lisbon. Just focus on your job there as Main Master. And be careful. Some will view this as a weakness on your brother's account. They'll test for power. They may even try to escape. Hell...they may try to kill you to take over. Do not for one moment trust anyone. No one."

"I definitely won't." Again, I glanced at the witch, blinking through the realization that my migraine was almost gone. I felt...good. Better. "I should go. Call me tomorrow or sooner if you find out anything."

"Will do."

I hung up.

"I thought you said luck? I didn't learn anything."

"You learned a lot. How is your head?"

"Better. Thank you."

"Water. Drink. You're going to need it."

At her tone, my head cocked to the side. "Why? What now?"

"Not luck. More of a pain in my ass. Water."

I didn't argue. I didn't even question her as I headed over and grabbed another bottled water from the mini fridge and began chugging it.

"Now, we wait."

"For your pain?"

"Yes. It won't be long."

"Do I get to know what it is? I mean, obviously you know. Couldn't you give me a hint or warning so I can prepare?"

At her eyebrows lifting, I took a seat back in the desk's chair.

"It's not so much of a pain for me. Inconvenience, yes, but… the pain isn't mine. It's hers, and this very moment it is feeding on everything that is wrong with her. Fear. Insecurity. Inexperience. Life will not be kind, and Death does not forget. I see, but only so much. The…paths are plentiful. The future does not have many happy outcomes. It'll take every ounce of fight from everyone. The days are dark, new Main Master. Heed your friend's warning. You are no safer than your brother. Than me. Than anyone. They all watch, and they all wait. Blood will be spilled today."

"Who's blood? Who is 'her'? What are you not telling me?"

"You will find out soon enough. But in case you don't and the paths shift, I will not speak another word. Fear the things you cannot see. The voices you can't hear. Not every threat has substance. Even luck can turn its back on you. Not love. If you follow that, you will find your way."

I leaned forward in the chair as I stared at the floor.

"You speak in riddles."

"I tell you what I can. The rest will play out. For now, we sit and wait."

# CHAPTER 11

## LAYLA

"You're sure he said he wanted me to help you? There are tons of other servants that can fold. I'm on a schedule. If I'm running behind, I'll be in trouble." Havaan threw Mandy a look.

"No trouble. We don't have much. This won't take long."

The slave seemed to relax. "Well, if that's the case, then fine. I've always wanted to come to this tower. It's as beautiful as they say. You don't think he'll close it up for good, do you?"

"No. I don't think so."

"Good. I can't believe everything that happened. I've never seen the Main Master so…devastated. The deaths of his family. Burning the slaves on the field. He scares me. It's hard to imagine that all really played out like it did. It doesn't seem real."

"It was horrible," Mandy choked out. "I still can't believe it."

Havaan got quiet as I watched her rock in the chair and fold clothes I'd worn before I started showing. I'd never wear them again, they were so small. I didn't even feel like the same girl anymore. A part of me even resented my younger self for reasons I couldn't process. Innocence? Naivety? Regret for not embracing my babies sooner? The room blurred through my angry tears.

"What does he want done with all of this stuff, anyway?"

"Storage. He wouldn't dare get rid of it. It took everything I had to convince him to let me pack this, and he only allowed it because he plans to put the nursery here."

"For the dead babies? That's a little morbid."

"Those were his children. He loved them very much. He just wants to keep their things for a while, that's all."

"But he didn't even know them. Not really."

My nails bit into my palm as I tried to stop the shaking that was taking me over. It didn't appear Havaan suspected that I was alive. I should have signaled for Mandy to get rid of her, but I couldn't as I stared her down from the large closet, listening to her callousness.

"He watched his children being born and then murdered along with his wife. He didn't have to know them; they were his. He spent months excitingly awaiting their arrival only to have the most horrific thing happen."

"I'm not saying it wasn't bad. I'm just saying it would have hurt him worse had he actually spent time with them." She reached over, snatching a pale blue sundress from the pile Mandy had placed down before them. "I'm sure it hurts him now, but he'll get over it." She paused. "This is the cutest dress. Do you think he'd know if it were missing? You wouldn't tell on me if I took it, would you?"

There was a threat underlining her question. She was testing Mandy, and I hated how my servant squirmed as she was put on the spot.

"He'd know. The Main Master specifically commented on that exact dress for Miss Layla."

"I'm sure he commented on plenty. Surely, he won't remember this one."

"If I remember, so will he. Fourteen-week ultrasound. She

was already showing with the twins. As she laid on the bed, he rested his cheek right against her stomach and talked to the babies. He told them how absolutely beautiful their mother was, and that he'd never felt love for anyone like he did for them." Mandy's lip trembled. "He said someday they'd leave this place and be the perfect family."

"And we see how that worked out." Havaan whipped the dress out with a hard pop, bringing it in to roughly fold. "I wonder if he'll decide to take another wife in the future or if he's learned his lesson? He isn't opposed to slaves obviously. If he's setting up the nursery, it might not be long at all."

The shock and pain on Mandy's face was something I should have held. It evaded me as I gripped the handle to the pocketknife even tighter, reaching down to withdraw the blade. I knew Mandy was back to talking again, but I barely heard the words at all. They weren't making sense as my gaze stayed zeroed in on Havaan's round face. Even her beady eyes sucked me in, filling me even more with rage.

"I can't believe you'd talk so ill about our Main Master. I can do this on my own. You need to leave. I've heard enough. You're the most hateful, ugly—"

"For speaking the truth?"

"For being a—"

"*Bitch*," I exploded, stepping from the closet. "Who do you think you are, talking about my husband like that?"

"M-Miss Layla." Havaan's eyes went impossibly wide as her head shook through the surprise and fear. "I-I thought…I didn't mean…"

"Didn't mean what? Didn't mean to imply my husband didn't care for his own children? Didn't wonder if he'd learned his *lesson*? How about how he could disregard us so much that he'd find someone new?"

"I only meant—"

Each step that brought me closer to Havaan was one I

couldn't take back. I was spinning down a dark tunnel of screams, and the demonic whispers in my mind were driving me on. They taunted me just like in my dreams.

"Get out of my rocking chair."

"Leelee, please." Mandy stood just as Havaan did, easing her hands up to try to calm me. "Why don't you give me the knife. You're already injured. I don't want you getting hurt worse."

"I'm fine." I pointed the tip to Havaan as she took a step away from me, trying to put distance between us. "Shut the door, Mandy."

"Leelee, please. Why don't Havaan and I go put you down to rest? Right, Havaan?"

"Shut the door!" I was shaking so badly, I couldn't stop my body from trembling. "Mandy, *now*. Do not make me tell you again."

Havaan went to lunge for the door, but I was faster, paying for it instantly with a sharp twinge to my stomach. I ignored it, fisting her hair and jerking her back. She fell at the force, bringing me down with her as my entire body seized with spasms. Still, I couldn't stop as I forced my way on top of her, holding the knife to her throat.

"My husband loves me. He loved our babies."

"I know. I'm sorry, Miss Layla. I—"

"Shut up. I didn't tell you to speak." I pushed in harder, watching as crimson began to stain the end of the sharp blade. "I almost died, and as I was facing death, do you know what I saw?"

Sobs left the slave, heavy wracks that shook her shoulders. "I'm sorry."

"*Do you know what I saw?*" She squealed as skin sliced under the edge of the knife. But I didn't see that. I relived Gavin's pain. My pain at losing my son and daughter. The emotions began drowning me, leaving high pitched whimpers mixing with deep grunts as they choked themselves out of me. "I will tell you. I saw an unbreakable man become weak. I saw love melt to loss. I saw what it was to lose everything. I will *never* risk that again. Never."

As if my hand was not my own, it jerked, cutting right through the flesh of her neck. The smoothness of the glide was almost beautiful. Had it not been for her gasp or the flailing that accompanied the laceration, I may not have moved at all. Blood squirted across me, pouring over her hands as she rolled on top, pushing to get away. Her flight response had her trying to run, but she was gurgling on her life as panic sent her standing and spinning in circles. I pushed to my feet, swaying as the room tilted underneath me. Red. Blood. Red. It was dropping and spraying on me as Havaan grabbed my loose dress, nearly pulling me back down and collapsing at my feet. Mandy was crying, but time was drawing out. I blinked, pushing my hand over the location of my incision. Wetness registered and I looked down to the blood that was beginning to soak through the material of my dress.

"I think. Mandy." I tried to continue standing but collapsed down hard to my knees as my servant rushed for me. Havaan was jolting and jerking on the floor, her sounds getting more hollow and wet as the room began to fade. Just as Mandy helped me to stand, the door flew open. The face I saw was one I didn't expect. Immediately, I dropped the knife.

"Son of a bitch." Luke glanced at Havaan but ran to me, pulling me in his arms as he spun us for the door. The Babke was a blur as she kept her pace just behind us. I was lowered to the bed, but something was wrong. Words didn't make sense. Yells erupted. Metal glistened in the light as the knife I'd used for Havaan flashed in my peripheral.

Silence.

Colors.

Screams.

Red. So much red.

It bled into the fog that manifested in the corners of my room. It was as if my repetitive dreams were leaking into my reality.

"Girl, get my supplies. Everything has been prepared. Do not hesitate. Go!"

*"Why the fuck didn't anyone tell me she was alive?* And what was she doing, killing that girl?"

"Luke." I reached to him, trying to pull him in closer. I was hyperventilating. I couldn't breathe. "Tell Gavin I love him. If I —" My mouth flew open as pain took over my stomach from the Babke pushing around my incision. "I love him."

"Save your goodbyes, Layla. No way in hell I'm letting anything happen to you. My brother would kill me if you died on my watch."

"I love him. I...love..." The fog was growing thicker as it ate the walls and grew closer. Red spread among the patches of gray, stolen by the black edges. I could barely speak as the whisper in the depths laughed and chanted words I couldn't make sense of.

Tugging rocked my body as pressure eased to push against my insides. Was I cut open again? Was I bleeding to death? I went to scream but nothing came as I was swallowed by the darkness. It sucked me under so fast, I was left freefalling into emptiness.

Words returned.

Visions appeared.

The voices grew closer.

What quickly started out as drums turned into a more familiar pattern. A thump-thump I recognized as not music but my heartbeat. It slowed. It stopped. It started, only to stop again. The vibrations tingled against my skin as a child appeared from the darkness. It was a small child, only a year or so as it tried walking towards me. The steps were unsteady, and the dark-haired little boy swayed as he reached his arms out towards me.

"Jamison?"

But I was already racing in his direction and scooping him in close as I started to cry. I was crying so hard yet laughing in relief as my heart thumped from the love. I could smell his sweetness. Feel his warmth as he let me cuddle him close. It wasn't enough to have him in my arms. I pulled back, soaking in every expression on his tiny, beautiful face.

"Jamison, it's Mommy. I love you so much. I'm so sorry. I love you."

Light brown surrounded specks of gold. Flames came alive in his eyes as he lovingly looked up at me. I could see a mix of me and Gavin as I cried even harder and kissed his rosy cheeks. Over and over, I kept repeating my love. I couldn't say it enough. I was too scared if I stopped, he'd be taken from me again. And he was. One minute I was hugging and kissing him, and the next, I was falling again. The drums were back. My heart was alive. But it wasn't full of love anymore.

Anger returned.

Hate festered.

My need to release it grew.

"She's awake again. Layla, can you hear me?"

"Luke?"

My voice sounded so far away.

"You passed out. Don't worry, you're going to be okay. You tore open some of your stitches, but you're not bleeding internally like we feared. You're okay. God, you're okay."

# CHAPTER 12

## THE DRAGON

*I*t was nearly dark by the time the King Fish finally made it to our fishing vessel. Spotlights lit up the deck, and the older teen slaves made their way back and forth, working the nets. Where I feared the boys might give us away by their nervousness, it appeared quite the opposite. The group looked relaxed, even jovial with the occasional joke or prank. Just seeing what the difference in our presence made didn't make me happy, it made me sad. How could an impending massacre be better than a day on the job? Why…because my slaves were being hurt by the men who were responsible for them. They were in hell, and that was my fault. I never condoned abuse on my ships, but I hadn't put a stop to it either.

"Lui! Lui, *where are you?*"

Laughter exploded and voices grew louder as the crew finished tying the boat alongside ours. With the seas eerily calm, it wouldn't be that way after a while. Given the clouds in the distance, we only had a few hours before the seas grew rough. A storm was coming, but not with more wrath than me.

"Lui!"

I kept my voice low, more growling in the ear of my captain

as I held to the back of his neck. It was just me and him in the wheelhouse, and my men were waiting for my signal. "The door is open. They can hear you. Call them over, Lui." My grip tightened making his shoulders draw in. "But if you so much as give us away or make them suspicious, you'll be my bait for this trip's catch. *Got it?*"

"Y-Yes, Main Master."

"Call them."

The captain was shaking as he yelled out.

"Come on over! I'm getting a drink! Who wants one?"

More cheers went up as I watched them begin to step from their boat to ours. Some men already appeared drunk, barely able to walk straight. My teeth bit into each other repeatedly as the heat inside me reached fiery heights.

"How many crew? I don't see Willard."

"Usually eight, Main Master."

I pushed the button on my radio, keeping my voice low.

"Eight crew. We seem to be missing two, Willard being one of them."

"On it, Double M. I'll bring them over."

I caught a flash of Fallon already slipping onto the King Fish.

"Lui! Where the fuck are you at?"

There was a nervousness in the man's voice, and it had nothing to do with his thick accent.

"*Walk.* You're going to go to the door and calm him down."

The captain obeyed as I stayed a good distance behind. When he reached the door, I could see from the large window the man relax and smile from the deck. With the spotlight below, I knew he couldn't see me.

"There you are. Are we good to go? Where's my drink?"

"Damn kids must have stolen mine. I can't find my bottles anywhere. I'll get them to bring some up from below. You all been out long?"

"Eh." The man threw up his hands. "Few weeks. We'll be heading in soon."

"Where's Willy? He isn't flaking out this time is he?"

"He's coming." The guy's face drew in, beginning to look up at Lui suspiciously. "Are you coming down?"

"Go," I said, lowly. "Take your time."

Lui laughed. "Of course I'm coming down. I hurt my leg while we were at the island. It's a bitch for me to walk."

I kept my eyes on him as he limped to the edge of the steps and started to make his way down. He wasn't halfway when movement caught my attention, and I stepped closer. Fallon had two men at gunpoint, leading them onto our boat. The six men on deck went to scramble, cut off as Pattinson, White, and Lopez surged in, weapons drawn. My head shook, and I headed for the door, watching Willard jerk to a stop as I began to walk down the steps. The horror on his face sent his color dropping to a deadly white.

"Main...Master."

Lui joined the group of men who were huddled in the center of the deck. I stopped midway down, taking a seat on the steps.

"It appears I'm seeing a ghost. You look a tad bit surprised, Willard. Or should I call you *Wesley*?"

"I-I can explain." I pulled my gun from the holster on my hip, not hesitating as I put a bullet through his outer thigh. Screams rang out around us, and the crew bumped into each other, not sure what to do.

"No need to explain why you faked your own death. I won't go into a lecture on how you're a fucking idiot. That's not why I'm here. I'm not even here about you hurting my slaves, or how all of you are piggybacking off me. What I want to know is, who have you talked to about *my wife*."

Willard's eyes jerked to his crew, confusion playing out as he nervously came back to me.

"Your wife?" He whimpered and cried out as he held pressure to his leg.

I was off the stairs and had his dingy white shirt fisted in my hand in four steps. "Layla, the slave you delivered to me. The one that almost died under yours and Ram's care. My wife!"

"I didn't know you married her. I n-never mentioned her, Sir. I..I swear I never told no one about her."

Letting the rage drain from my face, I let go of his shirt, patting against his chest as I stepped back. The teens were still sitting off to the side, and I called a thin, tall, dark-haired one over with my finger.

"You speak English?"

"Yes, Main Master."

My eyes bore into his as I stepped in, lowering my voice.

"Go to your captain's cabin. Right by the door, you'll see a black backpack. Grab it and bring it to me. Do not go in the room. Don't even glance inside. Do I make myself clear?"

"Yes, Main Master."

I nodded, watching him run off as I turned back to Willard.

"I'm going to give you a minute to think about your answer. Maybe you'll suddenly remember popping your mouth off about her. About me. Maybe it'll come back to you on how you overheard someone else talking about her. Or maybe I'll just let you bleed out while I wait." My hands clasped behind me as I let him groan and shift around through the pain. "I find it very suspicious how shortly after she comes to me, and I kill your deck boss, your ship goes down and disappears. I have a feeling word would have gotten around that Layla was pregnant by then."

"No. Main Master, *I didn't even know about the pregnancy.* When I left Red Island, I put everything behind me."

"Is that right?"

"I swear it."

"Oh…the island, just not my slaves," I said, gesturing to all the boys around and coming back to shoot through his other outer thigh. Screams echoed over the water as he collapsed. White immediately reached down, jerking him back up to stand. "You couldn't part from those boys. Isn't that why you're all here?"

"N-No, I mean—"

"No? Then it must have been me and the work you were *contracted* to do!" The back of my hand connected to his cheek in a powerful blow that sent his face snapping to the side. "Contracted, Willard. *Your life belongs to me.* Just because you supposedly died on that boat doesn't erase you from your debt. You. Are. Mine. Until death. But guess what?"

"…W-what?"

The slave ran up handing me my backpack. I unzipped it, removing the mini blow torch stored inside. "You've been replaced. You bled to get in. You'll bleed to get out."

Yells went up from multiple men, but none so loud as Willard's.

"Wait! Main Master, please! I may have heard some talk. Mentions of your slave—wife! Your wife! I think I heard some captains talking about her."

My eyes didn't lift. I continued adjusting the settings on my toy. When I didn't speak, Willard tripped over his words, rushing to get them out.

"There was talk of shipments. Medical stuff. Uhm. There were whispers."

"From whom?" Still, I focused on the weapon. I brought it up, pulling the trigger as the bright blue flame shot to life. One of the captives began praying between English and another language I wasn't sure on.

"Everyone." A shorter man yelling out in the back had my head shooting up. I gestured to Pattinson to bring him to the front.

"Continue. What do you mean everyone?"

The deckhand shrugged. "Your business is no secret, Main

Master. I've been on these boats for over five years. Captains talk. Almost every single one of them. Not threateningly, but they talk. Deadlines. Who's running what. What's fair or not. They talk shit. A lot of it. I don't even work for you, and I know who you are. I'll admit, I thought you were a myth or something. You never quite know what to believe, but I see I underestimated the stories. You're as terrifying as they say."

His accent had me stepping closer.

"You're American."

"I am."

"You're honest."

"I'm that too."

"But you're not stupid. You know you're all going to die today unless I get what I want."

His lips puckered, only to twist. "I do believe we're going to die anyway."

I scanned his face, shaking my head. "Maybe. Maybe not if I get information worth saving you over. Say…if you proved you were of use, I may let you live and come work for me. You'd have to sign a contract. There would be no getting out of it. *Ever.* Your life for your life."

"It's not as bad as he says," Willard bit out. "We know what to say and what *not* to say. We're not stupid. I never said nothing to no one about any wife or babies."

My hand jerked up as I pointed the end of the blow torch at his pale face. Willard grew tense, holding his breath.

"Repeat that."

"I…I-I said I never said nothing to no one about any wife or babies."

"Babies…More than one."

Willards jaw tightened as he smeared blood over his face to wipe the sweat collecting on his skin.

"Main Master, I heard a few weeks ago that it might be twins, but I didn't say nothing."

"*Heard from whom?*"

"Austin Birch, of course. He was the one going around boasting about how he was shipping some equipment over for you. He was giving me shit because he thought I...that I was still working for you, and I didn't tell him otherwise. We didn't talk long. It was only in passing while we were in port."

"Austin Birch?"

"Yes, Main Master."

"You're going to tell me what he said word-for-word or I'm going to start melting those bullets inside of your legs to help you remember."

His hands shot up.

"It was in Dubai, one of my first stops for my new employer."

"Dubai." I gave him a dry look.

"I swear. He even asked why the hell I was there, and I told him it was official business, and I couldn't say. That's when he laughed and said, '*Oh, you must be on a secret mission for the brats too.*' I was confused, and said, '*What do you mean?*' He told me to stop playing stupid. That everyone knew *The Dragon* was playing house. That he'd knocked up a slave who was having twins."

Repeatedly, my jaw flexed, and I could barely contain the fire that licked up my insides, towards my eyes. Had I been so careless? Or had I been too trusting?

"Everyone?"

"That's what he said, Main Master, but at that point, I hadn't heard it from a single soul. Just him. A few weeks later, I heard Leftie, from Summer Sway, mention how in love you looked playing daddy. That your slave was showing a lot. He'd seen the two of you on your balcony when he was parked at the island."

Trusting? Careless? Did I need to hear anymore? It was no wonder I'd been such an easy target. I'd been both. I had put my family at risk, and there was no one to blame but myself, and *Austin Fucking Birch.*

"I've heard enough." I took a step back, trying to ignore how my legs were weak. "String them up. All of them."

"...What! Main Master!"

Yells exploded from the group, and a shot rang out as one of the crew tried to run. Chaos ensued, and I pulled out my knife, leveling it against Willard's neck. "One move and I'll split you clean open like I did that bitch who killed my wife. I'm not letting you die by some fucking bullet because you're a coward. You betrayed me. For that, you'll die a death far worse than any measly nightmare that comes to you at night. Does the name Aamir sound familiar to you? Do you remember him, my wife's twin? I'm going to send him your head, Willard, and he's going to see what it means when I say I take care of family. You fucked up by running away. You fucked up even more by returning to my domain."

# CHAPTER 13

## LUKE

*I* was lost. Confused. Relieved. I was fuming that Gavin hadn't told me his wife was alive. I didn't know Layla. Not really, but not because I didn't want to. My brother and I hadn't been close since his death on the outside world. If I wanted to tell the truth, we weren't necessarily close before that. We were, but there was always this wall between us, and I'd come to take it for what it was. As I looked at Layla, I felt that wall coming down. My brother loved this woman more than anything on the earth. He adored her. Put her on a throne so high it was unreachable. Yet…it hadn't been, because they'd gotten to her. They almost killed her and killed one of their children. Gavin's pain was my own as I stared down at the dark-haired sleeping beauty before me. She was everything to him, and he was trusting me to keep her safe.

*He was trusting me.*

"She shouldn't be…this well." The witch woman paced, keeping her fist at her mouth. "I didn't see us taking this path. Death is growing a fondness for the Dragon. How will Death feel when the Dragon is finished? There is no balance right now. He kills, she kills. There must be balance."

Layla groaned, stirring.

"Ga-Gavin."

Her head flew up before her eyes even opened.

"Shhh. It's Luke. You're okay. You have to lay back so you don't tear open the stitches again."

"She was so cruel. My babies."

The last was mumbled through the silent sob, barely audible as she turned her head away. Had I not seen her body shaking, I would have never known the tears she cried. It gutted me to see what her and my brother were going through. I mourned the loss of my niece and nephew, but I didn't know that pain as they did. I did know what it was to love someone and not be loved back. To yearn but not have them. *I knew that, and it hurt.* It still didn't come close to comparing to Layla's grief.

"I'm sorry she was cruel. You don't have to worry about that anymore. I won't let anyone hurt you. You have my word. You're safe with me until Gavin returns, Layla."

She sniffled, turning to study my gaze.

"If only that were true. I have to leave, Brother. I have to go."

"Go?" My tone rose, even though I tried to keep my voice calm. Brother. The word did things to me that I hadn't felt in a long time. I longed for family. I had Everleigh and Bram, but it wasn't the same knowing my own brother distanced himself from me. Now, Layla, accepting me. Claiming me when that's what I needed. I loved her in that moment, and it was a love unlike what I felt for Everleigh or those closer to me. It was a comforting love. A consolidating one with no expectations other than unconditional acceptance. "Layla, you can't leave."

Glancing to the witch woman, Layla gave me a confused look.

"I don't have a choice."

"What do you mean? Of course you do."

Her lids closed for a few seconds as she shook her head.

"Gavin has ordered me to stay with the tribe until he returns."

"The tribe? You're kidding." My hand rose to the Babke. "No offense, but I don't see how that would be good for you."

"My husband believes it's for the best. I didn't agree with him until Havaan. Mandy and I can't be here. People will begin to figure it out. We have to leave…tonight."

"We will not," the witch woman blurted out walking quickly to the bed. "This is not the way. This is not the path."

"It is now," Layla ground out. "We leave tonight. It is the safest for Gavin. I will not put him at risk a moment longer. I did that today, and I will not make the mistake of doing it again."

Foreign words left the older woman as she walked away, shaking her head. I lowered my voice, focusing on my sister-in-law.

"I can keep you here, Layla. I can keep everyone out of this wing if I have to. No one will find you."

"I know every single servant and guard in this castle. They will be suspicious if anything changes. They must believe Gavin is out to avenge his dead wife and children. Dragons protect their treasure. Gavin says that all the time. If I'm discovered and killed while he is away, he will have nothing left to live for. The Dragon will fall, Luke. We don't want that. I will leave this place, and as far as you're concerned, I am dead. If I'm dead, Gavin lives. I need him to come back to me. I need him."

Her voice cracked and again the sobs shook her body. I kneeled by the bed, gripping her shoulder as I kept my head down. The woman had just given birth to twins. She lost one, and not only did her husband leave, but she could end up dying too. Now she was going to go live with a tribe? In a place with no running water or the simplest necessities? I couldn't see how I was going to let her do that. Layla and I were family. I hadn't had that in so long, I coveted her endearment. Just hearing it sent pings to a heart that had done nothing but love others with little affection in return. I'd given every part of me, and now the smallest sliver inside wanted to force Layla to stay. I could take care of her for Gavin. I could make sure she had the best damn care. That's what I did. It was my fucking job.

"If Gavin ordered you to the tribe, you will go to the tribe. But—"

"No." Her hand shot out to grip my long-sleeved black shirt. "No buts, Brother. I will go there, and I will stay. I will not return here no matter how hard or terrifying it becomes. My Dragon is making his mark on the world. It is time I do the same. Even if my mark is seen by nobody but me. I have to do this."

I grabbed her hand, holding it in both of mine as she let go of my shirt. It was a finality I could barely accept. I hated it. I didn't want her to go, but I gave her a squeeze, standing and walking over to her vanity where I'd laid down the bottle of water when I'd rushed in here from the witch woman's warning.

Movement eased in and I glanced over to the Babke. "I worry more for her than your brother. It is not time to go."

"Can you convince her to delay the trip?"

"Convince? Ha." The witch woman rolled her eyes. "There is no convincing that one. I can make her sleep, but I fear the woman who awakes. She changes by the hour. The voices grow loud."

"Voices?"

I glanced back towards Layla, but it was her servant's soft words that had me tearing my gaze away.

"Demons. The Babke tied them to her when she used the spell to save her life. Leelee isn't the same. I don't—" The girl's lip trembled as she quickly wiped away tears. "I don't know the woman who killed Havaan. Layla is not herself. She'd never speak a harsh word. She...murdered her. Attacked and slit her throat. The demons rule her when she gets upset. She scares me."

"You fear your Leelee? You better think long and hard about the title you've so generously given to your queen." The Babke's voice was harsh as she leaned in. "If you abandon her now, the darkness will grow. You are her light. Be her light or there will only be one thing left. That amount of dark *will* find you, and when it does, those demons you fear will come after you too."

Small arms latched just below my elbow as the servant, Mandy, clung to me. Although she was young, I was guessing she was older than Layla by a year or two. She had a unique beauty, but not one I'd classify as usual. Her brown eyes stayed down, and she kept her curly hair tightly tied back. She was always in white, but it looked good against her deeply tanned skin.

"You have so far to come, girl."

Mandy seemed to catch herself, quickly putting distance between us. She was still afraid. It showed in the way she held her arms around herself as she peered around skittishly. Looking between her and the condition of Layla, how in the hell were they going to survive out there? I didn't know much about the tribe on the other side of the island, but I did know one thing. It was a good five miles away at least, and that was just getting there. What about their rules? Their lifestyle? Their…diet? Hadn't Bram mentioned on our first trip to the island that they were cannibals or at least had cannibalistic tendencies?

"Babke."

The woman's laughter filled the room. "Bab-kah. Kah," she said, putting emphasis. "Kah. Bab-Kah."

"Bab-*kah*. Woman," I growled. "How safe is my sister-in-law in that tribe of yours? I'm going to be blunt because I don't have time not to be. Will she be safe? Taken care of? Where will she stay? What will she eat? Will she have plenty of access to food and water? These are things I need to know."

"Layla, your *sister*, will be as good as she makes herself."

"Wait." My hand shot up. "What do you mean?"

"She's a woman. She's capable."

"Are you kidding me? She just had two babies. Did you see that gash on her stomach?"

"Did you not just see me sewing it? Of course I saw. Who do you think fixed her to begin with?"

My lips pressed into each other.

"She can't be expected to fend for herself."

"She has her servant. I am not that nor anyone else."

A deep breath left me. "Alright. What about food and water?"

"The girl, Mandy, can hunt. She's capable."

My jaw dropped. "The woman huddling in the corner looking at the shadows for demons? Are you serious? She's no more of a hunter than Layla is."

"The girl packed well. They have food to hold them over for a while. It was taken to their hut earlier today."

"Will it be there when they arrive?"

The Babke shrugged.

"Jesus. Okay. I will send more food. I'll keep sending supplies."

"You will not. You heard the order. When the girls leave here, they die to you. No supplies. No help." The witch woman leaned in. "They must grow. They must learn to survive. If they don't, your sister will surely die, and not from our way of life. The winds are at work, new Main Master. If you stop it, they will fall. We all may fall."

The Babke left me there as she headed for a black makeshift bag in the far corner of the room. Layla was drifting off and on, almost appearing to cry in her sleep. My eyes closed, only opening as footsteps passed. The witch woman moved in next to Layla, lifting her head. There was resistance but whatever she said had my sister finally drinking. I let out a deep breath, checking my watch. My phone still hadn't rung, and I was going to lose it if I didn't get a location or some sort of video on my brother soon. Bram was doing what he could, but I wasn't sure if we were ever going to make it into Gavin's system. If anyone could do it, it was me. The Babke mentioned luck. I could sure use it.

# CHAPTER 14

## LAYLA

The screams were worse than the conspiring voices. I could hear them in the distance. The volume never rose, but it didn't have to in order to stir the madness that was building within. The longer I was here, the worse my dread became. I was spinning in circles, running nonstop through the thick fog that kept me prisoner to the snickers and constant screams.

Calling for help did nothing. Trying to find Gavin got me nowhere. I'd stopped walking what felt like hours ago. I was defeated, screaming back at no one. Everyone. How long had I been here? It felt like an eternity. I was in so deep, I didn't think it was going to release me any time soon.

*"She wants to quit. Look at her."*

*"She's going to cry again. Boo hoo. Boo hooooo."*

More laughs. More whispers. More screams.

My stare lifted from the daze I'd been caught in. Walking might help, but I'd done this so long, it would get me nowhere. Didn't the Babke say I needed to stop running anyway?

What had she told me to do? Face it? Face what? I couldn't even remember her advice. I hadn't wanted to. I'd been so angry that she was in my dreams to begin with. Now I was stuck, and I had no idea what it was I should do.

*"If we put her by the cliff, do you think she'll jump?"*

Multiple sets of laughter.

*"Let's throw her off instead. We'll dangle her and make her afraid."*

Angrily, I glared around the fog. There was barely any red, and for the smallest moment I felt like I couldn't breathe through the blanketing patches of gray and black smoke.

*"I want to see her scream. She'll scream if there's no ground to stand on. She'll fall."*

*"Fall!"*

*"Fall!"*

*"Jump!"*

"Shut up!" I collapsed to the ground, refusing to move an inch. "*Stupid* voices. I hate you! You think this is so funny. It's not! You don't scare me anymore. Just hearing you makes me angry. You're lucky you hide." I moved out my leg, kicking down hard to the surface underneath me. "*Do you hear me? You're lucky!*"

A dark hood thrust through the fog, even with my face and twice the size. It was so fast and close all I could do was gasp as it threateningly growled. Inside the hood was…darkness. A dark so thick and consuming it had no color. No black. No substance. It was a hole of nightmares, and it was staring right back at me.

*"What are you going to do?"*

I didn't think. I screamed and surged to my feet, running in the opposite direction. My pulse was pounding against my chest, and I was pushing my feet as fast as they would go. The laughter was back. Voices carried in the air, spinning around me. Where the screams had been a constant, they were suddenly gone. For some reason that scared me worse than their presence.

*"Let her fall!"*

*"Fall. Fall."*

*"Down she goes."*

Snickering. Evil giggles.

The ground began to shift down, and the fog gave way showing the cliffs ahead. The black robed figure was still there, watching. He was huge and growing bigger every time I stole glances. Was he getting closer? Was he coming for me?

*"Jump! Jump!"*

*"I want to see her fly. Fall!"*

The need to scream out to Gavin was there. Every part of my being cried out to him for help, but I hid the need. I kept running, knowing I needed to stop. I had to, but I couldn't. My arms were clawing the air.

Fear grew and I twisted, scraping, tearing at the fabric of the haunting scene. My legs didn't slow. I didn't even feel it was me that had control over them.

"No more running."

"Babke?" I was crying. "I can't stop! I'm going to fall!"

"Don't fight it; control it."

"Listen to me, Babke! I'm going to fall!"

"Only if you allow yourself to."

Emptiness was but mere feet away. Louder I screamed, bracing myself to plummet to the crashing seas below. Five feet. Three. I ran out of ground and the sky sucked me down. I kicked and screamed through the freefall, feeling it disappear as my piercing scream woke me from the pit of unconsciousness. I was so heavy. So out of it as voices buzzed unrecognizably over me.

"Shh, Leelee, please. I'm here. Please, stop screaming, they're going to hear you. *Leelee.*"

I gasped, my nails clawing into my servant as she tried to keep me laying down. I was swallowing big gulps of air, and my eyes were searching the room wildly for the robed figure I knew wasn't far away. His presence was suddenly a weight in me. He was here, even if I couldn't see him.

"Mandy. M-Mandy." I broke down sobbing as her wide eyes

stared into mine in horror. Still, I held to her in a deathgrip. I was soaking wet with sweat, shaking so hard I could barely speak at all. "He's here. I can feel him."

"Who, Leelee?"

"The cloaked...thing. It was so big. He was...he was in my face, growling. Waiting for me to..."

"One of the demons?"

I opened my mouth, clamping it closed. "I...No. I..don't know. It was nothingness. It was—"

"Death."

My head whipped to the side as the Babke seemed to appear at the bottom of the bed from nowhere.

"You can't give Death a gift and expect him not to be intrigued. You killed a woman today, Layla." The Babke grew closer, keeping her eyes on mine. "You committed murder. You planned it. You wanted it."

"*No.*"

Her head tilted as I felt shame and guilt heat my skin. It wavered as something hotter inside flickered to awareness.

"You did, and there's no going back. Look at me when I tell you, child...you took a life today. Any part of innocence you had left is now long gone. You've summoned Death and drew him in close. You can never outrun the tie that now binds the two of you. If you thought your dreams were bad before, you've now invited a force even I can't rid you of. Only you have the power to fix this, and only you will know how to do that."

Tears appeared and I groaned as Mandy helped me to sit.

"You did something to me when you saved me. I've heard you all whispering. I know it was something bad." Streams of hot wetness raced down my face. "I died. I know I died. What you did...was it the only way to save me?"

A long moment of silence passed before the Babke sat on the edge of the bed.

"It was, and I knew it was coming. I dreamed it long before

that day. But I fear what I did. The paths seemed so clear before. There's never a guarantee, but even I wasn't prepared for the direction we've taken. Nothing's the same as it was hours ago."

"*Gavin—*"

Her hand lifted, trying to calm me.

"The blood he spills will make him a very lucky man. Death deals in favors, but eventually those will disappear. When they do, Death will find ways to cause chaos. That only poses a risk for your Dragon...*and you*. Death will collect one way or another, and he cares not for who's on the other end of a blade. The steady supply is what he wants, and he'll do what he can to keep it. There is much...unbalance."

"It's all my fault. I keep ruining everything."

"Not ruining, child, altering. Nothing is ever ruined. Never think that. What sets us back can propel us forward. You showed great strength today. Spilling blood is never easy, but that doesn't mean it isn't necessary. You did what you felt you had to do. You took action to protect the person you love. A sacrifice for a sacrifice. The Gods can respect that. Death sure does." She paused. "You were not dealt an easy life, nor will it get any easier. You will find power in your purpose. Listen closely...*never lose yourself in it*. Things can appear good and go bad just as fast. Awareness is key."

"Babke, will Gavin and I be alright? Will he come home to me?"

She closed her eyes, taking a long but deep breath in. "I'm afraid I can't tell you more until time passes." Her eyes opened. "Every decision is a shift. Every path is a possibility. Time is the only thing we can rely on anymore, and it's not always our friend. One day after the next."

The Babke stood, heading for the door.

"Speaking of time, you gave me something to sleep. It feels late."

"The sun just set. I will go get your meal now."

There was an uncertainty in the Babke's voice I hadn't heard before. I stayed quiet, letting Mandy fix the pillows behind me so I could lay back against them as I weighed her words. I was still so tired and heavy, it was almost impossible to think. What I did know was I had altered our path, and it was up to me to get it back on the right track. I had to use my head. I had to make the right decisions. She said there was power in purpose. I wasn't sure what that meant, but I wanted to find out. I wanted power. *I deserved it.*

# CHAPTER 15

## THE DRAGON

The sunset had come and gone. Seeing the beautiful colors paint the sky as I splashed such rich shades on the deck was almost…invigorating. Calming yet energizing. Or maybe that's how I'd felt gutting and burning the crewmen alive in my needs for vengeance. It had been me and Layla's time, and I couldn't think of the next best way to spend that time since I couldn't be with her. Even now, I held her close in my heart as I watched Willard's ghostly, headless body sway upside-down in the increasing winds. The storm was getting closer, and it wouldn't be long now. I was running out of time.

"Main Master, please. I was stupid. I wasn't thinking. I-I'll never—I never."

Lui had been going for hours now, stuttering over his words. He was in shock after what he'd seen, and he knew he was next. If only I could stop staring at that headless corpse. It had such beauty in the way it moved with the boat. Wave after wave sent it swaying with such grace. Or maybe it was I who had an almost elegant method of death.

"Double M."

I brought my attention to Fallon who was suddenly blocking

what was left of Willard's body. I didn't say anything which had him continuing.

"The head is packaged up like you requested. I know you're busy, but I really think you should eat something. The cook's made a special dinner just for you. I can take care of this piece of shit captain if you want me to."

My stare went to the dark skies closing in. "Lui doesn't die yet. Untie him and send him with the other men. He is not to be alone." My eyes turned to slits as I took him in. "I swear, if I see you near another kid, so help me, I will make your death the worst of all."

"Oh, God. Oh, God. Never again. Thank you, Main Master. Thank you."

"Fuck you. Don't speak to me unless you have to."

I could have removed his tongue for the way his voice grated my ears.

"Come eat, Sir. It'll help clear your head."

"If only." But I didn't continue. I stood, motioning for the older slaves to take Willard down. They knew what to do. "I've got some stuff to check on my laptop first."

Fallon's hand waved. "Go ahead. I'll bring you a plate."

All I could do was nod in thanks. I headed for the cabin, relieved when it was empty. I opened the laptop, typing in my password as I took a seat, and watching it come to life. I grabbed the earbuds, sticking them in as I pulled up the surveillance in our room. What I saw didn't have me smiling. I cursed, barely able to stop my hand from slamming into the small desk. What the fuck was Luke doing in my room, and why did my wife still look pale and weak?

I turned up the volume, making the window fullscreen.

"You have to eat it, Layla. I know you don't want to, but Babke said you must."

"She's drugging me, Brother. You know she is. I refuse to go back to sleep. Death, he…" her face turned hard as she looked away from him. "I told her I want to leave. I understand the walk is long. There has to be another way. I don't expect to be carried, but a cart or something will do. Anything. I can't stay here."

"Another day or two isn't going to hurt."

Her face swung back to him. "It will if someone happens to come this way and sees one of us. I've killed once. My body can't take doing it again so soon."

The chair scraped the floor as I shot to my feet. I had no idea what the fuck I was doing. Had she said she killed?

I was patting my black cargo pants, moving up to blindly feel over my belt. By the time I got my phone free, I couldn't even hear words anymore. Layla killed? A person?

"Sir?"

I slammed my laptop closed, squeezing the phone in my hand. Fallon stood at the door holding a plate of food. Fuck, I wasn't hungry. I sure as hell could use a drink.

"Thank you." I took the plate, putting it down. "I'm sorry, I need to make a call."

"You swore you weren't going to do that."

"I know. Fuck. Fuck!"

"Do you need my help?"

I paused, seeing no other way. "I do. Dammit." I gestured towards their laptops. "Make sure I'm safe on this call. I don't want anyone picking up this conversation, including you. You hear nothing, Fallon. Do you understand me? I don't care what I say or what you think I'm speaking about. *You hear nothing.*"

"You have my word, Double M." He shut the door, nodding as he eyed me cautiously, sitting down. It took him a good minute or two as I paced. When he nodded, I dialed Luke's number. Heat was baking my insides as my brother answered.

"Who is this?"

"Someone you're probably pissed at."

"Gavin. Jesus. You're right. I'm downright fucking livid at you."

"I figured you would be. It couldn't be helped. You're standing next to the reason. Do you see why I needed you there, now?"

"You're watching us?"

"As much as I can. I don't like what I just heard. Did I just hear that right? Tell me she didn't say what I think she did."

He paused. "You heard right. A maid, I think. Havaan. Layla thought she'd—"

"Luke, I said give it to me."

"She wants to tell you herself. If I don't give her the phone, she's going to bust her stitches open again trying to get to it."

I didn't get to say a word before heavy breathing sounded over the speaker.

"You're okay." She sniffled. "I've been so worried."

"You killed someone." It wasn't a question. At her hesitation a growl left me. "What were you thinking?"

"I didn't have a choice. Havaan saw Mandy on the fourth floor gathering supplies. She would have put it together, and that would have put you at risk."

"Not good enough. *You killed someone.* Luke said you busted your stitches open. *Lovie.* Anyone could have taken care of Havaan. *Anyone.* Not you. Never you."

"I'm not a baby, Gavin. I will not risk your safety. I'll do what I must, just like you."

"What I do will mean nothing if something happens to you."

"My thoughts exactly!" My eyes widened at Layla's explosion, but she continued, not close to being finished. "I'm so sick of everyone treating me like I'm fragile. Maybe I was. Maybe I was weak. Never again, Gavin. If I lose you—"

"You won't."

"You don't know that."

"I do. I'm not going to die."

"You better not. The moment these drugs wear off from Babke, I'm leaving here. I will not be the reason you're discovered, and I sure as hell am not going to take the chance with anyone else. I killed. *So what.* I'd slit a million more throats if it meant you'd come home to me. To hell with the world. Let your flames burn anyone who wants to keep us apart."

A smile pulled at the side of my lips for the first time in what felt like years. My voice softened.

"The world will burn for you, Layla. Every time you look into the fire, know I'm looking back at you, keeping you safe. I love you."

"I love you too."

"And Lovie, I never thought you were weak. I just didn't want you to have to be strong. If you were in love with me, and you had everything your heart desired, I figured I could blind you from the life we truly lived. I was the one who couldn't see, and it cost us. I'm so sorry for that. I only ever wanted to protect you from who I was. I failed."

She sniffled, clearing her throat.

"We both did. I allowed myself not to see for far too long. I was living in a fairytale, trying to cope with what happened. Even when it came to treatment, I distanced myself. I never liked that bitch doctor. Not from the moment I met her. I should have put my foot down then. I didn't and..." Even though she went silent, our pain was loud. We didn't need words for that. "From here on out, no more fairytales, Gavin. The only way our love will survive is if we protect it. Let's focus on that. One day at a time. I'll be at the tribe, so we won't be able to talk again until you return." She paused. "Don't worry about me. I'm going to be fine out there. I have Mandy and the Babke. I'll be waiting. I have your heart. Mine is with you."

The sniffle sounded further away, and Luke's voice was suddenly coming back over the line.

"What do you need me to do?"

I glanced at Fallon who kept his eyes on the screen.

"Be me. Has Rich called you yet?"

"No."

"I'm sure he will soon. Watch the staff and kill anyone acting remotely suspicious. No one can know she's alive. Kill as many as it takes. I don't care if I get back to an empty island. No risks, Luke. Promise me."

"I promise."

"I have faith you have this under control. Be safe, Luke. I have to go. I'll talk to you soon."

"*Wait.* Gavin, I need the password so I can get in the system. I need eyes on this island. I need them on you."

My lids closed as I battled rules. To give the password was forbidden. It was for the Main Master only. But I wasn't the Main Master at the moment. Luke was. And besides...he might need it.

"Three-thirty-one-nine-forty-two-seven-fifteen. The time I was born, the time you were born, and the month and day I died."

Luke paused. "Gavin, you didn't die July fifteenth. You died in August."

"Not in the military. The day I truly died. The same day I was reborn into a Main Master. It was after more than a year of teachings and torture. Almost two. They almost couldn't bring me back. That day, Luke."

"July fifteenth."

"That's the one. I have to go. Love you."

I hung up before he could say anything more. Fallon hit buttons, standing and heading over.

"Try to eat, Double M. I'll be with the men on deck if you need anything." He gave me a nod, sympathy, respect, maybe even a slice of relief embedded in his tight features.

"A storm is coming. I'm sure they know but remind them. It's going to be a rough night, if not a rough few days. After I finish eating, we'll head back out. I want Lui back on top with me and Lopez. I don't trust that son of a bitch to breathe. The moment this passes, Lui's dead. I can drive this boat in far enough for us to jump ships, but I'm going to need a captain to take it back to Red Island. Talk to White and have him make the call. Find us someone."

"I'm on it." Fallon walked over, pulling open the door, but pausing as he stood in the threshold, looking back at me. "If you need someone to help gut that motherfucking captain, I volunteer."

I gave him a nod, letting out a deep breath as he shut the door behind him. I grabbed the food, taking a seat and opening back up my laptop. Soon, I wouldn't be able to see her at all. I had no cameras covering the tribe, only the land, and I doubted I'd get lucky enough to spot her on those. She was truly about to be gone, and the thought nearly killed me. Layla mentioned she wouldn't be the same person when I returned. I hadn't been gone long and that was already true.

It was startling.

Unsettling.

How different would we both be when we finally did reunite? Would I even recognize the wife I'd left behind, or had Layla truly died the day we supposedly buried her?

# CHAPTER 16

## LUKE

*he day my brother died.* I could still hear Gavin's words. His tone haunted me. It cut into places so deep, I couldn't begin to locate them. Died. The sorrow still lingered inside from his military death. To think he truly did die instead of only faking his passing…I didn't want to think what he must have gone through. I'd seen hints of the thick scars he carried from the burns he had on his upper chest. How much of his body was covered in proof of that torture, I wasn't sure. What I did know was that the fire left the biggest impact. It was his trademark. He'd adopted and became what he knew. He became the fire and the Dragon behind it.

"She fought hard. The girl is strong."

"Layla's a warrior. The fight is all she has left." My eyes eased up from the laptop screen I was staring at to take in my sister-in-law. She was peaceful…for the moment. I turned to the Babke. "She's one of the strongest people I know."

"It's only beginning. Her life won't become easier. Not in any path I see."

My frown was immediate. I didn't like that, but maybe I could do something about it. Now that I had eyes on everything from the ships to the fortress to the island, my mind was racing. The insight was great, but I didn't want to leave any chances. I was soaking everything in, letting myself calculate every possibility. I had to know the lay of the land. I needed to learn routines and what these slaves were up to. The housekeeping. The guards. The tribe she was going to stay with. There was so much to keep tabs on, and the faster I came up with a plan and routine, the more I could help out my brother and Layla.

"There's no cameras on the part of the island that holds the tribe."

The Babke raised one of her thin salt-and-pepper eyebrows.

"No. There's not. That is not the Main Master's land. That is ours."

"What would you say to temporary cameras? None too close, just...closer. I promise to have them removed when my brother returns. I." I stopped abruptly, taking in the witch woman's defensive stare. "I have to see for myself that she's okay."

"No."

"No? Babke."

"Bab-*kah*."

My eyelids shut as I took in a deep breath. When I opened them, I matched the stubbornness she was projecting.

"Please. What would I need to do to convince you to allow in a camera? Not a lot, just one. One camera that gives me eyes on the tribe, but far enough away it isn't imposing. Anything. Just name what you want."

"Privacy cannot be bought, new Main Master."

"It won't be imposing on anyone's privacy, I promise. It won't be that close. I just have to see the camp or huts in the distance. I need to make sure the tribe isn't getting raided, or your village isn't burning down. I have to watch and make sure no one is sneaking up and spying on you all. Layla is in danger. They want her dead. I need to make sure some big massacre isn't taking place so they can get to her. Please, Bab-kah."

It took a few seconds but a smile appeared, and she let a good minute pass while she stared off into space.

"The air is good. You are honorable in your request. Perhaps I can think of some things I need."

"Thank *God*. Thank you. I am honorable. I will not betray your trust. One camera, that's it. Name whatever you want."

"Name? You won't remember. I will make a list."

"Perfect." I went to continue, pausing as the phone for the Main Master started ringing. A frown came to the Babke's face, and her lips peeled back as she flicked her hand towards the cell. I wasn't sure what she was reacting to, but I knew it wasn't good as I stood and answered it.

"Yeah?"

My tone was deep as I grabbed the laptop, walking to a table at the far end of the room so I wouldn't wake Layla.

"Main Master, this is Tillin. I have your daily report."

I glanced at my watch, not missing the way his voice was slurring.

"It's after midnight. You didn't think I might need it hours ago? Do you call my brother this late?"

There was a pause.

"I must have got distracted."

"By a bottle, no doubt. What is there to report?"

I clicked through buttons, browsing through the cameras covering the slave huts, moving along until I got to the decent sized wooden building I knew the guards and captains gathered in. It was like a bar, but not one I'd ever seen. The night we burned some of the slaves, I'd heard stories of the fights, rapes, and opened torture held there. The place was a free-for-all, and Gavin hadn't thought too much of it. I did. It was too risky having a place like that when Layla wasn't in my care.

"I wouldn't say there's a lot to report. Four captains remain on the island. Nelton's ship should be fixed here in another week, and then he'll be good to go. There was a complaint by one of the female slaves, but I squashed that. A storm—"

"Go back. A complaint about what?"

Tillin paused. "Uh, she said one of the soldiers attacked her outside the wash house."

"Attacked her. Elaborate. Beat her? Raped her?"

Another pause. "I believe both, Sir."

"A soldier. Not one of the guards from the fortress?"

"No."

"As in the ones who live underground?"

"That's right, Sir."

"Name of the soldier?"

A small laugh echoed. "Mills."

"You seem to be familiar with this man."

"He has a history. It just 'is'. The slaves know not to be behind the drink-house after dark anyway."

I bit the inside of my lip feeling my pulse pound harder. I had been a soldier once before too, when I'd gotten the news of my brother. I'd fucking loved my duties, but I lost myself after I lost Gavin. I became unrecognizable in my grief. I fell in with some very bad people. It's what ultimately led to me working for West Harper. I didn't regret that. That led me to Everleigh, my boss to date. She'd married that monster of a man. She'd also killed him before she took his place that day on the plane. I loved her with everything I had. And she…she loved Bram Whitlock, her new husband. Life wasn't fair. Neither was karma. Tonight, I'd be both.

"Anything else to report?"

"We got the island prepared for the storm. It should be hitting late tomorrow, into the early hours."

"Excellent. Next time, call before nine. If you're a minute late, I'll have you brought in to see me, personally. You won't like what will happen inside these walls. My brother may be lenient, but I am not. Nine o'clock. Not a minute later."

I hung up, not even waiting. As I stood, the Babke made a clicking with her tongue.

"Beware the paths, new Main Master. They open before you. Choose wisely."

Grabbing the laptop, I tried to control the slight shake to my hand. Anger was within so many of us, for so many different reasons. Mine had nothing to do with revenge and everything to do with order and justice.

"I shouldn't be here in this room, and I won't be back. It's too risky for all of us. I will not continue to have Layla drugged either. Come morning, I will make arrangements to have her carried or moved through the tunnels. I'll figure out what is best for her so I can keep her safe."

She grabbed her black bag, walking slowly towards me.

"You don't threaten, but your words are no less a threat."

"Babke, I'm trusting you with her life when I feel I'm the one who should be protecting her. I can do that," I ground out. "I can make sure she's safe from anyone."

"Even herself?"

My lids narrowed the smallest amount as she continued.

"Layla battles demons, new Main Master. They live in her now. They fight for power over her actions. *Her decisions.* Soon, she will not know herself from them. She has Death stalking her every move. He almost had her once. I fear if she doesn't sate him, he'll find more appeal in taking her than accepting what she can supply. Obstacles are nothing more than a game for the dead. They arise, and their keeper waits like a spider to see if we fall. Death will be with you too, tonight. He already is. Do you feel him, Luke? Can you feel Death standing behind you? Murder serenades you. It whispers sweetly to the killer within. *That is him,* like a lover you can't resist. I'll say it again…Beware the paths before you. You don't want to take the wrong one."

I grabbed the door's handle, shaking my head.

"There's only one path, and that's the one that keeps my

family safe. Even on this fucking hell of an island. I won't have the men outright attacking and raping slaves under my watch. Maybe my brother was different. Maybe he was too distracted, or he didn't care. I do. If they can rape slaves, they can rape the tribal people. If they can rape the tribal people, they can rape Layla. Over my dead body. Over theirs—those out of control fucking soldiers. That is not our way. That is not what we represent. I'll fix this. I don't have a choice."

*"New Main Master."*

I opened the door, pausing as the Babke came up at a fast pace.

"Your heart is in the right place, but your mind is not. I disagree with what you're about to do, but this path is yours, and not mine. I will walk you to the tunnels and direct you to the soldiers. It's not a straight shot. You will have to go up top onto the field, and then back underground in their entrance. I must go to the tribe and prepare them. I am in charge, but I also do not like what that means. Both of our nights are about to take a turn. In which direction, I do not know. Follow me."

And I did.

The halls were quiet due to me repositioning the guards hours ago. I couldn't have them in Layla's wing. Not with me there, and surely not with her. When we arrived near the kitchen area, the Babke took us into what appeared to be a large wine cellar. The maze between rooms and wooden barrels were disorienting. I felt like we were turning in a big circle or square. Four rooms straight, two over, four rooms back. Over. Or were we not really turning anywhere at all?

If it wasn't for the pressure in my ears, maybe I wouldn't have even known we'd somehow been descending the entire time. The floor kept appearing to shift beneath my feet and the musk of mold and possibly grain kept me wrinkling my nose.

"There's a guard ahead. It's dark in the tunnels. He is...trustworthy."

"That's good to know. So, we're not in the tunnels yet?"

The Babke threw me a look. "Does this look like a tunnel?"

"Of course not. But we are underground?"

"We are."

She didn't go into further detail as we made a turn, bringing us into a blackness that was darker than any night. My instincts went into overdrive, and I was ready for anything that might pose a threat. The Babke had to have sensed it. She grabbed my wrist, leading me around another turn. My free hand reached out, feeling nothing, expecting the worst. The air was different. The energy was off. I could barely think into it as a glow appeared in the distance. It was a muted yellow, almost white. I strained as I got closer, wondering if the stolen colors were swallowed by the darkness as well.

"Zo've[1]."

A foreign language sounded, no doubt tribal, as the Babke communicated with the guard. The closer I got, the more I realized the man in the dark guard uniform *was* tribal. Or had been at one point.

"This is Va-hen. He knows where you are going, and he will bring you back when you return. *If*…you return." She grabbed a wooden torch from the guard, and I watched as flames shot to life at the end. "Follow me, new Main Master. It's not much longer of a walk."

But hadn't we already walked a good mile just to get here? I didn't speak as I obeyed, weaving even deeper in the circular void that seemed to go on in front of us forever. It wasn't the only one. Every few hundred yards, a big hole appeared off to both of our sides, leading in other directions. We had to of passed a good five tunnel openings before the Babke turned us into one. More darkness, but not for long. Stairs appeared, and we headed up two flights before she secured the torch and led us up a third flight. There, she opened a hatch. What it led us into was an abandoned village in the middle of a field. Even with as dark as it was, the moon gave me enough light to see the five other structures next to us.

"You'll want to go into the last hut, closest to the forest. You'll see the hatch. They don't hide it. They dare anyone to enter. Most who do that aren't a part of them, don't return." The Babke's hand lifted almost as a sign of peace, but I didn't think that's what she meant as she faced me. "Your aura grows dark. Be safe, new Main Master. Until we meet again."

"So, I live?" I could barely see her features, but I knew she wasn't sure, and she wouldn't answer. "I guess this is goodbye. Keep Layla safe. *Please.*"

"You beg but pray. It is in your tone. You should be praying for me, not your sister. I must go. The wind shifts. I will not return to follow Layla down. You must do that." She paused as she went to leave. "My people won't take well to your camera. I make no promises how long it will survive. You'd do best to conceal it as best you can. Expect my list, soon."

She didn't wait as she disappeared ahead in the darkness. I loosened the tie at my neck, cursing the suit I had to wear for my position here. I usually wore one anyway, but this time it represented something entirely different. It held power, and unlike my brother, that was something I had never wanted. Not like this.

Debris crunched under my feet as I headed through the empty doorway. Nothing was left but the structure and half of what I could only call a wall. As I headed for the last hut by the woods, goosebumps drew in my skin, and a chill raced down my spine. I wasn't a superstitious man. I didn't believe in most mystical stories. But I wasn't stupid either, and something was different on this island.

Laughing suddenly appeared. I walked faster, making it inside the collapsing hut just as two men were leaving the opened hatch in the floor. There was light below. It wasn't a lot, but more than I'd seen since I left the fortress.

"We all need to talk. I'd suggest going back down."

At my deep tone, the soldiers looked at each other, obeying and disappearing back below. I took in the pitch-black surroundings, cursing myself as I tried to see if there were any onlookers or threats I couldn't spot in the distance. What the fuck was I doing? I knew better than some spontaneous meeting with killers. This was dangerous. Stupid. Yet...here I was, praying my position wasn't about to get me devoured by an army of deadly soldiers who could easily chew me up and spit me out.

As I headed down the nearly vertical metal stairs, I could hear the buzz of voices decrease. What I came to face, I wasn't prepared for. I knew my brother had a lot of soldiers. I'd even seen some before when they came with us to Whitlock. That amount didn't compare to this. The bunker I was in wasn't just a large room. It was a small damn city, filled with beds and walls and...tunnels. So many tunnels, but apparently not connected to the main ones. At least, *not yet*.

The whispering grew as I walked more inside. Dozens of faces looked at me. Some from their bunks. Others from tables strewn out in the large main area. Card games were going on. Dominoes were laid out. Beers and bottles were aplenty. Where I should have been scared amongst all the men in camo, I wasn't. I felt at home.

"Does anyone here know who I am?"

A dark-haired man in what looked to be his early forties stood from one of the tables.

"The Main Master and Lopez filled us in. You're the brother. You're the temporary Main Master. You got some balls coming down here. I don't think any of us expected to ever see you. Aren't you supposed to be keeping your identity a secret?"

"I'm afraid I wasn't left with a choice. That's gone now; I'm here, and while I am, we all need to go over some rules."

"Rules?"

Another voice had my head turning as a younger soldier appeared from one of the tunnels.

"That's right. Rules. Gavin left me in charge, and if I'm going to keep him alive, we all need to have a serious talk. Let's bring it in. All of you over here so I know you hear me."

I walked over grabbing a chair and standing on it as the men began to head in my direction. It wasn't a quick task. Soldiers quickly surrounded me, but they kept coming from directions and spaces so deep back, I wasn't sure where or how many was crowding the space before I finally let out a breath and began.

"Before I get started, I need a soldier named Mills to come to the front. Do we have a Mills here?"

Shifting erupted, but that's all it appeared to be before a man in his early twenties eyed me suspiciously, walking forward. His uniform wasn't squared away like almost all the other soldiers. The buttons on his blousing shirt were undone and the black t-shirt he wore underneath was half untucked, hanging down the side as if it were two sizes too big. The closer he got, the more confrontational he seemed to become, even bumping his shoulder hard into another soldier as he got feet away.

"I'm Mills, what's it to you?"

My eyebrows rose at the attitude thickly laced in his tone.

"You come stand in the front, next to me. I'll be showing you what it is soon enough. First, I'm going to ask everyone a few questions."

The soldier obeyed, not becoming any less dramatic in his approach. He sighed. He huffed. He moved in a foot from my feet. It was his mistake. I pulled the knife from under my jacket's suit, leveling it to the side of his neck as the fingers from my other hand fisted into his dark hair.

"Respect has to be earned. *I get that.* But I don't have time, nor the want, to get respect from a piece of shit like you." My eyes cut up to the soldiers staring towards me uneasily. I spun the soldier to face them, keeping my hand buried in his hair as I lifted the top half of my body higher to see them all. "A few questions. Do any of you speak to the Main Master the way he just spoke to me?"

There was a pause, but men were shaking their heads, some even saying 'no'.

"I didn't think so," I said, jerking the soldiers head around as he squirmed. "I know my brother. He'd cut out your fucking tongue if you showed him such disrespect. Another question. Does he allow you to rape slaves? Are those not his merchandise? Does he not sell them out to people who visit this island?"

Silence.

"We're not allowed to be near them."

My head turned as I took in a soldier that had to be around the same age as my early thirties.

"That's what I thought." My body lowered again as I brought my face inches from the man's head as I stood above. From the chair, I had perfect position. "You raped a slave last night. Did you think I wouldn't enforce my brother's rules? Maybe you just don't give a shit about your Main Master."

"N-No. I" He stopped. "That bitch is fucking lying. I didn't do shit to her."

I leveled my blade back against his neck.

"Now, you're going to lie to me, on top of already disrespecting me?"

"Sir. Main Master—"

I pressed in harder, tilting my head more to watch the blood that began to stream down the column of his throat.

"My brother is all I have left. If you think I'm going to risk his life when he returns by leaving a lying, cowardice, piece of shit like you alive to stab him in the back at the first opportunity, you're mistaken." My body lifted again to stare the soldiers down. "My brother has taken care of you. Now, he needs you to take care of him. I'm sure words gotten around of what happened to his wife and children."

Faces went from cautious to hard as they took me in. If I

knew anything, I knew soldiers, and they needed a mission. They needed a leader like me.

"Those people who wanted to hurt my brother may return. They may even still be here amongst us now. We're going to find out. I need you. *He needs you.* From here on out, we're going to protect what's ours. We're making a schedule, and we're all doing shifts. Even me. We're going to use our skills, and we're going to look for answers. Anyone who isn't proud to be here, or loyal to my brother and what this island's about, get in line right next to Mills." I jerked the boy's head back, letting skin and muscle split open as I sliced the blade with almost all my strength. Skin tore at the hard pull against his hair, and blood poured from the gash, splashing and spraying across the cement floor as the weight from his flailing, panicked body pulled against my hold. Hands secured and positioned weight against my legs, covering almost every inch as I stared down at their contact. The large group of bodies shifted to get closer, and the soldiers moved in, keeping me from falling from the chair through Mill's thrashing. In our moment, I knew they accepted me. I knew their loyalty to Gavin was everything to them. And that…*was everything to me.*

# CHAPTER 17

## LAYLA

*E*ven though I knew it was daytime, it didn't look that way as Luke pulled me through the suffocatingly dark tunnels. Maybe it was my uncertainty over the entire situation that had me not arguing on my form of transportation. I felt like a child again. Like Aamir was pulling me around our backyard in our red wagon, except…it wasn't dark then, or so bumpy and uncomfortable, or…eerie. I didn't like it. Death may have stayed out of my dreams last night, but he was always close now. Or maybe I was just losing my mind in general. I mourned. I was sickened at my reality. I just wanted to sleep and never wake again. Not until I had Jasmeen and Gavin back. If I ever would.

The ache in my chest added to the claustrophobia from darkness. I could barely breathe through the oceans of emotion I was drowning in. If I wanted to be truthful, I was terrified beyond words at how life would be with this tribe. I was trying to be strong, but inside, I still felt like a little girl. Like…I had no idea what the hell I was doing.

"It shouldn't be much longer now."

Mandy's voice was quiet as she glanced back to look at me.

She was ahead with one of the tribal guards who held the only torch lighting up the space. We had to have already walked miles. It was as if hours had passed. Hours of self-loathing and sadness. Gavin may have blamed himself, and maybe he was even responsible in ways, but me…I was the mother. I was the one who was supposed to be the ultimate protector of my children. My mother had been. Sure, my father was overbearing and hovering, but my mother was the true shield for me and Aamir. She had kept us safe. She had fought and sacrificed to give us a good life. Yes, we had gotten taken, but that wasn't her fault. She'd been halfway around the world from us when we'd been trafficked in Greece. Me…I'd only been half a room away. *I'd been right there.*

"Layla."

My eyes lifted, and it was only then I heard my sniffles. My face was soaked with tears, and my shoulders were shaking through the silent cries that came whether I wanted them to or not.

"Are you okay?"

"I'm okay." I wiped my face, taking in a deep breath. "I'm good. I'm sorry. I can't seem to control it."

"Don't apologize." Still, Luke looked back at me as he continued to pull. "Never hold in pain like that. It'll do more damage than good. It's okay to cry. What happened…" He trailed off. "I still can't find words. I'm sorry."

"I feel like a parrot. I don't know if I keep saying this out loud or in my head."

"What's that?"

"That it was my fault. I keep going over it all. It keeps replaying, over and over." I couldn't speak through the sob that wanted to explode from me. I barely manage to hold it off as I continued. "I saw Jamison. I saw him, Brother. *He was alive.* He was looking at me. Starting to cry. I should have never let her leave with him. If I would have taken him or made her give him to me. I…He was blue at first, but he was breathing when I saw him. I swore he was—or maybe if I—or if I would have—" There were too many what-ifs. Too many things I could have done differently. "She killed my son, *my child*, and I didn't stop her."

"You didn't know she was going to do that. You thought she was there to help you."

"No." My voice cracked, breaking into a million shards like my heart. "I never liked her. Deep inside, I knew she was bad. I knew."

Luke grew quiet, hiding his face from me in the darkness as he stared ahead. Me, the tears wouldn't stop despite focusing more on the anger.

"I'm sorry. I know you don't want my help. You've made that clear, Layla. There's so much I wish I could do or say. I tried thinking over everything but." He stopped. "All I could come up with was the bag you're holding. *Just in case you need something*," he rushed out. "You said you didn't want anything, but I couldn't help trying. We can leave it here at the base of the stairs, and you can eventually get it or not. I'll leave that up to you."

My eyes lowered, but I was barely able to see the black material I was clinging to. I hadn't even given the bag much thought when Luke set it on my lap. Now, I could feel its weight, and it wasn't necessarily light.

"What's in it?"

"A few waters, a survival kit, a knife, a gun, and a cellphone with my personal number programmed into it. It's a safe phone that has a special battery that doesn't require it to be plugged in. It won't call most numbers, but it'll call the ones that matter. I've left instructions in the bag on how to use it."

I looked down, my lips twisting as insecurities once again melted in.

"You made this for me?"

"I told you I want to help you."

"Thank you. That was very kind." I kept my gaze on the bag, my mind racing. "Will the phone reach Gavin?"

Luke frowned as he glanced back.

"I'm afraid not. He left his personal cell behind, and I don't have his new number. I don't think anyone does. I'm not even sure it can be called."

I nodded, already knowing it was impossible.

"You're probably right. I..." Cautiously, he glanced back, and I knew he was trying to read me. "I really appreciate this. I think maybe...I think." I sat up a little straighter. "I think I'll just take it with me now. Just in case there's an emergency."

His shoulders seemed to relax as he turned to stare ahead.

"I like that idea. You can never be too safe. The phone is on vibrate. If you want, you can check it nightly to see if I call. If I do, it's because I have news that I think you'll want to hear. And just so you know...you can call me anytime." He slowed, stopping to crouch and face me. For a moment it was so dark I couldn't see him, but I knew Mandy and the guard had come in closer to us as his concerned features were suddenly illuminated. "I know you're determined to stay with the tribe, but I can keep you safe if and when you're ever ready to come back. I will come and get you at any time. I don't care if it's three in the morning and you've decided you've had enough. *Any time. Any day.* Do you understand?"

I wiped the tears quickly nodding.

"Thank you."

"You never have to do that, Layla. You're my sister. My family. I'll always be here for you."

I pressed my lips together, biting down until pain had me reaching for his hand.

"You are a good man."

"That's debatable."

"You are, and I'll never forget what you're doing for me and Gavin."

He forced a grin, turning to pull me again. As we continued to walk, I let my mind wander. Not on my son. Not on Gavin. Not on Jasmeen or Aamir. To go there hurt too badly. Instead, I focused on the plan I'd come up with after I killed Havaan.

No dependency.

No trust.

No fear.

That's all I had ever had, and it destroyed my dream. If it was a nightmare I was being forced to live in, I wouldn't be the one having it. I'd be the darkness that ate up the light. The howls and cries that drove the dreamer to run. I'd be the terrifying face they saw as they prayed to wake up. This was my new path, and there was only one thing I could do. *Embrace it.*

"Almost there."

Whether Mandy kept repeating it for me or her, I wasn't sure. I kept my mouth shut and my mind going. I would be the real Layla. I'd become this new me. Independent. Strong. Nothing would stand in my way. I could do this. I wouldn't be scared. I was strong. Strong. A killer. I was that now too. Strong. A force. *The force,* just like my husband.

Minutes passed. Longer. It wasn't until we slowed that I tore myself from the haze of my thoughts to see us stopping at the base of some stairs. The bag was lifted from my lap, and I took Luke's hand as he helped me to stand. The moment I was steady, he lifted me in his arms. I was so caught unaware that I couldn't stop myself from fisting his tie right at the base of his throat.

"Layla."

But I didn't ease my hold at his strangled tone. I couldn't.

"I appreciate what you're doing, Brother, but put me down."

"This is no time to be—"

Tighter, I held.

"The only man that carries me is my husband. I *will* walk."

Luke lowered, putting my feet on the ground as he coughed and rubbed his neck.

"Gavin said you were stubborn."

"He underexaggerated. I'm worse. I'm sorry. I...I didn't mean to hurt you, but I'm doing this on my own. I can do this. I'm strong, and what you're doing doesn't coincide with how I was raised." I looked up to the flights of stairs that disappeared into the darkness. "No man will ever touch me but my husband. Ever. Period. It just is, and I will not bend on that."

Luke's features were tight as he took me in.

"I'm not just *any* man, Layla. I do not have bad intentions."

"I know."

"Then let me carry you. You can't walk those stairs. Not all of them. You're going to hurt yourself worse."

My head slowly shook even though I knew he was probably right.

"I won't. I'll go slow. You can help me, but you can't carry me."

"Like hell I can't. I know for a fact if my brother was looking in, seeing this, he'd tell me to pick your ass up whether you approved or not. If I wasn't afraid you'd fight me and tear open the stitches, I would. So, again...I'm asking you, nicely, can I please carry you up the stairs?"

His arms came out expectantly, but I took a step back.

"Layla."

To argue was a waste of time. I stepped up, holding to my stomach as he rushed in, grabbing my bicep securely.

"There, see. You're helping, and we're moving. It's fine."

"It's not, dammit. We both know this isn't safe for you."

"It is. Let me go slow. Be at my side. Hold to my arm if you must, but I will make it up these stairs by my own two feet. The

Babke even said I can walk, so long as I'm careful. Am I not safe with you by my side?"

Luke's brow creased as he moved up one step with me.

"You are."

"Then let's keep going."

And we did, but not without Luke's other arm hovering behind me just in case I fell. We took it slow. I was sure I was going to have to stop halfway up. I didn't allow myself. The new me didn't give up. She didn't tap out just because fear influenced the weakness. I went slower. I put in more focus on my feet. I made it to the top, tired and covered in sweat despite the slight chill.

"When you're better…"

The threat was clear in Luke's voice, but all I could do was smile up at him as he shook his head in aggravation.

"Thank you."

He made a sound, close to a growl.

"Underexaggerated is right. My God, Layla. I'm not sure who is more stubborn, you or Everleigh. You're both…overwhelming at times. You drive me damn crazy."

"I take that as the highest compliment. Gavin's told me stories about her. I think she's amazing."

I saw Luke soften immediately.

"She is that. And strong and passionate for the wellbeing of others." Luke's eyes cut over to me. "Everleigh is also the biggest pain in my ass. That woman." He let out a deep breath. "She means well. It's just…sometimes even she needs to allow others in. It's hard for her, but Bram and I are trying, and she's getting better."

"As long as you're there. Everleigh is smart. She'll know when it's time to call you both in."

"That's what I'm hoping, too. I'm not always so confident."

Luke reached above, flattening his hand on the hatch. "I can't go out there, Layla. This is where you and I say goodbye. Don't forget to check the phone…if you want. Call me if you need anything. *Anything.* Take care, Sister, and be safe."

"You, too. Trust *no one.*"

He nodded and stepped up to the small ladder, taking a step up as he pushed open the top. Light flooded in, and my heart slammed into me as he stepped down and allowed me to take his place. Each step up was harder than the next. My legs felt like water and the pull against the stitches was a concern with every step, but I made it to the top. I was barely crawling out when Luke stepped up, easing the bag against the ground. He was gone just as fast. Soon, Mandy appeared, and where I thought the tribal guard would follow, he didn't. Mandy shut the hatch and for the first time, I looked around. And around. And around.

I spun in a slow circle, not sure how we were even on the same island. Trees were thick. Where I was used to the tropical beach, bungalows, and cliffs by the fortress, this was anything but that. I felt like someone had dropped us off in a rainforest. Sounds were alive all around us from birds to the rustling of leaves. The humidity felt thicker, making me sweat even more. Even Mandy was wiping sweat away as she gazed at our surroundings.

"It's been a while since I've been here, but I think I remember the way. Come. We have to go. Watch for ants. They can be bad. And the bugs; they'll eat you alive. I had spray taken to our hut. Lots of spray."

"You don't want to be here."

"At Harper's Hideout?" She gestured to huts barely standing. "No. Nor this far out in the forest." Mandy quickly picked up the black bag not meeting my eyes. "I do not have fond memories of this life. We're being watched. We must go." Her arm looped through mine, offering support, but I leaned in, kissing her cheek. She stopped again, and light brown eyes scanned mine, full of anxiety. But something else too. Fear? From our location…or from me?

"We're okay, right?"

Mandy's mouth parted, and she hesitated before a genuine smile appeared.

"I've been afraid for you."

"I'm okay. I know I've been—ouch!"

I lifted my foot, sweeping the large ant from the top. The burn had me wincing but not as bad as the pull to my stomach.

"Come, Leelee[1], we have to keep moving. Always moving. Never stopping. That's when they get you. The village is right through these trees."

"Good. Not far?"

Her arm wrapped back through mine as we started walking at a slow pace.

"It's a little ways but not too far. If you listen, you might be able to hear the mamans[2] humming. They're always humming and singing."

"Mamans?"

"The older women of the tribe. The...mother's mothers. Mamans."

"Grandmothers," I said, smiling.

"Yes. Older but wise. They're nice. Or they were when I was little." Mandy got a worried look on her face again. "I haven't been back in a long time. I fear I'm an outsider now. They'll think I turned my back on them. I guess I did."

The last was nearly silent as we weaved through the trees. What I thought wasn't going to be a long walk was longer than I expected. Just as I was about to ask Mandy how much further, foreign words drifted in the distance. I listened as the hypnotic tune put me at ease.

"Not much further. The men will be." Mandy stopped, glancing up, her tanned face darkening with red undertones. "I know you've probably seen them at times in the trees, but some won't be dressed. Especially if they're going through palla[3]. Mating age," she said quickly.

"Is that why they're naked? They don't wear clothes during that?"

"No. The men must…earn and entice. He must be worthy to the one who chooses him. Mating is different here in the tribe. Different than." Her head nodded back towards where I assumed the fortress was.

"Different? You mean less promiscuous than the slaves? Like, they choose and marry for life here, right?"

Mandy laughed under her breath, shaking her head.

"Not exactly. There are more men here on the island. A woman is able to take many husbands if she needs to."

"Needs to? Why would she need to?"

"To keep the tribe flourishing. So we grow."

"I see." I nodded, keeping my stare ahead as the trees opened up to show a good dozen or more huts. Fear grew in me like a wall. I hadn't even realized I'd come to a stop until Mandy's step tugged against my arm. Maybe she'd tried to prepare me, but words were words. Seeing was something else entirely, and I wasn't sure if I should close my eyes and turn around or try to run the opposite way. I wasn't innocent, but aside from my husband and Ram, the man who'd raped me, I'd never seen another man without clothes on. And this wasn't just nudity a few feet from where we stood. A woman was laid back and propped on her elbows on what looked like a wooden tabletop, her head thrown back in pleasure as one of the men buried his face between her legs. His cock was hard, dripping precum as he moaned against her. People were everywhere, walking in groups with baskets of what looked like corn and something green. And then, there was the couple, enjoying their own buffet.

"This way. Fast."

Mandy was red again as she led me around, deeper into the tribal village. Kids yelled, running around the different groups of women. Where a group of seven seem to handle the food, another was focused on sharpening weapons. Even the older group, the mamans, hummed and built different things with wood. Arrows. Utensils. Even things that looked like toys. Each was engrossed in their craft, ignoring us and putting me more at ease as we passed. That comfort was fleeting as we headed around a hut right into the Babke arguing with a group of men whose ages ranged from twenties to what had to have been in the seventies.

"*Ye pa gnelp.*"[4]

Mandy halted, pulling me in closer. The Babke was speaking so fast, I couldn't begin to know what about. She was in the middle of arguing something when the majority of the group turned towards us. An impatient, aggravated sound left the Babke, and three of the younger men narrowed their lids as they headed in our direction.

"Don't look at them, Leelee. They're angry we're here. He said something about a traitor or traitors. *Gnelp.*"

"Traitors of what? We mean them no harm."

"Don't look at them. Just—"

"*Phunze eh ilya e me?*"

"We should go," Mandy rushed out. "Let's just—"

"No." I forced myself to stand tall despite that I wanted to run away. "What is he saying?"

Mandy's face turned more into me as the man kept speaking.

"He wants to know why we're here. He says we don't belong here. He's mocking…the Main Master for not taking care of us. Something about protection. He wants to know why we're not hiding in our…I think he's saying castle. He says something about weakness. Flowers. Like we're flowers."

"Flowers? I don't think so." I looked at the man who couldn't have been but a few years older than me. He was tall with deeply tanned skin. Where it appeared most of the tribal people's eyes were darker shades of brown, his were more a gold, like Gavin's. His lips were full, softening the hard angles of his jaw. I knew he wasn't wearing clothes, but I could barely care as my own anger surged to boiling heights as I stared him down.

"Mandy, tell him we are not flowers. We're strong, and the Babke is in charge. She wants us here. We're staying."

"Don't make me talk to him, *please.*"

"Tell him," I snapped.

Mandy's voice rose in pitch as she translated, but I didn't stop, and she didn't either as I continued.

"Tell him also that we are not traitors. We all live on this island. We don't bother them, and they don't bother us. As far as I know there's peace. Am I mistaken? Is there not peace between the tribe and the...Dragon's fortress? Yes, tell him that," I said, lowering my voice. "Also, I don't want his protection. I can take care of myself. I just need a place to stay while things get sorted out. As far as I'm concerned, he can stay far away from me and just...be. Away. Far away."

Mandy looked between us, finishing up her fast words, but that didn't stop the man from nearly stepping in so close that his body was almost touching mine. I was intimidated, but I wasn't backing down. I couldn't with this tribe or else they'd view me as weak and that might be even worse.

"I..." Mandy said something else causing the man to expose his teeth to her threateningly. But he didn't to me. His head tilted for the smallest moment, and he turned back, raising his hand towards the sky, going off more on a rant. Mandy quickly pulled me off to the side, racing us towards a hut as fast as I could walk.

"This is my mother's. Was...my mother's. We'll be safe here. We have enough food for a few days and—"

"I'm not hiding in the hut, Mandy."

"Can't we though? Just for a little while until everyone cools off? They wouldn't even look at us as we walked up, Layla. This is so wrong to them. I just...I." She swung open the wooden door, jolting to a stop at the crowded space. Aside from two small beds off to the side and what looked like a tiny pot-like stove, crate after crate was piled on top of each other. There was barely any room to even get inside. "Oh. I might have overprepared. This place is smaller than I remember."

"What did you have brought here?"

She turned to me, cringing as she went back to taking it all in.

"Everything to keep you safe. Everything I could think of."

# CHAPTER 18

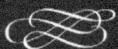

## THE DRAGON

The rain was unforgiving. The seas were hungry with wrath. For days we rocked, waiting for the storm to let up. Where we were hoping to meet up with Breezeway, we found ourselves a day closer to my fishing vessel, Sea Serpent. Lui was barely hanging on by a thread, and I couldn't help myself. I couldn't stop as I continuously beat him down. To look at him made me sick. To remember the fear on that little boy's face made my blood boil. I stayed in a constant state of rage, and even unconsciousness wouldn't save Lui. His face was no longer recognizable. His body was bruised and bulging in random places from the beatings I kept giving him. Lopez stayed quiet. Fallon and White came and went as Pattinson drove the ship a few feet away from me. This wasn't torture to my captain anymore. This was the actions of a robbed father. Of a broken husband and human being who had nothing left to give but a plethora of pain.

Hate.

Fury.

Disgust.

It festered and grew inside of me with every second I drew breath.

"Wake the fuck up."

My fist smashing into his already shattered cheek did nothing to wake the captain. A jagged piece of bone protruded from the lacerated skin on his cheekbone, shifting against the muscle and flesh as I V'd my other hand over his chin and unhinged jaw, squeezing. It shifted loosely under the pressure, feeding my anger even more.

"*I said wake up!*"

A groan merged with an incoherent slur. The captain stayed limp on the chair, not even able to raise his head as I shoved and let his head fall back down to the side.

"More smelling salts?"

Lopez lifted his hand, but I knew we were running low. I'd already used enough over the last few days. I'd be lying if I said I wasn't surprised he was even still alive.

"Not yet. Save it for his grand fucking finale. He'll feel every degree of that."

"Good idea." Lopez looked back at the screen, shifting. "Boss, I know you're...busy, but we need to talk."

"About what?"

I couldn't deny the slight irritation in my tone. I stayed lost in my mind. In the anger that kept me going.

"Luke, your brother, has taken a liking to the soldiers. He gives them purpose. He even stands guard with them."

"*What?*"

I stepped in, lowering to peer into the screen of the laptop. Luke was underground in the soldier's quarters. A large group was huddled around watching him point towards a dry erase board on the far wall. I squinted, taking in what all was written out.

"That's the island drawn out. Most of it, anyway. You said he has them pulling guard?"

"He does. I've been watching off and on over the last few days. He killed Mills. Slit his fucking throat in front of them all."

My brows drew up. "No shit? And they took it okay?"

"Better than I thought. He did something we've all contemplated, just haven't pulled the trigger on."

"Yeah he has. Well shit. What happened? What did Mills do?"

"He was himself." Lopez paused. "The kid didn't just harass a slave this time; he raped and beat her. I went back and confirmed it on video. Your brother didn't hold back. He set an example out of him. Luke isn't fucking around."

"He never has; that's why I knew he'd be perfect." My mouth pursed the smallest amount as emotions flared. "Luke was always the more disciplined one. He was braver. Smarter. Luckier. Had they not found me when they did, they would have jumped for Luke. I'm glad it was me," I breathed out. "The burden takes its toll. If it wouldn't have been for Layla, I…"

I stopped at the groaning that filled the wheelhouse. My fist swung and connected before I could even think. Lui bounced at the hit, sliding down in his chair even more as he went unconscious again.

I wouldn't be here…*but what about her?* She may have saved me but being with me almost killed her.

The bow of the ship came up as we rode the wave, tipping down as another crashed over the front. The structure of the boat shuttered at the force, jolting us forward as we held to what we could at our sides.

"Pattinson, how are we doing?"

"Shitty. I fucking hate boats. Did I ever tell you that, Sir?"

I laughed. "Only about a hundred times these last few days."

"I'm not going down from a fucking storm. It's not happening."

"We have too much blood to spill. Death won't take us today."

He glanced back. "You sound like that witch woman."

"You met her?"

"Once. I didn't meet her, per say, but I saw her. She was talking to some soldiers a few months back about elements and air. Water. Fire. All that shit. It was as if she could communicate with them. Even influence them. I would have laughed it off and ignored her if the wind didn't arrive right on her cue. Wind. I don't think at that point I had felt wind in weeks. It was summer. Hot as hell. You couldn't breathe. There was no damn wind, but she called it and it came. And it was cold. That freaked me out even more. *It felt like ice.*"

"The Babke is…I like her. She's okay."

Again, he looked back. "And she says we won't die?"

"No. She didn't say that. I did. But she spoke of Death as… not a person, but a force. Right now, I'm feeding it, you could say. It might like that and spare us."

"Or eat us too."

I laughed at Pattinson. "Maybe, but I think we're going to be okay."

"You know who's not okay? White. He's been throwing up for days. I think Fallon had him hooked up to an IV last night. Did you see how pale he was when he came up here to check in? He could barely walk. This storm needs to stop soon."

"We have pills for that. Did he take them?"

Lopez laughed under his breath, holding on and sliding in his bolted down seat as another waved crashed over us.

"What's so funny?"

"How stubborn he is, not to mention superstitious. He worries more than that damn tribe. White will eat anything you throw at him. Herbs. Tonics. Tinctures. It doesn't matter what it is. Try to give him a pill…" He shook his head. "He won't take it."

"So, he's suffering because he won't take the pills?"

"Yep. They're not natural. I told him he'd feel better if he just bit the bullet. He refuses."

My head shook, and I quickly braced myself as we pitched up a large wave. "Stubborn ass. I'll go down and get him." I cringed but breathed out as we didn't hit as hard as I thought. "I'm going to have him up here. He needs the window. Besides, I'm getting sick of looking at this piece of shit." I kicked at Lui's feet. "He's not doing anything but taking up space. And I'm bored, so…" I shrugged to Lopez. "White can assist."

"Be careful making your way down. The steps inside this ship are steep. And remember, give the door a good push. It sticks pretty good on this side."

I nodded to Lopez, holding to the railing of the top bunk as I moved deeper into the interior of the ship. I took the steps slow, holding on as we rocked up. When I turned to the right and grabbed the knob to the inside door of the captain's room, the force from us colliding with another wave threw me back. Pain flared along my side as I connected with the metal stairs. The door immediately swung open.

"Holy fuck, Double M, are you okay?"

I growled, pushing to stand as I took in Fallon.

"I'll be fine. You and White get your asses up to the wheelhouse. I'm not waiting for the storm to end. I'm finished looking at Lui." I grabbed the railing as we went up again, and Fallon braced himself in the doorway.

"You got it. We'll be right there."

I didn't wait. Nodding, I held tight as I headed back up. With every step, pain burned and throbbed. Nothing was broken, I knew that, but there was going to be a hell of a bruise if not many.

Grabbing the bunk, I stepped into the wheelhouse, pulling up my shirt as I cursed at the dots of blood and purple swelling that was already appearing.

"Fuck. I told you to watch those damn stairs."

My look had Lopez's hand flying up.

"I was off them already. It was hitting that wave that threw me right back into them. I should have braced myself. It's nothing."

"It doesn't look like nothing."

"If it's not broken, it's not a concern."

Minutes passed before Fallon appeared. I moved up, allowing him and White to enter the small room. White immediately climbed on the bunk, bracing himself on the edge as he sat down and held on.

"You look like shit."

"I feel like shit, Main Master. I fucking hate boats."

"You, Pattinson, and the rest of us. You've refused the pills. That's your own damn fault. You're going to get your shit together because I need your help."

"I'm ready. Just name it."

I took in his pale face and the sweat that was beginning to coat it. He took slow, deep inhales, watching me. Waiting. I pointed to the window.

"You look there. It'll help you feel better. We're starting, and I'm giving you fifteen minutes before you take over for Lopez. *If Lui lasts that long.*"

"Thank you, Sir. I'll be ready."

Fallon's stare was devouring Lui's unconscious body. Fallon was the easiest going guy there was until he wasn't. He didn't like my captain, and from the look deep in the glare, he was dying to get his hands bloody.

"Lopez, take his shirt off and get on one side. I want him standing. Get the smelling salts ready. Fallon, you get on his other side. It's time Lui pays for what he's done."

I turned, reaching into my bag to retrieve the small blow torch. It wasn't the safest weapon with how violent the seas were, but even now I felt as if we'd already passed through the worst of it. The boat hadn't shuttered in minutes, and although we were still pitching up, it wasn't anywhere near as high. We were finally breaking free. Maybe Death knew what was coming and had calmed the ocean for his gift. Maybe he'd soon reward us with the sun.

The shirt hit the floor, and each man wrapped around Lui's side, lifting him to stand.

"We're ready when you are, Boss."

I turned on the torch, adjusting the flame. As I stared into a vibrant blue, I nodded, exhaling my anger, and stepping into it as my eyes cut up.

"Wake him."

Lopez obeyed, moving his hand right under Lui's nose. His body jolted and swollen eyes tried to open, barely managing as deep sounds groaned and filled the room.

"I've always been too lenient with you captains. If you did your job, you were safe. You had rules, but I never strictly enforced them. That was my mistake. Yours was feeling comfortable enough to break them."

Moving in, I braced my feet through the decent swell, riding the wave down as I brought the flame just close enough to have him screaming.

"I said it a million times, Lui. Do not hurt or touch my slaves. Discipline within reason, yes, but nothing sexual. Nothing extreme."

Flesh singed, beginning to bubble and blister over the flat muscle of his pec. The smell was immediate. The meat cooked, the marbling melting and broiling as I leaned in closer. "It's amazing how long it sometimes takes a body to burn. Some places will peel back and disintegrate immediately. Others..." I didn't continue as I lost myself in the past. In the present. They merged as time ticked by and bone became exposed. I moved up, watching as skin darkened as I moved back down. I took my time covering the space until the area was blackened and cratered. High pitch screams of my name filled the room, breathless and barely there by the time I drew my hand back.

"Main Master, p-please. Main—"

I cut off the barely recognizable words. "You neglected another rule as well. No one on my ship who's not crew. Not only were you piggybacking from me, you brought a child on board to satisfy your sick needs. *A child!*"

The last roared from me as I put the flame not an inch from his sternum, moving down his chest and stomach in a steady path. Hair burned with flesh, perfuming the room with a stench I knew all too well. One that had become my home, once. Lui's broken jaw slid to the side, flopping this way and that as he began shaking and screaming violently.

"Mast—Ma-st-r! M-M-M."

"No! *You did this!* You're going to feel that boy's pain. A pain he'll no doubt carry for the rest of his *life*. If you ask me, you're getting off easy." I drew the torch back, using my other hand to rip open the buttons and to jerk his pants down enough to expose his genitals. The captain's head bobbed as he began to pass out. With Lopez ready, he wasn't able.

"Someday that boy is going to ask questions. He's going to want to understand why you hurt him. You've doomed any decent life he could have lived. You condemned him to Red Island. Now, he's mine, and it's not you he has to fear. *It's me.* His savior—his enslaver. You have no idea how much I wish I could burn every inch of you until there was nothing left. It'll never be enough for the hate I have for you for doing this to that little boy."

My hand leveled with his cock and the tone of screams ranged, dropping low as saliva bubbled and dripped from Lui's mouth. He was fighting again, trying to break free and not pass out at the same time. My head shook and my arm shot up right to his face. Facial hair caught on fire, bursting into an inferno as his busted lips almost seemed to pop under the heated pressure. The beaten face boiled and cooked but the blue flame almost stole my focus. It called me. Or maybe I could hear Death urging me on. Eyes yellowed and charred, and pieces of his cheeks hollowed out. I saw all of it. I soaked in every second as I held steady, still not sated or content with how I was ending things.

Sound faded.

Movements stopped.

Even as I knew Lui was dead, I felt far from finished. The radio went off and we all turned towards it.

"It's the Sea Serpent. They've picked us up on radar. They're about twelve miles out."

I nodded to Pattinson, finally drawing my hand back to turn off the torch. My heart was racing with rage. I wasn't done. I'd never be done. "White, run down and get Kenneth, the deck boss. We'll have him radio over that the captain is dead and he's in need of their assistance. It's time to get ready. We're about to take this new boat over, and I better like what I see."

# CHAPTER 19

## LUKE

"Are we sure it's not just a fisherman or someone stopped to rest for a while? It's not like they're coming closer. They're a speck. We can't even tell what sort of boat it is."

I glanced at Tillin, who stood the closest to me. Out of the four other soldiers who'd taken a lead in this new guard schedule, Tillin proved to be the most proactive. And that surprised me, given our first conversation where he'd called me too late and too drunk. Maybe he was testing me. I wasn't sure, but I kept my eyes on him regardless that he was proving extremely helpful.

"We can't be for sure on any of it. They're too close, and they're not ours. They're not even pinging in the system. I don't like it. Anyone who doesn't want to be seen as a threat would have their tracker on. They don't. We'll watch them. If they get close enough to identify, I want to know."

Juarez, a soldier in his late thirties, pointed to the far right of the ocean, making a path towards the boat.

"We launch off the far side where they can't see. We can drive a day or two out and come up from behind. If they are keeping tabs on the island, maybe they won't expect that it's us. We don't even have to get close, just close enough to see what we're dealing with."

My face drew in and twisted as I weighed his plan.

"Fuck that," Barkley said, moving in closer. "That takes too damn long. We have drones. Let's put one up. They won't even know. We'll stay high and out of sight. That'll give us the answers we need, in half the time."

"Too risky," Tillin mumbled.

"Is it?" Jones shook his head. "I'm with Barkley. If it is a threat, we need to know sooner than later. We have to prepare."

"We are prepared," I said, bringing the binoculars back up. "We stay prepared. There's no other choice. I want the island guarded at all times. I want the slaves to stay away from the beach. We can't go to the far side of the island, but we'll have to keep eyes on it as best as we can without imposing on the tribe there. My brother made it clear. We are not to go anywhere near that tribe. That could be worse than some boat. Their privacy and way of life is to be honored, and I plan to do just that. We all will."

"Or they'll eat us," Barkley growled out. "They have darts. They have powder. They have...*words*. Soldiers have crossed them before. I don't care how big and bad you think you are. The soldiers weren't ever seen again. I have no intention of becoming their next meal."

I straightened. "That bad?"

The soldiers, including Tillin, all looked over at me. Their expressions said it all. They didn't like the tribe, and each had their reasons. Something told me it was more than hearsay, and it was sure as hell a lot more information than I was finding trying to search the answers out myself. These men had experienced something at some point and those meetings left their mark. I didn't like that Layla was with them, but it's not like I could bring her back. The Babke would protect Layla, and I needed to allow that. I also needed to check on her. It had been days. How was she adjusting to her life there?

"I have to take care of a few things. Keep eyes on the boat and anything else that might seem suspicious. That goes for soldiers and slaves too. If something feels off, tell someone. Don't hold it in and try to investigate it yourself. No stupid moves. We work and analyze everything as a team. From there, I'll decide the direction we take."

At their nod, I returned it, turning to leave the luxury bungalow we were camped out in. It was evening and would be dark soon. I didn't soak in the beauty of my surroundings as I kept a fast pace and headed to the fortress in the distance. Maybe I shouldn't have been so active on the island, but I had things under control. The slaves, the soldiers, everyone here knew me. They'd known me when Gavin was here, and most of the slaves weren't even aware he was gone. They didn't need to know anything but to stay in line and do what they were ordered to. The soldiers were a different story. They were on strict orders to protect their home, and it was the only one they had left. This would work. I'd keep this island safe not just for Gavin, but for Layla too. My brother would not return to a dead wife. Not because of anyone who snuck in after her.

The two guards posted at the large fortress doors in the front opened them at my arrival. I didn't pause as I passed. My strides were wide and fast. Determined as I withdrew my phone and bounded up the flights of stairs, passing more guards. Just as I was entering my room, I punched in Layla's number, half surprised when she answered on the third ring.

"Luke."

"Layla." My brow creased at the slight anxiety in her tone. "Don't worry, I don't bring bad news. I just wanted to see how you're doing."

It was her turn to pause. "I think we're okay. I mean…the tribe isn't very accepting of me and Mandy. They pretty much keep to themselves. The women won't even look at us. They whisper. I don't pay much attention to it, but it seems to bother Mandy."

"I'm sorry. I'm sure over time they'll accept the two of you."

"That would be nice." She seemed to hesitate. "I'm sure it's fine, it's just…"

At her trailing off, my head tilted with concern.

"It's just what?"

"There's these men. Well, one really aggravating one. I'm sure it's nothing, it's just, the first day we arrived he was arguing with the Babke. He called us traitors. The way he stared me down." Again, she got quiet. "I'm sure it's nothing. We're imposing. They're not like us. We'll all adjust."

Even as she talked, I was already pulling up the footage of the camera I'd set up in the area. It wasn't close, but closer than the Babke would like. Although I couldn't see actual features of the tribe, I could make out people walking around in the distance. And there was a fire already going. It was faint, but I knew the colors. Dinner? I was getting hungry too.

"If you feel the least bit threatened, you come home, Layla. These tribal people are not to be messed with. I have no idea why Gavin would want you there to begin with. The soldiers, they're very weary of them. I want you to be safe. One call. That's all it'll take, and I'll come get you."

"Thank you, Brother." She let out a breath. "Have you heard from Gavin?"

"No. I'm sorry."

"It's fine. He's…fine. If he calls, will you please let me know. Can he call me if you give him the number?"

"I'm not sure. I can try, but I really don't think it'll work. That phone is connected to Bram and Everleigh. It's part of our system and the people we keep close. An outside caller might not get through like we could. It's rather complicated."

"It's okay. Please give him the number so he can try. I miss him."

I closed my eyes.

"I'm sure you do, and I'm sure he misses you too. I'll let him know the number next time he calls."

"Thanks, Luke. If I don't answer, I'll call you back when I'm able. We'll be out a lot in the next few days. We need meat, and Mandy mentioned something about an outing. I guess the Babke needs help gathering herbs or supplies for her weird potions. It should all be interesting, to say the least."

I laughed at the sarcasm coating her words.

"If truth be told," she continued, "I think the Babke just wants to get us out of the village for some reason. Maybe she'll explain what's really going on."

"What do you mean?"

"I don't know. I just feel like something is off." Her tone softened. "I think I've just had too much time to think. I am looking forward to getting out. I need fresh air and some decent food."

"Just be careful. Don't overdo it. How *are* you feeling?"

"Better. Walking is easier. All I do is pace this room. The days drag out for what feels like forever."

Knocking had me looking towards the door.

"Someone's here. I have to go. Be careful and call me if you need anything."

"I will. Take care."

The line went dead, and I hung up, swiftly walking to the door. When I opened it, my mouth parted.

"Aren't you supposed to be getting ready to search out herbs for secret potions?"

The Babke handed over a list, sweeping past me. As I shut the door, I couldn't ignore her lack of humor. She didn't smile or even look at me as she headed to the wooden shuttered window next to my bed. She didn't open it, she just stared ahead.

"Babke, what's wrong?

Silence.

I grew closer, slowing as she turned to face me. Worry clouded her eyes, and her lids were narrowed with uncertainty.

"The paths…they change for the worse."

"Worse? For whom?"

"For all of us."

"Wait." My head shook. "What do you mean? Can you be seeing them wrong?"

"I see what I see. I don't like it. I don't like any of it. This is not what was supposed to happen. This is not what I agreed to."

"Whoa." My hand lifted to try to calm her through the anger and panic in her tone. "Why don't you slow down and tell me what you saw?" Her head shook. "You say all. Who specifically? Gavin? Layla?"

"*All* of us. There's…" Her lids closed as she took in a deep breath. "The dreams grow darker. Blood fills the sky; the black clouds protect it. I know it's there, but I can barely see it anymore."

"I don't know what that means."

Frustration sent her pacing past me. She doubled back, trailing back and forth with quick steps.

"What it means, I can't say. I don't know, either. But I can *feel* it. We are reaching dark times. There's a watcher. He oversees, but he doesn't act. Not yet. Not like we…suspect. I can't find him. I can't see him. Be careful of the company you keep, new Main Master. Not everyone is who they appear. Same with me. Same with our Dragon. The timelines are shifting, looking for their place. I hope for all of us, the location isn't amongst the paths that come. If it is…"

The fear that took over the Babke had the hair on my arms standing on end. Something about her and her insight set me on edge. I didn't like it. Whether I could trust it or not, I wasn't sure, but I wasn't stupid enough to overlook it. The warning wasn't much different than Layla's own worry. Maybe they were over two different things, but what I did know was they were cautious, and that wasn't a bad thing. The emotion would keep them on edge. That was lifesaving, and maybe we all needed to watch our backs a little more.

"Layla has a phone. If for some reason you don't feel safe in the tribe, you can have her call me and you all can come back here. I'd actually prefer it. I think we're safer if we stick together." I walked over to my bar, pouring me a drink. "There's a boat pretty far out, but we're watching them. I have the soldiers pulling guard every hour of the day. If you were all here, I'd sure as hell worry less. I could keep the guards and servants far from Layla's wing. We could make it work."

I took a drink. The pure hesitation from the Babke's had me slowing as I brought the glass down.

"You're truly thinking about it. Your feeling is that bad?"

"I don't know what to feel anymore. I should have never come here." She stopped, mumbling under her breath. "There's no going back." A shuddering inhale. "I will not return, new Main Master, but Layla. She…she."

"She what?"

Her head went back and forth, and her hand came up to press against her stomach. The dark brown dress she wore swayed as she abruptly headed for the door, jolting to a stop.

"*Babke.* Layla what?"

"I have to go check something. Just know, Layla lives in all timelines. I can't say that for the rest of us. The quality of life, or what she becomes will depend. She'll either be stronger from all of this." The Babke turned to look at me. "Or she will break, and I can't say that's better than her staying alive. Watch the boat, new Main Master, but be aware, the greatest threat is not what's out there. It's what's here."

"What does that mean? With the soldiers? What about my brother?"

The Babke's didn't answer, nor did she turn to face me. She headed for the door at a fast pace, not even pausing as she disappeared through it. She gave me no answers. No insight. I was drowning in questions, and apparently there were greater threats closer to home than some ship we could barely see.

# CHAPTER 20

## LAYLA

"It's been almost two hours, Leelee. We've bathed. We've talked and talked. I think I was wrong. Maybe she meant tomorrow. I don't see the Babke anywhere. We should return to the village. It's getting dark. We're not safe. There are animals out here that will try to eat us."

I paused in tracing my foot in the water, content in the dimness and calming sound of the small, running river. I was tired after I'd spent hours analyzing me and Luke's conversation. I barely got any sleep, and the day had gone just as long. I prayed Gavin would call, but so far, nothing. I was on edge. All I wanted to do was relax away from the pounding drums and smell of smoke that was never ending.

"Maybe, but it was the Babke's idea to come out here at night. Why is it any different whether she's here or not? If a wild animal attacks, I can't see her doing much to save us. I think we're fine. Besides, I have my knife."

"I'm not sure what good that would do. We need to learn to shoot."

My lips twisted at the thought. I knew she wasn't referring to a gun, and I couldn't imagine shooting some sort of bow and arrow. And me, blow a dart? Life was too surreal. Nothing seemed plausible or easy to grasp.

Standing, I took a step, jolting to a stop as three men walked out from the trees in the distance. Mandy spun at my reaction, quickly jogging to my side.

"Let's go the long way around." She cupped my bicep as she moved in closer, lowering her voice. "Maybe they're here for water."

"They don't look like that's what they want. You're right, though. Let's walk around wide so we can avoid them."

But I was already walking, pulling her along with me as she kept her head down and hid at my side.

*"Te kluq ve gnelp?"*[1]

The tribal man who had stared me down before carried on in his language. I led us around a big rock, noticing the men stopping, feet ahead.

"What are they saying?"

Mandy held on tighter. "They want to know where we're going. He's calling us traitors again. He's saying...he says..." Her fingers dug into my arm as the men started to stay even with us. The man kept going, each word becoming angrier than the last. "Not traitors. Just one. He's talking about me. He says they should have never let me return. I turned my back on them to be a slave to you. He calls me names that I don't know. Bad names. Angry...names."

"Hey, *back off*," I snapped.

My lids narrowed at them as I tried to ignore how the men were now following behind us. I wanted to run. To cry. Worse, I wanted to scream and attack. I couldn't do either. Being the Main Master's wife didn't allow me to cower, and I had to be smart. I was strong like Gavin. *Like the Dragon.* I was a leader. Brave. So much more than before. I would not show my fear.

Holding the knife in the deep pocket of my tan dress, I clutched to the handle. It was a little bigger than the one I'd stabbed Havaan with, which I'd left in the hut. This one was the one Luke had packed in the duffle bag, and it was big enough to conceal, but also long enough if I opened it to do some serious damage.

"Leelee, I don't like this. I'm scared."

"I know. Don't let them see your fear. It'll make things worse."

"I'm trying. *They're getting closer.*"

Anger ruled me. It surged, exploding to a mass I couldn't contain. I spun, ripping from Mandy's hold as I stomped to the tall, nude man whose eyes seemed to spark with...challenge? Again? Had this been the look he'd held before? It was so hard to read him.

"You need to back off. I don't know who you think you are, but you are not going to intimidate us. Do you have nothing better to do? This is just petty. I'm starting to see culture and language have nothing to do with people's ingrained need to stir up drama. It's bullshit."

"*Leelee.*"

All three mens' heads whipped to Mandy, and her fear had a small cry leaving her mouth.

"Zu bev Leelee?"[2]

Mandy's lips parted as she backstepped. I thought she was going to run, but instead she rushed to my side. The man's arm shot out to grab her, but so did mine as I kept her behind me and flicked the knife open to point at him.

"Back. Off."

More language I didn't understand. It roared, blanketed with increasing violence. Even the man's deeply tanned face held a tinge of red.

"I disrespected him. *We have to go.*"

But we couldn't. With every step, the men moved in closer.

"I said get back or so help me."

Another step.

His arm swiped towards me, and I jumped back fast enough to dodge it.

"If you don't get back from me, I swear I'll kill you. *I'll kill you all.*"

A smile came to the man's face, not at all welcoming. There was an underlined threat. And pleasure? Dark eyes held mine, looking so much deeper inside than I could process in the moment. I didn't like the way the man made me feel. As if I were dangling by a rope that could break at any moment. He could get this knife away from me if he wanted. He could do so much more than that.

"*Layla.*"

The Babke's voice had my thudding pulse registering. How long had it been hammering into me this hard? I was shaking. Craving for a fight I knew I wouldn't win. And the man was spewing tribal words to the Babke as she came up to stand next to us. The word Leelee kept getting used, but other than the meaning, I had no idea what they were talking about. Whatever it was revolved around me, and no one was backing down as they argued.

"I'm sorry." Mandy spoke the tribal language, seeming to repeat her words. She kept on and on, explaining something, apologizing, but the men weren't backing down. It was another woman walking up that had them growing quiet.

"Is there...problem?"

The English had my eyes widening. The woman couldn't have been much older than me. She was beautiful with long, curly hair and dark skin. Her eyes seemed kind, and she walked with her shoulders back in confidence. I quickly folded up the knife, putting it back in my pocket.

"I think there's been a misunderstanding. Mandy and I just want to go back to our hut."

Confusion flashed, but I could barely see as the darkness grew. The Babke was still talking to the men. Her authority couldn't be mistaken, and I felt as though she was winning whatever conversation they were having.

"Mis-understand?"

"We want to leave," I said slowly. "We don't want to fight."

"No fight." She smiled. "*Aven.*" The name came out like a bark as the tall man who kept staring me down snapped his face to her. She didn't say another word. All the girl did was point and the man's top lip peeled back. His lids closed and he took in a deep breath, not opening his lids again until he let it out. When he did, the hardness on his face was gone. He walked to the woman, slightly bowing as he reached for her hand, bringing it to his lips.

"Ke ki yaz ze vu. Lu me wanu. Gnelp buva. Ye bev leelee. Pal ke voy leelee?"[3]

There it was. Another challenging look, but not to me. *To her.* It had her face transforming to anger as he and the men started to walk away. At the man's eyes coming to mine, I couldn't stop the way my blood turned cold. Something was happening. Something I couldn't begin to understand, and I didn't like it. I had every intention of sticking it out at the tribe, but I was suddenly wondering if it was even worth it.

"Mandy." I tugged her closer, lowering my voice. "What did he say?"

"Later."

The word was breathless, and her eyes were as round as saucers. The Babke nodded to the woman as she took one last look at me and spun off after the men. There was no kindness like before. We were the enemy. I felt it in my bones as the Babke groaned and turned to us.

"You can't threaten the future king like that, Layla. He could have killed you on the spot for even pulling out that knife."

"King?" It was my turn to be surprised.

"The previous king died a few years back," Mandy said, lowly. "I was still a child."

"Yes," the Babke agreed. "We have no real leader aside from me at the moment and won't until a rightful queen takes her place. Aven can't be king until that happens. The position must be earned. There will be no question to all whom are part of the tribe. It will be right. Feel right."

Mandy sniffled, wiping her tears. "I can't call you Leelee anymore. Not here. Did you see how angry he was? I called you his queen. You were never that, but you were always...more to me. Queen of the island. The Main Master's queen. It was natural to say that. It—" The tears spilled over. "They're going to kill me."

"No." The Babke shook her head, putting her hand on Mandy's shoulder, but my servant didn't seem to believe her, and I wasn't even sure the Babke believed herself.

"I made a grave mistake. Aven doesn't like me. The names—"

"Are just names, girl."

"You heard the last, Babke. What he said to that woman. I showed so much disrespect. It would have been no different than if I would have spit in his future queen's face. Did you hear what Aven said to her? I can't get over it. It scares me. He said, 'She's the Dragon Master's chosen. He thought her worthy. Maybe she's the one who I should make my queen.' He said that about Layla. And it was said with such disregard. He meant it. Or... he...he made her think he did. Aven made her our enemy in that very moment. This isn't good; I can feel it."

"I'm married and he knows it, Mandy. He can't marry me too. He's just trying to turn everyone against us."

"That may be true. Regardless, you will make amends, girl." The Babke nodded to Mandy and led us back towards the village, continuing on. "Jahee will understand when we can talk to her without Aven. He's angry. He has every right to be." The Babke glanced over to me. "You have to understand what our tribe has gone through. Although we have shared this island for over a hundred years, it wasn't until your Dragon took over that we had peace. It's been an adjusting period. Not all of the tribe want to continue to share, Layla. This was always our land. Some want it to continue that way."

"You mean Aven. He wants it to belong to the tribe again."

The Babke hesitated but nodded.

"It's been creating great conflict. We're split in half. The men want this to be our island. The woman…we're good with how things are. There's peace. To fight would be certain death to a lot of us. Aven…he doesn't *see*."

"And he has to be king? No one else can replace him?"

The Babke didn't look my way. She stared ahead, a mass of emotions making her face eventually draw in with sadness.

"I've seen many different versions of our future. I don't see many that doesn't involve Aven." She glanced at me and Mandy. "I think it's impossible, but you two must make peace. Tomorrow, we'll figure out how."

The smell of smoke thickened as we got closer. The drums were still going, and with what had happened, I knew our herb gathering was a plan of the past.

"Babke, have you seen anything more on my husband?"

We came to a standstill on the edge of the village. A roaring fire was going and random men danced around the flames. Aven entered the circle, smiling, yelling something as he began to join in on the dancing. He didn't appear as the angry future king anymore. Just a man.

"Your Dragon has spent days in rough seas. That has passed, but he works with Death, and Death favors him for now. Let's hope it stays that way."

With that, she started walking to the far side of the huts where hers was located. Mandy slid her palm under my bicep letting me lead her to our own hut. Laughter and singing merged with jovial yells as we got closer. Aven left the fire, joining in with the others that made up the circle, but it didn't stop him from looking over at us. His wide shoulders were squared and the muscles on his chest rose and fell with his exerted breath from dancing. I quickly led us to the door, pushing it open. The moment she was able, Mandy scrambled inside. Tears stained her face, but she wasn't overtly crying. She was scared, and she had every reason to be. This wasn't good, and despite what the Babke said, I couldn't see it getting any better.

# CHAPTER 21

## THE DRAGON

S ilence. Days. The two merged, mixing and morphing into torturous hours of festering hate. Although I couldn't find the Sea Serpent guilty of anything, I wasn't satisfied to sit across from a man I didn't trust. And I'd be a fool to trust Antonio Barchey.

The dark-haired man was my youngest captain. He was former navy, and deadlier than anyone in his position. Smarter, too. He was not from the US, but France, and although he appeared clean from any sort of suspicious activities, I wouldn't allow myself not to stay on guard. I couldn't afford to relax. Not that I'd be able to, even if I did believe the man was truly working. Whether it was his thick accent, the long ponytail he kept messing with, or his attitude that was triggering my temper, I wasn't sure. Now that I knew I had no reason to kill him, I wanted to be alone. I wanted a moment to think about how my wife was doing. I wanted to stew in my silent fantasies of mutilation and murder for the next person who wasn't going to be so lucky. My soldiers and Antonio were making it impossible, even if they weren't directly talking to me.

"Austin Birch? I have no idea where he is. Not out here or

anywhere close. At least not that I've heard. I don't understand. What does he have to do with Lisbon?"

"None of your business." White's eyes were cut up as he nibbled on crackers. He was still pale, and the sickness was bringing out his temper.

"I keep getting that from all of you. Am I not supposed to know what's going on? Frankly, I'm fucking confused as hell. You get on my ship. You tear it apart. You grill the hell out of me and my crew. We haven't done anything wrong. I know I'm a few weeks late, but that's because I wanted to meet quota first."

"We're not here because you're late," White said, deepening his tone.

"Then what the hell is this about? Main Master, please."

"No. You talk to me," White continued. "Did we announce our arrival before we took over this ship?" At the aggravation growing in Antonio, his stare narrowed even more towards White, but he stayed silent as my soldier kept going. "If we wanted you to know why we're here, we would offer the information. We haven't, and we won't. And correction…this is the Main Master's ship, *not* yours. You answer what we ask and stop asking questions."

The captain's gaze cut over to mine. I hadn't said a word up to this point and didn't want to now, but I had to keep any trust and loyalty this man had to me.

"My wife and our twins were killed."

"I…" Surprise. Shock. Antonio couldn't hide them as his gaze lowered.

"You didn't know."

"No, Main Master. I'm…sorry. I got the call to come back early, but I didn't want to show up without my numbers." His eyes jumped to mine. "Fuck. I'm so damn sorry."

"You're taking us to Lisbon."

Slowly, his head nodded, gaining speed as he seemed to put everything together. "Lisbon. I need supplies anyway. Are you wanting me to stay in town a few days while you…do whatever you need? I can wait around to take you back."

"No. You don't have to wait. I'll find my way. What I do want is for you to try to find Austin Birch. He had some part of this, and I want him. Do you hear me?"

"I'll find him. You have my word. I'll figure out where he is. I'm good at getting information without it seeming obvious."

I nodded. "He's hiding from what I can tell, and he has good reason. Thing is, I have bigger fish to go after at the moment. You find him, and you either somehow get his ass to my island or figure out his whereabouts. I'm going to give you a phone number. When you find that piece of shit, you call and let them know everything. They will find a way to get to him if you can't."

"Yes, Main Master."

I reached over, jotting down the number to the Main Master's cell and handing it to him. The captain didn't waste any time as he turned and left the room at a fast pace.

"Do you think he'll have any luck? Can we trust him?"

I shrugged to Lopez. "Keep the radio on. Keep listening to it. We'll see."

I kept my arms over my chest as I stared back across the small table I was sitting at. It didn't take long for me to zone out as I stared at the off-white metal walls of Antonio's personal quarters. Silence had me sighing and seeing her. It didn't matter that my wife wasn't here. Even in a memory, I could lose myself in her eyes. In her beauty. The moments she was happiest was what I held to. Her smile was my own personal sun which was odd since I detested the damn thing. The heat was a constant at the island, when all I'd wanted for so long was to lose myself in the darkness of night. In the cold, not tropical. Layla made the warmth real. Inviting. She could make anything manageable. Anything…but this.

My eyes closed as my heart twisted and ached. How was she

doing with the tribe? How were Luke and the soldiers? I should call. I should message Aamir and check on Jasmeen.

Tears threatened, and my jaw flexed while I tried to hold them in. One more day. Maybe two, and then I'd be on land. I'd be swift and unforgiving. Land saved me time. Once we got to Lisbon and out of possible sight, I'd be able to use planes. I had three locations to visit and four people to kill including Austin Birch. Any would be an impossible task given where I was going to achieve the three Main Masters' murders, but I wasn't worried. I had Death on my side, and there was no failing. I would return to Layla and make this right. My devotion and love to her left me no choice.

Sliding against wood left me opening my eyes. Lopez placed my laptop and the earbud case down in front of me. All I could manage was a nod and a half-ass, pathetic grin of gratitude I could barely muster. The squeeze to my shoulder said everything he didn't as he walked away. From where I was sitting, off to the side, I didn't worry about anyone seeing my screen as I opened the device. Lopez was already back at his own laptop, giving me the go-ahead that I was safe whenever I was ready to do whatever I needed.

Aamir. Again, my chest ached as I put the earbuds in.

I brought up the messenger, trying to force composure.

Me: You around?

Seconds passed.

Aamir: I'm here. I was starting to worry.

Me: I'm still alive. We ran into some bad storms. I'm almost to land now. How's my girl?

There was a pause before the video appeared. I took in her big eyes and full lips. In black hair and a beauty so familiar that I could barely hold myself together. Jasmeen was awake and so alert as she stared up at Aamir from a little white bassinet. *She was changing in such a short time.* Where I'd seen Layla before, all I saw was a mirror of...myself. Pieces of me and Layla together. Undeniable truth awakened the possessiveness in me. It wrapped around love so intense, all doubt I harbored over my actions faded. My lips parted and my breath got caught in my lungs. Tears did escape then, but I quickly wiped them away before they could make it down my face.

I was right in doing this. I didn't have a choice. Jasmeen needed to be safe. She'd never have any sort of future if I didn't set things straight now. I wasn't to be messed with. My family was off limits, and they were all going to see that real fast.

> Me: She's so perfect. I can't wait to see her again. Soon.

> Aamir: I hope so. I'm ready to come home. I need my sister. How is she?

> Me: I'm going to check on her next. She's safe. I've made sure of it. Anything on your end? What has Bram learned?

> Aamir: There's a party in London. I guess some big people are going to be there. I didn't catch names, but Bram mentioned some big bids were going to be dropped. Something about the caviar of cradles or cradled caviar. Something weird like that.

My eyes closed for the briefest moment as I took in a deep breath.

Me: An elite child. Probably one of their enemies. It'll be on the dinner menu for a hefty price. It's quite popular in London. Depending on who they have will be telling for who arrives. I'll look more into it. I have to go. Take good care of my daughter. Tell Jasmeen I love her with everything in me, and she'll be coming home soon. I'll message again when I can.

Aamir: I know it's probably impossible, but if you talk to my sister can you make sure Layla knows I miss and love her, and me and Jasmeen will be home soon.

Me: I'll tell her if I get the chance. I stole another glance at the thumbnail of Jasmeen. Protect my daughter, Aamir. Please keep her safe.

Aamir: With my life.

I ended the message, not able to go on a second longer. I went to create a new one for Luke but stopped, pulling out my phone instead. I kept the earbuds in, connecting them to my cell and calling my brother.

*"What."*

The power in Luke's voice had me smiling.

"Don't tell me you're regretting your new job already."

A deep sound filtered over the line.

"Dammit, Gavin. It's about time you called. Those storms looked crazy on the radar. I was starting to get worried."

"You and everyone else. I'm fine. Another day or so and I'll be on land. Tell me." I stopped, glancing at the men in the room who all appeared to be busy on their own devices. "Update me. I want to know everything."

"There's not much to report. We're watching a vessel on the

horizon. It's been there for a while. Sometimes it moves, but not far."

"I don't like the sound of that."

"Some of the guys took a boat out a few days ago. They're going out wide and are going to come back around and see who it is. I expect a call from them anytime now."

"Good. Stay on top of it." I glanced at the men. "What else?"

"Still no call from Rich."

"He might not call. He doesn't always. Keep going."

"The slaves and guards seem to be following orders well enough, but I'm keeping my eye on them. I trust the soldiers more than I trust them."

"As you should. *What else?*"

Luke paused. "The food shipment—"

"I don't fucking care about that."

"Gavin, I have no news on her. At least not any that you'd want to hear. I haven't talked to her in two days. The Babke…"

"What about the Babke?"

"She came to me. She was speaking about bad things to come. She wasn't happy and was worried. I'm sure everything is fine. I have a camera on the tribe. It's not close but—"

"A camera? Does the Babke know?"

"Hell yes, she knows. I bribed her and you should see the damn list she gave me. I can't even pronounce half the stuff she wants. Anyway, I've put in the order, and I'll call Layla tonight and check in on her. I'm sure she's fine. Your wife…she's a tough one. And stubborn, and *aggravating*." I laughed. "I begged her to just stay here. She refused. I really wish you would have trusted me to keep her safe. The tribe is…dangerous."

"Exactly, Luke. That's the point. No one can get past them. No one."

"And if that backfires?"

My lids narrowed. "What do you mean?"

"Nothing. You don't worry about us. I've got this."

Back and forth, my head shook. "You're not telling me something."

"I said I got this."

"And I believe you, but if you know something you're not telling me." I stopped. "Luke, what is it?"

A loud exhale sounded over the phone followed by clicks from his pacing.

"It's nothing. I just don't like how the Babke was acting. That woman doesn't appear to be a person who gets afraid often. Gavin, if you would have seen her. She was downright terrified. Panicked, even. She fears the tribe, and from what I heard from the guards, she has damn good reason to. They're not taking well to Layla and Mandy being there. Layla even mentioned that she had a bad run-in with one of the men. She tried to play it off, but I heard her fear. Tension is tight in that tribe, and it'll only take one thing for shit to hit the fan."

I blinked through his words, feeling my heart thundering in my chest. Had I made a mistake sending Layla with the Babke? From what I understood, we were on good terms. I gave them their space. I made sure my part of life didn't interfere with theirs. Of course, I hadn't thought it through either. I was devastated in my grief. I knew if anyone could keep Layla safe, it would be them. I never considered how they'd feel about it. After all, hadn't the Babke helped keep Layla alive? She made it sound like it would be okay. She even said she'd prepared for this moment and knew it was going to happen. She hadn't been alarmed then, but now she was?

"Now you're worried." Luke let out a groan. "See. This is why I didn't want to tell you. You have enough shit on your mind."

"No. I'm glad you told me." Still, I paused as thoughts raced through. "Make your call. If all is good, nothing changes. If things aren't better, we'll take our chances at the fortress. I trust whatever decision you think is best."

"I can decide all day long, but it doesn't mean Layla will. Did I mention how stubborn she is? The woman walked up multiple flights of stairs because she refused to let me carry her up them. She choked me with my tie, Gavin. She refused to let go until I put her down. She said the only man who'd ever carry her would be her husband. That woman—"

"Is amazing. Strong."

"Stubborn."

I couldn't keep the smile from my face as I stared blankly at my screen. All I could see was her. *I could feel her.*

"That is the truth."

"She loves you. God, she *really* loves you."

I blinked through my brother's words, my happiness vanishing with the guilt that wouldn't subside.

"I should go." I lowered my voice almost inaudibly. "Tell her her brother loves her, and our daughter is the most beautiful little girl in the world. I'll call again soon. Be safe."

"You, too. *Wait*...Layla would kill me if I didn't at least try to give you the number to the phone I gave her. I don't think it will work, but it's worth a try. I'm sure she'd love to hear from you."

"What's the number?" I pulled up my notes on my laptop, pushing in the digits as he spoke. "Thank you for taking care of her for me. It seems like you're on top of it over there. I'll try to give her a call."

"Of course. Keep in touch."

"Will do."

I hung up, glancing between the men and my screen. I shouldn't call Layla. Everything in me was saying not to. What if it put her at risk? So many questions came and went. Nothing would process as I saw a temporary fix to try to fill the hole inside me.

Punching in the digits, my eyes closed, waiting. Hoping. Praying.

Nothing.

Seconds went by.

Time seemed to stall and not exist in that moment as I waited for a ring. For anything. The line was just as empty as I was without her.

"You okay, Double M?"

My lids opened, and I took in Fallon's watchful gaze.

"I'm good."

I hit the end button, shoving the phone back in my pocket. My bleak afternoon was quickly taking a turn for the worst. Between the Babke's sudden fears and my own, I wasn't sure what to think. I was sure Layla would be safe in the tribe. Now…I wasn't so sure.

Fear burned the edges of my heart, and I quickly pulled out my phone again, trying the number once more.

Nothing.

I cursed, biting against the inside of my lip as I headed into the cameras that were tied to the island. Luke had said he put one by the tribe. As I pulled it up, I couldn't stop the way my skin seemed to crawl with some sort of warning I couldn't begin to decipher. The fortress put Layla in more danger. It risked more exposure. But if the tribe turned, they'd kill her without a second thought. At the fortress, the threat would have to get through Luke first, and those odds were better than Layla trying to fend for herself against men deadlier than most. But that was if…if the tribe turned. From everything I knew, they were fine. According to the Babke, maybe not anymore.

# CHAPTER 22

## LUKE

*I*f there was one thing I learned from this island, it was that days could go by with nothing, but when shit started, it came from all directions. Nothing happened in order. There was no such thing as one issue at a time. No. When the ceiling fell out, everything came tumbling down with it.

"So, what are you saying, Tillin? You can't reach them because of connection issues, or they're just not fucking answering?"

"They're not answering, Main Master. The phone rings, but no one picks up."

I cursed, jerking the binoculars down. I still had my phone in hand to call Layla, but with the barrage of bullshit that had gone down after Gavin hung up over an hour ago, I had yet to find the time to call her.

"The boat is still there. It hasn't moved, and I don't see another. Maybe it's connection issues, or maybe…" I trailed off, squinting to see if I could spot any other boats. "Maybe…no. It's not the connection. Fuck. Try it again."

"Main Master."

I bit against my bottom lip lowering the binoculars. When I turned to meet the soldier's gaze, he cringed.

"Sorry, Sir. I thought you should know that we finished rounds on the back side of the island. We didn't make it all the way down."

"What do you mean, you didn't make it? You just said you finished."

"The tribe." He bobbed his head back and forth as if I should know.

"The tribe, what?"

"They were there, fishing, Sir."

"But that's our part of the island."

He shrugged. "They were there, so I left them alone."

"Okay." I brought my hand up, my eyes widened even more as Jones headed up with another soldier I wasn't familiar with. "You're early. There's no way you made it all the way down to the north side of the island and back. Even on ATVs. You've seriously been gone ten minutes, tops."

"I can't do shit. The tribe is fishing, and the kids are all playing around. They're everywhere."

"On the north side too?"

He, too, shrugged.

"What the hell are they doing? Do they do this often?"

At them shaking their heads, I ran my hand over my face.

"Let them fish. Maybe they need food and can't find it on their part of the island. As long as they don't make this a fucking habit, I think it'll be okay. Tillin, keep calling. I have to go check on something. If you get a hold of them, let me know."

Jones went to speak but I waved my hand, dismissing him. Was Layla down there too? Surely, she wouldn't risk being seen. I took out the phone, more stomping to the fortress than walking. Layla's call went through, making it to the fourth ring before she answered.

"*Luke.*"

"Yep, it's me. You wouldn't happen to be out by the beaches, would you?"

"No, I didn't go."

"Good." I paused. "I talked to Gavin."

"*You did?*" Eagerness laced her tone. "How was he?"

"He's okay. The storms were pretty nasty the last few days, but he's almost to land."

The guards opened the doors, and I swept in.

"Thank God. What all did he have to say?"

I headed for the stairs, taking them three at a time. No one was in view, and I kept my speed at a fast pace as I headed for my room.

"We didn't talk long. I updated him on the island. He worries about you." I paused. "We're debating on bringing you back. Has it gotten any better there?"

It was her turn to get quiet.

"About the same, I guess. We've been staying inside for the most part. Mandy refuses to go out unless she has to. Even the Babke has been absent. I think she's stopped by once since I last talked to you. We had plans to go try to make peace with the tribe, but she showed up earlier this morning and told us we needed to wait until after the ceremony tonight."

"Ceremony?"

"Yeah." Layla cleared her throat, quieting her voice. "I guess it's the future king's birthday or something. They called it a weird name, but I can't remember now. They're all out now gathering food."

"I know. They're fishing on both ends of the island, exactly where they're not supposed to be."

"Then it's already started."

My brow drew in as I shut my door.

"What's started?"

Commotion had me listening even harder.

"I...Hold on." Movement. Rustling. "Mandy, what is that?"

"Layla?"

"Give me a minute, Luke. Something is happening outside. Noise. I'm trying to see what it is."

Hammering. That's what it sounded like as I strained to hear.

"What in the world?" A gasp. Whispering.

"Can you see what it is?"

More whispering.

"Yeah…They're bringing in structures or something. Not too big. And lots of wood. They're…one of the women out there are starting to shape it. I think they're going to make something out of it. She just started. I can't tell what it is yet. I think it's for the celebration."

"Oh, okay. What were you going to tell me?"

The whispering between the women continued.

"I don't remember. I'm sure it's fine. Hopefully after we make peace tonight, everything will get better. Did Gavin say anything else?"

"He did. He talked to Aamir. Your brother loves you very much, and Gavin says Jasmeen is the most beautiful little girl in the world." A sniffle. "*He saw her?* I'm so happy he got to see her. Do you have Aamir's number? I want to see my daughter too."

"I don't. I'm sorry. I think he got the phone from Gavin. I even gave my brother your number, but if he hasn't called you yet, I don't think it worked. Aamir's won't work either, and it's too much of a risk to get him to call you from Ev's phone. They're not supposed to know you're alive. But if you come back, you can use mine. It'll be less suspicious that way. I think we could pull it off."

"Come back? Luke, I told you I can't. Not if it puts Gavin in danger."

"Danger? Are *you* not in danger?" She didn't answer. "No one will find you here, Layla. We'll do everything we can to prevent it. You'll be safe, and Gavin will be too."

"We don't know that."

"I do. I would not jeopardize my brother's life. When I say no one will know you're here, I mean it. I'll send everyone out but us if I have to. I don't care. We'll do what we must to keep you hidden and my brother safe. You have my word."

A sigh came over the phone. "Let me think about it. I want to at least try to make peace before I go. The Babke deserves that. She saved my life. I don't want to ruin hers because I came here."

"Call me tomorrow. I want to know how it goes."

"Alright. Talk to you then."

Layla hung up, and I collapsed on the chair. Within seconds my phone started ringing.

"Yeah?"

Tillin. "Sir, I got a hold of our guys. They're not far out from the boat."

I bolted upright from slouching in the chair.

"Did they mention why the fuck they weren't answering the phone?"

"They said they never received any calls. Our conversation was pretty broken. Service isn't the best out there."

"Bullshit," I said under my breath, pushing to stand as I headed to my laptop. "If they weren't receiving calls, someone was preventing it. What did you say when you talked to him?"

Tillin hesitated. "I asked what the fuck was going on and why they didn't answer. That we'd been trying to call now for four hours. They were confused. Barkley had no idea what I was talking about."

"Did you mention the boat?"

"Well...I said target."

"Okay." I brought up the cameras, beginning to scan through them. "Be careful what you say. You need to somehow get the word to Barkley that his phone may be compromised. They need to be careful out there."

"I'll let them know. I'll call back when I have more news."

"Roger that."

I hung up, heading to one of the cameras that was positioned at the north end of the island. The tribe was still there fishing. Most were women and children. There were only a few men and they looked more on guard, watching over the families as the women worked to catch the fish.

As I headed for the camera at the opposite end of the island, my brow drew in at the black screen.

"What the hell?"

There was no picture. No view whatsoever. I went back through the recording, pausing it as color flooded back in. Dark eyes were glaring right at me, only a foot or so away. I could see the man's face, and what I saw went far beyond disapproval. There was anger. A lot of it. Hate. It only revealed itself even more as he reared back, stabbing the end of his metal-tipped, wooden spear right into the lens causing the flood of blackness.

"Dammit." My eyes closed, and I breathed through my own frustration concerning the nonstop issues. I pulled up my phone, hitting Tillin's number again. He answered almost immediately.

"Yep?"

"The tribe busted out the camera on the south end. I need it replaced. Send two—three men down there to take care of it. I want them in groups from now on. Something is happening with that tribe, and I don't like it."

"Will do."

I hung up, dialing Bram's number.

"Main Master."

"Fuck that title and fuck this position," I said, smiling as he let out a loud laugh.

"You're not already tiring of the almighty power, are you?"

"I've never cared for power. What I'm tired of is not knowing what the hell is going on with my brother. Have you heard anything about the men who did this?"

Bram let out a breath. "I've heard some things. Nothing good. It would seem the Main Master of London is having a party in a few days. A lot of important people will be there. Especially since the identity of the child they're going to feast on is out."

"I'm sorry, what?"

"You heard me right. It's the norm for London. Each place has their...preferences. Maybe it's culture, hell I don't know. London has one of the oldest undergrounds. The older and more established the hierarchy, the darker the preferences. At least in some instances."

"And, of course, Gavin is going there. I believe that's one of the Main Masters who tricked him into using that doctor."

"It is," Bram confirmed, "and if he thinks he can waltz right in without being detained and killed, he has another thing coming. They'll be looking out for him. Redmond may be quite the carefree socialite, but he's not stupid. He's been a Main Master now for almost thirty years, and he's survived that long for a reason. If he is guilty of being a participant in this, he's going to be ready. He'll be waiting."

"I could beat the hell out of my brother for leaving me out of this. To do what, run this damn island? I should be there helping him. Instead, I'm watching secretive boats and dealing with a cannibalistic tribe that's throwing red flags I don't like. They took over the beaches today, and I had one bust out a camera on a part of the island they're supposed to be forbidden from. They're testing the limits to see what they can get away with."

"Do they know Gavin is gone?"

My mouth opened only to close.

"Yeah. I think they do."

"Well, that's not good."

"No. I know I should put a stop to it before they go further but fuck if it's not a double-edged sword."

Bram made an agreeable sound.

"Take it from someone who learned lessons the hard way... put a stop to it now. The last thing you want to do is show weakness. They'll devour you whole."

"Literally."

"What about this boat you mentioned?"

"Fuck, I don't know. It's been parked out on the horizon for quite a while now. Sometimes it moves, but not far. It could be drifting. I can't really tell. I can't pick it up on radar, either, which means they don't want to be seen. I don't like it. I have people out there now getting eyes on who it could be. It's not you, is it?"

"I'm afraid not."

"Damn. That would have been nice." Crying in the background had me smiling. "How is she?"

Bram didn't even ask as he turned on the video calling. I followed in his actions, turning on my video as well. The inside of a familiar yacht came into view, and I smiled.

"You're home."

"For the time being. Jasmeen needed a little stability. Didn't you, precious?"

Everleigh turned, beaming a bright smile as she came to face us. She was holding Jasmeen, appearing happier than I'd ever seen her. My heart swelled only to ache.

"Is that Luke?"

I waved at Ev, seeing her grow even happier.

"It's me. Someone sounds upset."

"Aamir's making her a bottle." Everleigh turned Jasmeen more to face me and my lips parted through the shock. "Holy... shit. I mean. I see—"

"Her father?" Bram laughed. "I can see Gavin too."

"Isn't she the most beautiful baby you've ever seen?" Everleigh was stuck staring down and moving in a soft sway. "I'm soaking in every minute I can. She's such a good baby. She hardly ever cries."

"She's. I can't even find words. I can't believe how much she's changed in the last two weeks."

"Has it been that long already?"

"A little longer than that. Closer to three." Aamir walked up, pulling Everleigh's attention. Aamir's eyes widened as he saw me, but he looked conflicted or confused.

"Luke. Hey."

"Aamir. How are you doing?"

He shrugged, handing the bottle to Ev. "I'm okay. No offense to the Whitlocks, but I'm ready to come home. Have you talked to Gavin? Has he said anything?"

Aamir had no idea that I was aware of Layla. He didn't know anything me and Gavin talked about.

"Actually, yeah, but nothing about coming home. I...I need to talk to you in private about something he brought up with me."

The phone shifted, and I knew Bram handed it over. Colors blurred until it became bright from the sun outside. Aamir didn't stop until I knew he was far enough away.

"Is it bad? What did Gavin tell you?"

"He gave me a message... I relayed it."

Aamir's lip quivered. "You know."

I nodded. "There's a lot we can't say with you on that phone. It's not safe. Just know the feeling is mutual, and all is well."

"I'm not so sure about that. I don't like it, Luke. I don't like it at all. I know where she's at, and I've been at that island long enough to tell you it's a bad fucking idea. They can't be trusted."

"I couldn't agree more, and hopefully by tomorrow that will end. I'm waiting on some information now that could change things. You know me. Safety first, and I'm doing what I can to make that possible, okay? You need to trust me."

"I do."

"Good. Do me a favor when you go back. Put the camera up to Jasmeen so I can screenshot some pictures and send them."

229

"*She has a phone?*"

"Not one you can call. At least not on the one my brother gave you. You'd have to use Ev's or Bram's, and they'd know, Aamir. For their safety, we can't risk it. At least…not yet. If we did a call like this and I had her here, maybe you could go out like you are now. That could work, but it's going to take some time."

"Do what you have to. I need this. I need it, Luke. I've been losing my mind."

At the tears filling his eyes, I nodded. Aamir had almost died on countless occasions just so he could make it back to his sister. Being away from his twin now was not going well for him.

"I'll try my best to do what I can. Now, go back and get some pictures of my beautiful niece. She's the only light I can see right now, and I think we all need that."

# CHAPTER 23

## LAYLA

"*She won't do it. Let's push her. Make her jump.*"
            "*Jump! Jump!*"
"*Make her fly. Fall. Fly. Fly.*"

Hot wind blew at my face as I stood on the edge of the cliff. The sky was tinted a deep red and moving. Moving like blood pocketed inside the clouds. Sweat was covering my skin. I felt soaking wet as the ground shifted under my feet. Fear spiked, and my gaze shot down, watching as the earth gave way beneath the tips of my toes.

"*Jump! Fly! Die!*"

I tried pushing against the invisible force at my back but nothing I did would get me further away from the cliff.

"*Babke! Babke, help!*" Harder I pushed, trying to twist without falling. "*Babke, please!*" But there was nothing but the laughter and snickering just out of sight.

I had to get out of here. I had to get safe and go…somewhere. There was something, but I couldn't move. I was trapped, and here I was, back at the one place that didn't want to let me go. A force kept pulling me here, putting me right on the edge.

My head shook through the questions I could barely process.

More earth gave way just under my feet and I screamed. It morphed with another sound. A distant sound. One that was...familiar.

*"Look at her. I'm going to push her."*

*"Yes, yes!"*

But I didn't feel fear like I should. That sound. I knew that sound. What was it? Where was it? Was it coming from below?

Voices. Crying?

*"Hello?"*

*"She's so weak. Such a baby. Let's kill her."*

Baby. Baby. Baby.

The word repeated, making my heart thud in a rhythm so quick, I wasn't sure if it was adrenaline or panic.

Baby. Yes. My baby. I saw her in the pictures Luke had sent me. My daughter. I had to get to my daughter. She needed me. Did the voices have her? Were they trying to keep her away from me?

*"Jasmeen? Mommy's here. Jasmeen? Keep crying. Mommy's coming."*

Harder I pushed against the force, putting a strength I wasn't aware I had in trying to break through. Although I couldn't, something was different. Stronger, inside of me. The fear was gone. All that remained was pure determination, and I'd never felt so driven towards anything before in my life. I needed to get to my daughter. I had to make sure she was safe.

*"She fights too hard. Watch her fall."*

*"Yes, fall. Fall!"*

Chuckling sounded but all I heard was crying again. It hadn't come from behind me, but...beneath? Ahead?

I scanned the dark red clouds, moving down to gaze at the shadowy raging waters below. Was Jasmeen in the water? In the darkness where I couldn't see? Maybe there was a boat or she was somewhere down on the beach? It wasn't below me, but it wasn't far away. Was she there with Gavin? Aamir? A stranger? Why couldn't I think!

*"Jasmeen!"*

More earth gave way, but it was the increasing volume of the cry that stole any concern I should have harbored. My daughter might be hurt. *She might need me.*

With one last push to my back, I didn't think, I jumped.

Laughter turned to screams.

Snickers into roars.

The water opened like a void, morphing to fire, and all I could do was swing my arms and kick my feet as I screamed my daughter's name.

*"Layla. Layla."*

I was still screaming, choking through my gasp. My eyes shot open as Mandy rocked me awake. The sound of a baby was crying in the distance, and my long, loose dress was covered in sweat despite a chill in the air. Drums paused, turning to silence before they started going again. Tribal language buzzed, and I pushed it away as I tried to focus.

"I fell asleep?"

But I knew that answer. I'd been crying, looking at the pictures Luke had sent me of Jasmeen. I couldn't stop looking at them. My daughter. She was the most beautiful baby I'd ever seen. That she wasn't with her brother did things to me even the voices didn't dare provoke. Rage had edged in as I drifted off. Blood begged to be spilt. I had none to take. *Yet.*

"The ceremony is going. I didn't want to wake you, but you were screaming. I think maybe they heard you. Did you hear them get quiet?"

I wiped the wetness from the sides of my face, forcing myself to sit.

"Maybe. I don't know."

My voice was hoarse, and my throat felt raw. I grabbed my water, taking a big drink as I tried to catch my breath. The anger was back, drowning out the fear with the flames I could still see before me. I wasn't afraid of them. I had only feared falling. The fire was Gavin. It was home. In those moments, maybe even a part of me wanted to burn in their depths. What was the longing inside? My chest ached. It was crushing amongst the need to scream out with madness.

Mandy lowered her voice as she leaned in. "We'll have to make an appearance to offer peace soon. I believe all the ceremonial stuff is already over. It's the celebration now. *I don't want to go.*"

"We must. The Babke needs this. She's done nothing but fight for us. We have to at least try to get on the king's good side and maintain it for a little while. For her."

Mandy's face drew in. She paused, nodding.

"She has done a lot for us."

"For me," I corrected. "You should have never had to come back here against your will. I'm sorry for that. You've done so much for me too. I haven't overlooked that. That's why I'm freeing you, Mandy. You're no servant, you're my friend. You've always been my friend."

"But the Main Master——"

"I'm freeing you. You're free now. Right now."

"But—"

My head shook as tears collected in her eyes.

"Free. You can stay here, or you can come back and have your own room in the fortress when we return. The choice is yours."

"You're...*sure?*"

"Absolutely."

Arms flew around my neck as Mandy threw herself into me, hugging on tightly. Before I could say more, the cadence of the drums transitioned into a deeper, slower tone that had Mandy drawing back with wide eyes.

"What is that?"

I eased up to look out of the window but was stopped as Mandy tightened her hold.

"Don't look. Don't go any closer. We have the light on and it's getting dark outside. They may see you. They can't see you."

"But what is it?"

"Lu sitan va.[1] *The death call.* Or…Death's call. He's here to lead someone forward as a sacrifice to the king."

I didn't have to ask who *'he'* was. "Sacrifice?"

"Shh." Mandy pulled me to the ground, closing her eyes as she started praying, transitioning from English to her own native tongue. "I thought that was over. If he sees you. If he thinks of us." She stopped, tears dropping from her eyes as her stare shot to mine. "Or maybe…No. The scream. I think he heard. He'll say Death—he'll—"

The door flew open, and like a vice, Mandy clung to me as I forced us to stand. Large men surged inside, not slowing in their approach.

"What are you doing? No one said you could come in here." I tried to make it to my bed where I had my knife hidden under my pillow, but Mandy's hold wouldn't allow me to move. "*Get out!* Mandy, you have to let go—Hey!" A hand reached out, almost grabbing me. "What the hell do you think—"

She was pulling me back, screaming as a man with long hair came to the side, trying to reach around me for her.

"Don't you *dare* fucking touch us." I slapped the larger man's hand away, stunned as he reared back, connecting his fist with my cheek. The force sent me crashing to the ground, dislodging me from Mandy's hold.

"Layla! Don't let them take me. Layla!"

The Babke's voice was shouting in their language. I knew that, but I could barely process it as I fought against hands that were trying to lift me. Blood. It was on my tongue. It was all I could taste and oddly…smell.

"Layla! Layla, p-please!"

Blurred colors righted, giving view to Mandy's terrified face as she fought.

"*Let her go.*" I tried to stand but was snatched up and was being pulled in all directions. I kicked against the grip that had one of my legs, twisting in the arms that held me from behind. More men were crowding in, grabbing at me, not stopping until their hands were touching me. And we were walking forward. I could barely see Mandy fighting as they headed out of the door while we followed.

"This is not the way! Ye, no pa gnelp. *They're not traitors.*"

"Babke!"

I barely caught a glimpse of her as I was carried outside with Mandy, right towards the large bonfire blazing not a hundred feet away. It was taller than us. Taller than the two of us, and we were headed right for it.

"Aven. Aven!" I looked around wildly, jerking in their arms as I tried to search out the future king. Tribal people were everywhere. Men. Women. Children. Flowers were heavy in the long hair of the younger women, and the children were smeared with red. Blood? The more I looked, the more I caught it on their deeply tanned skin. It was on all of them, in one place or another. "Aven!"

The drum grew faster, sending my pulse speeding up with it. White blurred through the flames, and I tried twisting, locking eyes with the one man whose stare wouldn't leave me. For seconds I couldn't speak. The evil I detected in his cocky gaze left me screaming in a tone I hadn't heard from myself before. He wasn't going to listen. He wasn't going to see reason.

"Babke!" Back and forth I rocked, fighting against the restraint of the mens' hold. "Babke!"

"Here! Layla, here!" My eyes searched the crowds in the dark, spotting her pushing through the thick group as we neared the fire.

"He's going to kill us. You have to tell Gavin I love him. My daughter. You—"

Screams pierced the air, so high pitched and full of agony that my voice disappeared. My heart...it stopped. Lifting my head to see over the crowd, I fought to find some sort of oxygen. Mandy was clawing her way out from inside the flames. Charred skin bubbled over her arms and face, melting like wax as the men took turns pushing her fighting body back into the fire. Her mouth was opened, and she was still screaming as the orange and reds licked past her lips.

"Mandy! Mandy, *no!*"

But I didn't hear my screams or words over the drums in my ears. I couldn't tell the difference between my pulse or the music anymore.

Flesh oozed and fell free, and the crevices hollowed in her cheek bones. I knew she'd fallen back into the pile of wood, but I could still see her limbs moving as she appeared to scream. Or maybe she was dead and the haunting howls I imagined were my own. I was crying. Oxygen was barely existent, and I was moving forward. But I wasn't afraid; I was enraged as I fought. Aven stepped closer, and I locked right onto his face.

Hate.

It fed the frenzy inside. I was thrashing as hard as I could again, but not to break free to live. I was fighting to bring death. Fighting to spill blood. His blood. He killed my friend. Aven took her away from me just as the doctor had taken away my son.

"I curse you. I curse you to a million deaths before your soul finds peace. *Death favors me.* You can kill me, but you will never escape me just as I will never escape the demons that are inside me."

The Babke's loud voice boomed their language, barely breaking my focus.

"Continue Layla. I will translate."

"If you kill me, I will curse you," I repeated. "I will come back in spirit, and I will end your reign before it even begins. You will have no heirs. Disease will find you. It'll eat you from the inside out. *I will eat you*," I growled. "I will be you; you will be me…even if I'm dead. *I'm the Leelee*, and I will not be rid of so easily. This is my fucking island. Death saved me for a reason. It is part of me now, inside me. I hear him. Feel him. *Do you? Can you say that?*"

The drums had stopped and the silence was haunting. The tribe looked around, moving in closer together as they scanned the surroundings. Aven didn't move, but I could see his uncertainty.

"He's so close to you. He's practically breathing down your neck. Kill me if you want. *I dare you*. But if I were you…I'd let me live. Allow Death to work through me. You wanted a sacrifice. Lu sitan va. I am the death call. Me: lu sitan va. Allow me to give you a gift."

Aven's lids narrowed through the suffocating silence that had taken over the tribe. Worry clouded their faces and even some of the children cried as they stared at their future king. Even the men under me shuffled nervously. If the tribe was anything it was superstitious. The entire island knew that, but I didn't think my words were rooted from hope that this king would believe them. What I spoke was the truth in every fabric of my being. I would devour this man like the black hole inside of me, and even my death wouldn't prevent the stain I'd leave on his life. Somehow I'd make sure of that, and a part of him could feel it.

"Put me down." I jerked against the mens' hold. "I said put me down!"

A translation wasn't needed as the men practically dropped me with no order from their king. They feared me. They should.

"You killed my friend."

Aven stood taller as he stared me down. He didn't move when I took a step forward. I wouldn't have seen it if he did. My eyes locked on the knife at one of the men's hips. He wasn't wearing clothes, but he was armed, and I took advantage of that as I jerked the knife from the leather sheath. The group closest scattered, moving closer to Aven.

Tears were soaking my face and continued to fall as I glanced at the fire. What resembled a body cooked under roaring flames. It twisted my stomach as I turned my attention back to him.

"Layla." The Babke's voice was soft as she stepped in. "Hold the knife if you must but do not point it at him. Make amends. Let us leave."

"Leave. *No*."

At Aven's words, the Babke and I snapped our attention to the king. Could he understand us?

"You won, Aven. You wanted the traitor dead."

The Babke translated, and Aven's voice was filled with rage as he yelled back in their language.

"He says she deserved it. It is done. But you...you can't leave." She shifted, gripping up to hold her necklace as a choked sound left her. "You called yourself his queen in front of everyone. You took your place and gave yourself to him, Layla."

"Bullshit. I did not. I said I was queen of the island; *not his queen*, and this is not his island. This is our island. We share it. Besides, I'm married. That's forever. Tell him that." But he knew. They all knew who I was.

More argument, back and forth.

"He won't listen to reason," she said, quietly. "He claims you gave yourself to him. He's blaming you, saying you did this. That it's your fault."

My eyes shot to his as I glared.

"You can't take someone that doesn't belong to you. I choose to be with my husband. Not you. *Never you*."

"Zu ke vemzeka?"[2]

The Babke swallowed hard as his tone turned angry, filled with disbelief, through his question.

"Aven said." She stopped. "He wants to know if you find him unworthy of you?"

"Unworthy? Hell yes he's unworthy."

"*Layla.*"

But I didn't listen to the Babke's warning as I closed the distance to the king. He may have towered over me. He may have made up two of me in width. I didn't care as I met his glare.

"You will never compare to Gavin. It's not even close. Unworthy?" I nodded. "Yeah. I wouldn't choose you if you were the last man alive. *Murderer.*"

"*Stupid girl.*" A hand pulled at my loose dress, and I stepped back, allowing myself to move in closer to the Babke. "Tell him you're sorry. Tell him you didn't mean it."

"What does it matter? It's not like he knows what I'm saying."

A small laugh left Aven as he took his turn closing the distance.

"Murderer," he repeated in amazingly good English. "Very stupid girl. Perhaps you're right."

"You…You understand me? You—"

"Am a savage, yes? Tribal, so therefore I'm…stupid? I'm not stupid."

Babke pulled us back, inch by inch. She was terrified, and she was no longer trying to hide it. Had she known before now? It hadn't appeared so.

"Why are you doing this? You know I'm married. You don't want me. Why kill my friend and keep me here against my will?"

"Why not?" He shrugged.

"*Because I'm married.* Because my friend did nothing wrong."

"She chose…your slave life over her tribe."

My head shook back and forth through his slow English. He

knew it, but he wasn't very fast as speaking more than a few words at a time.

"That didn't mean you had to kill her."

"I'm a murderer. You said so...yourself. Your turn. I want my gift."

"*Gladly.*" I turned, searching the crowd for the man who'd grabbed Mandy and hit me. The long-haired man was standing behind a few others close to his size. I pointed the blade, biting down as I singled him out. "You. You're first."

"No."

Aven's voice was deep. I turned to the king, lowering my lids.

"What do you mean, no? I get to choose, and he's the one I want."

"You want him to die?"

"He took Mandy. He threw her in the flames. He killed her on your order. He dies."

"Alright." Aven moved in even closer, lowering his face inches from mine, but his eyes weren't on me. They were on the Babke. "He dies...*but her first.*"

# CHAPTER 24

## THE DRAGON

*L*and. It didn't matter that we had been held up inside a small hotel now for hours, the ground still rocked under our feet. It didn't bother me so much, but I could tell the trip took a toll on the men. If they were going to be of any use, they needed to adjust. At least another few hours… or…shit.

I glanced down at the message from Bram. I had to have read it a good five times. Confliction swayed, just as I did as I scanned the message one more time.

> Bram: Gavin, there are two jets waiting for you. I included their numbers. They arrived only this morning and are standing by. The address is below. One will fly you just outside of London. The other will take you home if you've changed your mind about this mission. The first is full of men to help assist you should you choose to face down Redmond. You have your soldiers, I know that, but a few trusted extras won't hurt. If anything, they're willing to be a distraction. You're going to need it. We both know it's a death sentence if anything goes wrong. It may be one if all goes right. Regardless of your decision, I'm here for you however I can be. You have my number. Never hesitate to call.

Home. God, I'd give anything for this to be over with, so I could be on my way back to my wife and daughter. Until they were safe, I didn't have a choice. I had to make an example so big, no one tried coming after us again. It was the only way in this world.

I brought up my phone, dialing Luke. He answered almost immediately.

"Brother."

"We made it."

Luke let out a sigh. "Bram told me about the planes. Did you get his message?"

"I did."

"And? Are you going to London?"

"Luke, you know I have to."

"I suppose, but I don't like it. Not one bit. There's no other way to get this guy without going into his territory?"

"Possibly, but I won't know until I make some calls. What's happening there?"

Luke made a sound, not at all happy I was changing the

subject. Voices were light in the background, but none were female like I was hoping. Was Layla not back yet? Was all going well with the tribe?

"The business part of the island is fine. The captains are accounted for. There's been no issues that's come up. As for the super yacht on the horizon, the boat's abandoned. Which makes no sense. We've seen it move. Someone was in it before today. Not to mention, this thing had to have cost hundreds of millions of dollars. It makes no sense. They must have picked up on our suspicions."

"Super yacht? Interesting. If they abandoned it, they had reason. That's not something you'd easily walk away from; unless you could afford it. Money is power. Money equals trouble. I don't like it. Great. Keep your eyes open. There's no telling who it was or what they want."

"That's what we're doing."

"Luke…what else?"

He got quiet. "I tried to call her last night. She didn't answer, nor has she returned my call. They were having a big celebration for the future king. She mentioned making amends before they came back. When I sent the pictures of Jasmeen, she said she might not be able to call for a day or two. I guess she wanted to put in a good effort to win the tribe over. Lots of socializing. Of mending bridges. That sort of thing. I didn't think she was serious though. Layla's been pretty on top of my calls."

"No call." My face drew in. "She's never cared for technology, but still. I can't really see her not calling after a few hours. She would have checked the phone before bed, right? I mean, for sure when she woke up this morning."

"That's what I was thinking, but I don't know her like you. Should I head down and go check things out, or would that cause issues with the tribe? How does that work? I'm not sure how to handle them. They took over the ends of the island, Gavin. They were only fishing for the afternoon, but you said that was our territory and they knew better than to go there."

My lips parted. "They do. That doesn't sound like them at all."

"They know you're gone. Do you think they're just pushing the limits, or is this something more? A tribal man...he busted out the camera at the north end. The hate on his face. I couldn't help but have a bad feeling."

Straighter I sat up, my free fist clenching through the anxiety that made itself known.

"Send soldiers to the line. Have them put their hands up to each side, slow and unthreateningly, and call out for the Babke. She's the only one that speaks English. When she arrives, have the soldiers tell her to get back to you."

"If she doesn't?"

My gaze drifted back to Bram's message.

"They're not to leave until the Babke appears. If for some reason she doesn't, they're more than capable of completing any mission you throw their way. And you know what I mean. But *you're* not to go. You don't need to be a part of that. You're the Main Master now. You are the last one to face the tribe. Do you hear me, Luke? The only way you're to go is if everyone else on that island is dead."

"Got it."

My jaw flexed. Could he hear how hard it was for me to say that? I wanted Layla safe at all costs, and although I knew the soldiers could hold their own, I trusted my brother to get the job done. Duty came first or there'd be no island, no wife, or any brother for me to go back to.

"Fuck." I let out a deep breath. "Make the call now. Keep calling. I'll call you in five minutes. Maybe she'll answer if it rings or vibrates back-to-back. Hopefully it works."

"Alright."

The line disconnected, and I hadn't realized how hard I was

breathing until I looked up to see my soldiers staring at me. They knew something was wrong. It wasn't anything I could clue them in on. Not yet anyway. Not at all, if that were possible. Lopez and Fallon knew...no one else would.

I moved my attention back to the cameras, pushing buttons as I went through the different views. When I got to the one of the tribe in the far distance, I squinted, trying to see more. From what I could tell, all looked mostly the same. Random members of the tribe came and went. Some appeared to be cooking by the fire. Nothing appeared out of place or suspicious.

"Sir? Is there anything we can do?"

I took in White and his question, glancing at Fallon, Lopez, and Pattinson. My head shook, but I had more going on than Layla. Who the fuck would be scoping out my island, staying on a super yacht? No one important would be that stupid. Unless they knew something I didn't.

"You want something to do while we wait? There's a super yacht that's been on the horizon for a good week now. Maybe longer. We sent a ship out to come up from behind them, but when we got there, the yacht was abandoned. They don't think that was the case days ago." I paused, glancing back at my screen. "I need to know who it belongs to. Call your buddies back home. We have technology they don't have access to. Get the info and figure out who the hell owns it. This thing is *expensive*. It belongs to someone. I want to know who it is."

"On it." Fallon pulled out his phone. "Fifty bucks that I find out first."

The race was on as all the men jerked out their cells. The distraction was exactly what I needed as I pushed to stand. I had to move. *To do something.* Why hadn't I left a phone for Layla? I had left one for Aamir. Why hadn't I thought to keep better tabs on her? Why? Because Layla brought out my killer. Protection and revenge drove me. And trust...My brother was always the better planner, and a part of me had known that in the back of my mind. He thought of everything; I took care of it. Our first instincts were opposites, and that wasn't doing me any favors.

Voices layered on each other as the soldiers buzzed for answers. Me…I kept pacing. Cursing myself. Cursing life and how slow time could go. When I felt enough minutes had passed, I quickly dialed Luke back.

"Well?'

A groan. "Nothing. I called repeatedly. Layla's not answering."

"Dammit." I moved back to my chair, taking in the fire in the distance. Luke had mentioned a celebration. Although there were what looked like more wooden trunks positioned for seating, I noticed nothing different. If there had been some big party the night before, I couldn't detect it. "Send the soldiers. I want them there until the Babke meets with you personally. Preferably with her *not* alone. If she still seems afraid, you put your foot down and end it. Make it clear I'm not in favor of it anymore. Safety comes first. That's with you. I trust you'll do what you can to…"

"Hide her? Protect her? With my life, brother. You know that."

"I do know. It should have been you to begin with. It was a bad idea. One I didn't think through. I assume…I mean…" My eyes swept back to the soldiers who were focused on trying to get the information. "Just bring her back."

"I will. I'm sure everything is fine. She might even be back home before the sun sets."

"I hope so. Keep up the good work. You're doing great. I'll call back as soon as I can."

"Do that, and be safe."

"Will do. Talk to you soon."

I hung up, shutting my laptop and sliding it in my bag. I couldn't sit here a moment longer. There was a plane waiting for me, and I was ready. The more the unknown questions settled in, the more my impatience ruled. I needed to hurry and get to

London. I needed to end this so I could be back with my wife. So I could heal and function again. Three weeks were three too many for the part of me who held love. My love wasn't normal —my emotions towards her weren't safe enough to contain. Layla *needed* me. For my own sanity, and the wellbeing of the world around me, *I needed her more.*

# CHAPTER 25

### LUKE

"What do you mean, no one is coming? You asked them for the Babke, didn't you?"

"*Two hours ago.* I've missed lunch. No one listens to me or Jones. Not the random person in the distance. Sure as hell not the man standing twenty feet away holding a spear and eyeing us like dinner. We keep telling him, but he just stares at us like we're stupid."

It wasn't like the Babke not to respond. "Keep asking. I want her located today. I want her either talking to me on your phone, or I want you escorting her and her companions here, yourself. I'm trusting you to take care of this, Juarez. You are not to leave until one of those things happens. Understand?"

"Yes, Main Master."

"Good. Keep me updated and stay near that fucking camera so I can see."

"Absolutely, Sir."

The sureness of the soldier's tone put me at ease as I caught the edge of the two soldiers on the tribal camera. He'd obey, and he'd keep trying. That's all we could really do if we didn't want to start a war with this tribe.

I hung up, calling Layla's cell for what had to be the fiftieth time. By the fourth ring I wanted to slam my fist into the wall. I wasn't sure what was happening, but I didn't feel like this was her ignoring the phone. Something felt...off. Especially after what I just discovered.

Lowering to stare at my laptop screen, I took in the only lighting in the distance. The fire the tribe had going looked normal. The three women and two men around it appeared... normal. Where the hell was Layla, Mandy, or the Babke?

"Tillin," I mumbled, lifting my phone and hitting the leader's number. It barely rang before his voice came flooding through.

"Nothing yet on the super yacht, Main Master."

"I figured that. I've got more pressing matters at the moment. Are you aware I sent soldiers to the tribal line for the Babke?"

"I heard the men mention it. Why you'd want to see that witch woman again is beyond me. She's been around a lot lately. It gives me the creeps."

"Good, that's the point. Tillin." I bit down hard, wiping my hand down my face. How was I going to explain the situation enough to stress the importance, but not hint that what we were hiding was a person? My eyes went back to the camera. "That witch woman is holding something very special for my brother. Something people may want for themselves. It's rare and if it fell into the wrong hands, this entire island would go down. We have to find the Babke as soon as possible. My brother got word that something might be wrong. I need to see if he's right."

Silence.

"What do you mean, the island could go down?"

Did I say too much? I couldn't take it back now. "It wouldn't exist anymore. At least under my brother's rule."

"This...thing she has...it could do that?"

"Revenge will not be enough. This is important, Tillin. I know my brother, and I cannot fail him in protecting the only thing he has left."

"He's already lost everything. What has that much power if not…if…What…?"

"Trust me when I say it may not make sense to us, but it is important to him. *It is everything.* Nothing matters aside from that. I need your help. Juarez and Jones are waiting for the Babke. To send more people would cause panic. The tribe would get defensive. We need to figure out a way to get into the village and see what's going on without raising an alarm. Do we know anyone in the tribe that can get to the Babke for us, so that I can talk to her?"

Hesitation.

"Have you spoken to the guard in the tunnels?"

"That's where I just came from. The man…the one who led me through before, he's gone. I don't know where he went."

"Fuck," Tillin breathed out. "That's not good."

"I was thinking the same thing."

"What about the servant girl? The one who was the companion to Layla? Mandy. Where's she?"

I groaned. "She went back to the tribe shortly after Layla was buried. The girl wanted to go home, and it's what Layla would have wanted, so my brother allowed her to return."

"Right. Well, shit. There may be another slave or two from there? I'm not sure. I can go check."

"That would be great. I'm going to brainstorm and see what I can figure out. Let me know if you find anyone."

"Will do."

I hung up, going right back to calling Layla's number.

One ring.

Two.

Four.

I tried not to crush the phone in my fist as I hung up. I shouldn't be panicking. It was one day. Damn this feeling that I couldn't shake. If I was overreacting, maybe it was a warning. Layla needed to come home. She needed to be here.

Forcing myself to sit, I took in the monitor. Juarez and Jones were still standing there. Juarez's hands were lifting, and he was clearly speaking to the tribal man, who didn't care to even look at him at the moment. It was movement further down by the fire that drew my eyes up the screen. White. Flowing. I squinted, moving in closer as two figures, a tall man and what looked to be a woman wearing a hooded robe, passed the fire. It was too far away to make out any details, but I held my breath as they came closer and closer to what looked to be now a yelling Juarez. He had his hands cupped by his mouth, and the tribal man was glaring as he watched both the soldiers become more animated. Up and down Juarez jumped, waving to something in the distance. Was it the couple they were screaming at? Could they even see them that far away?

They must have.

Minutes went by, and closer the couple got, coming in clear enough for me to growl as the man started speaking tight-lipped and angry. Without the woman looking up, I had no idea who was under the hood. I quickly dialed Juarez's number.

"Main Master." He answered quickly. "I think it's her. I think the witch woman is coming."

"I can see that. Listen to me closely. The man with her, he's not to be trusted. He's the one who busted out the camera at the north end of the island. I don't like this guy, and he sure as hell doesn't like us. Keep your distance from him."

"I'll be careful. They're coming up now."

Juarez's head tilted, trying to peer into the robe.

"Are you the Babke? The Main Master wishes to speak with you."

No words of acknowledgement. The hooded woman's hand lifted, and she took the phone, bringing it into the cloth that shrouded her features.

"Luke."

"*Babke.*" I sucked in air, not even realizing I'd been holding my breath. "What the hell is going on?"

"I...Everything is well."

"Bullshit. Your voice is trembling. Take off the hood and look at the camera so I can see you."

"I said I am well." Her free hand came up, easing the hood back. White hair stood out wildly as she allowed a few seconds to pass. When she looked up to where I had the hidden camera, I half expected to see her beaten. To see her bloody and her face marred. It wasn't. "What is it you wished to speak to me about, Main Master?"

"I want Layla."

"She is not ready."

My teeth bit into each other.

"I don't care. It's a direct order from Gavin. She comes home, *now.*"

She glanced up to the man, speaking in their language.

"I can let her know. I cannot promise she will return. Even the king says she's not ready."

"*King?* I don't give a shit what he says. You tell her—"

"New Main Master, do you so easily forget who you're talking about? She is queen of this island. She makes her own rules."

My lids lowered. Queen? "Tell Layla it's an order from her husband. If she wants more time, she can return after Gavin gets home. For now, she needs to come back."

"Impossible."

My mouth parted.

"No, it's not. It's quite easy, actually." I slashed my hand through the air, cutting myself off. "You know what, you and I are not going to argue. I'll take it up with her. You go back and tell Layla to call me. If she wants to stay, let her try to convince me."

"Impossible."

I went to argue once again, clamping my mouth closed. For seconds I didn't speak. I couldn't as I tried reading the situation.

"You said everything is well."

"Yes."

"Is it?"

A pause. "I would like my list."

"It's on the way. Are you and Layla in trouble?"

"We are well."

I growled. "Are you going to have Layla call me like I asked?"

"No. Like I said, impossible."

"*Why?* You tell me everything is okay, but you're speaking in code.*"

"If there's nothing else, I have to go. We're in the middle of a sacred ceremony. A very old practice, really. We stopped to come here and put you at ease." Her voice softened. "Be at ease, Luke. We are all playing our roles. It must be this way."

Aggravation had my head shaking. "I have no idea what you're talking about or what's going on. You tell Layla that she better call me. If not tonight, most definitely tomorrow."

"Impossible. The ceremony lasts three days. We are not to break practice once we begin again. Three days, Luke. Not one day more."

"A ceremony. You're sure you're okay? Layla's okay?"

"She grows into her fate by the hour. She is strong. I will tell her you wish her to call, but I cannot promise you in three days that she will. I must go."

"Babke, if she doesn't call me in three days—"

"Yes."

The line went dead and a roar left me as she handed the cell back over to Juarez. What the hell was that supposed to mean? Yes? Yes, to what? Did she know I was going to threaten to take over her village if Layla didn't call? That I was going to send every soldier in to massacre anyone who stood in their way? Yes? She couldn't have known the lengths I meant to go if my sister-in-law continued to play her games. Layla was coming home one way or another, and I'd make sure of it.

# CHAPTER 26

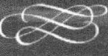

## LAYLA

To say I wasn't afraid was like saying I would forgive Aven for everything he'd done. There was no way in hell I'd forget watching my friend's flesh melt down to bone. Hours I stared into that fire. Not moving. Not speaking. *Seething.* Even now, I was restless knowing her bones were lying amongst dirt and ash. Traitor. If I never heard that word again, it would be too soon. Mandy wasn't a traitor. She was smart to steer clear of this tribe. They weren't good people, even if they were tolerable. That would end soon, and it would all be because of me.

"You know it must be done."

I wouldn't look at the Babke. I wouldn't even speak to her. She seemed to think the only way for me to be saved was for her heart to be at the end of my blade. I refused. Aven bought my excuse that he wasn't worthy enough yet, but only by a miracle. Where my words had come from that night, I'd never know, but they were the truth, and my decision would not change. Aven wasn't worthy of the Babke's death. Neither was I.

"Layla, I've seen it. I've made my peace. It's okay." She paused waiting for me to answer. When I didn't, she continued. "Three days. That's all you have, and truly not even that. If you don't kill me before Luke comes to get you…you *will* die. We both will, and with our death comes nothing but heartbreak for your Dragon. He already holds so much guilt over what's happened, and this will be no different. Gavin will blame himself for sending you here. He will never see his daughter, Layla. He will never recover from your death, and he will die, but not like you imagine. He dies by his own hand, and it is a slow, agonizing death. Here, on this island. You can stop that. You can have your family. Layla."

My eyes cut over, but I couldn't see the Babke. The tears wouldn't allow me to as I turned away from her again, curling into myself even more as I leaned against the wall. With my ankle restrained by a thick metal cuff, leaving was impossible. I felt like I was stuck in the twilight zone of some medieval nightmare that was only just beginning.

"You can be as stubborn as you want, girl, but it will do you no good. I must die. It is the only way you and my tribe survive. *Don't you see?* If you kill me right now, the paths can't change. You have to do it before our fates get worse."

She got quiet as the door to Aven's hut flew open. The king's stride was fast, his feet thumping into the ground in heavy steps as he paused at the small table by the bed he had me in, coming to kneel at my side.

"You didn't eat."

"I'm not hungry."

Fingers dug into my cheek and jawline as he turned me to face him. I could have attacked. I was on the verge, even if I did know it would make things worse.

"When I bring food…you eat."

"I eat when I'm ready."

Harder he dug, moving his eyes from mine down to my lips. There was no thinking. My palm shoved against his wrist, knocking his hold free and breaking any spell he'd started to go under.

"King or not, you touch me like that again, and I'll cut off your hands."

"I could say the same."

A cry left me as he fisted my hair, jerking my head back so that I had to look up at him.

"We…pair well."

"No we don't. You've done nothing but find ways to bully people. You did it to Mandy, and now you're doing it to me."

Aven's expressions changed as he took in my words. He may have spoken decent English, but it took him time to piece together what it all meant.

"Bully is mean?"

"Yes. So is asshole. That's what you are."

"Layla."

I ignored the Babke, but Aven didn't. He spoke quick sentences, not appearing happy at all when the Babke replied in their language.

"I see. You think me so…bad. Why make yourself my queen?"

"You know I didn't. Queen of this island does not mean queen to you. I've already explained that. Not to mention, you know I belong to someone else. I'm married. I just gave birth only weeks ago. I have babies." Tears welled. "A baby."

Aven's head tilted as he slid his thumb over the tear that rolled down my face.

"Why many? Then…one?"

"Layla, *no*. The paths."

With my hair gripped so tightly, I couldn't turn to the Babke, but the warning didn't go unnoticed. Not even to Aven as he bit out two sentences to her that sounded like a threat.

"One birth? How many babies?"

I sniffled, trying to move back into the wall as I ignored him. He didn't let me go far as he untangled his hand free of my hair.

Again, he came to grip my face, easier this time as he turned me to look at him.

"Answer, Leelee. Two babies? One birth? Or more?"

"What do you care?"

"I...*care*. Why many, and then one?"

"Because some bitch killed my son the moment he was born. She would have tried to kill my daughter if Jasmeen had been close. The doctor almost...she..." My eyes closed, squeezing the tears out through the memories I couldn't bear to relive. "I should be dead too. A part of me wants to go. *My son.*"

Tears forced their way free from the burning hole in my chest. Aven didn't speak. He just stared into my face as I opened my eyes to peer up at him.

"My daughter survived. One."

"You *do* have...magic? Luck. Special."

"What?"

"*Layla, please.*"

The worry from the Babke had me glancing over but turning back. The king's face was filled with wonder. With awe and something new.

"Two babies, one birth, yes? That's what you're saying. Boy and girl, together. Magic. Special."

"Twins are not magic. I'm a twin. I think it's mostly genetic."

"Genes...or blood. Special."

My lips parted. "Maybe."

He smiled, sliding his fingertips across my cheek as he dropped his hand from my face.

"Special, Leelee. You killed this...bitch doctor woman?"

"Gavin did. I was dead. Or dying. The Babke saved me, Aven."

"Hmm." He grabbed the flat piece of wood holding the fruit. "With demons and Death? She saved...my mother for a little while too. With demons and Death."

He didn't face the Babke, but his scowl told me everything.

He didn't like the medicine woman, and there was anger behind what she'd done to his mother.

"She saved me. I will not take her life. She's the reason I'm still here for my daughter and husband."

Aven grabbed a handful of berries, eating one, and then holding one out to me. He didn't speak. Not after a few seconds of me refusing, and not even minutes later as I kept my back plastered to the wall. It was the Babke that broke the silence.

"Aven, your mother was different. I never wanted—"

"De!"[1]

The vibrations and power of his voice had me jumping and pushing back into the wall even more.

"Do not speak anymore. You killed her. You made her..." He said something in their tribal language, appearing to curse as his head lowered. He was thinking, trying to find the right word to use.

"Crazy?"

My voice was quiet, but his head jerked to me morphing between anger and calm. More, he pushed the berry in my direction, and I finally took it, popping it into my mouth.

"Crazy. Yes. Do they make you crazy too? The demons? Do they...speak to you? Tell you things? Live in...dreams? Is that why you wake, screaming?"

All I could do was slowly turn to the Babke. For as much as she wanted me to kill her, she didn't appear so brave now. Her white dress was over her drawn up knees, and she hugged around her legs as she stared over at us. Her face was stoic, but I could almost feel the anxiety radiating from her.

"My dreams are a result of my trauma. They're from losing my son and not being able to save him." I grabbed another berry as he offered. "The voices. The demons..." My brow creased as I tried to decipher if I truly believed they were real. If any of this was. Certainly there were explanations, but I was losing myself in the ways of this tribe. I truly believed Death was an actual entity instead of a result of dying. My grief was scrambling right and wrong until I wasn't sure which was what. Reality. Illusion. I didn't know what to believe anymore. Was I even here right now? Maybe I died the day my son did and that's why I didn't have Jasmeen, Aamir, or Gavin anymore. Not even Mandy. Maybe this was hell.

"Leelee."

My gaze lifted to Aven. The intensity had me swallowing hard through the tingling of my lips.

"Don't call me that. That was Mandy's nickname for me. *You killed her.* You can call me Layla."

"You're Leelee, now. You can thank her."

My fist clenched, but I pushed back the need to explode. "Fine. Listen, I know you're angry at the Babke, but you're going to have to put that behind you, Aven. I won't kill her. If you want your gift, you're going to have to choose someone else. I will do that, but then I want us to be at peace. We don't have to be enemies. You can let me go home. We'll forget any of this ever happened. I'll stay on my side of the island, and you can stay on yours."

"This *is* your home now."

"No." My head shook as I forced myself to sit a little taller. "I live on the other side of the island with my husband. That is my home."

"No. You're Leelee now. This," he said, gesturing around him, "is your home."

"Here? With you?"

His hand came to his chest. "I am King." His finger came to settle on the skin just above the hem of my dress, easing into my sternum. "Queen."

"*Babke.*"

My voice cracked, and for the life of me, I couldn't turn away from Aven's dark eyes. Fear. It was beating out every other emotion as I took in the determination on his face. This king wasn't going to accept anything I told him. Gavin wasn't a concern. My children, my daughter, weren't even a deterrent. If anything, the knowledge only fed this odd sudden need for him to try to force me into being his queen.

"Babke." My repeated calls didn't go answered. The words that left her were...hollow...distant. It helped me break Aven's stare.

"Hair like the sand. Eyes like the sea. Death is near." The Babke choked on the last of her words as her legs drew down and she rose to her knees. "Trouble nears with the rising sun. It builds and grows." Her hand outstretched, and I knew what she saw, we couldn't see. "Strangers. One? More? I...I don't know. Close. He's...close. One day, Layla. The paths. One day."

"Strangers?"

She didn't answer as Aven spoke harshly in their language. Still, she stayed in a daze, reaching forward and moving her hand blindly through her vision. I didn't care. I focused on putting distance between me and the king. My hands went back, and I lifted my bottom, sliding my weight to the side.

"Zu bak.[2] Lie. You lie."

"No."

"*You lie.*" The king's palm clamped to the back of my neck, gripping hard and stopping me. "She lies," he said, turning to face me. "Zu bak. Remember that, Leelee. You learn my language too. Bak. Lie."

"The Babke wouldn't lie about strangers coming." My head shook in his hold, recalling mine and Luke's conversation. "The new Main Master in the fortress...I talked to him the other day. He said they're watching a boat. A big boat. Someone is out there. Aven..." I glanced to the door, returning my gaze to his. "I think they're back. They're going to try to finish killing me. I came here to hide, but they must know I'm alive." I gripped his forearm, projecting terror I barely felt. "There could be a lot of them. What do we do?"

"Hide? Here?"

"You never listen," the Babke rushed in. "I told you she was in danger. That we had to help her. You dismissed me. You wouldn't hear my reasons. *They've come to kill her.*" The Babke stood on shaky legs, holding to the wall as she reached for me with her free hand. "Layla has to leave. She has to go. I must take her to safety. She needs to hide in the tunnels while Death decides a path."

"Death will favor my Leelee."

"We don't know that," the Babke said, shaking her head. "Death wants her just as much as he wants to work through her. You've seen Layla's power. He has not chosen which he wants more."

Aven stood, looking between us. Seconds passed. A minute. "Strangers?"

"Maybe many."

"If you lie…"

"I don't," the Babke said breathlessly. "Someone is here. He…is here. I think he comes with others."

His former anger vanished into suspicion as he headed for the door. The moment he surged out and shut it behind him, the Babke slid something under a small table not far from her and rushed to my side. Orders were being shouted in the king's deep tone, and footsteps came alive, padding against earth as people began to move at a fast pace.

"We don't have much time before Aven returns. Today, I will die. You—"

"I told you, I won't—"

"*Not by you.* It's too late. My fate is sealed. Listen to me. What I speak is the truth. I *will* die before the sun sets. Time will become long for you. Each hour may be worse than the last. You will beg to join me. You can't. Just hold on—"

A growl roared from Aven as he burst back through the door.

"They search. Wall! I told you…not to move."

"Aven." I reached for him, trying to get his attention off the Babke. "You could take me to the tunnels. You could protect me until Death has decided."

"I know the answer. Death will protect you. With you as my Leelee...he protects us all."

"It doesn't work like that."

"It will."

Aven turned to the Babke, speaking their language in a jumble of words. I tried studying her expressions, but she showed me nothing. The older woman remained stiff. Still. Her face held no emotion at all.

"You saw the strangers. The tribe is waiting. Go show them where they are. This...man...the one with fair hair...of the sand." Aven's glare only narrowed. "He comes here. He dies first. No one is taking the Leelee. She stays with me, and we will feast on him for...thinking to hurt her."

My mouth opened to argue, to try to keep the Babke with me, but she didn't hesitate. She was gone before I could so much as say goodbye. The sudden emphasis of her words made it hard to breathe. If she was right, I'd never see her again. I wouldn't get to say thank you or tell her I was sorry for everything I'd done. I'd been wrong about her. I'd been...mean and angry...

Fingers swept over my tears causing me to rear my head back. I was still staring at the door, stuck in a truth I couldn't bear to face. I'd lose another person close to me. She'd be gone from me forever.

"Bring her back." My ankle caught as I tried to scoot closer to the door. Metal clinked, feeding anxieties that were growing without the Babke's presence. "Aven, please, bring her back. I need her. I need her with me."

"She's a traitor. Evil."

"*No.*" My head shook. "She's not. Please, bring her back. I'll go. I'll go look and work with Death to kill these men. Just keep the Babke here to be safe. She can't die. *I need her.*"

"You're the Leelee. You have the tribe. You have me. You don't need anyone else."

"Aven."

Large hands cupped my cheeks, and his fingers pushed into my hair as he held me almost crushingly. I tried to pull back but couldn't.

"We start the ceremony at dawn. Without her."

I jerked hard. "Bring her back. Don't do this."

"My mind is…set."

"Unset it. Change your mind."

"*That woman.*" He stopped, speaking in his language deep and fast. "She kills," he said, changing back to English. "She is not for this tribe."

"She is for me. Am I not queen? *You said.* You won't let it go. Do I get no decision? Is that how you rule your tribe? If so, what's the point of even having a queen?"

His stare bore into mine, searching my depths. What the hell was I saying? Desperation was ruling me. I could feel myself pulling against his secure hold as I battled how far I should go to save the Babke's life. Could I, or was I prolonging the inevitable?

"You're…influenced. You have the demons. They beg for her. I will not give in. She is not good." He paused, weighing his words. "You hear them. What do they say to you?"

I tore my gaze away. "Bring her back, and I will tell you."

"No. You will tell me now."

"I will not."

His fingers drew in, pulling and squeezing my hair. Strands came loose through the force and burning raced over my scalp until I was crying out. He didn't stop. He had my head trapped in his grip, exposing my neck as he leaned in, raking his teeth over my skin. I swung, pounding my fists into his sides, but he only squeezed and bit into my neck harder until I was screaming and clawing down his back. It didn't seem to faze him. Over and over, I dug into his skin, and he took it. Even making small sounds of pleasure as he endured my pain.

"What do they tell you, Leelee?"

"They w-want me to die. To kill myself. They say I'm weak." A sob tore from me. "*I am not weak*," I said, hitting him again.

"No." He lifted my head, jerking my face in until we were only an inch apart. "You are not."

"Then you have to know if you go any further, I will kill you. I love my husband. I belong to him. I am his queen, not yours. You know what you're doing is unacceptable. It's kidnapping. Forced. This is wrong. It's illegal."

"Like your island? Like your husband?" Aven bared his teeth at the end. "Do you think I don't know what he does? *What his men do?* Wrong? Maybe. Forced?" He shrugged. "Only at first. We all learn to...obey."

# CHAPTER 27

## THE DRAGON

*A* lot had triggered me since I left Red Island. Lui. Willard. Myself. Rage. Sadness. Guilt. I'd emotionally been all over the place. Nothing could have prepared me for the rollercoaster of emotions I felt when I stepped on that plane. I couldn't believe it as my head went back and forth. I tried to hold in conflicting sensations that left me wanting to do everything from explode to cave in on myself.

"What the hell are you all doing here?"

Aamir glanced at Bram, who was on the phone, not hesitating to come up and throw his arms around me.

"We knew you wouldn't come if we told you. It's my fault. I begged him."

My hand fisted Aamir's shirt between his shoulder blades, holding him to me as I put my mouth next to his ear, growling through my whisper. "You're supposed to be keeping Jasmeen safe."

"With Everleigh, she's the safest baby in the world. Besides, I'm not raising my niece without her father. You need me. I don't care what you say."

"Dammit, Aamir." I pulled back, acknowledging Bram's

gesture that he'd be another minute. I nodded, taking us to the far side of the plane, away from everyone as I lowered my voice even more to Aamir. "This is dangerous. You could die. I can't be responsible for that. I can't...I won't do that to Layla. I've already—"

"Don't you fucking say it," he breathed out, quietly.

"It doesn't matter how you want to look at it, Aamir. We both know this is my fault."

"Your fault? *My fault.*" A shuddering breath left him as he searched my eyes. "God...I'm fucking sorry. I...I saw her. She shot up Jamison with something, Gavin. He was starting to cry, and I thought she was trying to help. I watched her kill my nephew, and I did nothing. *Nothing.* I can't unsee it. I can't try to believe it was anything other than what it was. I can't...the dreams. Fucking nightmares. I'm so sick over this. It's my fault just as much as it is yours. Do you think Layla is going to blame either of us? We didn't know. I swear I didn't know. My sister." He stopped, wiping his eyes. Only then did I realize I was still holding onto his shirt. Clinging to it so that I wouldn't spiral into a hell I wouldn't be able to climb out of. Shot. Shot. He'd never said that before. I hadn't known. Now that I did, *I couldn't breathe.*

"Gavin, let's sit down. You're pale. Have you eaten anything? Slept at all?"

"Probably no better than you. I'm fine. Give me a minute." My legs were weak. I looked to Bram again, running from the mental images that I knew would haunt me. Images courtesy of the man who lived it. Shot? I wanted to vomit. To be sick and collapse. "Bram's off the phone. We'll talk more about this later. It's not the time." I headed to Bram, despite eyeing the white leather sofa Aamir had mentioned. Truth was, I couldn't remember sleeping more than an hour or so at a time. Food had no taste. Liquor did, but I couldn't stay drunk if I wanted to stay alive.

"I can't believe you came."

"*No?*"

I shrugged, not able to answer. "How much longer?" I pointed to the cane he held, watching him lift it from the ground.

"I can go without it, but I've sort of grown an attachment."

With a twist of his hand, the top came free, revealing a sharp blade hidden inside. I smiled, nodding.

"Very smart and convenient."

"It really is. Gavin." Bram's eyes went to Aamir, who was now sitting on the sofa, looking down at his phone. "He thinks he's the reason we're here. You know me better than that. We need to talk."

"About Redmond."

Bram nodded, taking his seat in a matching recliner as a voice came over the speaker. I didn't hesitate to follow in the other. Soldiers and guards shuffled around the large jet, finding their place, but steering clear of me and Bram.

"This party. I've learned it's not just any party; it's a celebration. It goes beyond the child they intend to prepare. They're donning a new leader. A new Main Master."

"A new one? For which location?"

Bram leaned in, lowering his voice, but keeping his eyes on me.

"Mine." His fingers drew in once. Twice. He was worried. "I think I made a horrible mistake. They chose him. Elec, my cousin. I told them to, but I wasn't sure they would. He's going to be heading up their new location, wherever the hell that'll be."

My lips parted as I took in the information. I'd never gotten an invite, and those things came out months in advance. There were preparations that had to be made. Arrangements that needed to be dealt with. All the Main Masters were technically invited, even if they chose not to attend...but not me. Not this time. What did that say? What did that mean?

"I see I was right. You had no idea."

"No."

"It seems you're not the only one."

"Who else wasn't invited?"

A smile tugged at Bram's lips.

"Someone you want."

"Kaun? From China?"

A short shake came from Bram.

"He won't come to London. You won't need him anyway. He's not a part of this. That was all Austin Birch, whom, from what I hear, is taking money under the table from Redmond. But…Ramiro. I got word hours ago, he's on his way from Chile, and he is beyond pissed off that they left him out. Like you, he's suspicious. Especially after what he did to you. You can say guilt is driving him right to the source of all of this."

My stare lowered as I weeded through the new information. "Redmond is behind Layla?" A pause from Bram had me taking in his troubled expression.

"Redmond. Maybe who rules him. Maybe his entire circle. Possibly higher than that. You helped me, Gavin. No one else would have. You saved my life when I was meant to die. They wanted Whitlock to fall. They have now for some time, but they couldn't be the ones responsible for it. Not directly. That goes against policy and vows. But if it were to fall from other means, it's fair game. How else would they get a better grip on the machine? With me gone, they'd have more control, and you interfered with that. You chose a side, and it wasn't theirs. For that, I'm sorry."

I couldn't address what Bram was saying. I couldn't even make sense of the words. Only one thing came to mind, and that was this cousin. He'd be the replacement. He'd be part of this machine. Elec would have power. More than most of us. He was a direct link to the source. Maybe even to the Collective High Council, themselves. "Tell me more about your cousin. How is he part of this machine?"

"Elec...he's...always been part of them, I guess. I just never realized how much until recently. I've always overlooked him because of his nature. He never appeared a threat. We got along fine. He was quiet, courteous, respectful...fuck, he was perfectly out of sight, out of mind. That's exactly what they wanted. What *he* wanted. I never knew him at all. Not that I would even though we were family. We didn't grow up close. The Wexlers were in deep with the other elites. My dad didn't play their games and hated my uncle. The only reason I was allowed to be around Jerry at all was because he was my mother's brother. Jerry was always squandering money. He had a huge gambling addiction. No one liked him; not even Elec."

"Anyway," Bram said, continuing. "As we got older, my cousin and I ran in different circles. I was a Whitlock. *Popular.* Powerful. A God in the outside world. He wasn't. Elec ran more with the...intellectual crowds. The times we were in the same room, he was like a friend to everyone. He blended in with every group he mingled with. I keep thinking back. Elec was so nice. He laughed at the right moments. He showed concern when he needed to. He was a fucking chameleon. Maybe the best damn one I've ever seen. Always there, yet not. Always saying the right things. Always getting you to talk but never doing much of that, himself. The guy studied different types of psychology in college. I even think neuropsychology was what he had aimed to get his doctorate in. But I remember a rumor that was whispered to my mom. Before Elec could finish, he got in trouble for something. It wasn't normal." Bram paused. "I got the impression from what I heard that it was...mad scientist type shit. It was odd, but with what I was raised around in Whitlock, I didn't give it much thought. Truthfully, I figured he'd just end up over there with the rest of us. The next thing I had heard was he'd quit school and started working for the government, doing something psychology related. But what, I don't know. I just figured he was analyzing bad people. I never thought maybe he was one of them. Not all psychology is good. It goes deeper than that. Darker and more...manipulative. I never gave it a second thought until he showed up with Gabriella after my attack. Even then, I never imagined he was in with them so deep..."

The plane took off and Bram sighed, still appearing perplexed. "I called Elec a few weeks back to check in on things. I was curious how it was going and whether they were going to choose him. The man who answered...I almost didn't recognize him."

"You're sure it was Elec?"

Bram nodded. "Without a doubt. Elec's voice sounded different, but only because he wasn't pretending anymore. He was cold. Detached. He spoke with a voice full of purpose and power. *He sounded like the old me.* I knew immediately who he'd become. My cousin was the new Main Master, and he had such hatred towards me. I've never heard Elec talk that way to anyone, but I wasn't just anyone to him. I'm his enemy now." Blue eyes turned dark. "He thanked me for being weak and caving to love. The way he said it...*weak, love.* There was such disdain. The idea of love angers him. It's no secret in our circle how Elec's girlfriend went missing back in college. A body was found, but it was unidentifiable. Some say my uncle killed her to get her out of Elec's future. She would have gotten in the way of their plans. There's even whispers Elec killed her, himself. Given his change in personality towards me, maybe he did. I can't help but think, though, if his role as a Main Master was planned, and I believe it was, he'd know what an impossible task he was facing. *What a dangerous path.* If there were any feelings inside of him, he may have planned for this. Vivia may still be alive, and maybe he knows exactly where she is. That could be something to remember. Something to possibly investigate for future collateral."

My fingers came to press against my lips.

"If she is alive, and he loves her, he won't be hiding her here.

Not above ground. He'll have her. No one will know he does, but he'll keep her close in a place where no one can see. After all, if there's no proof, there's no truth, only speculation. You can't hurt what you can't find. What doesn't exist." My brow drew in. "If he knew this was his path before she supposedly died, he's already won. He's made sure of it."

"But that's a big if," Bram said, shaking his head through his thoughts. "We're talking years. God...ten years now? Fifteen? There's no way. Maybe it wasn't him and she is dead. All I know is Elec just turned into one of the most powerful men in the circle. Hell, in the world. If you're going to try to negotiate anything, Gavin, it has to be with him. Kill Redmond. I don't care. If you go after Elec, you're dead. He's too well protected. Don't even try. It accomplishes nothing. Play his game. Learn what you can. Do *not* speak of love. Speak of property. Of rights. Of ownership. These will be terms he's comfortable with. With love, you lose. Connect to him as the leader you are. Make peace. State what you want. The man prides his position, and he'll respect you even more if you take that approach. It's probably all he's ever wanted. Use that, but tread carefully. Elec is one of the smartest men I've ever known. If you slip up, the game is over. There's no coming back from that."

# CHAPTER 28

## LUKE

*P*icture after picture I scanned my phone, shaking my head through the mystery of such luxury and grandeur. This wasn't just any super yacht. This one was even nicer than the Whitlocks, which I thought was impossible. Thing was…it was sitting in the middle of the ocean, abandoned. Someone had been on it, but it wasn't the owner. The yacht didn't have one. According to the registration, the yacht had never been purchased by anyone and was currently supposed to be in Miami, for sale.

"You're sure you want to leave it out there?"

"Tillin."

My voice was clipped as I continued to scroll through the pictures the men had sent.

"Sir…have you seen that thing?"

"I'm looking at it as we speak. The answer is not just no. It's hell no. Someone may come back for that boat. We're not giving them a green light to come here. Fucking trojan horse shit. Nope. If anything, we should have the men drive it even further away." I nodded. "That's exactly what we're going to do. Tell them to take it a day's drive out and torch it."

"What!" Tillin's eyes flared. "You want them to burn it?"

"Do you want to risk someone leaving behind prints if it was stolen? Take it further out and light the bastard on fire. I'm done worrying about this fucking thing. I have more pressing matters than an abandoned spy boat. How about who the hell was on it? Do we have anything on that? No. We don't, but we need to."

Tillin let out a huffing sound as I waved him out of Gavin's large office I had taken over. I continued pacing, but I didn't put down my phone. I hit Layla's number for the millionth time. It barely started to ring when Tillin barreled back into the office with the phone at his ear.

"Sir. *Sir.*"

"What is it?" I hung up, taking in the alarm on his face.

"Jones is on the phone. He says he just saw a large group of tribal men and women headed north. They're on our side again, and from what he says, they're armed more than usual. They're acting strange." He paused. "The Babke is with them."

"*What?*" I headed to the laptop. "What the hell are they up to now? She mentioned a ceremony. Maybe..." My head shook as I dismissed it. That couldn't be right. She made it sound like the ceremony was happening within the community, there amongst their huts. Not out by the beach. And Layla, was she with them?

I clicked through the cameras, shuffling through as fast as I could. Trees. Beach. Luxury bungalows. Beach. Walkway between the trees and beach. I jerked to a stop, focusing on the crowd that came onto the screen, not feet away. I quickly scanned the men and women. The Babke was easy to spot with her wild, white hair. As I took in the crowd around her, my stomach twisted with an odd sense of warning. Layla wasn't amongst them. Neither was Mandy. *Neither was the king.*

"Something is off. Tell the men to steer clear for now. I want to see what they're doing."

Tillin relayed the message as I projected the feed onto a number of larger screens mounting the wall.

"What...*the hell* are they doing? Why are they all carrying rocks? Are they fishing? Don't they use spears?"

The phone came down as Tillin moved in closer. The tribe was scanning the tall grass lining the dunes. Some were even crouching down to disappear and move within it.

"They're looking for something. Maybe somebody. Do we have soldiers out there?"

I glanced to Tillin, who was bringing back up his phone.

"Jones, do we have any soldiers out towards the dunes on the north end?"

"Right." Tillin shook his head, lowering his phone as he disconnected. "Not that we know of. They're not after any of us. At least not actively. They may be making sure they're alone. It's hard to say. I've been here ten years, and I've never seen them act this way."

Lifting my cell, I hit Layla's number, even if I knew she wasn't going to answer. Ring after ring went by, and I cursed like I did every time I called.

"I can't fucking stand this. Something is not right. I should send them back to their end of the island. I would if I wasn't so damn intrigued by what the hell they're looking for. The Babke. She sees things...If they're looking for something, perhaps it's something related to one of her visions."

"Do we really want to know what it is? How does that pertain to us?"

My eyes cut over.

"Did you forget me mentioning her importance? What she has is irreplaceable. Maybe it has something to do with that. I don't know. That's why we're going to watch."

Silence filled the room as we took in the tribe. The Babke wasn't standing but maybe twenty feet from the camera. She'd come to a standstill, staring towards the water as the other members swarmed the area. White hair blew back from her wrinkled, tanned face, and her hands were palm up, facing towards the sea. It appeared her eyes were closed, but I couldn't really tell from the angle.

"That woman gives me the creeps."

I ignored Tillin, taking in the mysterious way her dress shifted as it blew back. Watching her was almost hypnotizing. I hadn't known the woman well, but I liked her. Or had until she'd become just as stubborn as Layla.

"What's the movement back there?"

Zooming in, I tried to grasp the blurring further off in the thicker section of trees. Had it not been for the odd expression of a woman standing up from the grass, I might have tried to keep viewing the colors. The way she moved like a predator, I panned back out, seeing it wasn't just her who's body language was changing. The tribe was heading back to the Babke. They weren't speaking, just...moving. Sleek. Slow. Watchful.

"Uh...Main Master."

My hand lifted as they neared the Babke. With as still as the witch woman was, I couldn't begin to figure out what the hell they were doing? Was she saying something I couldn't hear? It didn't look like her mouth was moving. Her palms were still out, facing the water. Her eyes appeared closed. Wind was whipping her white dress around a little more forcefully now. White hair blew back, lifting from her head with the constant gusts.

"I don't like this."

Tillin was shifting on his feet. The sensation was one I couldn't begin to describe. The hair stood up on my arms, and I knew a threat when I saw one. My eyes zeroed in on the rocks they held. Of the painted images on them in deep earthy shades. Faster my pulse raced as they got closer to her.

"Call the men. Get them out there right now."

Tillin shuffled as he began to pace, but I couldn't turn around to see him. My heart was in my throat as a man reared back, slamming the side of the thick rock into the side of the Babke's head. The force sent the older woman flying to the side. A dark red blurred with white as she hit the ground. The tribe rushed in, starting to strike her as well. Tillin was speaking. Even yelling at some point, but I couldn't stop clutching my phone. Shock kept me frozen as blood sprayed back thickly out from the strikes. It painted the faces of the tribe. It stained their hands and forearms as I caught glimpses of the Babke's sunken in face. Her nose, mouth, and eyes were nothing more than a mushy crater. White specks of bone and teeth were scattered at the repeated blows, and the tribe wasn't stopping.

*"Oh my God.* Fuck."

Tillin made it to my side, but I could barely see him in my peripheral as metal flashed.

"They're too late. Call the soldiers off. We have a worse problem now. Tell them all to meet me in front of the fortress. All of them. Every single one."

"They're cutting her apart. They're…going to eat her. They're—"

*"Call.* I want them lined up in front of the fucking fortress *now."*

At my order, Tillin didn't just call. He rushed from the room. I couldn't tear my gaze away as I brought up my cell.

"Come on, Layla. Answer the fucking phone." Nausea sent me pacing. "Come on. Come. On!" Ring after ring…nothing. "Jesus. Jesus, fuck. Fuck."

Sweat coated my skin, soaking into my shirt as I walked the room back and forth. I pulled off the jacket, jerking the tie free. They were in trouble. They'd been in trouble the entire time, and the Babke hadn't told me. Hours. Hours upon hours. But not more than a day. I'd talked to Layla maybe twenty-four hours before to send her the pictures of Jasmeen. Maybe she was okay. Maybe—

My mind wouldn't go there. It couldn't. Why hadn't the Babke said something? Why hadn't I just gone and got Layla when I felt something was off?

Five different people were sawing through the Babke's limbs. Her insides were tossed to the side, still slightly hanging from her stomach. My eyes closed, and I focused on my breaths, slowing them through the reeling what-ifs. When I opened my lids, they were gone. All of it. All of the Babke, except for her blood and entrails...gone.

I didn't go through the cameras to follow them. I shoved the phone in my pocket, surging from the office and heading down the stairs as fast as I could. When the guards saw me rushing towards them, they quickly opened the doors. What I was met with on the front lawn of the fortress was men for as far as I could see, and more were lining up.

For what...? Even now, I couldn't tell them Layla was alive. Not all of them. I had to think of a plan. A mission that would get them in without getting them or Layla killed.

"Anyone here special forces?" My hand shot up. "And don't fucking bullshit me either. I need the best. There is no room for error."

Jones was already pushing through the crowd. Tillin was headed through with two other men, but I was too busy scanning everyone around. I lifted both hands, raising my voice so that they could hear me.

"From here on out, we're on high alert. There is something going on with the tribe. They are not stable, and they are not to be trusted. I want the perimeter of our land to be protected at all times. You're to stay in groups of three. Everyone sees everyone. We keep our eyes on each other. Camp out fifty feet apart. You make a line, and you keep it. No one from that tribe is to make their way through. We have enough soldiers to pull twelve-hour shifts. Maybe this will last a few days. Maybe less. We're taking it a day at a time until I say otherwise. Got it?"

The loud acknowledgment had me nodding as I headed for Tillin. He was speaking to a group of at least twenty-to-thirty men. It was too many for what I needed, but then again...this wasn't going to be an easy task. We might have to send more than one team. The first could completely fail. They may all die if what I heard was true.

"No one likes this tribe, and we all know why." I stopped in front of them, watching as their intense eyes locked on me. "These people are deadly. They're hard to read. They're damn dangerous. Tillin and I just watched them murder the Babke. You've all been here a lot longer than me, so you know how bad this is. The woman was the only thing keeping that tribe in line. Without her rule, there's no telling what's going to happen. It appears they have a new king. This king is responsible for smashing the camera on the north end of the island. Hear me when I say he had no hesitation displaying his hate for us through that lens."

I paused as something tried to click. Something. Something. My head shook as the thought refused to come. "You're probably wondering why I want you here. Although I've been working with the Babke due to my brother's request, I'm not sending you in to that tribe for revenge against what they've done. Truth is… the Babke was protecting something for your real Main Master. She was guarding it to keep it safe. With her dead, that's now in harm's way. This king…." I stopped. "This…king…"

*She grows into her fate by the hour. She is strong. Ceremony. Queen of the island. Queen. King.*

My mouth opened. My hand lifted. Nothing would come. No words. No air. I looked at the men, seeing their face transition as they took in my shock. My fear. Surely, I was wrong. The Babke would have said something. She would have put a stop to it. Warned me. She…Three days. Ceremony. Three days.

"Gun up. *Fast.* We don't have much time."

# CHAPTER 29

## LAYLA

There was a deepness in the loud cry. A heaviness that surpassed the grief and heartbreak I'd had when I lost Mandy. I knew I was screaming. Crying. Yet all my mind could process as I took in the Babke's dismembered body hanging from the tribesmens' hold was the sound of my voice. I couldn't break my stare from her hollow, disfigured face. I couldn't even control my body as I thrashed against Aven's hold. Where I was trying to go, I didn't know. Where I was going to now that he'd taken off the metal shackle, I had no idea. My stare was locked on the mix of dark meat and jagged edges of protruding bone. I was gagging between calls. And yes…I called to the woman who'd saved my life. Calling and screaming and reaching for a body that was broken and unrecognizable. She was all I had left at this tribe. Now I was here, alone…*with him.*

"I knew it was lies. Good. Make. We eat. No more demons."

Aven's language quickly changed over to his own. It came out in fast, demanding sentences, but I barely heard them. My mind was getting fuzzy, and I was spinning. The brown colors of the walls and floors were blurring together, and I was beginning to move too. I was still reaching for her. Still…making sounds.

But my cries weren't human. They were something entirely different as I felt my knees weaken.

"Hasta te hul. [1]The demons are dying. That is what you are feeling, Leelee."

Feeling. It took a moment for Aven's words to sink in. He was holding me up, and gripping tightly to keep me back, but the only mistake was holding to me at all. My grief turned to fury as I faced him, swinging my fist into his cheek with everything I had. My hits were fast, coming one after another as he blocked the blows, wrestling me to the ground.

"The only demon here is you. *I hate you.* She did nothing wrong, and you killed her."

Tribal language roared as Aven panted and held me pinned. Blood from his nose dripped along my jawline, but all I heard was the sliding against dirt as one of the Babke's body parts drug against the floor. More sobs tore from me, and Aven's weight only increased, becoming brutally crushing as the door closed behind them.

"I told you. We pair well. You are strong. You have a good…hit."

I thrashed, trying to push him more off me.

"Let go of me so I can do it again. Next time I won't stop. I'll keep hitting until your face looks just like hers."

He laughed, wrestling one of my arms to pin between us. The smile stayed as he wiped his nose along my cheek, smearing his blood against my face.

"I like your fire. I hope it's there when they're gone. You will be free soon."

"The demons can stay if it means I'm rid of you."

Aven didn't respond. Another drip of blood splashed my neck, and he didn't even seem to notice as he kept his stare pinned to my mouth. The longer we were together, the more he kept doing that.

"Get off me."

I tried to buck my hips, but it only had him forcing his way between my thighs.

"Women..." Again his eyes locked on my lips. "They don't fight. They...want me. Throw themselves at me. Too easy. You. You don't want me, but I want you. Do you think, Leelee... maybe I can make you want me?"

My glare intensified.

"Never."

"No?"

"*You're a murderer.* You're arrogant. You're vile. You've killed two people who meant something to me. Let's not forget about the part where I love my husband."

"Hmm." Aven shifted, wrestling me even more as he adjusted his hard cock to rest on my stomach. For the loose pants he wore, they didn't do a good job of concealing or restraining anything. "How long from birth?"

"What?"

"Do you still bleed?"

I didn't speak. I fought harder. I used all my strength as I tried to find a way out from beneath him.

"Tell me, Leelee. Answer or I find out, myself. Not that it matters. Your body is ready. Even now. Do you think our babies will be special? Will there be two?"

"I'll kill you. Help!" My tone was different from before. I knew this scream. Desperation didn't sound like horror. "Get. Off!"

"The more you fight, the more I want. *I saw you.* Before. On your...place up high." Aven kept his focus on me as I grew still. "You like it up there. High. In the breeze. Watching the colors as night comes. The water. Do you want that back? Your place?"

"The balcony? What do you mean?"

"When this island is mine again...like it should be...I can give you that. We can go there. Live there. I deserve that...as mine. Leelee, you looked beautiful up there. Here." He paused.

"Closer, you're more beautiful. We can go. Together with the tribe."

No words came as I tried to calm the urge to scream and fight. This man...how long had he been planning this? How long had he been waiting for the right moment? That didn't matter. What did was that he had it. It'd been given to him in a collage of tragedies on my side. Somehow, our lives, our fate, had been intertwined, and it didn't feel real. The odds were unthinkable.

"How long have you watched me?"

"Many moons."

"Then you knew about Gavin. You knew I was pregnant. You had to have seen us together up there almost every night. And Aamir. You...*knew*."

"I hated, like you right now. I didn't want you here. I—"

"But you knew. You watched."

"Not every night. My view...it isn't like yours so high like a king's should be. Mine..." His hand settled to my chest, fitting between my breasts. At my thrash, he kept still, not moving but splaying his fingers out over my skin. "Trees aren't that high. But I could see this. From here, up. Beautiful, but not more than now."

"Enough. You're speaking from envy. Jealousy. I want to go."

"We're going, Leelee. Underneath, to prepare."

He stood, pulling me up with him. When he slid the low bed over, exposing a dark hole, I felt myself tug against his hold.

"Prepare for what? I'm not going down there."

He jerked harder, but I put my weight behind my own pull, breaking free and nearly falling as I raced for the door. Just as I went to reach for it, he swooped his arms around me, picking me up from behind as I kicked and tried to claw back against him. Aven's steps were fast, but he couldn't quite get a good enough grip as I twisted and thrashed. We hit the ground again, and I clawed into the earth, feeling one of my nails break as he grabbed my leg, sliding me back to him.

Large hands gripped and held, but I was drifting from my actions, detecting things that shouldn't have mattered. People were talking. A baby was crying again. Animals. Wild dogs? They were yelping. Barking. I could smell the scent of smoke changing as I realized the women were cooking again. *Cooking the Babke.* My nails were clawing into Aven as he spun and positioned himself on top of me, but I wasn't in my body. I was merely observing a woman I didn't recognize fighting for her basic freedoms. Freedoms that should have never been taken to begin with. Not here. Not on the boat that brought me to Red Island. My world was spinning as Aven forced up my dress. And time…it stopped.

My head rolled to the side, and the tears that escaped burned my skin like fire as they left. For such a small thing, my soul felt the path the wetness made as it escaped me. My arms were heavy. My legs barely moved. I was falling even though my stare was fixated on the lower level of a table not feet away. I could feel my body jerking through Aven's pull to my clothes, but I couldn't respond to the violation.

*"Look at her fall. Look at her fly."*

*"Fly. Fly."*

Cackles. Snickers and laughter.

*"I'm going to push her."*

*"Yes! Push her. Push. Her!"*

*"Die. Die!"*

"Die," I repeated, mumbling through the word. "Fly."

*"Such a baby. Look at her cry."*

*"Baby. Baby. She knows nothing."*

"Die…Push."

Aven paused from sucking on my neck, but I could barely notice as the voices took back over, holding me hostage. Keeping me so far away from where I didn't want to be.

*"Fall. Jump! She's right there."*

*"Push her!"*

"Die," I kept mouthing. *Die.* Yes. There was something I was missing. *Die.* Something I needed to do. *Fly.*

"Look at me, Leelee." Aven's palm slid against my cheek, bringing my stare up to his. "They'll die soon. You hear them now?"

Pressure against my lips had me trying to turn my head back to the table, but my brain wouldn't settle on what I was meant to know. Something. Something.

"See me, Leelee. Look at me."

Lips crushed into mine again and the bruising pressure had my arms shooting back up to press against his shoulders.

*"Fall! Fly!"*

"Stop. *Aven, stop.*"

"I'll make them stop."

"You, stop. I said no. You can't do this; not even as king. Your title does not give you that right."

He growled, lifting his head.

"Says who? I am king. You are my queen."

I didn't argue. I blinked through memories that blinded me. The Babke. She...

Aven lowered slower this time, moving his hand to settle on my thigh. My entire body flinched, but my face turned, going back to the table.

*"Fly. Die."*

Die. Die. Die. I blinked through seeing the Babke rush towards me as Aven left. She'd...slid something under that table. She'd...

I turned my upper body only to be returned to my back as Aven moved up to grip my hip.

"You could like this, Leelee. I can make you like it."

"I won't. I love my husband. I'm married. I'm taken."

"No. That Layla died. You said so yourself. The Babke brought you back. You're new. This you belongs to me."

My legs drew up, and I braced my heel on Aven's thigh, using my strength to slide myself more towards the table. My hand shot out, but my fingertips barely reached under the shelf before I was jerked back underneath him.

"It's okay that you fight. I bet you fought him too."

"My fight will not end for you."

"We'll see."

I grunted as he buried his fingers in my hair, roughly. More, I tried to find a way free, but Aven was all over me, holding me pinned under his body even further away from the table. He had every part of me restrained, and any hope I had ended as he let his weight settle even more.

Heavily, I breathed, tears of frustration threatening as my mind raced. Aven was back to rubbing his face against the side of mine. Moving his body erotically to add friction between my legs. My nails embedded in his side, hooking in, making him hiss.

"I will tear you apart if you don't stop. I'm warning you only because it's not too late for you to call this off."

"Zu bak, Leelee."

"I don't lie."

Aven lifted, smiling and capturing my mouth. My hair tore at my jerk, and I cried out as his fingers twisted even more agonizingly in the length.

"You learn."

Knocking had Aven's face lifting, but he didn't move. He called out angrily as a woman yelled through the door. Sentence after sentence, they went back and forth until finally Aven's expression changed, and he jumped to his feet, pulling me with him. I could barely get my footing as he dragged me to the door. Dirt was caked all over my back and arms, even falling from my hair with every step. When the door flew open, Jahee froze, looking between us.

"What?"

"Our language."

"No. My Leelee has a right to understand. I taught you. *Speak.*"

Again, her eyes came to me, dropping and taking in my appearance before she turned back to Aven.

"I don't like." She stood taller. "Not our ways." She glanced at me. "Not our tribe. I can't approve…of ceremony. She doesn't want it."

"Thank you," I rushed out. "I don't want this. I—" A cry left me as Aven squeezed me more into his side. "I want to go home. Find Luke, the Main Master. Plea—"

"We do not need your…approval, and I don't need hers. Everyone heard. She gave herself to me. She can't take it back."

"That's not what I meant. Jahee, please."

"Enough," Aven's voice rumbled, and the threat wasn't missed. "What of our meal? My Leelee needs to eat. I want the demons out of her."

"Cooking." Jahee lowered her gaze. "The Babke said it was…impossible. Demons don't leave. Ever."

"They'll leave *her.* My Leelee is strong. Death chooses her. Protects all of us. She has magic babies. Two in one birth. She will give me magic babies too. They will rule us. They will be…*unstoppable.*" Aven turned me into his body, hugging me tightly as I stabbed my nails into his back, ripping down his flesh. The tribal curse that left him vibrated my body, but he didn't let me go as he pinned me to him tighter. He laughed. "See? Strong. Now leave us. No one returns until it's with my Leelee's food. We're *busy.*"

# CHAPTER 30

## THE DRAGON

"Gavin, you're not paying attention. We're almost there. This is important. Repeat it back to me."

I met Bram's blue eyes, letting out a breath as I glanced to Aamir and then Lopez. My head went down only temporarily as I groaned and leaned back in my seat.

"Knightsbridge, near Hyde Park. I heard you. I know where Redmond's going to be. I've looked into him before. It was years back, before Layla, but when you said the address, it's the same. I've visited the area. I know exactly where I'm going."

Bram's brows drew in. "What do you mean, it's the same? It's the location of the party. It's not one of his private residences. It's not even near one of his companies. The flat is on its own floor and belongs to Harvey Loran, of Loran Industries. How would you have the same address from years ago? That doesn't make sense."

A smile began to appear on my face, disappearing just as fast. I tried pushing my worry over Layla away, but it was nearly impossible.

"Harvey Loran is just the newest dupe on Redmond's list. The flat is only Harvey's on paper. It's merely a safeguard to supply a paper trail. If you go back a few decades, you'll see the building belonged to Redmond's father. It would appear the floors got bought out, and still get sold to this day, but it's an illusion. The tenants are real; the purchase is not. Not like how it looks. They're special guests to London's Lair, contracted and leased out for however long they negotiate. Nothing more. Think of it as a guest admittance. A trial offer to see if they're a good fit for permanent residence."

"But it belongs to Redmond? He truly does live there?"

"I'm positive of it. My guess is the underground level. That floor has never been sold. No one would ever think to go there. Plus...it's awfully convenient, wouldn't you say?"

"I'll be damned. You found it." Bram sat up straighter. "You found the entrance to London's Lair."

I shrugged. "Maybe. At least a private one for Redmond, but I can't be for sure where the main one is. It's one thing to speculate. It's another to find the entrance face to face. But...we both know London's underground is full of tunnels and passageways. Not far from the building, there's a large area that's heavily restricted. No one can go down there. That must be where the main entrance is at. It adds up. It's conveniently close for Redmond. He'd have no problems traveling through the tunnels to make it back and forth. It's safer too, which may explain why he chose this location to throw the party. He knows I may come after him. He won't risk not being able to escape."

Bram nodded, keeping his hand at his mouth as he seemed to think.

"I want to look more into this. Gavin, I really think you're onto something. What do you think about maybe waiting until after the party to confront Redmond? Only a few days. His guard will be down by then. I think it gives you the upper hand."

My head shook. "I wish I could, but I can't. I have to get back."

Aamir nodded. "Me too. I'm with him. I want to go home."

"Home? But..." Bram looked between us. "Isn't Luke taking care of things? We want to play this safe. Is there really a rush?"

"There is. I have a super yacht worth more than yours abandoned within sight of the fortress. The tribe on the island is getting unruly. As much as my brother is helping me, I also know Rich, my boss, is probably on edge with me being gone. No one knows, but they will soon if I don't get back to take my place."

Bram wasn't buying it. One look at his arched eyebrow, and I knew he was calling my bullshit.

"You're hiding something from me." He looked to Aamir. "Both of you. You're not telling me something."

"What? We're not hiding anything." Aamir glanced to me but quickly pulled out his phone, pretending to browse through it for something.

"Bram—"

"Gavin, we both know how risky it is, being at the same place at the same time. If I deserve anything it's honesty. I'm trying my best to help you, and I want to do that, but if you're keeping something from me, I need to know what it is."

Lopez met my eyes, and I waved him to go stand with the other men. It wasn't until he joined the crew that I met Bram's questioning stare.

"You're right. You deserve that." A small sound left me, and I shifted in my seat as I searched for the right words. "I want to ask you something. You love Everleigh."

"Of course I do. More than anything."

"If she would have been killed—"

He threw me a threatening look, not even liking that I spoke the words.

"*If*," I said, continuing. "Do I even need to ask if you'd do the same?"

"No. You know I would. It's why I'm here and not with my

wife. I never leave her. You know that, but this…I had to be here for you."

I nodded. "And I appreciate it. I do. This means a lot. What if…" I glanced at Aamir, who's lips pursed at my pause. He wanted Bram to know. He didn't like secrets any more than I did. "What if," I said even quieter, "Everlcigh died but was miraculously brought back, and…lives, but she's hidden where no one would know?"

"*Gavin.*"

My hand raised. "Would it not be imperative to make a mark? One so big that even if the truth got out, you'd become untouchable? Would it not be imperative to do this and return to her side as quickly as possible? Bram, my wife needs me. The way I left her. How bad she was…" I swallowed back the fear. "The danger she may be in right now without me by her side…I have no time to waste."

"I'm starting to see that." He grabbed my shoulder, squeezing as his intense eyes stayed on mine. "We'll get you back as soon as possible. Damn, I haven't heard news this good in a long time. I'm so happy to hear she's okay." His smile was wide, full of a relief I was too afraid to feel. It wasn't safe until I was back on the island. Until I had her protectively in my arms so nothing could ever hurt her again.

"Thanks. I know I can trust you. I just want this over so I can go home. But now that you know, I'm going to need a phone. One from you. Layla has one from Luke, but I can't call it. Can you get me one, or can I use yours? I need to hear her voice so I know she's okay."

"You don't even have to ask. I have an extra in my room. I'll get it and then we can all come together and get the ball rolling on our plan. It's going to have to go flawlessly if we're going to get you back to Red Island in one piece. We don't have much time. Let's not waste another second."

*R*edmond should have been my focus. My anger should have overpowered everything so that I could zero in on my target. I wanted the bastard to pay. To die the most agonizingly horrible death ever known to man. Although I knew he would, he didn't have my attention like that. There was only one person on my mind. One that could assure my safety from here on out. Redmond's death would come. I knew that in my bones. But I needed Elec. I needed him on my side, and being close to Bram, I wasn't sure how I was going to manage that. Bram and I had a lot in common. Love, for one. But where I had love, I had an island. I had slaves. Elec would have his domain as well, and we were both in a business we'd die in. That kept my eyes on the screens as I sat in our newest hotel room, not a mile from our targeted destination. It was just me and my men again. Aamir hadn't been happy about that, but he listened. He was good at that. Besides, he wasn't part of this stage of our plan.

"Are we good?"

Pattinson gave the thumbs up, and White, Fallon, and Lopez followed suit as we went down the line. Nodding, I lifted the phone Bram gave me, knowing they were getting to work as well. We were safe. We were ready.

Ringing filled the line as I dialed the number Luke had given me on the boat for Layla. My heart was racing, and a stir of nausea had me pacing the dim room. Over and over it rang. I called again, but it was the same. My head shook, and I placed the phone down, trying to process what this could mean. Why the hell wasn't she answering? This wasn't like Layla. She'd want to know if I was okay. She'd be glued to the phone in case there was an update on Jasmeen. It didn't make sense. I didn't like it.

I pulled my laptop free of my bag, opening it to bring up the cameras on the island. The inside of my fortress looked bare. Only the random servant rushed from different rooms, which seemed odd. Were they panicked? Worried? My brow creased but I kept going. I looked at my office. Mine and Layla's room. The tower. I clicked the button again. What I saw immediately had my face shooting in closer to the screen. A line. A line of my fucking soldiers. They were in the distance, scattered in groups of three, surrounding my property. My head shook, but I kept going. Clicking. Clicking. Clicking.

The bottle of water I'd had went sliding to the other side of the table where I'd laid the phone. Fallon shot to his feet, and even Lopez was startled by my quick actions.

"Somethings wrong. The soldiers are out. They're holding the line. Lopez, *call Tillin.*"

I was already dialing Luke's number, trying to search him out and find him on the cameras. I couldn't, and he wasn't answering.

"Fuck. Fuck!"

"Sir, he's not answering."

My pulse was hammering into my body with a force strong enough to make me shake.

"Call again. *Call someone else.* Keep calling until someone answers."

And I did the same. I called Luke again, almost hanging up when I heard his breathless voice come over the line.

"It's not a good time, Bram."

"Try again. This is your brother. What the fuck is going on? *Where's my wife,*" I roared.

Hesitation. "Gavin, I'm trying to get her back."

"What do you mean, trying? Where is she?"

"The king had the tribe kill the Babke. They stoned her to death. He's got Layla. He's calling her his queen."

Words wouldn't come, only visions as I tried to recall any dealings I'd had with someone holding that title. It had been years. More years than I could remember. "There is no king. No real king. I mean...not yet. The king is dead. You must mean his son. He's king now?"

"Apparently, and it would seem he's chosen your wife to take as his queen."

My fist drew in as I brought it to my mouth, closing my lids through the engulfing rage.

"Luke..."

"I'm going to get her back, Gavin. I have a team already through tribal lines. They're the best we got. They'll bring Layla home."

"I swear to God if that motherfucker touches or hurts my wife— No. No. *Fuck this.* I'm headed home."

"*You're already there.* Put some trust in me, dammit. I got this. I said I'd bring her home, and I will. You jumping on a plane is not going to allow you to sweep in and save her. Focus on making those bastards pay. I'll do the same here. I have to go."

The line disconnected and I yelled, slamming my fist into the table and watching it break and crash under the power. The fury I felt had no end, and my men knew that as they stood and watched me try to get a handle on my destructive temper.

"Sir...Double M."

Lopez was talking low to someone on the phone as I tried to slow the breaths that left me wanting to go into a rage all over again.

"Give me a minute, Fallon."

What the hell had I been thinking sending Layla to that tribe? First, I put her at risk with the murdering elites of my world, and my solution puts her in danger as well? What the fuck was happening with me?

"Wait," I said, pointing to Lopez. "Are you talking to Tillin?"

"I am, but I have him on mute. He's currently talking to Luke."

"I want to know everything there is about this king. *Everything!*" I stormed to Fallon who was already leaning down, pressing buttons on his computer.

"I have records here somewhere, Sir. I document everything just in case. I know I have it here somewhere."

"It's not the former king, either. I think this is the son of the king. By tradition, they have to find a queen the tribe feels is worthy. Apparently, that queen is *my wife.*"

"She lives?"

Pattinson was cautious as he took me in, and all I could do at first was nod.

"She died, but we brought her back. Keeping it secret has been damn fucking impossible. One problem after the next. I thought by sending her to the tribe, she'd be safe. The Babke was supposed to protect her. They stoned the Babke to death, and now the king is holding Layla against her will. I want to know who this son of a bitch is. I want to know everything about him."

"I'll start packing."

My hand went up to White.

"Luke's right. We won't get there in time. We have business here. We have to take care of it before we leave, or my wife is in more danger than ever. Luke says he can handle this. He better hope he can. If I really do lose her..." Back and forth I shook my head. "Luke will save her. He'll get to her before anything bad happens."

To think otherwise would kill what was left of me. *It would kill her.* I'd done so much to heal the brokenness she'd held when she came to my island, and I'd do it again if I had to, but fuck if Layla could survive something of that magnitude again.

"Got it!" Fallon leaned in, peering at the notes on his screen. "Tribe. The king who died was named Pavou. He had two sons, but one was killed in the accident that took out the father. Aven was the one who survived. There's no exact date of birth, but my estimate would put him at around…twenty-to-twenty-five years old. It's been a few months, but I have pictures in my files of the tribe. Not with their knowledge of course. But like I said, I record *everything*.

I leaned in as he began scrolling through.

"Tribe. Here."

"Over four thousand pictures?"

Fallon shrugged. "I like to be thorough."

"Start with the most recent."

He scrolled to the bottom. "These were a few months back. Let me see…" Buttons were clicked, and crisp images popped up. Huts weren't but ten feet apart. The wood and moss aligning their sides were in amazing detail. Women of all ages were doing numerous different tasks. Where an older woman was stirring a large cauldron, another was whittling down some sort of weapon. Kids ran and chased each other. There was even a random dog here and there. If I hadn't known any better, I would have thought Fallon only feet away. There was no way he got that close, yet the pictures were immaculate.

"Here we go." He paused on a photo of a group of men. "Look for a necklace."

"A necklace?" I glanced over, and he nodded.

"The king wears a necklace with the tribe's symbol. It looks like lines, but no one else will be wearing a necklace but the king or future king."

"How do you know this?"

Fallon smiled but kept his attention on the screen as he clicked the next picture.

"I met a tribal girl. She spoke a little English. She was nice."

"I see."

At the disapproval in my tone, his smile melted, and he stopped on the next picture of men.

"Okay, necklace. That must be Aven." It was a picture of three men. Where two appeared normal height, the one he pointed to towered a good foot over them. He zoomed in, and I lowered even more, taking in dark eyes and tan skin.

"I...know this man. I. I swear I've seen him before. Watching. Always...watching. Never close."

But my words grew quieter as realization dawned. Watching, but not me. He'd been watching her. He'd been watching my wife.

The width of his shoulders were wide, and he was lean but more muscularly defined than the others. In the picture, he wasn't wearing any clothes which had me grinding my teeth as I glared down. I knew it was a common practice for males looking for mates to be without clothes, but...to see him now. To know what he might be trying to do. He didn't want Layla for nothing. He *wanted* her. *He wanted what was mine.* And he'd pay for that.

# CHAPTER 31

## LUKE

*H*ours. More hours. Long…torturous…hours.

They drug out, stretching into a blur of yells and orders. Getting the soldiers to surround the grounds had been easy. Coming up with a plan to breach tribal land for the secret team had gone fairly smooth. Getting updates? Now that was a fucking task. Patience and silence. The two were driving me crazy as I waited for some sort of word. It had been almost fifty minutes now since they last reported, and the team was barely moving a few hundred feet at a time. To cover more ground any faster brought on a risk we couldn't take. Not with how deadly the tribe was.

"Sir." Tillin pushed a coffee in my direction, refusing to take it back as he looked at me. "It's going to be a long night. You might as well settle in. They have miles to go. It's going to take a while."

"We don't have that much time. I need them there now."

Tillin frowned, shifting as I sipped the coffee.

"Do you think it's already too late? You said the king has what the Babke was meant to protect, but will he even know how special it is to the Main Master? Maybe her death wasn't over this? Maybe he just wanted more power than she was allowing him to have. The Babke was the one in charge. With her dead, he's king."

I glanced over, taking another sip before I could get the words out.

"He knows how special it is, that's why he has it."

"And the team will know what they're going in after? You didn't tell them. You just said, find the king and retrieve. Retrieve what? We're all confused as hell."

"And you'll stay that way. It's for the best. Trust me. You don't want the burden the truth will bring. The team will know when they get there."

Two clicks had me jerking the radio up. It was the signal that the team had reached their next location safely. I waited for them to speak but nothing.

Dammit. Gavin would be calling back soon. I could almost guarantee it. He'd want an update. I'd have nothing to tell him. I couldn't send him into a deadly situation without good news. I couldn't lie either. I needed time. I needed...a distraction. Something to have the king focused on anything other than Layla. It could help get attention off my men and make it easier for them to move faster. It could also make things worse. But worse for whom? Them? Me? We could take it. Layla? I couldn't see how stealing the king's attention away from her could be worse than what she might already be going through.

"Fire. We need a fire. Not too big. Something to distract them. They can't know it's us."

"Fire." Tillin breathed out, scanning and pointing off to the side of where the tribe was located. "We'll have to go the long way around. You can't get to their village by boat. The cliff is too tall and goes straight up. It's way too dangerous. But there's a river that feeds up that way. If we take it, we may be able to get close enough to burn them out from behind."

"I don't want to destroy their village. I want the king preoccupied and out where we can see him."

"But if you burn their village, he'll have nowhere to take this item. He'll have no place to hide."

"Bullshit. We all know how deadly and lethal they are. Besides, what about the rest of the tribe? Tillan, there's children. That village is their life."

He twisted his lips. "They'll kill you as quickly as their parents. Let me see...village or the Main Master's treasure? You said yourself, one can almost guarantee we're all homeless. That our island is gone. Fuck the village. They can rebuild. *We can't.* We need that treasure back."

My teeth clenched as I let his words sink in. He did have a point, and the longer I waited, the more danger Layla was in. Still...women and children. *Their homes.* Their culture and livelihood. We weren't the bad guys. Or...maybe we were.

"We set a fire. A small one," I emphasized. "We can't burn them out. We have no idea the condition or exact location of the treasure. It's too much of a risk. We need...eyes. We need to see what's happening. I fucking hate not being able to...I..." My head went back as I stared into the sky. "Eyes. Yes!" My gaze snapped to Tillin. "A drone was mentioned when we were talking about the super yacht. We need that fucking drone."

"Jones!"

Tillin spun, waving towards the second group of soldiers that were waiting as backup. Jones jogged over.

"Yes, Main Master?"

"You were talking about a drone. We need it."

"I'll get it right away."

A sigh of relief left me.

"Do that and tell your team to get ready. I want them to move upriver and get as close to the village as they can without being detected. They're going to need to start a fire. Not a big one," I stressed, "but big enough to cause a distraction within the tribe. I need the king out where I can see him. He has something that belongs to the Main Master. I need him away from it so our men can get in to retrieve it."

Jones nodded. "Give me a minute. I'll get you one of the drones, and the team can head out."

Another two clicks sounding over the radio had me jerking it up to my ear. Tillin stepped in closer, squinting as we waited for something, *anything* from the soldiers.

"They're way too early. Do you think they've run into trouble?"

I glanced at Tillin.

"I hope not."

Another click.

My brow drew in as whispering started.

*"Sir, four men. Fifty yards ahead in a clearing. We've already deviated from the path twice. They're out. I think they're looking for something or someone. It's more than them pulling guard. I—"*

The voice cut out and my eyes jumped to Tillin's.

*"More of them just showed up with three men. They're not from the tribe. They may be ours. I'm not sure. I don't recognize them. They're dressed...Wait. I might...hold."*

"What the fuck is happening out there? Three men? We're all accounted for, aren't we?"

Tillin glanced towards the soldiers in the distance.

"As far as I know. Unless a group left the line, but we would have been notified of that. Someone would have seen them and reported it immediately."

"Fuck." I glanced up as Jones raced towards us with a black hardcase. "Drone. Perfect. Maybe we can figure out what the hell is going on."

Just as Jones ran up, the voice started again.

*"Those are not our men. I thought I recognized one. It's*

*Austin Birch. Blonde hair. Blue eyes. We're following behind them now.*"

I jerked my head up, my blood going cold as morality melted from me. This man was the cause of the entire situation. He was the beginning. The start of it all. True, he may have had orders, but he did this to my brother and Layla. He assisted in sending that murdering doctor here, and I couldn't overlook that. Not for anyone.

"Kill the tribe that has them. Take them out, right fucking now, and half of you bring me Austin Birch and his men. The rest of you keep going. I need that motherfucker here. He can't get back to the king. He's the man who betrayed the Main Master. *He belongs to me.*"

"*Roger.*"

"Jones, put up the drone. Send out your team, but you stay here. I need you as my eyes. Tillin, get two groups of men. We're going to meet the team with Birch. No fucking way I'm going to risk losing him to the tribe."

"But…you're the Main Master. You can't leave."

"*Watch me.*" My lids narrowed as I signaled for Jones and held up my radio. "Stay ahead of us. You're going to be our eyes. If you see any tribal men, you let me know immediately. If anything looks out of the ordinary, you fucking tell me. We shouldn't have to go too far into tribal lands, but that'll depend on how fast we can get to the men." I glared at Tillin who was still standing there uneasy. "Our ride, Tillin. *Right fucking now.*"

"Yes, Sir."

The disapproval was clear, but I ignored it as I watched the drone lift.

"If you want to update my team, Main Master, I'll start scanning the surroundings before you take off."

"Sounds good to me."

I headed over, waving the men forward. They were ready.

Unemotional. As I took in their dead, empty stares, I knew when they left here they'd be ready for anything. Even death.

"You're to follow the river up to the village. Not too close. I don't want you getting detected. You're going to start a fire. Not a large one, but big enough to attract the attention of the tribe. I'm not stupid. I know fires can't necessarily be controlled. If it burns this fucking island down, I'm willing to accept that, but let's try to prevent that at all costs." I paused, taking them in. "The king has something very important to your real Main Master. Let's not risk that or else I'm afraid we'll wish this island did burn when he returns. We need to get it home. That's where you come in. You're going to try to draw out the king with this fire. I want you all hiding and watching. Try to get close to the village enough to see if he appears. I have a picture of him," I said, pulling out my phone to show them. "If you see this man... put a bullet in his head."

"Yes, Main Master."

The response was one, the voices merging in a monotone assurance. My heart was racing.

"Be as quick as you can." I grabbed the man who I could tell was taking the lead. Leaning in, I lowered my voice, but met his eyes. "If you see someone you recognize, you call me immediately."

A pause but nod. "I will, Sir."

"Good." I pulled back, scanning the soldiers. "You all be safe."

Again, they were in unison. I spun as Tillin pulled up in the UTV with one following behind. The four-seater utility vehicle already had two soldiers in the back with big guns strapped to their chest. The other had four men who were exactly the same. All were ready, but was I? I grabbed one of the rifles that was handed over as I climbed in. It was going against every rule Gavin had given me. I was breaking my word. My promise. I could live with that if it meant that I'd be breaking the bones of the bastard who destroyed my brother's life and family. I'd never been much of a violent man outside of necessity for my job, but I felt a different yearning taking over. I was going to make Austin Birch suffer worse than any enemy I had ever had. I'd break him. Destroy him in the most grotesque ways imaginable. He was going to see what happens when you mess with my family...and he was going to wish he never returned to Red Island.

# CHAPTER 32

## LAYLA

old. It was everywhere. Surrounding me in massive piles of rock and coins that had to be hundreds of years old. It decorated me in heavy cuffs on my wrists and ankles. It was even draped over my head, weaved into a neutral-colored scarf, covering my dark hair. I felt like a girl in a fairy-tale again. Like my mom was going to appear at any moment and tell me this was nothing but a dream. It wasn't a dream. It was a nightmare. One I'd been living now for weeks. There was no escape. Not from the reality of my life. Not from Aven as he adjusted the gold, multi-braided band on my forehead.

He didn't speak. Lights flickered in the dim underground space, and I kept eyes on the dress that was shrouded in long-dead flowers.

I wasn't meant to be here. This wasn't my ceremony. Not really. This tradition belonged to Jahee or another tribal woman who had been groomed for queen from her earliest age. Yet…here I was—dream killer—death bringer. I knew it was coming to the point of putting on the gold-woven gown, but I couldn't bear to think of wearing it. Not just because it felt wrong, but because that meant I'd have to undress in front of this crazy king. Aven couldn't see me like that. I wasn't even sure I could see myself. My baths in the river had been quick. To see the scars…To know…That was to face the truth of what I'd undergone. That was to admit I was almost killed, and that I'd lost my son. Maybe I'd never be able to accept it. Maybe the pain would always feed the rage I lived in. It consumed me, and the thought that I'd be so exposed in front of this man without a choice only fed that need to explode and lose myself in the grief. In the fury. Fear didn't sit well with me anymore. Fear made you miss the obvious. It stole sanity. I couldn't allow that if I was going to protect myself and live.

"Straight."

Aven's hand waved at the word breaking my stare from his injured neck. The amount of blood-infused clawmarks neck-lacing all the way around his throat and hairline on the back of his neck was startling. From his chin to his chest, from his ears to his shoulders, they raked down, standing out darkly as they overlapped each other. It was terrifying to look at, but he wore my fight proudly, occasionally tracing his fingers over the grotesque bruising of my rejected affection.

"Sit straight." He leaned forward, gripping my waist to pull me in enough to obey. "Leelee's don't…" his shoulders drew in, mocking me. "Straighten. You will have…pride when you wear the svua[1]."

At his gesture to the dress, I tried not to shift. "It's very pretty, but if you put that on me right now, it's going to be filthy. I'm covered in dirt from these floors."

A smile appeared only to morph into a scowl as he cupped my face, moving in inches from me.

"Dirty shows our history. You fought me all the way…down the steps. You sit there but still you fight with your excuses." His words slowed even more as he scanned my lips, sweeping back to my eyes.

"I'm supposed to be a queen. You'd present me dirty and a mess? Would that not cause instability with the tribe?"

Aven's lids narrowed.

"Instability?"

"Doubt."

Dawning had him nodding.

"Tribe is already...instable—"

"Unstable," I corrected.

"Unstable. They will be fine. They will adjust."

"I won't be long," I said, softly. "Please let me go to the river to clean up. I won't fight. You have my word. That dress is beautiful. I'd hate to ruin it."

One of Aven's hands slid to the back of my neck, tightening painfully. It was paralyzing. A small cry left me, but he let go. "I'll clean you here. River after the ceremony. I'll clean you good, then." The smile returned. "You'll need cleaning after we finish. Cleaning and food. More cleaning. Then food again. Babke. No more demons." He stood, bending his head at the low dirt ceiling. "Undress...I will be back."

"Aven."

His name was nothing but a threat as I tried to hold in the gag. It only had him smiling wider as he headed for the makeshift ladder. Quickly, I scanned the room, looking for some sort of weapon. Anything. My time of stalling was coming to an end, and I wasn't sure how I was going to continue to prolong the inevitable. If I did nothing, I wasn't going to escape, and I needed to. I had to get the hell away from this tribe and back to the tunnels before they found me. If I could just get back to my cabin, I'd have the ultimate weapon. A gun...*and a phone.*

Standing, I removed the band and scarf from my head and rushed to the matching golden dress, sliding it off the stand it was on. I ripped the dirty one I wore over my head, slipping the ceremonial one on just as fast. It was tighter than I liked, hugging to my waist and thighs, but I didn't care as I smoothed it down. Aven wouldn't get the satisfaction of dressing me. He'd get nothing.

"Did it take you long, Leelee?"

My eyes jerked towards the opening as he yelled down from above. Banging sounded, and something scraping against the floor sprung me into action. I raced around the small room, peeking inside crates of pottery. "Did what take long?" I didn't wait for his answer before I headed for a mound of coins and antique gold silverware. Metals clinked as I grabbed a fork to position in my bra between my cleavage, but I saw nothing else that I could use as a weapon as I continued to search the surroundings.

"Your special babies. Did they take long to come?"

My lip peeled back in anger. "To conceive, you mean?" At a guttural sound, I jogged to the other side of the room, hoping lies would somehow help. "No, but the doctor cut my stomach open when she tried to kill me. For all I know, I can never have kids again. Aven, I was thinking." I stopped at a pile of different types of fabrics, digging through them as I prayed something was hidden underneath or inside. "Do you think I can get my things out of Mandy's hut? I need my clothes. My...toothbrush and stuff. *Soap*. I—"

Creaking from the ladder had me jerking up. I quickly surged back to the center of the room, picking up the scarf and band to put back on my head, but I was shaking so badly, I could barely get them to stay. Foot by foot Aven appeared. The moment he turned around, I braced myself, and for good reason. The anger on his face as he took me in had me taking a step back. Water sloshed over the side of the bowl, but he didn't move. He didn't even speak.

"I used my dress to clean up. I...I would really like to go back to Mandy's to get my things."

Nothing as his lids lowered even more.

"You could go with me if you wanted. The...cloth thing you

use for teeth, whatever you call it, I can't do that to mine. I need my toothbrush, Aven. It's driving me crazy. I can't imagine how you keep getting so close. I feel…dirty. Are you sure we can't just go to the river now? I can…change again. I can—"

Water engulfed my face, soaking my hair, neck, and chest causing me to gasp. My eyes flew open as I sucked in air, but oxygen died just as fast as he threw the bowl to the ground and lunged forward. Pressure squeezed around my throat, and Aven was so close I could only see his eyes.

"If you trick me one more time…"

"Let go." I jerked in his hold. "You're *hurting* me."

I was barely able to get the words out as he tightened with his warning. Both of my hands locked around his wrist, but it didn't have him easing the hold. It was more secure than ever.

"Aven."

My fist slammed into his shoulder. Once. Twice. There was no cocky smile at my pain. All there was was hunger as his free hand clasped to my hip.

"Don't."

"I will. Wearing that dress makes you mine. The ceremony… just…for show."

His pressure forward had me taking quick steps and holding back to his wrist so I wouldn't fall. Cool earth met my back, and I quickly turned my head to the side as Aven's mouth missed mine. His rough cheek burned into my skin and suction to my neck had me pushing and swinging towards him. With how close he was, I knew I wasn't doing much damage. I couldn't as he kept squeezing to my throat. Fire burned inside and the restriction of oxygen was becoming too much. I tried to scream. I even started clawing my nails into every inch of flesh I encountered again. Everything was blurring. I was becoming heavier with every swing and strike.

"You will make a good queen. Better…mother. You fight good."

His thigh pressed between mine, and my chest cramped and burned at the lack of air. He moved his face back along the side of mine, and reality hit so hard, I wasn't sure if I was on the verge of passing out or I was breathing again. I let go of Aven's wrist, reaching between my breasts as I pulled the fork free. With a wide swing, I stabbed the pointed ends into his ribs repeatedly with a speed and force I couldn't process.

Air rushed in for me, and Aven jerked to the side. I didn't wait. I raced for the ladder, pulling myself up as fast as I could. Fingers brushed my ankle as I threw myself through the opening. I was screaming, clawing my way to stand as I stumbled and sprinted for the door. I was moving so fast, I could barely control my body as I crashed into the barrier. Hands locked on my hips, and I screamed with all my strength as he spun me for the ground. Twisting, I tried to turn towards the table where I prayed there was a weapon, but at Aven's hard shove, he pinned my back to the ground by flattening his palm between my breasts.

"*You*." His teeth were exposed through the deep breaths. I was trembling, shaking worse than ever as I took in the small puncture wounds that were bleeding along his side.

"I just want to go home."

Material tore along my shoulder as he latched on to the delicate fabric and jerked.

"More…proof for our story. You are home, Leelee. Accept."

"Never."

A growl left him as he grabbed the dress at my cleavage, jerking down even more. When he grasped my bra strap, I screamed again, bucking my hips and swinging my fists at him. I didn't stand a chance as he wrestled my flailing arms to pin over my head with one of his hands.

"You *will* accept."

"You can't make me. I said I loved my husband. Gavin *will* come for me."

Finally, he smiled, his cockiness mixing with an evil that turned my stomach.

"I hope he does. By that time, it'll be too late."

"He'll kill you. *I'll kill you.*"

"You both can try. He'll die. You will bow to your king."

"The only way I'd get down on my knees before you is to find a better angle to stab your heart with a blade."

Pressure from his hand moved from my sternum down my stomach. Harder, he squeezed to my wrists with his other hand. I bucked, again, twisting and adding strength behind my movements, even managing to roll us to our sides. It only gave him better access as he fitted himself directly against my most private part, rolling and returning me to my back. Voices rose outside, but Aven didn't hesitate jerking the dress higher on my hips.

"Aven, I'm warning you." I cried out as he shifted, easing his free hand inside my panties. "Aven, *stop.* I'll kill, I swear—"

His finger traced down my slit as he added more of his weight to the upper parts of my body. No matter how much I fought, he countered my movements making it impossible to escape.

"Keep going, Leelee. You'll kill me. You'll…pierce my heart with a blade." His finger eased in, holding still as he continued. "Are you not piercing it now? You fight what you cannot escape. I give you this tribe. I give you me. *Me.* And I'm not good enough? So, I pierce you," he said, forcing in another finger. "Today you bleed. Tomorrow…maybe me. Either way, we bleed together."

I screamed, thrashing against him as his face went back to my neck. Yelling increased, followed by banging on his door. Aven's head flew up and he let out a deep sound leaving me on the floor. I was crying, not even aware of the tears as I fought to see straight. But my eyes weren't on the distracted king. I rolled to my hands and knees, scrambling to the table. What I found as my hand shot underneath had my lids closing. The Babke. She died for me. Now, Aven was going to die for her. For Mandy. For ever thinking he had the right to take what wasn't his.

Tribal language was loud and fast as voices spun in a confusing web around me. They came from all sides of the hut. From the door. From behind the back wall. I barely heard them as I stood and focused on the center of Aven's back. Just as I took a step forward, the king barked something in his language, spinning to me fast enough to make me freeze.

"You stay with Pactu. I will be back."

"Who? Back? You're leaving?" I had the folding knife behind me, feeling hope surge as I fisted my hand around it. Was Luke here? Had he come to get me? What if he was in danger? "Where are you going?"

Aven walked past the small table I'd just left, grabbing a leather bag and throwing it over his shoulder as a man I'd never seen before stepped inside. He was older and his long hair was braided down his back. He wore loose pants like Aven's but they weren't the same light color as the king's.

"Aven. What's happening? Do you hear that out there? Children are screaming. They're crying and scared. What can I do?"

"Nothing. There's been no ceremony. It is forbidden. You stay," he growled. "There's a...fire." He paused if looking for the right words, but it was more than that as he searched his hut in what seemed to be a daze. What he wasn't saying said more than what he was. He was calculating. Maybe even worried? It had to be Luke. Luke was the fire. He was coming. That had to be it.

"Can I at least get my things from Mandy's real quick? It won't take me long. I'll be back before you return. If I can clean up. If—"

"Stay," he said between clenched teeth. His language transitioned over as he went back to speaking to the tribal man. He pointed at me, and at the man shaking his head, Aven snapped at him even louder, repeating something until the man nodded. "No more games, Leelee. He will not take you anywhere. He knows that. Sit…and wait."

Aven pointed to the bed, but he was already turning and storming from the hut. The door shut, and I met the tribal man's cautious eyes. I didn't waste a second as I ran to the window and pushed it open, but I didn't dive through. I knew I didn't have enough time as I flicked open the blade and threw my weight right for the running tribal man who had his arms outstretched towards me. We hit with a jolting thud sooner than I could prepare for. A waft of air blew back my hair, and I felt myself pulled forward as the man's knees buckled and he fell, pulling me down with him. The knife came free, and I barely had time to react as he reached back for me. This time, there was no way I could disguise what I was doing as an accident. I reared back, stabbing through the man's chest repeatedly, torn with emotions as his body stiffened through the pain.

Removing the knife, I couldn't stop the tears as I ran for the door. Opening it was nearly impossible. I had no idea where Aven was, and if he found me…it was over. I'd never get a chance like this again.

# CHAPTER 33

## THE DRAGON

*R*inging. Ringing.

It's all I could hear as cars and lights blurred outside of our SUV's window. I didn't hear the men talking. I didn't hear horns honking or the tires on the street from the vehicles surrounding us.

Ringing. Ringing.

"Double M, we're almost there. Do you want me to circle around again?"

I couldn't answer as I shot forward in the back seat.

"Gavin—"

"For fuck's sake. What the fuck, Luke. Tell me you have her."

"Soon."

"What do you mean soon? It's been hours. *Fucking hours*."

"No shit. Do you want me to update you, or do you want to sit here and keep riding my ass like I haven't been doing anything. I have, and truthfully, Brother, I'd much prefer to give you the good news.

"You have good news?"

"I happen to think so. Before I show you, I'm going to tell you what's happening. Your island is currently on fire."

"Fire?"

"That's right. I had a team go in and cause a distraction. It worked. The king is out with the tribe, attempting to put it out, but I make no promises of what will be left when it's all over with."

"I don't give a shit. Tell me about the king."

"The men can't get a good enough shot to take him out. If they get closer, they'll be detected. The foliage is just too thick, but the tribe will move. They have to with the rate everything's burning. But that's only one team. I just talked to the other soldiers, and they're making ground now that the tribe is mainly focused on the fire. They should be there in the next hour or so."

"Hour? No, now, Luke. I want her out *now*."

"You know that's impossible. Don't you fucking pretend otherwise. One wrong move and your men are dead and we lose ground. That tribe isn't just there because of fucking contracts, Gavin. They're still here because they know how to survive in that terrain. They're still here because aside from dropping a fucking bomb from the sky, they're deadlier than we are, even with the god damn guns. If we can take out the king, *maybe* we stand a chance. *Maybe*. But don't count on it. One hour and the men can get close enough to hopefully make a difference. We'll get her, and I'll bring her home. Now do you want me to turn on the video so you can see my good news?"

My jaw clenched repeatedly.

"Yes. I want to see."

"Good."

My screen lit up as color appeared. The camera was pointed at the floor as Luke walked. When a door sounded, more light flooded and it creaked shut as he turned, pushing the old, wooden door closed. I knew that location. He was by the cells.

It's where I'd kept Layla and Aamir when they were first brought to my island.

"You son of a bitch. I don't know who the hell you think you are, but you better let us go right now."

Slowly, my lips parted, and my eyes widened as I took in the voice. *I knew that voice.* I knew it so much that my head was shaking as I scraped through memories for exactly who it was. The echoing made it hard to pinpoint, but there was no mistaking my recollection.

Luke appeared on the screen. "Sound familiar?"

"Yes. *Yes.* Who is that? I know that voice."

"Hey! I'm talking to you. Do you know how much trouble you're going to be in? Where's the Dragon? Why aren't you letting me use the phone? Hey!"

My fist drew in at my title and heat flooded through my skin. The slight accent. The soft rolling of the r when there shouldn't have been one. Anger ignited into a blaze inside me.

"You have that son of a bitch, Austin Birch."

"Damn right I do. The tribe found him and was taking him and two others to the king. We intercepted before that could happen. Meet Mr. Super Yacht. How do you think he got all that money? Do you think he's truly a guest on the yacht like he said?"

Sweat was increasing as I jerked at the bow from the tux I wore.

"Take the phone to the cell."

Colors switched, darkening as Luke turned the camera around. The video moved and swayed with his every step, and I watched Austin's eyes narrow as he stomped his way towards me.

"What the hell is this, Dragon? I show up on your shore looking for help, and this is what happens? Why are you not ruling your island? And who the hell is this bastard calling himself the new Main Master? Do you see he has me locked in a cage?"

The heat inside spread, boiling in my veins as I watched him shift on his feet.

"I asked you questions, Dragon. You tell him to unlock this door."

I glanced up at my men, lowering to return my glare to Austin Birch.

"He's going to open the door." Austin smiled. "I'm going to have him take you to a special room. A room worthy of someone like you."

"I knew this was a mistake."

"Oh, it was. The biggest mistake I've ever made." Austin's smile fell. "I should have killed you when you offered to help me. I should have ripped your throat up through your mouth before you ever got out a word."

"Dragon—"

"Don't you fucking Dragon, me. This *Dragon* isn't there tonight. You know who is? *My brother,* and where I can't take my time removing your body parts just to burn them in front of your dying, worthless fucking corpse, he is. You killed my son. *My son!* You almost killed my wife. For that, there will be no mercy for you. If you have a God, you better pray like hell he's listening because by the time Luke finishes with you, there might not even be a soul left. *Luke.*"

The camera turned around, facing my brother as denials and yells filled the space. His expression was hard. He wanted this revenge just as much as I did, and I trusted him to take it.

"If you look to the left, there's a door. Have the guards take him in there. Put a bullet in the other pieces of shit he brought with him. You choose what happens once you get Austin in that room, but don't kill him or show an ounce of mercy. Not one. You make him pay for what he did to Jamison, Jasmeen, and Layla. *To me and you.* He stole something so precious from us.

My son. Memories. Moments. A life we'll never get back. When I watch this video of his torture back religiously, because I will, I want you to make me proud. I want him to suffer like we'll have to *for the rest of our fucking lives.* It's impossible for him to know this sort of pain, but not impossible for him to get a taste of it. Draw out his agony. Make Death beg for its next victim. You brand my heartache so deep inside that motherfucker that it's all he feels as he waits for me to get there. I don't want him to ever forget it. Not even if he's born again a million goddamn times."

Luke cleared his throat as he tried to hide his emotions from me. He couldn't. Life was tragic. It was full of painful sacrifices and raw ruination. We'd lost so much time together, and we were only just now getting it back.

"I'll make you proud. I give you my word." He cleared his throat. "You're dressed. You're ready. Make Redmond pay, and then *get your ass home.* Layla and I will be waiting. Be safe, Brother."

Nodding, I took a deep breath.

"I will. You, too. I'll call back as soon as I can. Get her, Luke. I need Layla back. *I need her.*"

I hung up, not waiting for a reply. My head was buzzing with the need to spill blood. After seeing Austin Birch, all I wanted to do was massacre anyone who got in my path to Redmond. And I'd get that once we arrived. But I wouldn't do it alone. My soldiers and I had a plan. We were a team, and we'd work as one to get to Redmond. If we even made it that far. The underground would be thick with the Lair's guards. One wrong move, and we'd be caught. That couldn't happen.

"Double M, I'm approaching. Do you want me to circle around one more time so you can—"

"I'm good. Let's fucking do this."

Fallon nodded as he took us closer to Hyde Park. Parking would be easy enough thanks to Bram's connections, but once we dropped into the underground, all bets were off. Even now, we were being watched. If I knew anything, it was the amount of protection that went into keeping one of these places safe and secret. The Lair's guards would be posted everywhere. I had no doubts Redmond bought out other places along the street just so they could monitor the surroundings during times like this. Nowhere was safe in a country that was led by your rivals. Especially ones who wanted you dead. I had something most Main Master's couldn't dream of. *Love.* Men would kill for an impossible dream. They'd also kill to keep it, and that was exactly what I was doing.

"We can trust your friend? He's good?"

Pattinson asked the question, but he didn't turn to face me as we pulled in and parked. It was a show of trust. My soldier was putting his life in my hands and his actions had me reaching forward to cup his shoulder.

"We can trust Bram Whitlock. I saved his life. Now, he's doing what he can to save mine. All of ours, really. We're good."

Pattinson gave a hard nod, letting out a breath as he unbuckled. I followed suit, sliding out on the same side as Fallon. Our walk once we got underground wouldn't be far. Not as far as the hotel would have been had we taken that route. There was no way we'd get to our destination had we tried. Not with the amount of guards between here and there. We were better off two buildings down. But would that still be too far away?

I refused to think about it as the soldiers moved in next to me. As we approached the large building, two security men in black appeared, opening the entrance's front doors, I tried not to question why the fuck I had a code to get in if they were here. It didn't make sense from what I was told, but I couldn't leave now. To do so would make a scene. It would set the guards off and that could be even worse.

"Keep steady but be ready. Something's...off."

"I thought you said—"

"Bram didn't do this. Just…be ready but don't do anything rash."

The doormen didn't look at us as we approached. They didn't do anything but stand like statues as we passed through. What met me had my feet slowing but not stopping.

"Well, there's no mistaking you. Dark hair. Tanned skin. You look like you've spent the last decade on vacation on a remote island. Lucky you. You really are what they say. I almost missed you. Fantastic connections on your part. I'm actually surprised. And disappointed." The dark-haired man's head cocked to the side as he took in the burn scars just above my collar.

"Is there something you want, or are you just standing in my way?"

"I heard what they did after they brought you in to become a Main Master. I even saw pictures from afterward. I imagine that hurt like hell."

More men dressed in black moved in along the side of the room, but they didn't draw the man's attention. He had complete trust and control of the situation, and he knew it. "You're not Westlow. This isn't your place"

The man smiled. To say he wasn't handsome was a lie. He was, and he was familiar on a level that had my heart racing. Dark hair. Blue eyes. Bram's blue eyes. He was taller than me, but only by an inch or so. The tux was perfectly fitted to his slim yet powerful frame. And his voice…smooth. Almost hypnotizing.

"No, it's not. I'm not Westlow."

"You're Elec. Elec Wexler."

His smile grew. "So, you've heard about me."

"Yes, I have. You've taken over the US. Congratulations."

"Thank you. It's a long time coming."

"I hear that too."

At my response, his lids narrowed the smallest amount.

"Let's not stand around all day. I hear Westlow has an excellent bar. Let's grab a drink."

My head shook. "I don't have time. I haven't come for the party, but I think you know that."

"Ah. Yes." He gestured, walking off and leaving me there as he headed into the next room over. I threw a look to my men, following, even though I didn't want to. At this point, I didn't have much choice. One word, and I was a dead man. All for what? Westlow? Did he run to Elec...or was Elec's power so great that it reached places unthought of before?

"You're here for revenge." Elec sighed, coming to a stop at the bar as he turned to face me. Two men with guns were already positioned in the corners at the back end of the room. I headed through the threshold, not even pausing as I walked over, grabbing the decanter from Elec as he finished pouring his drink. "Redmond, right? You're going to kill him for murdering your family."

I stayed quiet until I finished pouring. When I met Elec's eyes, I shook my head. There was no room for lies amongst Masters. Not when you were making alliances.

"No."

"No?"

The look he gave said he didn't believe me.

"I'm here to kill Redmond, yes, but not for killing my family."

Elec Wexler stood straighter, his gaze eating my reactions like dessert. He was good. He was studying my every move, and I saw the moment he realized I wasn't lying.

"Why are you killing Redmond if not to avenge your family?"

"Oh, I'm avenging them, they're just not dead. Not all."

"I don't understand. I was told they died. Were they not buried?"

"My son was. That was not my wife who went in the ground

that day. She lives, as does my daughter, and the world can know that for all I care when I leave. But they better not think of making the mistake of coming after them again. Next time, I won't be so trusting. Next time, they won't make it off my island. So yes, I'm going to kill him, and not you nor anyone else is going to stop me."

"You're very brave trusting me with that sort of information."

I tipped my glass towards Elec. "Would you have not found out anyway?"

"I would have."

"So what difference does it make? I'm being honest. Now, it's your turn to be honest. What do you want from me? Are you trying to stop me from killing Redmond?"

He laughed, drinking deeply.

"Quite the opposite. I'm here to help you. For a cost."

"Cost? I don't need your help."

"Oh, but you do. It won't take them long to find you. They're looking, trust me. I'm the only one who can get you and your men through. And I'll do that...for your word, your alliance, and your blood." Elec pulled a vial from the inside of his jacket pocket. "It's for the new system. Is literally your word *in* blood. You give it to me; I own you. But you're safe. You're free to live whatever life you want on that island. When I call or need something, you don't ask or hesitate. We're moving out with the old way and beginning something entirely new."

I took a bigger drink, weighing his words.

"No one owns me."

"I will. You'll do this Mr. Draper because if you don't, we both know you're a dead man."

"This was a setup. *All of it.* Me. Redmond. They've already replaced him with someone new."

Elec didn't answer immediately as he took me in.

"Maybe. Maybe not. The old system is a risk. Certain Main

Masters don't feel the need to comply or be ruled. We're changing that. We're a machine. Either we run together, or we fall apart. There's no way we'll allow ourselves to fall."

"Again, with the machine talk. Let me guess. I was one who wouldn't comply so now you've found a way to make sure I will."

"Not me."

"Not you, but you. You said *we*." I took a step to the side. "You mean the Collective High Council." It wasn't a question. "You're one of them?"

"That is something you'll never know. Identities are never discussed, Mr. Draper. Titles get you killed, or have you learned nothing? Each of us, no matter the hierarchy of this machine, live by orders. By rule. By taking the lead and doing what we must. Everything else is trivial."

"But this machine...it's new. It wasn't formed when I got in."

"Was it not?" Elec poured another glass. "It's always been there, but with time, we grow. We learn. With time, we evolve; and we are evolving, Gavin. You're either with us or you're against us."

"So that's it. World domination for this machine."

He smiled, clinking his glass into mine.

"Call it whatever you want, but...cheers to world domination. I know you'll make the right decision."

# CHAPTER 34

## LUKE

It really was a room of beauty. Light colored stone walls. Stone floors. Drains in the perfect locations. Racks. Tanks. Torture devices only one could dream of. From electricity to boiling oil, I had it all. Where did one start when everything was at their disposal? I couldn't think past the screams. Past the need to silence the man whose voice grated my ears.

"You're making a mistake, Mister. I didn't kill the Dragon's son. I didn't do shit."

"Hang him above the tank. Put weights on his ankles."

"Wait, the one filled with water? You're not going to drown me, are you? I said I didn't fucking do anything. I tried to help. The only reason I'm here is because I was invited on a special trip by some rich guy. He said he wanted to talk about shipping business with me. I didn't even know we were coming this way. I swear it! Fuck. Fuck, man, *come on.* He abandoned me and my men. He left us out on that yacht to rot. Let me go. Are you even listening to me? I've been set up."

I watched as the guards pulled Austin across the room

towards the two large tanks in the center. He fought with every step but didn't stand a chance.

"The Dragon said you were his brother. Please, you have to listen to me. This isn't right. Hey! I said—"

A yell left him as another guard approached with the weights. "Brother! Guy! Hey!"

"*It's Main Master*. Lies will not save you. Your reason for being here now may not be your own, but you originally came looking for information and you found it. You sold my brother out and as a result, I lost my nephew. I almost lost my sister-in-law. Do you think I'm going to forgive you for that? Do you really think I'm not going to make you pay for the pain you've caused?"

"It was information! I didn't sell—" He kicked and thrashed, but the guards held him still as the weights were applied. "It was shipping help. I helped him! I brought over equipment. Nothing more. I swear. The information was already known. They already knew!" The guards wrestled the harness on Austin, making him yell even more. When the buzz from the hoist sounded and he began to elevate, his pleas only increased.

"Anything else, Main Master?"

Austin swung at the top, his feet still kicking as he rocked back and forth. I took the remote from the guard, not taking my eyes off the man behind this. *Off of the enemy*, and in this world, he was that.

"I think that's it. Stand guard at the door. No one comes in. You're not to give this son of a bitch any of your attention. Don't talk to him. Don't answer questions. Don't give him anything. The moment I recover my brother's treasure from the tribe, his ass is mine."

"Main Master! *Please!* You're not listening."

No, I wasn't. I wouldn't listen to his pleas until I could unleash every ounce of pain I held. It was heavier than the weights on his ankles. Deeper than the water that awaited him. It constantly suffocated me. Soon, it would be drowning him as well.

Pulling the phone from my pocket, I replaced it with the remote as I hit Tillin's number. They were all watching footage from the drone, and I sure as hell didn't want to miss it.

"Talk to me, Tillin."

"Nothing yet, Main Master. We're close."

"How close? I'm on my way back. Tell me what we have."

"The tribe is still guarding the village. The men are trying to find their way around them but they're like a fucking wall. They're spaced out just enough that if you take one out, it'll set off a chain reaction down the line. We're working on a plan."

"But they're close?"

"Maybe less than a quarter mile. Maybe closer. I think they had a good run, but where we thought almost all the tribe would be going to put out the fire, that's not the case. They're smart. They're not taking any chances."

"I didn't expect them to. I can't believe you did."

"Well…I guess I didn't. I was sure hoping we'd get some luck on our side."

"That would have been nice. Maybe we still will."

Wind blew against my face as I jogged out of the side door that the guard held open. Dark clouds were beginning to fill the sky, and the smell of smoke was thick. It looked like a storm was brewing and it was going to start pouring rain any moment. I cursed, hanging up, and increasing my speed as I jogged to the main building we were set up in not far from the luxury pier. Tillin was staring down at his phone as I burst through the door. The large screen they now had the footage attached to had me swearing under my breath even more.

"You're settled over the fire. Jesus, it grew since I last saw it. It's getting closer to the village."

"It is. That damn wind. We'll be lucky the entire island doesn't fucking burn. I already have the men wetting down the line. Hopefully we'll get that luck you mentioned, and the rain will get a handle on it."

"Let's hope."

I narrowed my eyes, cocking my head as I tried to see down into the trees. Aside from a random blur of colors, getting a glimpse of a tribal member or soldier was nearly impossible. I waved my hand.

"Go back to the village. Fuck the fire for now. I want to see how many people remain. I want to see if we can glimpse any of their men or women standing guard."

Jones nodded, obeying as the scenery changed. The closer we got to the village, the less dense the trees became. Space opened revealing the tops of huts. At the center rested the circle seating that surrounded the fire that always burned. But no one stood by it. Not today. As far as I could see, no one appeared present. Not even the children who must have been close to their parents' sides as they attempted to put out the fire.

"This is good. If we can get past the line of tribal men they have on the outside, we can get in the huts to start the search."

Tillin's face tightened, displaying his angular cheekbones.

"That makes you mad?"

He glanced at me. "I'm worried the soldiers won't know what the hell they're searching for. What if they miss it and get caught because they're so damn confused."

"They won't be once they see it."

"No? I am. I hate not knowing what the hell—"

My arm shot up through the movement I hadn't seen before, and my stomach flipped as I tried to hide my action. The beat of my heart spiked and pounded into my chest at the long dark hair. Gold. This woman was shrouded in gold. Even as far up as we were, there was no mistaking the cuffs on her ankles or wrists. Regular tribal women didn't dress like that. And she was crawling between huts. Hiding, as I finally noticed the scatter of a few random women not far away.

"Out! All of you out right now!"

My outburst caused confusion to the remaining special forces soldiers sitting down, but they obeyed, crowding through the door. Tillin was so caught unaware by my yelling, he was focused on me. But not Jones. His eyes were wide as he zoomed in to the woman now skirting towards one of the far huts on the edge of the woods.

"What in the hell is wrong?" Tillin went to turn to the screen, but my arm wrapped around his frame as I led him to the door.

"Watch them. Keep a close eye on these men. Maybe take them to the line and put down more water."

"Wait one damn min—"

My arm flexed around him so hard, he stopped talking as I nearly threw him out the door.

"Go. I got this here."

I slammed the barrier, eating up the wooden floor as I headed back to Jones.

"Not a word. Follow her."

I reached over, grabbing the radio from the table Jones was leaned against, making sure the channel was still set on the special ops soldiers.

"The treasure is on the move. I repeat, the treasure is on the move. Look for gold. You won't miss it."

Two clicks sounded letting me know they understood but couldn't speak.

"That's...That's—"

"Jones," I threatened. "Not a damn word."

His eyes told me everything as he nodded and turned back to the screen.

"Come on, honey. Go a little faster." And she did. Layla was crouched, but she was running. I took in the location shaking my head, angrily. "Dammit, I think she's going for the tunnels. She won't make it in; just like we wouldn't make it out. They're guarding them. *They're going to find her.* Son of a bitch."

"We have men on the line not far from the opening there, Sir. Harper's Hideout. That's what we call the area. It's a good distance from here, but you could radio it in. The soldiers are ready. If they were fast it would cause a distraction from the tribal guards in that location. She could make it." He paused. "Some will die, there's no question about it, but she may be able to get in. At least she won't be in any danger from our soldiers seeing her. They'd have to make it through the tribal guards, and she should be able to enter the tunnels before that."

"We have to try." I lifted the radio, switching over to the main channel all the soldiers were linked to. "Everyone start pressing forward. Those close to Harper's Hideout, make ground and be quick about it. You will be in enemy territory, and they *will* try to kill you. Shoot on sight."

My jaw clenched through the order making the words clipped and forced. I didn't like this, but I didn't like Layla in trouble either. If the tribe saw her, they'd either deliver her back to the king or kill her. We couldn't risk either one.

*"Roger."*

I lowered the radio through the repeated responses. Jones was still following Layla. She slowed as she approached a clearing that met the main trees. She was almost there. We wouldn't see her very well once she was hidden by the thickening canopy, but we could follow her heat signature and that would be enough.

"That's it. Just a little further."

She looked to each side, pausing before she raced to the line of trees. I reached towards the large screen, my lips parting as color blurred to her side, tackling her with a brutality that took my breath away. They hit hard. Too hard for me to stomach. Where the hell had that man come from? But as I looked closer, it wasn't just any man. It was him. *It was the king.*

As Layla thrashed under his large frame, I could see her mouth opening as she repeatedly screamed. Jones was zooming in, and I couldn't breathe. Maybe I'd said every curse word imaginable, or maybe my mind had just gone through the motions as the entire world shifted. Layla wasn't going to make it out. We weren't going to get to her until we went through him.

Jerking the radio up, I couldn't speak fast enough.

"The king has the treasure. I repeat, the king has the treasure. Everyone push forward as fast as you can. He's taking it back to the village." I paced as I watched him begin dragging her towards the fire. He was yelling, rage filling his face as he waved his hand towards some tribal men and women who approached without hesitation. "What the fuck is he doing?"

"I don't know, Main Master. It looks like he's...he's taking her to the fire."

The strain in Jones' voice was a feeling I felt in every cell of my body. This tribe had no regard for outsiders. If he couldn't control her, would he kill her? Layla was fighting with everything she had. More than once he had to stop to regain his grip or get better control of her. Marks already completely covered his top-half. They were so thick along his neck and back. Jones and I couldn't stop looking at each other as we took him in. They didn't escape either one of us, and it was something we couldn't ignore. She'd fought him. *A lot.* From the position and angle, it wasn't hard to imagine where he'd been when she was fighting.

"He's ordering them to do something. Look at the tribe moving closer. Some are...What are they getting? What the fuck is that?"

"It's like..." Jones lowered, allowing the camera to zoom into the scene even more. Where I thought I'd seen too much, what I saw as we got a better view of her turned my blood cold. Layla's dress was torn across the top, exposing half of her bra and breasts. She even looked to have dark bruising littered across each side of her face. Tear stains were evident as she cried and swung her limbs at the king even more fiercely. "Oh God."

Jones' head shot to me as the tribal man who held a long rod stuck it into the fire.

"Is that a brand?"

I couldn't speak through the horror.

The king was waving his hand again, yelling at them with authority. The red glow at the end was turning bright, but he had Layla by the hair now, standing in front of her. I moved in closer to the screen not having to wait long as the man withdrew the poker. A gray-haired woman was speaking, making symbols in the sky, reaching towards the heavens in some sort of...ritual. Layla was fighting harder, but I kept my eyes on the king as he braced himself, nodding. The rod lifted and the king looked up to the sky. His eyes were closed, and he was...smiling, almost in pleasure as his skin melted on his chest. The pain did nothing to distract him. He didn't flinch. He didn't so much as move. His eyes opened, and the smile wavered, only to grow as he locked his stare on the drone.

Jerking up the radio, I couldn't stop the sickness from swarming.

"We've been spotted. Get to that tribe, now!"

"Sir. *Main Master*."

But I already saw it, and I was frozen as I watched the king spin Layla, angling her neck with his secure hold. Layla went wild. One of the tribesmen rushed up, grabbing her arms, but the moment he touched her the king reared back, striking and sending him sliding to the ground. He was wrapping one of his arms around her, holding to her bicep as he pinned her to him. The moment his lips crushed to hers, the brand found its home on Layla's neck. Her body stiffened and she was powerless in the seconds it took for them to pull the rod back. Her knees gave out, and I watched her body collapse in his hold. Layla was gone from us now. I just prayed our men could get to her before she woke up.

# CHAPTER 35

## LAYLA

*H*ad the flames kissed my neck? Had Gavin's fire caught up with me? Kissing. Gavin. Fire. Kissing. Yes, I felt lips moving against me. The slight suction was nice. The hold on each side of my ribs was firm like I preferred. Kiss. Fire. Gavin. Moving down. Fire.

The burn intensified as I tried to blink consciousness in. It was so…quiet. He wasn't though. I could hear words, even if I couldn't make them out.

Suction.

Kissing.

Fire.

Fire.

The blur of visions started to come only to fade in the background as the heavy darkness pulled me back under.

*"Gavin?"*

A soft moan sounded as weight pushed harder into me. Touching. Rocking. I blinked him in, reaching up to cling around my husband's neck as we were suddenly back in our bed at the fortress. Dark hair was almost black as night in the dimness, but his golden eyes were bright as they soaked me in between kisses.

*"Are we home?"*

A finger slid inside me, and I sucked in a breath as he hungrily met my mouth. He was doing so good teasing me, stretching me with a second finger. I arched, crying out as I clung to him tighter.

*"You know the rules. If I kiss you, you kiss me back. We'll always love each other. I love you, Layla."*

*"I love you, too. We're really home? I...want...I."*

A gasp left me as his mouth took in mine, only to lower to my neck.

Fire.

Fire.

*"Gavin?"*

*"Spread wider for me, Lovie."*

And I did, opening my legs and trying my best to pull him back up. The spark of hope unleashed a tidal wave of need. It stirred in me, building as I waited for him to position himself. Time seemed to blur and skip, leaving me confused at Gavin's sudden thrusts. As soon as concern surfaced, it disappeared, melting into pleasure.

*"Gavin. Yes. Gavin."*

*"Me and you, Layla. It'll only ever be me and you."*

*Snickering. Laughing.*

I blinked in the sounds, spinning as colors morphed. The rooms of our walls disappeared as everything went dark. The voices only got louder.

*"We'll bury her in the sand."*

*"Drown her. Make her fall! We'll hold her down."*

*"Bury her!"*

I spun in a circle, suddenly thigh-deep in black water. The sky was so red and bright, and the sand was as white as salt. It was so bright it was glowing as I looked between it and the small boat in the distance. Dread surfaced, and my heart sank.

*"Come back to the sand."*

*"Bury her."*

*"We'll dig a hole. We'll put her in it and fill it until she cannot breathe."*

*"Shut up,"* I mumbled, trying to clear the confusion. If I was somewhere seconds ago, I couldn't remember. I was lost. Alone. My stare went to leave the boat, only to go back. There was something…something I needed. Something I was looking for… wasn't there?

I was back here. Back to the void of unanswered dreams. I was dreaming. I somehow knew that, but I was suddenly here for a reason.

*"Babke?"* Stepping towards the boat, I came to a stop, choking on emotion as I suddenly recalled she wasn't here anymore. "Gavin? Luke?" But I didn't have access to them either. I was alone, and I was in trouble. There was a panic so deep inside, and it was growing by the second. Why couldn't I remember? What was happening?

*"Let's pull her under. We'll grab her ankles and watch her drown."*

*"Pull her. Pull her!"*

*"You touch me, and I'll kill you."* Anger tinged the hollow fear inside. I was alone. All alone. No one was coming to save me. Not from the demons who whispered pleas for my death. Not from Death, itself. Not from the water or the…fire. Fire. Fire. Alone. Alone.

*"Grab her."*

The water rippled around my legs, swirling as something rough slid against my thigh.

*"I said enough!"* I slapped at the wetness, almost falling as I tried to get away. Again, the boat caught my attention. I took a step, feeling the movement slide between my knees. Fear surged and I tried running towards the boat, but the water was suddenly so thick, I could barely make any ground. I hit at the ocean

again, screaming as I scooped and looked for any grip I could get to move me forward.

*"Make her fall."*

*"Do it!"*

*"Fall. Fall!"*

Chuckling. Whispers.

Weight clipped behind my knee making the top half of my body crash down into the water. The ripples sent the boat drifting further away. Fear vanished, transitioning to frustration. I took another step. And another. Again, the force hit against my leg, almost seeming to grab it as my thighs were spread.

*"Fall. Drown. Fall!"*

*"Fuck you! Leave me alone!"* I punched down, growing still as the boat got even further away. It was pointless to escape. Where was I going to go anyway? I had to stop running. It wasn't saving me. Nothing was going to. I was trapped in every faucet of being. I didn't know the logistics, but my soul did, and it told me running wasn't going to work. Even the Babke had said the same thing.

*"Where are you hiding? Hey!"*

I turned, easily gliding towards the sand. There was no resistance when it came to facing fear. That only came with escape. You could run from the most troubling situation, but until you faced your demons, you'd never overcome them. And I had to. Mine were real.

Each step was easier than the next, and I walked more determined...until I saw them.

*Snickers. Growls.*

I slowed, feeling the fear return. Still, I stepped, trying to ignore my racing pulse.

*"You don't scare me. This is my dream. My mind."*

*"Is it?"*

The demons. They were laughing again, but it wasn't them who spoke. The hooded figure stepped from the shadows, halting my advance. Water brushed against the back of my heels as my toes pushed into the wet sand. My hair was sticking to my face and neck, pulling me from the brinks of terror as the tall figure approached. For the life of me, I couldn't focus on the red glowing eyes as the heat on my neck increased. Fire. Fire. Fire.

*"I gave you souls. I killed for you. I want to go home. I want my husband."*

*"You're not finished."*

*"I am finished. I can't do this anymore. I don't want to. Get out of my head. Get. Out!"* I turned my attention to the red eyes watching from the darkness. *"All of you. Get out! You don't belong here. I'm done. Finished!"*

More laughing. *"You can never be finished. We are you. You are us."*

*"No...I want...I...want."* I stopped, the heat becoming overwhelming as odd pressure took away my words. Something was wrong. Something...

Flashes of my dream with Gavin returned, but I suddenly felt uneasy. I felt real terror, and I couldn't face that. I couldn't let my mind go to my biggest fears. *"I want to go home right now. I...can't...I can't."*

Was I rocking? Moving? Still in the water?

*"You can...with one more."*

*"More death?"*

*"One. More."*

But it wasn't Death's voice I suddenly heard, nor was Death before me. White hair was wild as I stared into kind, pale blue eyes.

*"Babke?"*

My arms clutched around her as I pulled her close. *"I'm sorry. I was wrong. I'm so sorry."*

*"No."* She gave a shake, pulling back. *"I was wrong. It's time to wake and to put Death and the demons to rest. Release or own them. The choice is yours."*

*"I want to go home. I can't wake up. I...don't want to."*
*"You're ready. You're strong. Release or own."*
*"But I don't know what that means."*
*"Release or own."*

Burning pulled me from the Babke's arms throwing me right into a nightmare far scarier than demons and Death. Aven was on top of me, whispering tribal words as he fisted to each side of my head. My eyes rolled as I tried to bring him in clear, but what I couldn't see, I could feel. Him, on me. *In me.* And fire. Fire so intense that my scream was half agony, half murderous rage. My body came to life with a vengeance as I pushed against his shoulders, drawing my legs up to try to wedge between us. I was screaming again as I began to dig my nails into his skin as viciously as I could. And Aven didn't stop me. He kept his position, thrusting only through the motions of trying to keep me at bay.

"You're dead. Dead. Dead!"

"Leelee, you see I am not."

I tore my hooked nails through his biceps, beginning to pound into the only part of him I could get a good angle on. With the way his arms were positioned, I didn't have the right movement. My upper body twisted, looking for reach. It went wild, but he held steady, waiting for me to tire myself out.

"Slow. Breathe."

I spit in his face, screaming as he lowered to wipe the wetness along my cheek. When he turned, flattening his tongue against it, licking it back up, I hit him even more. I didn't make it far before the grip to my hair sent pain racing down each side of my scalp.

"Are you finished?"

"I h-hate you." The sob came from nowhere, and yet everywhere as it left tears racing down the sides of my face. "I want you off me. I did not consent."

At his confusion, I thrashed.

"I did not say yes to what you're doing. *You have to ask.* I have to agree. I have to want this. I don't want it, Aven. I don't want you."

"You don't have to. I'm the king. I do not have to ask anything. Not from you. Not from the tribe. What I want, I get."

Moving my hips back and forth, I tried getting my knees between us but failed at every attempt. The Babke couldn't have wanted me to wake to this. Release or own made no sense. Release the demons? Release death? To what? How? The only way I was going to release anything was to see Aven's blood on my hands. Own. I'd own that. I'd own it all if I could kill him. Death wanted one more, and I was going to do everything in my power to give it to him.

"There." His voice was low and smooth as he dropped one hand from my hair to grab my hip. The thrust was just as slow and gentle, but it did nothing to stop me from crying out at the pain.

"I don't want this. *You're hurting me.*"

"It wouldn't hurt if you…let go. You could like it, Leelee. I want you to."

"Never. Never!"

With another hit, I turned my head, taking in our location. My heart seemed to shoot to my throat, only to nearly stop entirely.

"We're in Mandy's hut. We—"

"Did you want to finish our ceremony next to a dead man? You killed one of your own, Leelee. *For nothing.*"

I couldn't speak right away. It was impossible knowing my knife was under my head, just below my pillow.

"I didn't do that. You did that, Aven. You killed that man by leaving him alone with me. I'm death's call, remember? It's your fault."

"Maybe it is. I can't say I didn't…suspect. I came back. I knew." He withdrew, taking his time sliding back inside me. I groaned, not able to bear the sensations through every inch. I almost would have preferred him to be rough. Brutalizing. He wasn't, and that made it a million times worse.

"Please stop. I'm begging you." I applied as much pressure as I could to push him away, but he only added more weight against me, gripping to my hip with crushing force. The pain was sobering. It was stimulating, but not just to my body. My mind raced in a new way. I was in pure survival mode, and if I was going to make it through this, fighting wasn't going to help me. It would only prolong the inevitable, and my sanity wasn't going to allow that sort of time.

"Aven." My lips parted as my head rolled to the side. Without the pressure from my hands, he began to thrust. The friction left me shaking my head back and forth. I didn't have to pretend to be in an internal battle. I was there, but I knew where I stood. "Aven, you have to…" My hips arched, giving way for him to slide deeper. I cried out for reasons that screamed murderously in my mind.

"Shh. It's okay. See." He withdrew, increasing his speed only the smallest amount as he pushed deep again. His mouth was opened through the pleasure, but his possessiveness or attentiveness didn't escape me either. The king didn't trust me. He was watching my every move. My every expression. I didn't focus on that. My head tilted back, and I sucked in a breath, pushing my breasts more into his chest as my nails dug into his sides. I flexed my grip, moving them between us as my legs lifted a little higher. He'd see my dilemma. My want…yet fight.

"Aven. Please. This isn't right…we can't…" My head swung to the other side, and I shifted my hips, even trying to tilt them away. Another sign of my resistance, but the fake moan and squeeze of my fingers helped cancel it out.

"This is right. You're mine now."

"No," I moaned. "I…*can't*. He'll kill us. He—"

Lips crushed into mine, and I opened to him long enough to

sink my teeth into his bottom lip. Blood tinged my tongue, increasing, but Aven had me in his hold just as fast, squeezing my jaw opened so I couldn't turn and tear through his flesh like I wanted. The pain was excruciating, causing me to cry out.

"I could *beat* you." Harder he squeezed my lower face, crushing his lips into me again. My legs lifted giving him deeper access and he took it, slamming his cock into me with all the anger he had bottled inside. I cried out, but not in pain. He detected the pleasure, grounding his hips into my thighs as the rocking of my hips urged him on.

"I'm going to kill you, Aven." I gasped, letting pleasurable, little sounds leave me as he began to thrust. He eased his weight so he could shift to cup my breast. I didn't fight it as he began massaging the fullness. I didn't even react explosively when he tore more of the material from the dress so he could slip under my bra to roll against my nipple. "Aven. Stop. Aven."

"Yes. You're going to kill me." His thrusts were getting faster. As he lifted the top half of his body, I didn't react immediately. I kept my hands on his chest, moaning and continuing to shake my head. It was an act, but one I wasn't getting through unscathed. Tears left me.

Hot.

Branding.

Burning.

Tears.

They scorched my skin, merging with the cries of ecstasy that I'd heard once upon a time when I'd get so lost in Gavin. My husband. Gavin. The Dragon. Fire. Fire. Fire.

I lifted my arms up over my head, gripping to my pillow as I sucked in a breath. I was getting louder. My legs were lifting higher. Gavin. Gavin. Fire.

The words repeated in a mantra as I went through the motions of a woman trying to fight a pleasure she couldn't deny. Truth was, I almost didn't feel anything anymore. I saw my husband. I saw his smile and the adoring way he'd look down at me. He always had his hand on my stomach, including our babies through everyday conversations. All he wanted was our happiness. Us as a family. Safe. Healthy. Happy. He wanted what so many viewed as the dream. But here we were...

My hand came to my neck as I breathed and moaned through my parted lips. I was feeling along the column of my throat, moving to my throbbing jawline. Aven was losing himself in what we were sharing. His heavy lids and long lashes somehow softened his face, but I could barely notice as my fingers slid under my pillow. Just brushing against cool metal twisted my stomach in an odd tightening. I blinked through the realization, not able to stop the pleasure that suddenly hit me. My orgasm sent my eyes flying open. I was tightening around him and clutching to his cock with every erotic thrust of his hips. And he saw...*he knew.* The smile that tugged at the side of his mouth had me seeing red, but it did nothing to stop the spasms that had me screaming out. I was fighting. Fighting more than just the demons that were laughing in my ears at my betrayal.

"Leelee."

"No! I said I didn't want you. *I don't want you!*"

Grabbing the handle, I put every ounce of hate, of guilt, behind my swing as I stabbed up at his neck. The connection was solid and the moment I felt the knife bury, I jerked, ripping through pressure with a strength I didn't know I had. Hot, wet heat gushed down on me in a downpour of blood, splashing against my lower face and chest. And it wasn't stopping as I stared up at the laceration that exposed split meat and the white hints of bone. Aven's eyes were wide, panicking as he threw himself back, grabbing at his throat.

"*I said no.* No! No! You killed my friend. You killed the Babke!"

Air gushed in a gurgling wet hiss, but I was already throwing myself forward as I screamed. I broke through muscle and flesh in his chest, using my weight to send him flying off the side of the bed, onto the floor. I was stabbing him. Crying. Hitting barriers inside of him and cutting my hand from the blade. I couldn't stop.

"I said no. No! Murderer! I said no!"

Fire was consuming me. It stung my palm as I continued punching quarter-sized slices through Aven's chest. The heat intensified on my neck from his blood mixing with the brand, feeding me on. Large hands rose towards me, but I sliced against them, returning the five-inch blade into its home in his chest. In his heart. But it wasn't good enough. I knew that as I used the weapon to carve him open. I had no idea what I was doing. Emotions left me in a daze as I began using my hands to help rip into his being. I dug my fingers in tight wetness, slicing here and there to give me better access as I continued to saw. It wasn't until I was pulling his heart free that I even knew what I needed to see.

"You're taking these demons. Death can have you. I'm done. I…I'm done. I…"

Words were slipping. I couldn't think enough to even say them as I looked down at the heart in horror-filled fascination.

"The demons are yours. I…Death." I placed the heart to lie on top of the hole I'd pulled it out of. My hands were saturated in red stickiness. I took in Aven's handsome face. In the way his eyes were still opened, and how his full injured lips were slightly parted. Before I could stop myself, I stood, grabbing the heart and stumbling outside. I was mumbling words. Prayers?

Gray skies and green from the trees in the distance blurred as I fell back so deeply inside myself. My body moved. My mind was still. Content? Lost? Broken. Ruined?

Blue and orange from the fire danced, calling me forward. I heard tribal people talking, but I heard none of it. I saw nothing but the fire. Gavin. Fire. The Dragon. It swayed this way and that, luring me like the love of my life. Calling me. Drawing me closer.

Words. Words. Were they even my own?

"Lu sitan va. Lu sitan va. Death's call. Call of death. Death. Sitan. Satan," I growled. "Evil. Death. Call. Lu sitan."

My knees crashed to the sand circling the fire. The warmth baked into my skin, igniting the wound on my burned neck. Still the words flowed, and still my fingers flexed against the muscle of the king's heart.

"Release. Own."

Time slowed as I turned, meeting Jahee's worried eyes. She was speaking but I could barely make sense of what she was saying.

"What?"

"Release. Own." She lifted my hand that held the heart. "Release…evil. Demons. Death. Release and own them. No power over you. You…have power…not them. You call them if you need. But tell them…leave now."

"Release and own." My mumble was broken as a sob had me thinking through a sliver of sanity. "Release and own. B-Babke?"

Had she really come to me? Had that dream been real? Was this? Death. Demons. Did any of it make sense, or was it nothing more than superstitions and the delusions of grief?

"Burn, Leelee. Let…go."

Unclenching my fingers was the hardest thing in the world. The moment I opened my palm and tilted my hand, the heart rolled free, causing the fire to shoot up and stir as it settled into the same ash that held the remains of Mandy. Tears came, but I held in the remaining sobs as I stood. I couldn't stop watching the fire peel back the layers of Aven's heart. They rose. Boiled. Disintegrated. It was a voice behind me that caused me to break completely.

"Layla, honey…it's time to go home."

I spun, a sob finally tearing free as I met worried, green eyes.

Luke looked every bit as horrified as the soldiers who began to crowd in in the distance, but I couldn't do anything but throw myself in his arms.

Home.

Yes.

*I was ready to go home.*

# CHAPTER 36

## THE DRAGON

*B*ram.

Elec.

Bram.

Elec.

Bram.

I'd tried to warn him by calling. My men did everything they could to make it past the guards. We failed, and now all three of us were staring each other down in a room oblivious to what was about to go down. The hate that shown through from Elec was one I could understand. I didn't agree, but I did see how Elec was threatened by his cousin. Bram could have brought us all down. He could have tried. He didn't. Not yet, anyway, and wasn't that the ultimate fear? That he would? That he would at least attempt to expose us to the world? I knew he wouldn't. Not today. That didn't mean any of us were safe in the future.

"So that's how he got into Westlow's. I should have known *you* were behind this. How did you get in here?"

Bram approached the far corner of the crowded room, slightly limping as he held his weight with the cane. "I still have my ways. I'm a little disappointed that you didn't suspect me. I thought you were smarter than that, Elec. That is why I told them to choose you."

"Don't pretend my position was all your doing. Who do you think they were grooming for this very thing? Your choice made no difference to them. It does expose what you've always known."

"And what's that?" One of Bram's eyebrows lifted, but he threw a smile towards his cousin.

"I was the better choice. We both know it. Whitlock would have never fallen had I ran it. You could have left it to me when you supposedly died. *You could have taken your slave and disappeared*," Elec snapped. "No one would have known otherwise. Instead, your greed allowed West Harper to step in. He almost ruined everything. I could have accepted that, but you managed to destroy things just fine on your own. *Traitor*."

"Is that what this is about? Whitlock? Maybe I should repeat the name since you fail to realize that you are not one. *You're a Wexler*, Elec. You were born into the wrong bloodline. That is not my fault. I couldn't leave you Whitlock when that is not who you are."

"But you'd raise a toddler cousin in that hellhole to make him your heir? Or are we forgetting how Alvin was brutally disemboweled because of your decision? Three years old. Degraded and hung like a puppet on a string because of you."

"Watch it, Elec. I've killed men for less."

"You try to kill me, and there's no walking out of here for either of you. I was the right choice. *I've always been the one.* You said I wasn't born into the right line. That your blood is superior to mine. Say that to me when you're begging to retake your place in our circle. In the underground. Because you will. You can't help who you are or what your slave—"

"*My wife*," Bram cut in, threateningly.

"You can't help what your wife is. Your actions made her into the monster she's become." Elec's shoulders squared.

"When the world can't contain her, and the walls are closing in, you'll be on your knees begging me to take you both in. To save you. We'll see whose line is at the top, then."

"We're never coming back."

"You will." Elec's anger melted into a smile of contained rage. "You won't have a choice. You're elites. Both of your bloodlines are needed, unfortunately. Plus, you're here, aren't you? You can't help yourself. You'll return to our world, and when you do, you'll get to see how a true Main Master is supposed to run things."

"Alright, enough, you two." I threw them a look as they held each other's glare. "You both need to move past this. Bram is finished with his duties. He's on good terms with those that matter." My eyes narrowed at Elec's in case he was thinking of turning on Bram. "Your cousin is no threat. Not to me, and most definitely not to you. Where is Redmond, Elec? He should be here. If you're playing me…"

The Main Master laughed under his breath, completely transitioning his aura and behavior as he reached over, grabbing a drink from a waiter walking by.

"Redmond thrives on making an entrance. Just wait. He'll be here. You'll be smart to stop looking around. If someone recognizes you as one of my guards, he's definitely not going to show." Elec turned his blue eyes back to Bram's. "They actually let you in? As who you are?"

"Of course. They know better than to blacklist me. I may have fallen in your eyes, Cousin, but I have their fear. As I should. I'm a Whitlock. That will never change."

Elec didn't speak until he finished off the dark amber liquid. "You may have the majority's favor, but not everyones. Someone's going to try to kill you tonight. You know that."

"Of course."

"So, you're hiding by me to prevent it." Elec rolled his eyes, sneering. "You were always smart. *And conniving.*"

Bram shrugged. "I do what I must. If you think I came here alone, unprotected, you're sadly mistaken. I'm probably safer than you."

"I doubt that." Elec's jaw flexed as he scanned Bram's face. "I should just kill you now and beat them to it."

"We both know what will happen if you do. You might as well kill yourself. Harming or coming after me is forbidden. Besides, if I'm dead, you lose out on your game of being everything I'm not. Where's the fun in that?"

A deadness darkened Elec's stare. "You have no idea the amount of fun I'm going to have proving that exact thing. Just wait, Bram." He stepped closer. "Remember this moment, right here. You think my hate will pass. That I'll get over it or be won by your superficial charm. I've watched you my entire life. I know your fears. Your weaknesses. I know what makes up your nightmares. Unbeknownst to you, *I've lived it.* You'll never be the man I am. You'll never know what it is to sacrifice like me. You think you've been through hell. I've been through worse than that. This game you speak of so nonchalantly, it's only just beginning, but I want you to know..." He stepped in closer, not inches from Bram's face. "It's going to destroy your world. And the funny thing is...*I've already won.*"

For seconds neither of them spoke a word. It wasn't until the music went silent and trumpets started playing from each side of the large French doors that both men turned their attention to the spectacular happenings at the opening. Confetti was raining from the ceiling in gold, shiny slivers, and balloons just as rich looking were released as Redmond walked through with his hands lifted above his head, as if we should all bow to his feet and thank him.

"Here we go." Elec glanced over to me. "Remember your word. If you think to betray me after this—"

"Don't you fucking threaten me. I gave my word. I keep it. You worry about keeping yours."

Bram looked between us, but kept silent as men in black moved in close to Elec. The blonde-haired guard I knew as Nineteen smiled at Bram, and what passed between them was something I couldn't quite put my finger on. I knew Nineteen was appointed High Leader during Whitlock's fall, but I had no idea he took the lead for Elec too. There was no mistaking it. Nineteen wore the pin placing him as High Leader.

Keeping my head down, I fell in line with the guards that were following Elec. Redmond already had a huge smile on his face, holding his hands out and showing his welcome to the new Main Master. Celebratory music was playing and clapping was loud as the Masters and Mistresses cheered at our approach.

"There he is," Redmond announced. "I've heard such great things about you, Elec Wexler. Know that you have the Lair's complete support as the New Main Master of the Garden of the Gods. We're going to do great things together in this new era of change."

"Me, most definitely. You...well. I don't think so."

The smile fell on Redmond's face as Elec approached. The new Main Master gave a small signal with his index finger as he bound up the four white and black marble steps Redmond stood on. The large doors shut behind the Main Masters, and the crowd was only just starting to realize something was off. Redmond's head snapped to the guards throughout the room, but as he peered into the faces of the men wearing the red uniforms, there was no mistaking that they didn't belong to him.

"What the hell is going on here?"

"Change, of course."

"What? What do you mean? *You can't do this*."

"I do believe I already am."

Elec reached for his bicep, gripping firmly as he practically dragged Redmond down the steps. I could feel Bram's presence move in behind me, but my sights were zeroed in on the man who'd sent Austin Birch to my island. Who'd assured me the woman doctor was safe for my wife. She may have not come directly from him, but if there was anyone responsible for setting the hit in motion, it was Redmond.

"Mr. Wexler." Redmond tried jerking his arm out of Elec's grasp but was met with the tip of a knife just over the artery on his neck. Blood was already starting to run the tiniest stream down into the collar of his white dress shirt. "Fine. Fine! If you just tell me what this is about, I'm perfectly sure we can—"

Redmond's eyes met mine and he jerked to a stop. The spin was so fast, he managed to break from Elec, but there was nowhere for him to go. The room was completely surrounded by Elec Wexler's guards. I should have been nervous about that, but all I could focus on was the hate that was boiling inside me.

"I can explain. Dragon. Draper. Please. I..." Redmond was slightly crouched through his panic, his arms outstretched to the sides as if he were ready to flee or attack. Even as he watched me remove the black baseball cap that was part of my uniform, there was nowhere for him to go but in a wide circle.

"Don't make me come after you. Stop fucking being a coward and hiding behind people and come face me."

"It wasn't my idea. Not directly. If you let me explain maybe—"

My hand shot up, cutting him off. "If you don't walk over here to face me, I'm going to get out my torch and give you a reason. You can't walk if you have no feet to walk on. Get. Over. Here. *Now!*"

Redmond jumped, along with other Masters and Mistresses that were part of the crowd. Some held flashes of fear in their expressions, others were masked in pure lust at my threat.

"Dragon." Step by step, Redmond inched closer. "You know how things are run. You know what's right. Our position." He stopped, weighing every word he spoke. Closer, he got, but he was still feet away. "Having a wife. Kids. I mean, you can't expect to live some sort of life with those. Look at what you do? It was for the best. You have to agree with that—"

I lunged, wrapping my hand around his throat as I jerked him towards me.

"Who are you to decide anything? You think because you've held this position for decades that you're untouchable? Do you think yourself better than the rest of us?" I roared, shaking him and tightening my grip. "You do not make the rules. Nowhere in those rules does it state anything about a wife or kids. We choose our fate, and yes, most of us choose our position over an outside life, but it is *our choice to choose*. If anything, family and kids are off limits. We know this from those who have taken that path. You didn't, but you couldn't stand that I did."

Redmond's face was turning purple as he fought against my grip. I didn't loosen until his mouth was opened and I could see consciousness leaving him. Even then, I barely provided him enough air to hang on.

"What you've done cannot be forgotten, and sure as hell not forgiven. When I leave here tonight, what *I'll do* will stay with every Main Master until he has the title no more. Everyone will know. Everyone will *see*. From the largest underground establishment to the thrones the Collective High Council sit upon, every single person in this life is going to witness and live your torture with you. They will know what happens when you try to take a man's family from him. There will be no question or opposition of choice from here on out. Our lives as Main Masters are not always chosen." I glanced at Bram but returned my gaze to Redmond. "But you can bet your ass after today our position and rights will be honored."

"Dra-gon."

Redmond forced my name out in a whisp of oxygen. It only had my lip peeling back in disgust as I pushed him hard enough to have him sliding across the floor. My eyes came up and I saw Aamir nod in approval from across the room in a red uniform. It had me pausing as I turned to my men. I was pacing, but they were already pulling out their devices, getting the equipment set up. I didn't miss as they did, the nervous shifting Elec did as he watched on from the side. I hadn't told him this part. He had no idea how I was going to livestream Redmond's death to those who mattered the most.

"Double M, we're good here. What do you want me to do?"

Fallon headed up to me, not tearing his gaze from mine as he awaited orders.

"My tools?"

"Over by Lopez, Sir."

I nodded. "I need to make a call before we go live."

"I'll let them know."

Swallowing hard, I took out my cell, hitting Luke's number. Ringing had my stomach twisting and turning in knots I could barely handle. When a familiar voice answered, my own breath wouldn't come.

"Gavin?"

"Oh fuck." My palm leveled over my mouth for the briefest moment. "God, I was afraid he didn't have you yet. You're okay? You're home?"

"I'm home." A sniffle. "Is it done?"

"Not yet. I'm about to start. Talk to me. Don't you fucking lie to me either. Are you hurt? Did...Did the king...did he hurt you? Does Luke have him?"

Silence.

"*Lovie.*"

"The king is dead. I killed him."

My mouth parted in a sea of suffocating emotions.

"You." It wasn't a question, and I didn't need her to necessarily say more. Her tone. The pain and hardness in it. The flat emptiness seared into me worse than any flame ever had. The ache and fury inside had my stare jerking to the one man I intended to take it out on. "How hurt are you?"

"Bruises. Nothing I can't handle." Another sniffle. "Try to hurry and come home."

"I'm sorry. For everything."

"I know."

"No." I turned my back to the men, closing my eyes. "I can't talk much now. We're about to start. But—"

"Gavin, stop. Listen to my voice. I love you. I've always loved you. And Luke says you're about to put on a show."

"Layla—"

"Don't even think about not asking me to watch. I just dug out a man's heart from his chest. He raped me, Gavin. He didn't...finish, but he violated me in a way I cannot even think about right now. *I need to watch.* I need to see that what we've been through wasn't for nothing. Prove to me that you're going to make it to where something like this never happens again. I can't...*I won't.* I want my daughter here where I can see that she's safe. *I need Jasmeen here with me.*"

"Shh, I know." My body was shaking so forcefully through the adrenaline, I almost couldn't see straight. "And I'll get her home. I'm going to make you better. I'll—" I swallowed back the hellish yell I wanted to unleash. The force for destruction was so thick inside of me, I couldn't even stand still as I paced and ate up Redmond. My men were holding him down as he fought against their restraint, but he wasn't going anywhere in those ropes. "I have to go, Lovie. I'll be home soon."

I hung up, grasping to the lapel of Bram's tux as I pulled him close. For seconds no words would come.

"My wife needs our baby. My wife needs." I took in a deep breath, trying to fight through the uncontrollable chaos that left me itching to tear Redmond apart with my bare hands. "The tribal king. She killed him. She tore out his fucking heart. He hurt her, he—" I couldn't say it. "She needs Jasmeen."

"Calm. Take a deep breath." Bram grabbed my wrist, easing me free from where I clutched. "We'll get Jasmeen home when it's safe. You don't have much time here. Look at me." I met blue eyes. "Do what you must to Redmond. I'll inform Everleigh and have her on standby. We'll all get back to the island as fast as we can. Okay?"

I nodded, taking a step back. My lids closed, and I inhaled slow but deep. When I turned, I didn't head for Redmond; I stalked to Elec. To the one man who I'd sold my soul to. Maybe not him in general, or maybe it was. All I knew was he could pull strings I couldn't, and right now, I needed that.

"You said I could come to you if I needed something."

"That was fast." He had a hard stare, but there was intrigue in his depths as well. "Who were you talking to?"

"My wife."

"And how did that go?"

At my silence his lips tightened. "What do you want?"

"To meet with the Collective High Council."

"Impossible."

"Is it?"

Elec's lids lowered but the expression faded as he shrugged. "What do you want from them?"

"Their word they don't pull this shit again. You think I'd choose this for my family? Fuck no. But it's done, so here I am. If they want to replace me, they won't get a fight. I will leave on my own free will. I will never speak a word about this world. It's a risk on their part. I get it. But you have everything you need to completely destroy me, and that's worse than killing me. I'm at the Collective High Council's mercy. All I want is their word that no matter where we stay or live, my family will be safe. You gave it to me when I made our deal, but I want to hear it from them. I want *their* assurance."

Elec grabbed my hand, squeezing with just enough force to have me contemplating whether I should stop him.

"When you have my word, you have theirs. *Never doubt me*

*again.* Your wife and daughter will be safe. I'll even prove it to you."

"How are you going to do that?"

Elec dropped his hand. "Go have your fun. Give me a few hours, and you won't be asking, you'll find out for yourself."

# CHAPTER 37

## LUKE

The large monitors were a plus. I'd seen them when I had been in the torture room before, but I hadn't paid them much thought when I'd been so focused on Austin Birch. Now that I was just as deep into his torture as he was in water, I was quite enjoying watching my brother dismember the man Austin thought would swoop in and save him. And he had thought that, even if he didn't say it. Although he didn't know the rich mystery man who'd brought him on the yacht, he recognized Redmond the moment I turned on the monitors. The sheer panic he'd displayed upon seeing the older man on the screen told me everything. Austin Birch thought he was getting rescued. Any hope he had died the moment Redmond's restrained body appeared before us. But it wasn't much of a body anymore. Not a whole one, anyway.

"P-p-please." Water sputtered with the plea, seeping into Austin's busted-up mouth as he tilted his head further and spit it out. "Main M-Mast-er."

With the man's head completely back and his swollen eyes submerged, the only parts exposed were just outside of his broken nose and mouth. Even those weren't a sure bet. With every movement, the water stirred, and with every stir, he choked on the small amounts making their way in.

"You're going to want to see this." I lifted the hoist just enough to bring his head out of the water. Austin scraped in deep breaths, coughing and gagging as he threw up for the third time since we started. "If you take your eyes off that screen, I'll drop you in completely. The weights will drown you and when I'm sure you're dead, I'll revive you so I can start over again. We can do this all night before we move to the next part."

"I own a shipping business. I have money. Lots of money. It's yours. Every penny!"

I didn't wait for more. I hit the button, releasing the hoist so that the weights could drag him down. With Austin's hands tied, all he could do was twist and flop as he tried to fight his way back to the surface. It was pointless with how much weight was attached. Even if he was skilled in the water like I was, sinking to the bottom, only to push to the surface with both feet, wasn't going to work. There was no chance where he was concerned. It was death. And I could easily let him die right here and now. Had it not been for my brother, I would have teased the thought.

Large bubbles raced to the top of the tank as he screamed, going crazy. I put my focus on the large screen. Skin and muscle charred, turning black as it bubbled along the path of the torch. Bone protruded where Redmond's hands used to be, and his lips were long eaten away by the blue flame my brother wielded. I was so lost with how even tied to an armed chair, my brother managed to make Redmond's torture look poetic. It was a chair. And rope. But it was blisters and blood. Cooked meat and meticulous skill. He took his time burning the clothes free to expose even more skin he was about to inflict suffering on.

"You didn't tell me it started."

My head whipped around as Layla walked forward. She was wearing a pale lavender robe, and her hair was wet. Her skin was paler than I ever remembered, enhancing the bruising on her face and neck. The brand towards the front of her throat had me wanting to choke the hell out of Austin Birch just to feel his life leave him.

"I didn't think you'd want to watch. I figured you'd just go to bed. It's getting late. How are you feeling?"

She didn't speak as she walked to the tank taking in Austin's slightly bloated and beaten face. His eyes were wide, but he wasn't thrashing anymore. He was staring ahead at Layla as if he'd seen a ghost. And perhaps to him, *he was*.

"I've seen this man before."

My lips tightened into a thin line as I hit the button on the hoist, bringing him back to the surface. More gasps. More vomiting and cries.

"His name is Austin Birch. He brought over medical equipment for your pregnancy. He was the one sent in to get information about you and my brother. *He's a fucking piece of shit*," I said, loudly. "He was working for that man, right there," I said, pointing to the screen. "Austin's the one who dropped the doctor's name to Gavin."

"Is that right. All the while pretending to be a guest on this island."

It wasn't a question as Layla's eyes rose up the tank.

"Yes. A guest who took to its luxury and inhabitants greedily."

"The slaves," she mumbled, heading closer. "And you're going to kill him?"

"Gavin will do that. I was given orders to make him pay until he arrived."

"Main Master, please!" Coughing. "I swear."

The sobs had Layla's face going blanker than it already was. She didn't show fear. Not even anger where I expected it. I couldn't read what was going on inside her and that worried me after the condition I found her in. This Layla, I didn't know. What I was sure of was that the determined, sincere woman I had taken to the tribe existed no more. That Layla was gone, and maybe she'd never return. From the way she turned her attention to the screen like a lifeline only cemented in my worst fears. Trauma had her. It'd stolen and corrupted pieces of her innocence. Her humanity. I hadn't witnessed what Everleigh had gone through, but I saw the aftermath and watched what she'd become. There was no fixing her need for vengeance. It was more alive than ever, but at least she could control it. I wasn't so sure of that with Layla. There was a wildness in her eyes, and it only grew as she reached over, grabbing the remote to turn up the volume so she could hear the violence her husband committed.

"Some...Someone." Redmond's head bobbed as blood-curdling screams started again. With his lips gone, bloody teeth separated widely, and his head jerked back and forth. Gavin was watching, stalking in a path before him.

"Let's recap, shall we? Hands that dialed and directed the order. Lips that spoke the words. How about what you've heard. Was this really your idea, or maybe someone put the thought in your head? Who told you to do this?"

"I-I." A long howl left him as he continued to squirm the little amount the rope allowed. "Maybe I...Maybe Ramiro and I-I."

I couldn't see Bram, but his voice was unmistakable as it began to speak.

"Try again, old friend. That's not what I hear."

What sounded like doors opened. Yelling erupted as two men wearing full face masks approached, shoving another tied-up man down on his knees before Gavin.

"Ah, Ramiro. Thanks for saving me the trip. Was it you who came up with this plan to kill my family?"

Blood was already smeared on the man's face, and his eye was swollen as he swung his head back and forth from Gavin to

Redmond. The Main Master was fighting to run as he yelled in horror, but the guards kept him kneeling.

"It wasn't me. It wasn't me! It was Redmond's idea. He heard from Austin Birch that you might have a child on the way. That you fell in love with a slave. He thought it was hilarious. I was just told to say I used some doctor if you ever called. I had no idea what they were going to do," he said with a thick accent. "I swear it. I wasn't part of this!"

Me and Layla looked back at Austin whose lip was quivering as he sobbed and shook his head in denial.

"You knew," Gavin said, moving in closer. "Whether he told you his plan or not, you know how this works. Your word is your bond. I thought if anyone had my back in this world, it would have been you. What did he do? Offer you more money? Get you some delicacy you can't get where you are? What was more precious to you than the life of my family? Than a partnership or bond with someone who would have been fucking loyal to you?"

"Dragon, please. It's not like that at all. I thought it was a joke. It was a doctor. I—"

"The health of my children or wife was not a fucking joke. I think for too long all of you have thought yourself indestructible. You think by hiding in your underground world, with all your guards, you're safe. *You're not.* If you mess with someone's wife or family, nothing in the fucking world will stop the carnage that's coming for you. Take note," Gavin said, looking to people offscreen, only to turn and point right at the camera. "You fuck me over. You target my family." The torch shot to life. "I'll introduce you to the fires of hell. It'll be the last thing you taste before the devil, himself, meets you on the other side."

Layla sucked in a breath but didn't flinch as Gavin turned the weapon directly into Ramiro's face. The man was screaming and breathing the flame in as his skin caught fire and began to blister and melt. Back and forth his head turned, but that only caused more flames to ignite, running up over the top of his hair as his head turned into an inferno.

High-pitched cries had Layla's stare turning to Austin, but a knock drew both of our attention.

"You," I said, holding my hand up to Layla. "Not a sound."

She nodded as I headed for the door. When I cracked it, spotting Tillin, I slipped out, shutting the barrier behind me.

"What is it?"

"A man, Sir. He's just docked at the pier. He's saying he's not happy about us destroying his yacht after he delivered who we were looking for. He's...He's pretty well guarded. Looks fancy. Says he wishes to speak to the Main Master. He says his name is Rich. That this is his island."

"His...island? Rich. Shit." I glanced back at the door, turning to Tillin, hesitantly. "I see. I...I'm going to have to make some calls to verify his identity. Until I know for sure, I don't want him in the fortress. Get our own guards posted up. Take him to the soldier's hangout and watch him very closely. Make him a drink and sit with him until I get there. It won't take me long."

"You got it, Boss."

I waited for Tillin to leave before I headed back inside. What I saw when I walked through the door had me jerking to a stop. The water was so dark, you couldn't see through all the blood. Layla was sitting along the edge of the tank, her feet disappearing in the depths below as she steadied Austin's head between her knees.

"Hair like the sand. Eyes like the sea. Hair..."

It took me a moment to realize the motion of her hand. It was cutting along the lining of his scalp in brutal slices. She was on a mission to tear his hair free, cutting and pulling as she moved along. Cut, Jerk. Cut. Impatient tug.

*"Hair like the sand. Eyes like the sea."*

Austin's head bobbed through her positioning, going face-down in the water as she moved to carve just over his ear and then the back of his neck. Minutes passed as she swept the blade in shallow angles, digging underneath the skin, and scraping along his skull. Jerk. Tug. Pull. Frustrated cry. More repeating the mantra. Again and again. Over and over.

Had I moved? I had, and I hadn't even known it. I was at the top of the steps, and I could barely blink as I saw visions of Everleigh all over again. Blood had the water almost black as she finally ripped his scalp free, placing the wet clump of hair and flesh down beside her. The blade returned to the lifeless corpse, and I stepped forward, but I couldn't speak. Layla wedged the blade under his eye, prying it from the socket.

"Hair like the sand. Eyes like the sea. Death is near. Hair like the sand. Eyes like the sea."

"Layla?"

"Not yet, Luke."

"Layla, what are you doing?"

"I'm taking what's mine. The Babke saw him. She saw him coming. Hair like the sand. Eyes like the sea. Death is near."

"He's dead. I think Death already came and collected."

Layla pulled the eye free, cutting through the nerves as she laid it to rest near the hair.

"He did. He's still here. One more." She pointed the bloody blade towards the large screen as Gavin held the torch's flame to the inside of Redmond's ear. The Main Master's own eyes were nearly bulging out of his head. His body was convulsing as he violently thrashed through the pain. "I need to burn these. I'll burn them in the fire pit and the demons will never come back. Death will never come. It'll be finished. Release and own. I release these parts and own. I own them. *I own them all.* They'll burn. We'll burn everyone."

Shock. I knew it when I saw it. Layla wasn't in her right mind. That was going to take time. Whether she'd ever find sanity again on this island though was beyond me. If Death had a second home, it was here. With everything going on, it was easy to ignore the statistics I'd faced since I had arrived. The truth was: children were dying on those boats. Sex slaves were being attacked and raped and not reporting the acts. The resort bungalows were already booked and rented out for the season, and it still wasn't going to start for another few months. This island was full of secrets I had barely even been introduced to, and yet...my brother lived it. Now, he was going to live it with a wife and child? I couldn't stop that any more than I could stomach Layla turning into a stranger before me. She was holding both eyes. Clinging to the lock of hair as she lost herself to the images on the screen. Redmond was dead, and still my brother burned his body.

Silence.

It was worse than the screams. It was sobering. A reality call I couldn't stomach. We were all broken. Every single one of us was treading water that was waiting to pull us under. I couldn't let that happen to my brother or Layla. *To Jasmeen.* Who was I if I didn't at least try? There was only one choice. One thing that made sense to me or anyone who looked at the situation. I was the Main Master of Red Island...and I was going to do everything in my power to keep it that way.

# EPILOGUE

## LAYLA

*E*leven months later...

"*T*hat's it, Jazzy. That's it. You can do it."

Gavin had his fist at his mouth but his other hand an inch away in case he had to catch our daughter. I smiled from across the large, cozy living room we'd made in the fortress, glancing at Everleigh as I laughed and shook my head.

"She'll never learn to walk if he doesn't let her try. Mark my words, the moment she lets go, he's going to pick her up. If it's not him, it'll be Luke or Aamir."

"They look happy. Especially, Gavin. He's a lot better than the last time we saw him."

My smile fell and my own heart sank. "He took the decision of Luke and Aamir pretty hard. He blames himself. Maybe Rich had it planned from the beginning. Gavin seems to think so. Gavin even suspects maybe this entire thing was Rich's doing. We'll never know now. In a little over two years, Luke will run

Red Island and Aamir will be locked in as his High Leader.
Gavin…" I glanced back over at him. "Gavin says it's to secure
our silence. I can't imagine leaving here knowing they'll remain
to take over. I just can't grasp how it came to this. It was one
thing when it was me stuck here. Aamir…He didn't ask for this
life. I guess Gavin and I are both adjusting. Gavin is getting
better at accepting it by the week."

"He looks like it, but what about you?" Everleigh grabbed
my hand. "You weren't so well when we left you, either. I'm
sorry about what happened with the tribe. What you went
through was horrendous. Have you seen any of them since?"

"Some are still convinced I'm their queen. They come to me.
They…try to communicate but Jahee isn't the best at translation.
I've made her in charge until they can sort out what they're
going to do." I frowned, taking in Everleigh's genuine concern.
"I'm sorry. I'm sure you have so much on your plate. I just keep
doing this. I shouldn't have dumped what happened to me on
you. Not then and not now. I was just so…lost when you all
arrived. And now things are just hectic as we try to plan and
cope with all that's happened."

"Don't apologize. It's good to talk to someone. I've been
there. I'm always here for you, Layla. You know that. You're
never a burden, and don't be too hard on yourself. Nothing that
happened was your fault. *Nothing.*"

I nodded, but the movement was more of a shake, trying to
erase memories I still couldn't deal with. I was healing, but not
like I should have been. The numbness inside rarely left. It ate at
me. Some nights it swallowed me whole. Death visited, but only
during nightmares I couldn't wake myself from. Most nights I
was good. Others…I stood on the balcony, looking into the darkness towards the trees. Waiting to see him step from them to
come try to take me again. I could hear the clinking of shells.
See them sway underneath the branches. I dreamed of giving

into the cravings. The demons whispered such sweet songs of sacrifice. They lured me in with their snickers and bonfires. With the drums I could hear in the distance. The Babke visited me too, but only in the darkest nights. She eased the need. She made me see the light. I was content there. I had what I had always wanted for me and Gavin, a new life to look forward to, and yet... secretly...we had more.

We had an invitation for a grand opening in the future.

We had a guaranteed membership neither of us could quite speak fully about yet.

I didn't know exactly what that meant. I was afraid to find out, but the time would come. Then, there'd be no escape. There'd be no ignorant bliss.

"Gavin says you and Bram are leaving after dinner."

Everleigh smiled. "You know us. We're always on the move. Although, I can't really use that excuse." She paused, glancing to Jasmeen and the men who surrounded her. "Luke's been training pretty hard with...whomever he's working with to get ready for this place. He wanted to come here, and after what I can only guess is happening, I couldn't deny him. Even at such short notice. But I have an appointment I can't miss."

"Really? Hopefully for something good?" My head cocked to the side, and she shrugged, blushing.

"Not yet. Maybe someday. That's what we're going to see. Apparently, there's still a chance for us to have a family. Maybe. I'm not going to get my hopes up, but my doctor seems optimistic."

"That's great news. Gavin mentioned how Whitlock gave hysterectomies to the slaves. I'm so happy there's still hope for you."

Her smile was weak as her mind seemed to wander.

"Hope, yes. A decision?" She stopped. "Safety first. I don't think we're quite there yet for an actual family, but it'll be nice to know if it's possible. There's so much that has to be done. Places in society that we'll have to take due to who we are. I wish it was simple, but I'm afraid our status doesn't allow for anything to be easy. So...we'll go find out if it's even possible, and if it is, we'll start trying to decide on a path. Bram and I are in no rush. We're not even sure it's something we should do. We have people to save. Others to destroy. Until the pieces fall into place, and we know it's time, we'll keep playing our game. Then, maybe someday we'll have a baby just as pretty and as adorable as Jazzy."

"Lovie!"

Gavin had his arms out, waiting, but Jasmeen stayed strong with every step. My lips parted, and I rushed closer, placing both hands over my mouth. One step. Two. Three. Gavin swooped her up just as she was about to fall on her bottom. Cheers from Aamir and Luke had me smiling.

"Did you see that!" Gavin laughed, nuzzling his face into the junction of Jasmeen's neck, sending her into the cutest giggles. Bram smiled over at Everleigh, and I couldn't stop from soaking in our moment.

From out of the darkest of humanity, we all had been pulled together. What should have been a fate sealed in pain and blood became a bond that was only just beginning to grow. We were an impossible statistic in a world of lies and deceit. We were the anomalies. The ones who'd battled true evil and survived. That was all we could do, and Luke and Aamir's duties in this world were only just about to begin. Winning didn't exist when you were owned, and true sovereignty didn't come to those who appeared free. Gavin and I may have been handed our fairytale, but the nightmare inside of it still walked in the shadows of our pages. It was in the invitation, worded in a way we couldn't refuse. It was how a man named Elec called my husband at least once a month. It was in the new identities he created, in the blood he took from each of us, and it was waiting until our time ran out on Red Island. It was a new life, but in a circle of elites that I didn't know. I wasn't sure what that entailed, but Gavin assured me this was for the best. In a world where the rich ruled, I knew I'd have to be ready for their games. *I'd have to be ready for anything.*

THE END

# ABOUT THE AUTHOR

A. A. Dark is an International Bestselling Author. She doesn't reside in one place for long and is known to move at the drop of a dime. From mountains and snow to tropical beaches, she could be at one in the morning and the other by night. A. A. is a Goodread's Choice Award Finalist in Horror. She is also the President and CEO of Mad Girl Publishing, and the founder for the Pitch Black brand.

Mad Girl Publishing's rating system in levels of darkness.

PITCH BLACK ☒ (Level 1)
STATIC WHITE ☒ (Level 2-darker)
OBLIVION ☒ (Level 3- darkest)

# CAST OF CHARACTERS

### Red Island

Gavin Draper: Main Master of Red Island.

Layla Draper: Wife to Gavin Draper. First appears in the 24690 series. Former slave: 27009

Mandy: Layla Draper's personal servant and friend.

Gavin Draper's Personal Soldiers: Pattinson, Fallon, White, and Lopez

### Red Island Tribe

Aven (Sounds like Ay-Ven): King of the the tribe on Red Island.

The Babke (Sounds like Bab-kah): The tribal shaman/witch doctor.

Jahee (Sounds like Jah-hee): Supposed future queen of the tribe.

Va-hen (Sounds like Vah-hen): Guard of the tunnels.

### 24690 series

Bram Whitlock: Former Main Master of Whitlock. You can find him in the 24690 series

Everleigh Whitlock: Wife to Bram Whitlock.

Former slave: 24690.

Luke Draper: Everleigh Whitlock's main bodyguard.

Aamir: Layla's twin brother. Former slave: 27011.

## Garden of the Gods

Elec Wexler: New Main Master of the Garden of the Gods. First appears in the last book of the 24690 series. You can find him in every book in the Garden of the Gods series.

Nineteen: High Leader for the Garden of the Gods. Former High Leader for Whitlock. Friend to Bram Whitlock.

## A. A. World Characters

Rich Tilson: An 'Overseer'. The Master overlooking Gavin Draper and Red Island.

Charles Redmond: Main Master of London.

Ramiro: Main Master of Chile.

Kaun: Main Master of China.

# ALSO BY A. A. DARK

*24690 series in Reading Order:*

24690 (24690 series, book 1)

White Out (24690 series, book 2)

27001 (Welcome to Whitlock, 24690 series, book 2.1)

27009 (Welcome to Whitlock, 24690 series, book 2.2)

27011 (Welcome to Whitlock, 24690 series, book 2.3)

Or

Welcome to Whitlock Complete Novella Series (book 3)

Black Out (24690 series, book 4)

*Garden of the Gods*

*Vol. 1*

*(all standalones and can be read in any order.)*

Mistress B-0003 (Garden of the Gods)

Master B-1212 (Garden of the Gods)

Couple B-0001 (Garden of the Gods)

Master B-0077 (Garden of the Gods)

Master B-0999 (Garden of the Gods)

**Vol. 2**

Mistress B-0042 (Garden of the Gods)

Couple B-0019 (Garden of the Gods)

Master B-0491 (Garden of the Gods)

Master B-0113 (Garden of the Gods)

Master A-0005 (Garden of the Gods)

*Anna Monroe and Boston Marks series in suggested Reading Order*

Never Far (Boston Marks)

Mad Girl (The Chronicles of Anna Monroe)

MasterMind (An Anna Monroe and Never Far crossover)

Heart Lines (The Chronicles of Anna Monroe and Boston Marks)

Crossed Paths (The Chronicles of Anna Monroe and Boston Marks

# ACKNOWLEDGMENTS

To my FABULOUS betas…
YOU ARE AMAZING! You all rocked Red Island. You tore the
world apart and built it back up to shine beautifully. I'm truly
grateful for each of you.
Karen Preiato
Nicole Johnson
Elizabeth Jansen
Amy Martin
Kelsey Elizabeth Stone
Morgen Frances
Devon Brugh
Monica Anne Patrie

Also, to all the amazing readers, bloggers, TikTokers, and
Bookstagrammers who have reviewed and shown love to not just
this series but to ALL my books, I LOVE YOU! I appreciate
you. I can't thank you enough.

Last, but definitely not least, to Dee Trejo and Nadine Flotte.
We've been with each other from the start of the A. A. World,
and I can't wait to see where we go next. I love you both!

# NOTES

## 5. CHAPTER 5

1. Queen. (In tribal language.)
2. Hallucinogenic tribal soup.

## 10. CHAPTER 10

1. Tribal snack.

## 16. CHAPTER 16

1. Tribal greeting. Hello.

## 17. CHAPTER 17

1. Queen.
2. Grandmothers.
3. Mating age/traditional for the tribe.
4. They are traitors. (In tribal language.)

## 20. CHAPTER 20

1. Where are you going, traitor? (In tribal language.)
2. You call her my queen? (In tribal language.)
3. She's the Dragon Master's wife. He thought her worthy. The traitor does. Is that who you want me to take as my queen?

## 23. CHAPTER 23

1. The death call or Death's call.
2. You find me unworthy?

## 26. CHAPTER 26

1. No. (In tribal language.)
2. You lie. (In tribal language.)

## 29. CHAPTER 29

1. The demons are dying.

## 32. CHAPTER 32

1. Traditional name for the tribal queen's wedding dress.

www.ingramcontent.com/pod-product-compliance
Lightning Source LLC
Chambersburg PA
CBHW050023030726
47506CB00001B/92